In Pursuit of Balance

In Pursuit of Balance

A NOVEL

MARTA S. GABOR

OPTYON BOOKS NEW YORK 2000

THIS IS AN OPTYON BOOK
www.optyonbooks.com
E-mail: info@optyonbooks.com

First Edition

This work is a product of the author's imagination. Any resemblance with real persons, dead or alive, is purely coincidental. No reproduction of any real person, happening or dialogue was intended. Opposite to specific locales and private times, most localities and public events are geographic and/or historic facts.

Publisher's Cataloguing-in-Publication Data

Gabor, Marta S. [date]
In Pursuit of Balance: a novel / Marta S. Gabor

p. cm.
I. Title

L C C N 00-091045

813.6 —dc21

ISBN 0-9700207-0-8

Manufactured in the United States of America

To my children
Rita and Tom,
with love.

Perhaps if the future existed, concretely and individually, as something that could be discerned by a better brain, the past would not be so seductive; its demands would be balanced by those of the future. Persons might then straddle the middle stretch of the seesaw when considering this or that object. It might be fun.

—Vladimir Nabokov, *Transparent Things*

Part I

1

Doctor Nora Mann parked her car inside the company gate by the windowless wall at the end of the low building. She walked in the drizzling cold rain to a glass door that opened directly into the small waiting room, then turned toward the office on the right. At every step, the wet rubber soles of her boots made an annoying squelch as they stuck to the worn-out wavy linoleum and jarred the slender young woman's graceful gait. She often, like now, tried to convey more assertiveness in her stride to better suit her official position, while in the depth of her soul she wished she could get over appearances. Her round hazel eyes that usually received the world with a smile were now downcast under her thick eyelashes. Her fur hat was pulled low on her forehead. Her shoulder-length light chestnut hair impishly curled up over the fur collar as she nodded left and right. People seated around the room welcomed her with hushed greetings. *Isn't my failure enough to keep them from wanting my help?* She wished she could leave such thoughts outside the office. Be her usual energetic and optimistic self. Not a caged bird with shriveled wings and no courage to fly out the open door.

From time to time, gripped by spells of spastic crying, she ran to the back room and splashed her drawn face with cold water. With its perfect oval shape and smooth rosy complexion, even in this state, her face belied her thirty-six years. The barely noticeable tremor of her always purposeful and steady hands only brought more tears to her eyes.

At the recommendation of a psychiatrist colleague she had consulted the past week, she decided to take the first dose of Atarax that evening. The smallest dose that wouldn't even harm a newborn chick. Nightmares carried her to depths she had never been before, though she thought she had been everywhere.

The day after, at work, she took a second dose, when tears welled up in her eyes again, making them feel like bursting balls, minutes before starting consultations. Feeling hopeful that the medication would kick in, she asked Cornelia, the nurse, to call in a patient.

The man took the seat in front of Nora's desk and told her what brought him there. She listened dutifully, asked questions, took notes, and gave thanks that the employee was new at the Transit Authority and knew nothing about his company-physician. No danger of having to answer condolences. She rose from her chair to walk over to the consultation table where the patient was sent to undress behind the screen.

She raised her head. Felt dizzy. Looked down at a body dressed in a white coat, feet, wearing *her* shoes, elevated on a hard pillow. Had she walked to that table to examine herself? The blood pressure machine's cuff was being pumped tight around her arm.

She had collapsed two steps away from her desk. They caught her midway, like a tottering sac of potatoes, and laid her on the examination table, Cornelia informed Nora. "Your blood pressure dropped to 80 systolic. Now it's 110," she reported.

"Orthostatic hypotension," Nora gave her interpretation. Fainting was a side effect, though not expected with the minuscule dose of medicine she had taken. Not even a legitimate antidepressant. Her sardonic laughter shocked the people in the room, mostly the patient who sat petrified on a chair, holding tight a white sheet around his torso. "I shall never be sick. There's no help for me." Thinking of her consistent sensitivity to drugs, she sighed. "Cornelia, would you make me a coffee?"

The nurse responded with a conspiratory wink. The electric coffee maker and the black market coffee were hidden treasure, classified as illegal by fire security, and according to the Romanian Communist Party's slogan, symbols of "rotten capitalist immoral decadence and illicit creature comforts that soften the combative spirit."

Her colleague gave up the idea of treating her like *any normal disturbed person,* as he put it. Sick leave for stress neurosis was not the remedy Nora imagined she would need two weeks after Paul's death. She would have preferred work if she could face it.

Scenes of her husband's last days, the funeral, were indelibly imprinted in Nora's soul.

"Don't cry!" he had told Nora in the hospital room.

"I have a cold." Nora could barely utter the lie.

"You can't fool me . . . I'm fucking going this time." He punctuated his opinion with a curse delivered with his dry humor. As if nothing had changed. He could still make people smile. The patients in the two other beds smiled and tears ran down their wrinkled old faces. "You deserve a rest . . . your life will be easier . . . maybe . . . more time for the children . . . and yourself . . . I didn't tell you . . . there was no need . . . ," he muttered as he wriggled his hand out of Nora's to scratch his forehead. "Everything we had . . . until we did . . . made me happy . . . what we didn't . . . I hadn't missed." Words dripped from his parched lips like droplets of mercury during the brief alert moments of his uremic stupor.

"Where is that nut?" he asked later.

"Which nut?"

"The one I want to crack, right now, here," he mumbled as he sank back into coma.

The scene that she stumbled upon one morning. Nora couldn't and didn't want to explain. She had opened the door with trepidation. A man was sitting on Paul's bed, with a hand resting on the blanket where the feet raised it. The private duty nurse stepped away from the window and collected her bag from under Paul's bed. She met Nora halfway between the bed and the door.

"How did this man get here?" Nora recognized Alfred, a journalist she had met before.

"Paul asked me yesterday to call and tell him to come by. Early."

Nora's mind short-circuited. Paul wanted Alfred to visit *before* she came? Russian lessons for Paul's doctoral program came to her mind. When was that? The first year of their marriage. Lessons and more lessons. Long lessons into the night at Alfred's place. And what since? A life of cheerfully declared principle, that what's good for you is good for me, and what's good for me, should be good for you too. Mutual, wasn't it?

Alfred stood up, touched Paul's hand. Paul opened and closed his eyes. Alfred turned away from Nora and vanished like a ghost.

With supernatural self-control, Nora held back the erupting question: why were Manci, his own mother, and Sonya and Daniel, his children, banned from visiting? And this man was summoned. After years of practicing mutual consideration as a way of life, no question was worth as much as the time that words would have taken to utter it. Didn't matter.

The jar under the bed mattered. It was empty. A crack ran down its side. The crack gave Nora the absurd illusion that the urine had leaked out. Perhaps Paul could fill it again. The empty smudged glass container had become a symbol of mortality.

Nora managed to contaminate another colleague, Egon, with her frenzy. Against his better judgment, he accompanied Nora to the only dialysis unit. She begged. To no avail. A young mother clung to her dear life, hooked to the only dialysis machine in the city, her kidneys having failed due to complications of pregnancy. Chronic illness, like Paul's, had to follow its natural outcome, sooner or later. The realization hit her. Sooner or later was now.

"Why's it dark all the time?" he had asked.

Nothing contrasted more with the brightness of the rising sun than the darkness of the setting life. The lights were on, the room was quite bright. She knew that it was the retinal bleed that took his vision. "There's a blackout . . . it's night," she lied.

"Horse's dick, blackout . . . Tell me what the hell's going on!"

"One thing is, the kids would like to come visit."

"Don't upset me . . . I said no . . . What's to visit? . . . I have nothing to say . . . especially to the kids . . . They shouldn't remember me like this . . . no one should come . . . not my mother . . . I love her . . . tell her . . . she might not know . . . I never told her . . . life is a horse's dick . . . no, life's like a baby's shirt . . . short and full of shit . . . What's to eat?"

Hours of coma would follow other short vigil episodes.

"Come here," he called from the distance of an impenetrable mist.

"I'm here, right next to you." Her hesitant hand caressed his face, then returned to rest on his hand.

"Stand up."

"All right . . . I'm standing."

"Leave . . ."

"You want me to leave?" She was truly surprised, even though she knew his coherence was at best questionable at that point.

"No . . . no . . . stay . . . come with me . . . no . . . no . . . don't come," and he was out again.

"Doc. It's not good, huh?" The cab driver, one of her patients, asked. Everyone at the company knew.

"I think this is it. They didn't tell me when they called . . . I'd just got home from the hospital . . ."

"I'm so sorry."

Whether it was the result of her animal instinct to escape reality, or the subconscious connection of misfortunes, Nora was not aware, but animated scenes kept flashing in her mind, as if triggered by the parade of streetlights they drove by on the way back to the hospital.

Her parents. Feverishly throwing their only daughter's clothes in a suitcase.

Nora couldn't remember most of her childhood, but she would still shiver at the thought of having to go away in the middle of that night with people with whom she never thought she would have to live. That her parents would send her away and leave her.

"My dearest," her father, sitting on a kitchen stool, with little Nora standing between his knees, said. "You are a very smart seven-year old. You have to know that there are some things we can't explain to you because we don't understand them ourselves. You must learn some very important things fast." Nora knew only too well that her father did not put too many demands on her, but when he did, she had no choice but to obey.

"What happens if I forget?" Nora had asked terrified.

The warm weight of her father's big hands on her shoulders never left her. "Terrible things could happen. Your mother and I might never be allowed to see you again." She was petrified beyond tears. Her father looked up at her mother standing behind her, then talked again. "Your name from now on is not Mann. It is Kovács. Say: 'Kovács'." She did. "Good girl. If anyone asks you where you came from, say Kolozsvár."

"Where is that?" A sorry little smile on her father's face.

"It's where your mom's sister Adel and also Bori's sister live. Bori will be here soon with her husband and you will go with them in their nice horse-drawn cart to their place."

"I want to stay with you." Her childhood cry slit through the sleepy night. Nora knew Bori. Even liked the strong peasant woman with big skirts and beautiful colorful scarves tied around her head. Sometimes she would take off the scarf and put it around Nora who would run to the mirror to admire herself wrapped to her knees in the large flowery cloth. She loved to watch Bori as she smoothed the braids crowning her head before she would put back the scarf. Bori would leave a large aluminum canister full of fresh milk, and take away the empty one. She would chat a while with Nora's mother, then was gone until a few days later.

"You'll like their big family."

"Am I going to have sisters and brothers?"

"More like cousins. You should know that Aunt Bori took you because your mother in Kolozsvár is sick."

"Is Mother sick?"

"No, sweety, I'm fine," her mother answered.

"Is Aunt Adel sick?" Nora had asked remembering her aunt whom she was always pleased to visit.

"My dearest, you will be told everything you need to know. And remember, we will not see each other for a while. If you'll be a smart little girl, which no doubt you are, we'll see you as soon as we can." Nora couldn't realize then the desperation, the dilemmas, the pain of her parents. She couldn't see, but imagined later, the stream of tears on her mother's face. She would realize later that Mom and Dad, Bori and Feri protected her life at the risk of their own.

Burlap sacs loaded in the cart. A leather toiletry case. She used to play with the crystal jars and bottles, chrome soap dish, ornate brush and comb, all smelling of her mother's perfume. The expensive accessories were thrown in a careless pile on the bed. Later, perhaps a year later, Nora saw her mother's fur coat, their embroidered bed linens, and silver trays, and candleholders, coming out of those potato sacs in Bori's house. Nora never saw the toiletry case after that nocturnal trip.

She playing all summer with the many new cousins. More fun than her neighbors on Szacsvay *utca,* the paved city street, and even more than her classmates at the Jewish Elementary School in Oradea. Nobody tripped her when running for a ball. She didn't even get a bad scrape on her knees the whole summer though she climbed all the trees the others did and even waded into the creek for tadpoles.

Nora wore Bori's scarves whenever she pleased. Especially when she was sad that Mom didn't come to comfort her. She had cried a lot at dinners though she could recall Bori asking her what she would like to eat. Bori would make little braids of her thin hair in the morning and pile them on top of her head like little raised tassels, would take her in her arms and make the sad little girl laugh. Feri often put her up on Pityu, and held her as the old horse trotted around the yard with his big head hanging. They taught her how to milk the cow. She would dip her lips in the frothy milk, then run around to show everyone her big white mustache.

By the time school started, Nora had forgotten that her name was ever anything other than Kovács Nora. Like all the other girls, Nora wore loose-fitting ankle-length skirts under the light-blue uniform apron. Her hair grew longer. Bori would comb it into two scrawny, hanging braids tied with white bows and would say, "My cute little bug, now go to school and pay attention, so you'll grow smart and clever."

During the second summer in Telegd, Bori and Feri built a shelter. A sturdy-looking roof of beams over the entrance to the ice-vault in the back of the yard under tall poplars. Nora was told that they would be better off hiding underground if airplanes would drop bombs. They didn't know for sure whether they would ever be targeted. Nora could only vaguely remember years later, more from what she had been told, that she threw tantrums, kicking and screaming, trying to resist going underground. There were not too many occasions when they actually had the time to run for shelter when they heard the threatening droning of the approaching planes, which flew over the region headed towards some bigger, more important destination. People crossed themselves as the noise faded in the distance.

By the time the second school year started, Nora no longer cried. She would diligently do her homework. When she had finished, she would cuddle up next to Bori on the ledge of the hearth in the kitchen and watch with avid eyes the flying knitting needles.

In the lolling whisper of the tires rolling on the asphalt, Nora almost felt the short clumsy fingers of the child Nora trying to follow Bori's large skillful hands as she looped the yarn around the crossed tips of the dancing needles. The off-white, red-striped woolen scarf she had knitted by herself and how itchy it felt around her neck.

Wheat fields had filled again with the rough green blades of the promise of bread. Giggling girls ran along the shallow ditches separating people's parcels and picked bouquets of silken poppies, blue cornflowers and bright daisies. After summer rains the breeze was sweet and tangy with the scent of caraway and coriander. Gold took the place of green and sickles cut down the wheat. Dust clouds floated over the clattering threshers in the fields. Days were long and tiring.

It was during the third summer when Bori had read a letter to her. It was from Aunt Adel, her mother's sister. She was coming soon, it said. And she did, and took Nora away to where she lived, in one room and a tiny antechamber of the big villa, where Nora used to run around when visiting with her parents as a little girl. She was not little any more. She came of age at nine to understand that Mom and Dad will never come back. She felt guilty. It didn't help knowing that she never made a mistake.

By the time Adel returned from the concentration camp in Poland, her villa had been requisitioned and a few families were living in it. After numerous battles with the officials, someone was finally evicted so Adel could have one room in her own house. Before the war they used to sit in the garden on benches between hedges of trimmed boxwood. Now it looked neglected, like everything else in the city. Squat fruit trees rose above the tall grass.

One day they went out to dig in the back of the overgrown garden to plant some vegetables. Adel, who seen from the back could easily be taken for a teenager, had been kneeling under a dwarf pear tree, her slender body bent over, marking points with a measuring tape. "Nori, dig here and don't scream when you hit something hard," she had whispered with excitement.

"Is this a treasure hunt?" Nora remembered asking.

"You bet."

"But Adel, you don't have a map."

"I don't need a map. Uncle Jo and I buried this treasure."

"Did Mom and Dad bury anything?"

"No, sweetheart. They gave everything to Bori."

"Can I have those things?" She had asked, envisioning the toiletry case.

"Not really. You see. You are worth far more than all those things. Bori needed to sell them . . ." she said. Nora could not forget Adel's big sigh, ". . . to pay people off, so they wouldn't squeal. They were very courageous, you know, Bori and Feri."

During one such conversation—Adel didn't miss a chance to mention, again and again, how grateful she was to those people for saving her niece—Nora, a young teenager by then, broke down and wrapped her arms around her aunt's neck. "You are a very good Mom." They both cried hot tears.

The squeak of the brakes chased away Nora's visions. Moments later, Doctor Rhub, opening the second floor chrome-framed glass elevator door, took her in fatherly comforting arms. "Nori," he said. "I'm so sorry, Pali expired just before I called. I couldn't tell you on the phone."

She nodded. They had already removed Paul from the room and wheeled his bed into a treatment room against the rules. They should have taken him right down to the morgue. Preferential treatment. Before entering, Rhub handed Nora Paul's wedding bend.

"Do you want to see him?" he asked.

She nodded again. He lifted the sheet. "He looks like a baby," she said in a whisper bending over to kiss Paul's tight lips. Not cold yet.

Specters of the raw past were always ready to appear to Nora. The small chapel. Packed with people and flooded with floral tributes streaming with ribbons of emotional outpouring. The Reform Jewish cemetery was flower-friendly. Friends from afar. They came to pay their respect. During his last visit a few months earlier, Paul apparently presented the Geras in Bucharest, and the Feldmanns in Timişoara, with his lugubrious request, "Don't you dare not show at my funeral."

Manci's husky lament, more bone-chilling than the frigid wintery sunshine. "Now you can't stop me from looking at you," she said to the coffin, leaning toward the bier on the arms of two friends.

"It's not the custom, really," one tried to keep her back.

"It's not the custom for young sons to die. For the last time." She turned to Nora with imploring eyes.

Nora felt the unfairness of not giving her a chance to see her *Bubuka*, once more. "It's all right," she said and took her mother-in-law's arm. They stepped up to the coffin. The cover was lifted.

A silent blessing poured from Manci's eyes for an oppressively long moment. She didn't cry. "He's asleep. Now I want to touch him."

Nora was concerned for Manci. She could break down after all.

"Manci, he *is* cold, believe me," she said. *Colder than ever,* she thought. The occasion was neither accommodating nor appropriate to let her thought linger. Something felt like bubbling up—from how deep she couldn't tell—but she suddenly felt the yawning gap of the past opening to receive the future.

"Are you sure?" Manci asked.

"Yes."

"All right then. I never doubt you."

They replaced the lid. The rabbi gave his eulogy in Romanian after a very short prayer in Hebrew. More eulogies from colleagues, friends, and former professors followed. Nora listened to every word as if trying to find out something she might have missed in Paul that others knew. She saw people candidly touched and registered her gratification with a regained keenness, as if her perception was taking a deep breath between years of a losing battle with illness and coming times of struggle for a new balance in her life.

The frigid light was fading in the early afternoon hours of the short winter day when the family returned from the funeral. Nora was deemed unable to drive, at least that's what a concerned Doru said. It felt comforting to be taken care of, to be driven in her own car to Adel's place. The separation of a few hours from her children seemed criminal. She felt already sorry for taking some friends' well-meaning advice and not taking the children to the funeral.

"Cornelia told us that Tata is not coming back. Is it true?" was Sonya's first question as she lay on the cot, fiddling with a tiny stuffed bear, Daniel crouched like a hurt kitten at her feet.

Cornelia sat next to the cot, shaking her head, gesturing that she hadn't taken it upon herself to explain the events.

"Yes, it's true, my dear," Nora answered.

"Where did he go?" Dani asked.

"To a place from where he cannot come back," Nora said.

Sonya assumed a dauntless expression, and in a grave, unrecognizable voice she said, "I won't tell anybody. Ever!"

Perplexed, Nora couldn't find an explanation to Sonya's shocking statement. It would take years to grasp the growing child's—and later the young adult's—fight to overcome, outgrow and change the oppressive inferiority complex of abandonment that she was left with by her father's death. It would take many years before Sonya would accept the fact that her father didn't leave because she was a bad girl. Daniel was no exception, no matter how supportive the ones around him were, and would deal with his own problems at his time as well. But then, the adults looked at each other pained by their inadequacy to help the bewildered children. Nora only suspected that it would take more than a staunch embrace to alleviate her children's suffering and fear.

2

When Tibor Rozsavölgyi finished working on the last cab and climbed out of the pit, he was the last in the shop. *I'll be late, damn it,* was the first thought that flashed through his mind as he looked at the grimy face of the wall clock. *All these VIP jobs! Why me? My stupid ego should be flattered, right? And here I'm bitching. Another day I wouldn't. But today? Now rush my ass to school double-quick.*

Rubbing his hands blackened by machine grease with an oil-stained cloth, Tibor passed the row of pits gaping empty. Long strides took him to the locker room lined with narrow padlocked metal cabinets. Another mechanic was sitting on the only chair tying his shoelaces. A naked light bulb hung from the ceiling shadowing their tired faces.

"Any hot water?" Tibor asked snatching the oily black beret from his broad forehead. His straight, dark blond hair instantly fell over his face in a statement of regained freedom. He threw the beret to the bottom of his locker.

"Barely," the man answered.

"Damn it," Tibor shrugged. "At home it ain't any better."

He took his soap dish, the tube of shaving cream and the razor, unhooked his towel from inside the door and stepped into a smaller back room with one single shower head separated from the rust-stained sink by a gray metal divider.

Standing in front of the mirror, still dripping, he started to work the shaving cream into a firm lather with his fingers going carefully around his long sideburns. He wiped his hand in the towel tucked tightly in around his waist, over his muscular buttock. He worked fast with the razor, his green eyes fixed on the straight scar crossing his left jaw line, ending at the prominent ridge of the neck muscle. The scar and the vivid vision of that horrible night had more meaning than ever. He would still shiver recalling that nightmare. Always the same question. By thrashing, perhaps springing up as he woke, did he escape being more seriously injured? Maybe fatally? On the other hand, he might not have been hurt at all. Perhaps the knife had slashed his skin only because he jumped. He would never find out.

He was searching for the right words. Plain 'Marry me,' he was afraid wouldn't work. He felt a knot in his stomach, though he thought he was beyond the stage of visceral doubts. She was too cool. Always talking, more than he would have liked to hear, but saying not much of what he would have really liked her to say. He couldn't explain. After three years of dating Ibolya, the routine seemed so ingrained that he couldn't see beyond the details, beyond her reluctance to discuss future plans.

Proposing was not as easy for him as for someone who hadn't been burnt before. Yes, he wanted her as his wife. Not on a trial-and-failure basis. He had been there before.

He concentrated on his hands. The black crescents under his fingernails, the stigma of his profession he was not the least proud of, had to be left in the shop. Extra surgical brushing did the job followed by close scrutiny with hands lifted to the light bulb.

A last cockeyed look in the mirror to smooth a tuft of hair behind his ear. The slightly long hair suited his square face, high, prominent cheekbones. He liked to think he looked attractive to women with his greenish-gray eyes—sea green he had been told more than once—and his nose a tad longer than he would have liked it, and stronger, not to say slightly rearranged since his unsuccessful attempt at boxing took care of his perfectly proportioned profile. In a fresh shirt and dark slacks—chocolate brown, his favorite color—his impetuous long stride of a six-foot-plus man took him to the bleak street behind the company's fence, to his old weather-beaten car.

Sitting in class—a knitted hair band replaced the oily beret—reality totally eluded Tibor that evening. No time for socializing after classes either, not even the few usual minutes before running to meet Ibi, or buy something for dinner, or at least try. If he had anything waiting for him on his single shared refrigerator shelf, he would gladly skip shopping and get down to his homework before he collapsed after 17 or 18 hours of intense activity.

Too often he thought of the lazy boy who most of the time looked for subterfuges to duck class work, who often on the brink of being left behind to repeat a class, would go around to pals to borrow their work and barely pass from one class to the next, like a thread through the eye of the needle. His parents had given up, frustrated as he slipped between their fingers, like a lively fish, gone to play marbles or some other childish game. Never anything serious or big. No fights, no dangerous escapes, no over-fired imagination. Just play instead of homework.

Now he was pushing himself to catch up on what he had missed. Anything to get out of the pits. Literally. How happy he had been when his mother—despite his father's disapproval—took him out of school after the eighth grade and sent him to be an apprentice to an auto-mechanic uncle. His father refused to teach him carpentry. "You useless nitwit," she had told him. "At least learn to earn a living."

How unhappy he was now, and how aware of his limited abilities. Everything looked so difficult. His head as heavy as a watermelon. And as smart as a rotting watermelon at that, he would mock himself.

She was strolling with her chums as if he were not waiting there, at the corner of the Teacher's Academy. *Move Ibolya! What's her problem? Is this part of her hard-to-get play? Fuck her, isn't that behind us?* "All right," he mumbled when finally she directed her steps toward him. He saw in the approaching slender figure, frizzy dark hair tied in a pompon on the top of her head, the future mother of his future children. He smiled with satisfaction.

He wrapped his arm around her waist. They kissed briefly.

"Nice haircut," she said turning him around. "What's the occasion?"

"I've told you," he said. "We had the pictures for the yearbook taken yesterday."

"So, they didn't wait for you to grow a beard?"

"I was only joking," he said. "I've something serious to tell you."

"Maybe we should sit down so I won't faint?" she teased.

"Maybe we should lie down," he teased her in turn while pulling her waist close to his hip.

She was lying on her side on his single bed, palms together under her face. He returned from the shared kitchen, wearing a tank top and his trousers to disguise his nakedness, carrying a plate with two salami sandwiches. He sat on the bed. "Are you ready?" he asked after they munched awhile.

"Shoot."

He bent over her and kissed her on the cheek, "Will you marry me?"

She slid her arm around his neck. "I might," she said with a voluptuous embrace more feigned than her accompanying laugh.

"You might have joked around before, if you think that passing on my proposal last year was a joke. This is a proposal, in case you have any doubts." He was taken aback and thought he should have better said ultimatum.

"We could get engaged," she went on, not letting go of his neck.

"That's better," he paused. "I would like to ask your parents for your hand."

"Don't expect them to jump up and down." She sat up baring her small firm breasts.

He could only guess what her parents thought of a divorcé without as much as a high school diploma yet. Ibi made no secret of her parents' disapproval of her boyfriend, though they were willing to accept the pretense of his platonic dedication to their daughter as pure as a lily and as innocent as the gentle violet whose name she shared.

"All that counts is that *you* say yes," he said.

"Where would we live?" she asked instead.

"I'll make it up with my mother and in time we could build an extension or a separate structure in the back of their house." He couldn't imagine how he could carry out his plans in the totally nationalized and rotting Romanian economy of the early 1970s. An approval for private construction was as difficult to get as bringing the stars down from the sky. Procuring material and getting any work done was yet another problem. If one could not do everything with his own hands, or with the help of friends, it would not happen. He was well aware of this, but on the other hand the government could not take away his dreams.

"And until then?"

"Well." He felt cornered. "We could look for a bigger sublet," he admitted with hesitation. "By the way, I have to move out of here."

"When?"

"My landlord is exchanging this apartment for . . . to be exact, I don't know . . . but they're moving to a smaller one for money."

"Then what?"

"As I said, I'm moving back with my parents."

"Don't they have a tenant?"

"He's moving out. For a change something actually works in my favor."

The damage had been done. He had been on mere talking terms with his mother for years. His father could do nothing. It took Tibor long lonely years to overcome his disgust with his mother's meddling that had ditched his life.

He had moved away from his parents. In anger. It was the only thing that could alleviate the poison boiling in his veins. Now, in the squeeze, with no place to go, he was as humble as a wet puppy squealing at the door. Anger had taught him independence. Miserable as it was. Now his predicament crushed his ego. Of *that* he had plenty, not that he knew what to do with it. It was time to mellow even if he was slightly embarrassed that it was interest that pushed him to reconcile. His folks were getting old, his father arthritic, his mother doing her best to make ends meet with her sewing.

There was not much else he could do. His application for an apartment of his own on the company's waiting list was a joke. A bad joke at that. Many employees with families lived in rooms no bigger than his. The city—as the only hand of the government empowered to distribute the state-owned apartments—allocated only five or six apartments a year to the company of about two thousand employees.

He tried to look at moving back home positively. He had never brought a girl to the house. He was now committing to in-house-celibacy by moving back to the room where he spent his youth. And lived his tragedy. He could get proof how Ibi and he would weather under less-than-favorable circumstances to jump into bed. They would have to let less carnal aspects rule their relationship.

3

Nora leaned her forehead against the cold windowpane in Paul's room. She pulled at her hair. Her memory was blank as to Paul's departure and how she got back home the night he died. She shuddered in waves as if shaken by after-shocks of a catastrophic earthquake. She couldn't banish from her eyes' memory Paul's face distorted by his labored breathing. The scrapes of death in his heart and lungs still resonated in her ears. Tightly squeezed eyes, palms pressed on the ears didn't stop her hallucinations.

Details flashed like remote silent lightning. Obsessing memories all day, tormenting nightmares all night. Not an instant did the strobe lights allow her attention to turn away.

She couldn't keep away from the small room. His room. The need was irresistible. Touch and feel the writing pad on his desk, open the wardrobe, pat his suits, squeeze the fabric of his fleecy winter coat, hold between her fingers the paper-smooth starched collars of his shirts lined up on hangers. Waiting forever. Rearranging handkerchiefs and underwear, turning around suits, moving the blotter on the desk became part of an oppressive daily routine.

A spell of mysterious docility led her to the window again. Her eyes were blind to the rows of alternating tower-like and lower blade-like buildings with alleys gracefully snaking between and up the hill across the main dividing road, a sight that usually made her pleased to be living in the city's best new district. She leaned her forehead to the cool glass and lost her thoughts in the space outside. She sank deep in the abyss of oblivion. The sounds of the children running around faded as if a radio had been turned off. Silent echoes. That window in Paul's room, no other in the apartment, had *that* particular lure. It drained her willpower and replaced it with a frightening weakness.

A desire lingered in the dimness of confusion. She couldn't afford to be weak. Never. Not the least now.

To resist opening the door to Paul's room took as much of her will as if holding back a scream when tortured. But somehow that room promised relief—as it never did while Paul inhabited it—beyond her ability to imagine relief in any other way. Entering that room brought the relief of a scream.

She hesitated to accept, no, she downright rejected the idea that supernatural powers gained control over her. Mystic explanations never appealed to her. Now the elusiveness of her own feelings and the impenetrability of forces beyond her control devastated her already insecure balance. Peering out through the lace curtain she searched in her past for an explanation of the seduction of that particular window. She could not come up with anything. Insecurity, self-doubt, were uncontrollable reactions to the situation that molded her into an image that was definitely not her. An alien in an obscure world.

After prudently avoiding it for a while, Nora entered Paul's room again. She pressed her palm over her mouth, as if to hold back a scream. The frightening vacuum that paralyzed her logic was there waiting for her. A most befitting replacement for their existentialist marriage.

She was glued to the window by a heavy numbness. The gray void outside sucked up her strength. She didn't register the February blizzard beyond her own grief and chilling remorse. She stirred. Seeing the reflection in the smooth polished walnut wardrobe took her aback. Her own silhouette in front of the heavy bookcase, packed to the ceiling, stretching along an entire wall. The titles of the books in the mirror image made no sense. Nothing made sense, though Paul's death was not unexpected, as untimely as it was. She lost a very close friend. How close, she was now wondering. Close enough to bear the long years of misery.

It was quiet. Nora loved silence. When right. What was right? A long list of things that had always been right and important, and they had steadily stayed very much the same. *Why these doubts now? Why this feeling of despair?* She parted the lace curtain. She touched her fear. The blinding light reflected from the snow below stabbed her eyes and made her squint. She turned toward the bookcase. Every page held the memory of Paul's interests. The room held the echoes of his remarks, opinions, humor, and above all his hearty, thunderous, contagious laugh. Tears found their way up from Nora's throat. They were pooling there constantly creating a scraping feeling. Now, they were pouring in hot creeks burning their way down her tired face, blurring her sight and mind. She felt at ease with her lonely tears, but thoughts of evanescence and life's unstoppable calling failed to bring relief just then.

Nora kept fighting the returning painful images, while others, she was groping for, dropped out of her memory like marbles from a holey pocket. She rubbed her burning palms as if trying to get rid of a crust. Her hands wouldn't stop rubbing Paul's feet.

She had reached for *that* window knob not once before. Opening the window would allow the vacuum to suck her out of the eighth floor room and carry her away like a feather. The windowpane and her fortitude to keep it closed kept the vacuum away, but resisting it longer didn't seem worth the effort. That force out there was nothing less than physically alluring.

She shuddered at the thought of giving in to an unexplained urge clashing with her duties. She couldn't afford that. *But, what help can I offer now? I can't do anything for Paul any more. My mother is still young and self-sufficient. Manci? Maybe. Doru? Certainly not. The children? What help is a worthless mother?* She couldn't answer the simple question, "Did Tata have to go? Didn't he love us?" That's what made her feel discouraged, hopeless, empty.

Lucid again, she pushed herself away from the window, buried her fingers in her hair, grabbed it in her fists and pulled until it hurt. Time, the great healer! huh? Space too, perhaps? Space emptied of laughter? The void outside the window seemed to fuse and crush her like an ugly monster she could not look away from. The irresistible vacuum was grabbing her again just like she was grabbing at her hair. It was an almost glamorous feeling of forceful passionate embrace. To melt into the featureless gray void outside the window seemed just the right thing to do.

With the window open, she would have only the abyss to confront, silently beckoning like a welcoming and understanding friend. There was nothing else. No sound. Everybody had left. Looking for something better.

She closed her eyes to squeeze out the last tear. Her lips stretched into a sarcastic smile distorting her features. Captive in a thick, slimy cocoon filled with silence. She pulled the curtain to the side as if in a dream. Held the handle of the window lock. Her nails scraped the cold metal as her hand pushed down on the handle. The cold air rushed in around her, froze the cocoon and instantly turned the slime into shards of glass that crushed to the floor with a deafening noise. Life inundated the dead space around her.

"Mommy, what do you see out there?" Daniel was pulling on Nora's skirt as he tip-toed trying to look out that same window and see more than just the gray sky.

"Leave Mama alone," Sonya called to him sharply as she burst into the room chasing after her little brother.

"It's all right, Mommy dear. Let's all sit here on Tata's bed and talk."

Sonya sat on the bed putting an arm around her mother's waist as soon as she sat down too.

"Did you see anything out there?" Daniel insisted, turning his back to the window.

In the warmth of the innocent pair of wondering eyes waiting for an answer, things fell back into their rightful place; worthlessness thawed like ice in the spring sunshine. The hopeless vacuum curled up in a shameful ball of dust that shrunk into the horizon.

"Nothing special out there . . . Come sit here with us . . . I love you both a lot."

"I love you, Mama."

"I love you, Mom."

The following few weeks Nora resumed her work and all the activities that went with it, including meetings. Useless meetings she could barely stand. The essence of the Communist Party base organization's meeting was written all over people's bored faces. A session of rehashed, already overused slogans: Be a responsible member of the multilaterally developed socialist society; Build the blooming socialist economy; Fight the class enemy. The latest Party decrees, meant to prod health care workers into achieving higher productivity, did not interest anyone either. Anyone brave enough to raise relevant issues having to do with their work's real problems and substandard conditions would have been instantly declared an enemy of the people, a traitor of the homeland, a rotten capitalist collaborator. Members preferred to go home in peace.

Nora walked out of the room amidst clumps of whispering people. A friend and neighbor caught up with her. "You know, they took my assistant, they say there's no money to fix a sterilizer, not talking about getting a new one. What do they want from us? Miracles?" Doina complained. "What would be the merit in doing the work with everything you need? Mastery is to do it without," Nora said. They couldn't even laugh. "You wanna ride?"

"No, thanks. Meeting my husband, going to some friends. Good night," Doina's shrill voice faded, filtered by the pelting rain, as she ran to catch the bus that just pulled into the station in front of the Policlinic.

The rain painted glittering wiggly streams on the walls. Umbrellas popped open, puddles rose in cold splashes as people lunged erratically in search of islands of non-submerged asphalt. Faces and voices melted into the dripping darkness. The fog engulfed Nora and her car parked along the curb.

She hesitated. She would get home, Adel would leave, the children would go to bed, she would be alone again with her dreaded visions and her pillow soaked not by the cold rain. She pondered the imponderable on this particularly frigid spring evening that felt more like February. The February that refused to fade.

Her thoughts wandered between the images of herself that she still could not discern, like looking into a mirror with a peeling silver backing, and of her apartment. She could see Sonya bending over her homework, Daniel pushing around and buzzing over some new toy, and Adel, no doubt, adding more stars to her lace. Nothing and nobody was missing from that picture. The doubting of her own role and place was simply absurd. She knew that. She shrugged. Those days were over.

She pulled her umbrella shut, stepped in a cold puddle to reach the door lock and stood in the pouring rain absent-mindedly, showing no indication of trying to escape from the soaking downpour. Her arm, as if acting on its own, pushed the door closed. Her feet took her back into the lobby. She leaned into the corner. The black ebonite receiver felt warm in her cold trembling hand. She dialed her own number. "Hi, *Nyuszi.* How are things?" Since time immemorable mother and daughter had called each other all different sorts of *Nyuszi,* as affectionate terms for bunny. Ad-hoc additions of endearment cropped up from time to time. When playing together in the grass, *Ugri bugri kis Nyuszikám,* My-frisky-little-bunny, was the minimum Adel called Nora. All the bunnies disappeared if her dress would be torn. Then she was simply Nora. Not even Nori. A mother could not endear a child who asked for a slap! There were slaps too. A whole assortment of slaps, including slaps of protection and love, that meant to underscore words she feared to have failed.

"They haven't eaten well, but otherwise everything is fine," Adel said. "What are your plans for the evening?"

"Go home and watch TV."

"Is Arthur with you?" Nora thought of her mother's boyfriend, with his comings and goings to Adel's house shrouded in the mystery of the two old-timers' privacy.

"No. It's his backgammon night."

"I thought he plays chess."

"That's on Thursdays."

"All right then. Would you put the kids to bed and watch TV in my place?" Nora asked hesitantly. "I'll take you home later."

"Why?"

"The meeting's over, but I'd like to stay out a while."

"How long?"

"Not too long. Maybe ten?"

"All right. Wait, Sonya wants to talk to you."

"Mom, I got a ten in arithmetic," Sonya said excited.

"Good girl. Any problems with your homework?"

"Nope," her voice was confident. "Can we stay up? We want to play doctor and patient with Dani."

"All right. Who's gonna be who?"

"I'll be the doctor, of course, and Dani the nurse," Sonya said with all the seriousness of an eight-year old. "Tell Adel that we can stay up."

"All right, dear. Do you think you could call Dani your assistant?" Nora smiled.

"Because he's a boy?"

"Sure. Who's the patient?"

"Broomo," Sonya named one of her favorite bears.

"What's wrong with him?"

"I don't know yet. I have to examine him first," Sonya said.

"Good girl. I mean doctor." Nora smiled with satisfaction.

Nora dialed the second number with the demeaning intention of speaking only if Doru answered. It was he who picked up. Nora felt like a pickpocket. Yes, he could meet her in fifteen minutes; he expressed concern; she reassured him that nothing was wrong.

Nora's hesitating hand pulled away from the light switch. The streetlights strained through the curtains suffusing her mother's apartment with mysterious lacy islands. Strangely unburdened as in a dream, Nora lingered between the luminous patterns discovering with astonishment a soothing buoyancy for the first time since . . . Oh, perhaps years?

The tranquillity in the warm apartment defied the past commotion of Adel's life. A deceivingly peaceful haven *for an old wreck which was given a paint job.* Nora smiled, remembering Adel's favorite self-definition. Not far from the truth.

The apartment—with its two rooms, balcony, bath, kitchen, pantry and entry hall, all compressed into the scale of socialist construction style, but neat, and certainly comfortable enough for Adel—came as a conclusion to her mad adventures that Nora felt guilty about at the time.

Expecting the door bell any minute, Nora tried very hard not to think about how Adel had lost her motivation to exist when her duty with the daughter she'd raised had been finished, when that only daughter was out to destroy her own life against her mother's best judgement. Adel felt she couldn't be a witness to what she perceived as a tragedy-in-the-making, so she decided to leave the country not long after Nora got married.

"*Nyuszi.* We are not Siamese twins. You don't have to live with Paul." Nora had tried to make a joke when Adel didn't give her her blessing to marry Paul. Nora never got over the feeling that she had pulled the rug from under Adel's feet.

"You promised not to marry before you finish med school." Adel had been deeply disappointed with Nora's choice.

"Well. I'm sorry. I'm not Pythia. I couldn't predict I'll fall in love," Nora remembered now how she had retorted.

Adel's emigration papers came through fairly fast. So fast that Nora had the feeling that her mother disappeared like an apparition, as if she was never real.

"Israel is just another concentration camp," she wrote to everyone's stupefaction a few months later.

Two or three years later, Nora couldn't remember exactly, Adel had moved on and wrote from Canada. 'You think the climate is cold here? The temperature is hot in Toronto as compared with how friendly these people are. It's a pity. I'm making so much money that it makes me feel rich and I'm not even officially settled.'

A postcard a while later had brought another surprise. Adel was in Paris. Not for a pleasure ride. If it turned out that way it was not her intention. She tried to settle in France. She was finished with Israel and Canada. France was the place she thought could offer a niche for her troubled soul. 'I couldn't paint a place more to my taste. You might be wondering, because we never thought of the French as friendly. I don't know what was wrong with them during the war and I don't care. Maybe it's because I've met this man?' Nora had been happy to hear that finally Adel could find peace. But soon she had written, 'I have no other choice but to hang myself. No way that these bastards would let me stay. I asked Maurice to come with me to Romania, which is still the best place.' Nora's was in shock. Adel had left the country in the 1950s. Those bad years were dreamed about soon as *the good old times,* when by the late 1960s Ceausescu had shown his fangs. The exodus of Jews from Romania was massive. And her mother, safely out of the disaster zone, wanted to return. What else could Nora have done other than try in her letters to make Adel understand that they loved her, but she should try the United States or Australia. Anything, but come back.

In a few months time, the only thing left for Nora to do was to go to Bucharest to receive in her loving arms a broken-hearted *Drága Nyuszikám.* Dear-Bunny had left behind the first man she could relate to since the war. A sadly optimistic Adel was full of joy to meet her two grandchildren born in her absence.

The door bell interrupted Nora's thoughts. She walked with measured steps and turned the lock as if in slow motion. As if in doubt whether to open it at all. Doru stood in a dripping rain coat, an extinguished cigarette hanging from his lips. His bewildered blue eyes peeked over Nora's shoulder into the dim living room.

"I'm alone," she explained.

"You're never alone," he pushed the door shut behind himself and took her in his arms like a brother.

The sense of lightness abandoned Nora just as suddenly as it had embraced her before. She was again game to uncertainty, self-disapproval, futility. She had no compelling reason to keep her thoughts from Doru. Thoughts of an irreconcilable conflict in their relationship. She turned on a small reading light. Nora needed to express her doubts. "An equation cannot be the same if one factor has changed," she said.

"Nothing has changed in the way we feel about each other." His voice reached her as if coming from outside the room. Nora, remotely struck, was torn between arguing the undeniable truth and nestling in Doru's arms.

She untied his coat belt.

Anti-climactic, imperceptible, Nora realized, as Doru kept stroking her face between smokes, the incongruities of her life transcending their togetherness, past and present.

"I'm more doubtful than ever." She paused. "I had no right to hurt his ego—"

"How can you even think like that? Nobody could've done more to protect a sick husband's ego." His voice was firm and Nora wanted to believe him. She bit her lips.

"I wish I had someone as devoted as you to hold my hand when my time comes," he said.

"I can't make a second profession of burying the men in my life. No, thanks for the trust."

"But I need you—"

"I hate needs. Especially my own," she said with disgust. "I could be proud now, only if I were able to live with whatever our marriage was." During the pregnant pause, Nora resisted to make the connection with Alfred's image as he sat on Paul's deathbed.

Doru was looking at her through the smoke pleadingly. "That's another issue where I don't agree," he said.

She was not ready to switch moods.

4

It was perhaps the first time in Tibor's life that he had no doubts about passing. He couldn't pay attention though, no matter how hard he tried. Not as much because of his emotional state. A distracting itch on his back was getting worse. He scratched at it and was alarmed. More and more afraid, he decided to seek medical help. In his ignorance he was terrified. Having his father suffer from a bad case of generalized psoriasis, complicated with crippling arthritis, he was anxious to have the cause of his rash diagnosed. He headed to the infirmary to see Rodica.

At the age of 23, when admitted to the hospital to be stitched up, his disillusion with life ran much deeper than the slash on his neck. Vali, the nurse who took care of him on the ward, couldn't wait for Tibor to be discharged. Then she wouldn't let him out of her sight until she got what she wanted. Tibor himself. Rodica, a good friend of Vali's, was transferred to the Public Transportation Authority's Infirmary about the same time. Not only had the company gained a much-needed Physician's Assistant, but Tibor gained a badly-needed friend. She remained his confidante for years through his many tribulations.

Vali, years his senior, was not a novelty to Tibor. That's how he was started. Like a juicy green plum hanging on the tree waiting to ripen and unexpectedly bitten into by an indiscriminate poacher. Not yet 14, moderately confused—as he saw himself in hindsight—he didn't really mind being seduced by the married woman next door with a husband home from work only on Sundays. She most likely couldn't resist the sight of the tight shorts hugging the handsome neighbor boy's virgin loins as he brought over a garment his mother had altered for her. That's what he figured later, when, more confident of his newly discovered abilities, he kept going back for more to the "old lady" he had soon learned was 30.

A thread of logic followed him throughout life. He refused to spell it out, even to himself. School had always been at the bottom of his list of priorities, after play, street pals, little pranks, and many other distractions. Not stupid, no, he didn't think he was stupid in the sense of not being able to keep pace with the others. Just not excited about school. Then, SEX lit up with big throbbing letters on the top of his list and knocked SCHOOL off the page, as if it didn't exist.

Not only that, but the slightest boasting to his pals, the slightest attempt to enlighten them about what girls were really like, brought him nothing else but the boys' taunting disbelief. So, he soon stopped bragging, for he chose to lose his friends rather than give them the name of his seductress as proof that he was not just fantasizing. With Tibor's untimely departure from school in favor of a premature sexual experience, alone and without pals, his mother had had an easy job flinging him like a wet dishrag into any apprenticeship she pleased.

Vali, different than that neighbor, and Tibor, not at all a child lover at age 23, would have lasted together longer than they did, if it weren't for her marital problems that she could solve only by relocating. Both of them were chagrined. Both of them recovered. Life went on. Tibor and Rodica remained friends.

"Two things. Ibi said yes, and I want you to look at my back," he said now to Rodica.

"Wait," Rodica gestured with irritation. "You proposed?"

"Yeah."

"After all we discussed, despite all your doubts?"

"I'm 31 going on 50."

"Tibi dear, you're such an ass. You're gonna fuck up your life again. At least the first time it was not your fault. What's your rush? Yes, sweetheart, you're 31, but going on 12 not 50."

"With friends like you I don't need enemies."

"Forget it. Let me look at your back," she shrugged. "You dummy," she said after looking. "Firstly, this is not your back, it's your ass. Your back ends at your waist."

"I'm shy to call things," he joked.

"Sure. Are you shy to show your butt to the doctor? I don't know for sure what this is," she said.

He didn't have to wait long to be seen. "Rodica, you're right . . . this isn't psoriasis . . . it's a garden variety dermatitis," Doctor Mann told her assistant. "Have you ever had an eczema before?" She asked Tibor who was lying on his stomach on the examination table with his pants lowered. With his head turned to one side, he could see the doctor's figure bent over and engrossed in studying his buttock through a magnifying glass.

He imagined himself with embarrassment lying on his back and having his front items looked at that way.

"Not that I know of," he said. "I could ask my mother."

"That's irrelevant. I mean as an adult." Doctor Mann stepped back. "Eczema might be caused by some local agent, like motor oil in your case, but it might be also triggered by stress."

"Stress?" Tibor was surprised at the idea that stress could break out on his bottom. His mouth was agape with confusion. He was trying hard to apply the term to the mental inventory of his predicaments that could fit the bill of causing stress. He was pondering whether his bottom was a mirror of his amorous, school, or housing problems.

"Like being between a rock and a hard place." Doctor Mann explained teasingly.

Of course, she knew, Tibor realized. He occasionally joined Rodica in the back room of the infirmary at lunch time. They made no point of stopping their conversation when Cornelia, or on rare occasions the doctor too, joined in for lunch.

"Some place to show stress," he finally said, turned with his back and buttoned his fly.

"Would you have preferred it on your other cheeks?" He heard Cornelia mocking him. No, he wouldn't have. He listened to Doctor Mann's instructions, took the prescription, and thanked her.

Nothing worse than a nasty stress that itches to boot, and nothing better than noticing, in a few day's time, that the itch and redness were gone.

He could go on working his eczematous tail off and staying late into the wee hours of the night, his mind like a pendulum, moving to and fro between his planned speech with Ibolya's parents, class work and fantasizing about nonexistent choices to solve his problems.

"I thought you have *some* ambition," Ibolya said with a disparaging grin, when Tibor told her a few weeks after his high school graduation, that he will take a year off from school.

All his problems boiled down to money. A place to live, a new car. He needed to make more money. Attending school was not a good bet to earn the extra money he needed as soon as possible, which was sooner than right away. His bride-to-be refused to understand. He was fuming. *Fuck her. The professor. Big deal. She'll be teaching little nitwits. Well, she's right. Sorry, Ibi. I'm an oaf. I want more than anything to get out of the pits. She doesn't have to tell me. Why does she have to criticize me? I've ambitions. More than ever. Maybe that doesn't say a lot. But can't she be patient? Damn it. I want to do all these things for her. For us.*

"Tibi," the Chief-engineer yelled into the pit. "Come up for a sec."

He did, and there was Davidescu with Doctor Mann, standing in the open door of the shop, their silhouettes projected against the bright sunshine.

"Yes, Comrade Chief?"

"Gimme a break, mister," Liviu said in a friendly tone. "Doctor Mann needs her car checked before driving to the seashore. When can you do it?"

In the brief moment before answering, Tibor thought of his visit to the infirmary. *She could've asked me. Well, she wanted the best and she didn't know who that might be, huh! No, it must be because Davidescu and the Doc's late husband were school mates and good pals,* Tibor knew that from Rodica, *and the Doc's husband loved to work on his own car. Now her car. So, basically, I guess, it's normal that she doesn't have the slightest idea. She asked Davidescu for advice. Maybe he offered to help her just to be nice to her. Poor woman. I've no reason not to be nice too.* "When are'ya leaving, Doc?"

"Sunday," she said.

"How's tomorrow?" he asked thinking of his own vacation.

"Fine. Thanks in advance."

The climate of corruption entangled people in a web ruled by practices as ingrained as, say, greeting etiquette. Younger people greet the older, men greet women, people greet others when entering a place, regardless of who they or the people already there are. Anything short of the rules would make one a boor and a loser. Tipping etiquette was no less convoluted, just as mandatory, deserving to be taught in school, in case one didn't get it with mother's milk. A survival skill.

Tips crossed the boundaries of social classes. Roll my log and I'll roll yours, whoever you are. A universally accepted and expected social phenomenon, tipping was the grease of social machinery. A byzantine way to add to one's income. Also to obtain services. Not to say, dangerous to accept having your tip refused. A set-up for being used.

Good friends were just about the only exception to this law of the land. Even remote family was not automatically exempt. In Tibor's environment, taxi drivers surreptitiously slipped their tips into the mechanics' pockets for the official work they were hired to do. Otherwise waiting for the repair was longer and who knows what else.

Tibor was never quite at ease with the system, but no amount of discomfort could prevail when it came to the much-needed extra money to beef up his puny salary. That is, moonlighting in full daylight.

A dilemma flared up now, not because the Doc came with the chief. Work on both his and the Director's cars—not the Party Secretary who favored another mechanic, a Communist Party member himself, unlike Tibor—he regarded as company work. There was an ego part as well. Repairing VIP cars elevated a mechanic to a certain level of respect. The company infirmary staff provided important services which at the Transportation Authority, and opposite to prevailing custom, were not used as currency. Many company employees would have loved to get sick leave in exchange for a tip or return services. The workers were out of luck with two doctors in a row. You're sick you get sick leave. You're not sick, you go to work. No exceptions. Quite annoying, but respectable. Doctor Mann stepped right into Doctor Gold's shoes, a man whose memory everyone revered. Both very friendly. This one, called Doc by everyone, except the hard-liner assholes who addressed her as Comrade Doctor, or the non-conformists who dared to call her Madame Doctor, came around to the shops often to check on work conditions. She seemed to revel in congenial chats, mixed with the workers, told them and was told jokes. To indicate some camaraderie she often spied with an amused expression over her shoulders, as if to say, 'This is between us and we're bad. Isn't that fun?' Like equals. Not stuck up in her white coat. But back in the office, she knew no chums, only patients.

Now the Doc became a potential problem. Tibor was petrified by the possibility of having to deal with her tip. Why was her money different? The familiar and expected illicit fringe benefit suddenly felt to Tibor like a humiliating threat. He dismissed his confusion as soon as he put the Doc's car on the pit.

"Doc," he called through the open infirmary window later. "I've got good news and bad news."

"Don't tell me I need a new car," she joked.

"No, you can wait with that till tomorrow."

"It's that bad?"

"No, that's the good news. The bad news is that I have to do more work on it and it won't be ready till six or seven."

"That's not a problem," she said. "Here's the number where you can reach me." She scrawled on a piece of paper and handed it to Tibor. "I'll return by tram."

"I'd bring it to you, but I'll need a ride back." He realized that the words slipped out without thinking. He hadn't thought at all how she would get her car back. It was not his problem. He needed to explain this to himself and all he could come up with was that he wanted to be nice to the Doc. Just like the Chief.

"That's awfully nice of you Tibor," she nodded. "Thanks."

Indeed he found it very easy to be nice to a good looking woman. Then, he felt like slapping his own face. *That's stupid, you moron. You can't afford to think of her that way, she is . . . What? A pretty young widow. Right roundnesses, up front, back down. Hmmm. Long, bouncy hair, captivating smile, great legs and ankles . . . and I was not even looking. What a package! Enough. Go back to work, you fool.*

As agreed, he pulled the car into the marked parking spot in the gravel lot behind the Doc's apartment building. In the elevator he looked himself over and flicked at little pieces of dried gook stuck to his greasy overalls, as if that could have improved his appearance.

He had seen the children before. One Saturday morning, he recalled, they were playing in the yard under the infirmary window. Shortage of baby sitters, he had thought then. Now the little girl opened the door, a skinny twig with short auburn hair, huge gray eyes, sharp looking, and pretty in her red dress with big bright flowers.

"Good evening, little girl," he said, not knowing her name.

"Come in. I'm Sonya," she said and took off running. "Mama," he heard from the entrance hall. "I think they brought the Skoditza," she said, using a term of endearment for the car, that Tibor had never heard before and that made him smile.

The Doc appeared in the doorway of the living room holding a whimpering little boy in her arms.

"Good evening, Doc," Tibor said.

"Good evening, Tibor," Nora said. "We had a little accident," she said, pointing to a small area of redness on the little boy's cheek. "The window sill ran into Dani."

"Don't worry, Dani. Worse things happen and they pass," Tibor held up an index finger with a black and blue nail.

"What happened to you?" Daniel asked sniffling.

"Promise not to laugh at me?" Tibor gave him a conspiratory wink.

"Promise," Daniel lifted a hand in oath.

"I confused my finger with the nail I wanted to hit." Tibor shook his hand and hissed suggesting pain. Daniel smiled.

"Did you cry?" Sonya asked.

"A little, just like Dani," Tibor answered. "But men don't cry a lot, right?" He caressed the boy's soaked face.

Daniel smiled and scrambled down from his mother's arms. Nora looked appreciative for the relief effort and told the children, "This is Tibor, the best car doctor I know."

As soon as Daniel ran away as if nothing happened, Nora asked Tibor, "May I offer you a drink?"

"Well, thank you," he hesitated, not sure whether it was proper or not to accept. "I won't refuse. I don't need to drive tonight." Then he thought that was a silly thing to say. He was not invited for a night of drinking. "Do you mind driving me home instead of to the shop? It's even closer," he added.

"That's fine," she said opening the middle bar section of a slick combo wall unit and pointing to the armchair. "Have a seat. Do you like fizzy gin?"

"Yes, I do," he said, thinking how much better a cold beer would've been.

Tibor started telling Nora the bad news about the back of her Skoda when the kids, screaming, burst through the room chasing each other. He was not about to outshout them, so he raised his glass, "To your health," he said and started to sip, just when the kids stormed in again from the other direction. Sonya stopped as though on a hard brake and examined Tibor with a startled look. The next second she took a leap and landed herself in his lap. He held the glass out of the way but barely saved it from being knocked out of his hand. Now it was his turn to be startled, but it was much too soon. Next thing, Sonya stuck her index finger in his drink, then licked her finger and repeated the operation under the adults' stunned gazes.

"Sonya, stop that immediately," Nora yelled, yanking her daughter from the dazed Tibor's lap. "I apologize, she is such a lively child."

That's putting it mildly, Tibor thought disapprovingly of Nora's abilities to control her children. He felt suddenly uncomfortable and more than ready to go. He could tell her about the car some other time, now he wanted to get out. "No harm done," he said, placed his glass on the coffee table and got up.

"Are you ready for a ride, kids?" Nora asked to his relief.

In the tight cage of the elevator, Daniel tried to fend off Sonya's pinching-attack by whining and sawing the air. The small cubicle could not hold the little girl's bursting vivacity. Not altogether pleasant, no matter how much Tibor tried to look at her behavior as simply that of a child. He could barely hold back a disapproving sneer and stood frozen. *What a brat.* He saw the embarrassment on Nora's face and did his best not to stare at her. It appeared she was looking away too.

"Your car is fine for now," he said in the car, "but I'd like you to talk to me after you return."

"What's wrong?"

"Nothing that would be a problem on the road," he assured Nora. "Rust, as expected."

"Oh, well. It's not a Rolls Royce, is it? Thank you very much for taking your time," she said, stopping promptly where he told her to, in front of his parents' gate in the tree-lined street of modest family homes.

"No problem. Thanks for the ride," he said turning towards Nora, reaching for her hand resting on the steering wheel. He lifted it and kissed the back of it as any well-mannered gentleman would when taking leave from a lady. Very careful not to let his eyes linger too long.

He heard a nervous revving of the engine as he walked toward the house. He was thinking neither of the little brat of the daughter, nor the condition of the car, or the Doc. His fear of being offered a tip had passed. He felt relieved. He couldn't tell why, but he felt a deep pity for the skinny little chap with wide open, scared eyes and peachy cheeks, softly crying in his mother's arms. He felt some kind of kinship with this little person, whom he could comfort with such little effort. He had never felt that way before. It was more gratifying than . . .

5

Steam rising from the bubbling, boiling electric sterilizer filled the office with a scent of warm yeasty mist. It was a soothing background to the hassle of work, practically double than normal, or more, due to the raging flu epidemics.

Nora plunged into her work with determination. The stack of charts grew higher and higher on the side of her desk. Nora struggled to conjure up the concentration that, after a few hours, was under attack. A backache claimed her attention with a vengeance. The pain she had forgotten for weeks was as disappointing as finding a rotten core when biting into an unblemished apple. She could cry. Stretching didn't alleviate the pain drilling between her shoulder blades.

Nora faced the complexities of life, seeing herself as a puppet acting in an unnatural manner at the whim of an odd set of strings tugging her between professional and private demands. She was hard-pressed to reconcile her two selves. *Rotten apple, crazy puppet, which one am I?*

Driving to the day care, an elbow in the open window, enjoying the promising brisk spring wind, she was waiting for the light to change. She rotated her achy shoulders and rubbed her back against the wooden spheres of the seat back cover. Rolling spheres. *From a proton I became the entire nucleus, no energy adjustment to keep me together. I wish I knew how this works. My electrons share their energy with me.* She thought with warmth of her children. *What is this new atom? I'll call it an unstable Norium. I have to make it stable, find a new balance.*

Dragging home with Daniel, Nora remembered how humiliating it was to get him into the only day care in the housing development of thousands of families. The dilemma to bribe the officials, or to prostrate herself in front of them. No children of high income parents, even widowed ones, had a place. Nora had searched throughout the city for alternate solutions. There was nothing else in a workable radius, private or otherwise. There was no doubt in Nora's mind that the bright and inquisitive child belonged in a structured environment. Finally, after a humiliating pleading on Nora's part, the committee disregarded income as the ruling criterion in Daniel's case.

Other trials, those of a new evening, were waiting for her. She had to figure out a buffer, a diversion, to keep her moods, ranging from rigid inertia to jumpy hesitation, from taking hold of her for the evening. Extreme mood-swings tormented her and those around her with a totally illogical pattern. Fortunately this was not so at work.

"Dani, what do you think of dumplings for dinner?" She squeezed Daniel's hand as encouragement. The little hand that one cold Sunday morning . . . Nora shivered as the fierce scene burst into her memory. They were at the cemetery. Nora had just told her children that that's where Tata had to go. Soon Daniel fell on his knees and started to claw with his bare fingers at the burial-mound, fixing his gaze on the unyielding dirt and shouting, "It's cold and dark in there. Take him out." She again, as always, tried to alleviate the children's bereavement, to lift it off their tender souls and minds with hugging arms and caressing hands.

"Yummy," she now heard Daniel, giving his lips a funny lick.

She boiled potatoes, kneaded the dough, took a jar of prune butter from the pantry. And wept. She had made dumplings so often for Paul. He loved them. Apprehensive, captive of memories, she bit her lip. Some memories, would crystallize with time, to an essence of shared happy times. Through the years happiness had condensed to thin, few and far between, precious lodes in the somber rock of protracted misery.

She wiped her tears with the back of her wrist, keeping her dough-clad hand away from her face. She could not wipe away the dark circles under her sleep-deprived eyes. She laughed by herself like a half-wit. *Who will eat forty dumplings each the size of a small canon ball?* Her usually infallible sense of quantity failed. She filled a large bowl and two small dishes with dumplings rolled in buttered bread crumbs. She inhaled deeply, unrelenting in her need of using all her senses, then picked a dumpling between her index finger and thumb and bit into it. She nodded in self-approval.

"Dani," she said. "We have forty dumplings."

"I'll eat one," Daniel voiced his less than gargantuan appetite.

"I'd expect you to do better than that."

Nora picked up the phone. "Manci," she said with her voice as soft as she could manage, her eyes radiating affection. "You in mood for some prune dumplings?"

"You made them?" her mother-in law asked in her husky voice.

"All forty of them."

"You silly girl," Manci said.

Nora kept on joking. "If the kids eat three each, I should be happy. Me four, that's ten. Adel and Arthur another eight," she went on mocking her mistake and the distribution of the excess. "Are you counting?"

"I'll take the rest," Manci said.

Next she dialed her mother, happy that for once she had cooked for her.

A finger hesitantly held out as a gauge, Nora turned on the hot water faucet. A sarcastic victory sign acknowledged the water pressure. Warm to boot. She refilled the containers—buckets, pails and pots—lined up under the sink, empty after the two dry days before. The lack of water pressure became a crippling problem because of the ever more frequent power failures that left people in the dark and cold many evenings. Flashlights started to become useless too, as batteries were also in short supply. The good old candles had to do. Hope was high that matches would not disappear from the market. Touchwood was the next expected step back into pre-historic ages.

After the shower she walked to the hall, took an open bottle of beer from the refrigerator, poured a little into her palm and rubbed in into her hair. The juice of the single half-ripe lemon in her possession would've been better, but too scarce a commodity to be squandered on vanity. *This is ridiculous, I must get hold of some hair spray.* Cosmetic products smuggled from abroad, by people lucky enough to be occasionally allowed to travel, were sold on the black market for astronomical prices.

The night came and with it the unwelcoming pillow, as if closing her eyes to seek restful sleep did nothing other than open the door for relentless visions. Alone with her journal, tossed around by the ups and downs of her own moods, Nora jotted down shreds of incoherent thoughts.

The particularly erratic weather pattern of a wintery spring had turned into a boring wet summer. On Sundays it rained as if on a cue. The children grew frenzied with cabin fever, Nora kept slapping them as if that could calm anyone. A firm believer in the profound influence of meteorological changes on people's behavior and diseases, she started to blame the weather for her own extreme moods.

One morning, as the toothbrush touched the back of her gum, Nora retched. Her empty stomach kept heaving in pain. She pushed her hand against her belly, she took deep breaths. *Food poisoning? No. The kids are fine.* As if hit by lightning, Nora came to realize, that neither was her hormonal function suspended due to grieving, as she was inclined to believe, nor was she that lucky to have food poisoning turn her stomach inside out. Head hanging over the sink, the unpleasantness of retching shrinking behind the jolts of her thoughts, there was no doubt in her mind that she was pregnant. In that cold and rainy evening of loneliness that drove her into Doru's arms, she had carelessly dismissed the possibility of being fertile.

An unwanted pregnancy in the legal climate of a total ban on abortions, and the challenge of finding a way out, promised to be both a sensory and an intellectual agony. The unfairness and absurdity of the situation grabbed her with vicious claws, as she leaned over the sink trembling.

"Doru, could you take an afternoon off next week?"

"For something interesting? Sure."

"It's relative," she said first, deceiving herself with the intention not to divulge her secret. She felt punished, deeply embarrassed and angry. For being in trouble due to her own stupidity and carelessness, when deep in her soul all she wanted was to make a clean slate of her private life. "It's a business trip," she threw her arms up. "I'm pregnant." Nora blurted it out like a petty thief caught red-handed.

"Huh?" Dumbfounded, he forgot to close his mouth. "Would it be very nasty of me to say 'I told you so'?"

Why do people have this tendency of generalizing? Why does he have to chide me, now, when it's too late? He was never totally happy, not more than skin deep, about my rejecting the use of a condom. Fine. So much for that. "Yes, very," she told him after finishing her inner monologue. "No need. I am thinking more in terms of being punished. No, not for being sloppy, but for not ending this entire affair with you long ago—" She was getting all worked up.

"Now, wait a minute," he raised one hand in protest while he planted the other on his waist. "Is it my fault?"

"No, it's mine, of course . . . it's always mine, even when I can't figure out why . . . Now, at least, I have the consolation of knowing why," she said with bitterness, ringing her hands.

"I'm truly sorry . . . but . . . what do you want me to do?" He stood stiffly.

"I found a guy."

"Is it safe?" He asked with a tone of genuine concern. She didn't go into details of the tribulations she went through going from colleague to non-professional, and back to someone else who might know someone willing, to being lost in the maze of covert information she was never before interested in. Yes, it was as safe as it could be, to have an abortion performed by a physician in a sterile environment.

They met first at a patisserie. She was nervously spooning at her *savarin,* as he walked in with an attaché case in hand, well-dressed, jovial, oval blondish-reddish face radiating confidence. Too slick to be likable, was Nora's first impression. She was given instructions. The car had to leave after dropping Nora a few corners away from the district infirmary of Doctor X., who didn't want a car waiting there for two hours. "Why so long?" she had asked. "I'll give you a little Valium. I don't like to hurt anyone," he had assured her. "My fee is two thousand," he continued. His fee didn't surprise Nora. She hadn't really expected any courtesy in the medical underworld, contrary to the common practice, where payment between colleagues was totally unconscionable, and physicians were honored to be of assistance to each other.

She ran to the building in the pouring warm rain. The car revved up behind her. Doctor X. was alone in the rural dispensary, a lonely and simple building at the corner of two deserted streets. In a corner of the single room, a column of steam rose to the ceiling, emitted by a large size electric sterilizer. Besides the gynecological table at one end, there was a low consultation table, more like a cot, hidden half way behind a pulled curtain. That was all that caught Nora's attention. *I'm not going to ask questions. I have to trust him. I won't make him nervous with my interfering.* However, the calm she tried to impose upon herself evaded her in favor of an unsettling uneasiness. He took her coat politely. In the midst of pleasantries, he handed Nora the promised Valium and a shot glass.

"What's this?" she asked.

"Good old Romanian elixir," he said sneering.

"You mean *tuica?*" She couldn't imagine swallowing the liquid fire disguised as plum brandy.

"The best you ever had, I promise." He held the glass in front of her face and stared at Nora as if trying to hypnotize her.

"I don't think so. Give me some water, please."

"All right, as you wish, but in my experience the two together would relax you the best."

"Listen, I'm not used to either. The two together will knock me out for two days. You don't want me lying here for two days, do you?"

"I wouldn't mind having you here for as long as you want," he winked shrewdly. She despised both his words and his wink, but it was not the time or the circumstance to act upon her intuition, which was to leave immediately.

He poured the brandy down in one gulp himself. This worried Nora for more practical reasons than her primitive intuition, and she told him so. He reassured her by caressing her hands crossed over her stomach, as she was urged to relax on the cot, that he'll be fine and so will she, while holding the glass in front of her, full again. She shook her head.

She was getting sleepy.

"Drink only half," he said, lifting her head off the pillow and pressing the glass to her lips. She drank. She had lost her will. "Close your eyes now, I'll wake you up when the instruments are ready," he said. She drifted away.

Nora could barely part her eyelids when she heard his voice calling and felt crowded. He was sitting next to her on the edge of the cot and was reaching for her panties. She mumbled something, tried to get up. He only wanted to help, he said. Her limbs felt heavy and purposeless. She couldn't stay awake, kept drifting in and out of sleep. Nimble fingers sliding up her thighs woke her again, his helping hands, she remembered through the haze. It's probably time. She mumbled again, "I think . . . I can . . . manage that . . ." His reassuring voice, then quiet again.

Hands were pushing her knees apart. She fought to open her eyes. He was between her legs, lowering his erect pink penis to her crotch. Her weak, numb arms, like rubber bands against his chest, could not stop his thrust jolting her inert body back and forth.

"Monster. Get off me." She whimpered, suddenly awake, helpless and humiliated.

It didn't take him long. Minutes? She was not sure. What did it matter? He was sitting again next to her, delivering his warped logic. "Sorry, you were so beautiful in your sleep."

"Oh, shut your face . . . you pig . . . you monster . . ."

"Why should you get upset? . . . You'll be clean of everything in five minutes . . . I'll be very good to you . . . I guaranty . . . Nothing bad happened, forget it . . . That's how I am . . . It doesn't hurt anyone."

Nora's words froze, her eyes went blind, her tears dried up. A piece of dirt doesn't cry and doesn't think. Inertly she let him pour another shot of brandy down her throat. She was not sure whether she couldn't stand or was ashamed to move and walk to the table. In a few minutes, perhaps immediately after the brandy, she was being carried and deposited on the table like a corpse. He put her legs in the stir-ups, this time with purely *professional* motions, and went right ahead with the procedure. She drifted away again.

He woke her gently. He was pressing a bandage between her legs. She felt wooden and remembered no pain. She couldn't remember the scraping sound of the curette either, the sound that always raised the hair on her back and forearms whenever present at a D&C, regardless at which end of the curette she happened to be. The lightning of a thought crossed her mind. The flashing image of a blue-eyed baby in six months. *Did he do anything else than humiliate me?*

Nora put on her panties. He helped her with the coat. Not one more word was said. She could hear the car pulling up in front of the building. She handed him the envelope. He opened the door. She stepped out without looking back.

In the car Nora quietly broke down and hid her face in her palms.

"Are you all right? What's the matter?" Doru rested a compassionate hand on her knee.

She said something evasive. In the soporific whooshing of the windshield wipers she dozed on and off on the way home.

Rape, the hideous word, the monstrosity mankind invented. Worse than humiliation. Nora felt flayed alive, not just living stripped naked. A dispossessed and annihilated self.

If I could not defend myself against rape, if it happened to me, all I can ask is: does anyone escape it at one time or another? If not in the past, then what lurks in women's future? Why do men do it? Because they can? By their sheer muscle mass advantage, turning women into powerless children? All are rapes of children. She refused to accept that type of men as paradigm. Just bad luck of being in the wrong place in the wrong time where a brute with no self-respect lurked.

Her self-respect annihilated? She needed to find words to restore it, but words turned against her like a murderous weapon held by weak untrained hands. She couldn't confide in her own journal. The shame was too deep. Telling her story face to face to anyone was impossible. His name she forgot. Self-defense of the memory. A sign of his nothingness.

What did the nameless monster know, 'You'll be clean in five minutes?' Could she have entered the spheres of black magic of one of those legendary gypsy women, she would have fashioned thunderbolts of fury out of her blind rage, to strike and deliver an everlasting spell to torment his pathetic soul and slowly rot his vile body, forever burn his sick pleasures into a train of stinky smoke he would drag everywhere, until he wished he were dead. Her unquenchable impotent wrath, like a sagging dead serpent, was dripping its sticky juices. Burning her soul. Not his, of course.

How long and how deep can I let this affect my sanity? was the next question rising from a soul which did not easily give in to defeat. Restoring inner balance emerged as a paramount goal, no matter how destabilizing the present impasse seemed. A balance between the involuntary and voluntary. Involuntary: the monster's act. Voluntary: her resolve to rid herself of the damage. *I have to live with myself. I can't let a low life poison and destroy my self-respect forever. I have to put the violence behind me and go on with my life.*

"I can't bear myself," she told Vera, an old friend she had bonded to since Paul's death. Their singlehood that they had arrived at in their own ways, had brought them closer. Vera, a divorced piano teacher, had become what Nora always wanted. A woman confidante, a friend with whom to share her private thoughts. One of Paul's childhood friends, she emerged after his death as one of the not-so-many who really stood by Nora. The children would have a ball when Vera agreed to sleep over. Vera made the kids roll on the floor, and the walls bulge with laughter. She downsized her cynical humor and tuned it to the children's understanding with a musician's fine pitch.

"Nori, that's much worse than if you couldn't bear *me,*" Vera answered. "I could leave, you can't. Don't do it to yourself."

Though Nora was certain of her friend's unqualified support, she couldn't bring herself to disclose the reason for her dismal moods. She had ruminated the reason, as if rolling a repulsive piece of rotten meat around in her mouth, unable to swallow it or spit it out. She only said, "What makes you want to associate with a person who sways between moods of demented disposition and immature exuberance, without any warning or apparent reason?"

"It's fun. Don't you ever stop swaying." Nora was sure Vera would never have said anything like that unless she was ignorant of her current state of mind.

6

The meeting with Ibi's parents was less humbling than she'd predicted. Tibor put the engagement ring on her finger right then and there in exchange for them accepting him as a future son-in-law. A modest ring with a tiny ruby. So much for the event. Wedding sometime next spring.

He painted his old room, moved back home and fought his mother for every piece of furniture she wanted moved in and he wanted kept out. Any exchange with her felt like tightrope walking. He couldn't afford to offend her. Everything he wanted, or said, she could—if she wanted to—take as offense. Aware that his father was on his side, Tibor expressed his gratitude by taking him to the corner pub, where he slowly sipped his beer while his father drank one of his many.

"You'll never grow up," the old boy teased Tibor, obviously happy that his son did not turn out a drinker. Tibor shook his head as if saying, 'Nope.' "Good for you." The father tapped Tibor's knee with satisfaction.

Wishing he could build an extension to the parental house overnight was far from taking care of the issue. *How the hell am I supposed to round up connections to have my miserable little plan approved?* He was prepared that a good part of the expense would go into the pockets of officials as heavy baksheesh. Without greasing palms, handshakes meant nothing. Private construction was no priority. That is, no construction company would contract any private work before government-related ones were finished. And they never were. His father could have organized a team of construction pals to build a room, a bathroom and a kitchen. Of course, Tibor would have worked alongside, but then where would the construction material come from? As a private person, one had to wait until all the government orders were filled. They never were. *Fuck the government. They drop law after law, like horse shit on the road; they don't even have time to write up regulations for them.*

So much for building. He had the estimated cost down, it would have been around 40,000 Lei, which represented almost three years of his salary without having bought toothpaste or gone to a movie. Well, if he counted the tips he was getting, a year-and-a-half of income, still without having bought toothpaste. He was stretching his imagination trying to figure out a way to make more money. He came up with nothing.

To get an official apartment, the cheapest and best solution, was improbable unless some miracle happened. Tibor didn't believe in miracles. The waiting list was getting worse by the month. The company had his name because they didn't refuse anybody's application. It didn't mean a thing. A mere mockery of generosity.

Then there was the newly-instated opportunity to buy. The city started to sell a number of apartments per year. The same kind. Lilliputian everything. The waiting list for those was a little shorter. A year perhaps. The cost? A two-room unit—meaning a kitchen, a bath, and two rooms, all tiny—was going for around 80,000 Lei. That meant twice as long without toothpaste as with the extension Tibor couldn't figure out how to build.

Besides, his second-hand car that would have been in the scrap metal pile long before, unless owned by an auto-mechanic, was dying. He wouldn't compromise. He dreamed of a new car. Another waiting list of a year or so, another year without a single toothbrush, or toothpaste, or shoestring, or anything else for that matter, not even gasoline to run the fucking car. Steal like everybody else? He was afraid. Not that others where not—afraid, that is—but he lacked reliable friends to cover, when gasoline was being drained from parked buses or diverted before they were filled. He was sure that sooner or later he would have to do it too. The gas shortage was one of the worst ones.

He felt like a dog running in circles grabbing at his own tail.

"Ibi, would'ya explain to me how you are related to these people?" Tibor asked on their drive east towards the Sekler wonderland of forest-ringed volcanic lakes and spas with bubbly thermal springs.

Her hands were clutching the top of the seat back, elbows spread like wings. "Joska is a cousin of a sister-in-law of my father's sister and—"

"Stop it. Spare me the trouble," Tibor interrupted laughing. He could never understand how these relationships worked.

It was a long drive through the wide cultivated fields tapering into river valleys, water pouring over boulders and into calm eddies along the road. Fishermen waded hip deep, some waving to the passing car out of boredom when the fish wouldn't bite. Children sprung from under the trees and ran to the road with hands stretched out showing summer apples for sale. He slowed down thinking he might stop and walk around, breathe the fresh smell of the forest. Flocks of sheep took over the road from place to blocked place, staking their native claim with an immutable calm.

"When are ya gonna learn to drive?" Tibor asked from the blue, it seemed, but it was his aching tired body that triggered the thought.

"Don't worry about me. I'm fine," she said.

"It's tiring to drive alone." He looked at her. "Don't you want to travel and share the driving?"

"You don't look tired." She cast off his hint.

His elbow rested in the open window, his head tilted onto his fist. He gazed at the shadow of the car leading the way, away from the sun, as if it was towing the car. His mind escaped into the dark silhouette of the car running on the light gray asphalt. *She can't see the forest because of the trees. How was I at 24?* The sardonic smile on his face poured inside him bitterly. *What kind of measuring stick am I anyway? She'll have a college diploma in a year, she'll teach little children to write and add, and sing. So, she won't drive.* He would have loved to sing, but couldn't.

"Ibi, sweetheart," he blinked at her. "I'm getting sleepy. Would you sing something for me?"

"Hum, hum," she cleared her throat. "Debrecen has the best turkey, Let's go there and buy so many . . ." She went on animated, tapping her knees. He hummed along. Off tune.

"We'll make it before dark," he said as if to himself, passing slowly clattering ox-pulled carts loaded high with fresh hay.

In Tusnad, the evening seemed to come earlier in the midst of the thick dark pine forest. They found the villa, and, at the back of the dim entrance with peeling paint, the screeching wooden steps leading to the manager's apartment.

"My, my," the middle-aged pot-bellied man, a napkin hooked into his shirt collar, smiled and clapped his hands. "I can't believe you are the little Ibolya. Well, well, Bozsi, come quick, they're here," he called on his wife.

They were sitting at the dinner table before they could look around, the pilaf and chicken spooned right onto plates that appeared as if by magic. The overpowering hospitality left Tibor with mixed impressions. It was a little too much, though it looked genuine.

"It's fortunate that you came in June. I have a great room for you," Joska said to them.

"It's not too much trouble, I hope?" Ibi asked.

"What trouble? It's always nice to have family here, but later, during the main season, it might have been a problem for me to put you in any room."

"But of course, please tell us what's our part of the deal," Tibor said.

"That's silly, my friend," Joska motioned gently. "Anything for little Ibi."

After dinner they drove up a gravel road. They could see lights from buildings behind clusters of tall slender pines. The small villa at the end of the drive looked abandoned. Joska unlocked the door and switched on the weak light bulb in the hall.

"This little gem is not much at first sight," he said obviously proud. Tibor and Ibi were holding hands behind their benefactor's back. Squeezing gently. The place was, to say the least, romantic. "Only four rooms, and for now you'll be the only guests. Until a few years ago there was no indoor plumbing here. You'll like the bathroom. Right there," he pointed toward the darkest end of the hall.

"Great," Tibor meant more the absence of occupants than the common bath. He felt embarrassed for being an ingrate.

"And this is your room," Joska said proudly leading them into a little room filled with wicker furniture, the scrubbed pine floor covered here and there with colorful rag-rugs.

"This is truly charming," Ibi said appropriately excited. "Joska, are ya sure you won't have any trouble letting us stay here? We can afford it, you know."

"Don't be silly. I'm the boss. In season would be different. People come with assignment vouchers from their unions and I couldn't do a thing," he said. "Now, let me show you the boiler. You're family, you can help me and be in charge of your own hot water. Wouldya? I won't hold you to the official hours."

"Please, of course. Could we help with anything else?" Tibor offered.

"Be serious," he said with a wink. "You take good care of little Ibi."

"That goes without saying," Tibor winked back.

"That's a boy. Tomorrow I'll show you around. You'll have fun, I promise."

There was no time to stargaze. Hauling their bags, throwing them around the room, arranging the wardrobe, gave just enough time for the water to warm up, so they could wash off the dust of the road.

Tibor could go to sleep before his head hit the pillow, Ibi didn't look less tired either. They lifted the blanket, and sat on the double bed that creaked like an exotic musical instrument. They laughed at the opportunity of mischief to fill the house with live rhythms of wicker.

"No," she said pouting. "I wanna rest today."

"Didn't you like the hike to the crater yesterday?" he asked rubbing her hands placed over the blanket.

"Yeah," she said. "But, it was tough."

"Well, I'm sorry." He would have liked to enjoy a hike each day to hidden creeks and alpine meadows. The day before, arriving out of breath at the rim of the ancient volcanic crater, overwhelmed by the view of the sloping meadow sprinkled with pine trees and boulders encircling the crystal mirror of the lake, he had realized the magnitude of what he must have missed in his life. An avalanche of desire for nature swept him off his feet. *And she's not moved.* He felt sorry for her still missing what he had just discovered. Never mind that it was her idea and her connections that brought them there. "So, what would you like to do today?" He dropped the idea of the other trail he would have liked to take.

"Oh, just hang around."

"Hum," he thought for a while. "How about going bowling?"

"You must be kidding," she said sitting up surprised. "Me?"

"Why not? The bowling alley looks quite good. It's right next to the grocery store." He had checked it out the other morning when he went for provisions for the picnic they devoured at the crater, *Oh, was that good!* while Ibolya had turned to the other side to finish her beauty sleep.

"I've never tried," she said now.

"I'll teach you." He tickled her.

"Oh, com'on," she shrieked, swatting away his hands and jumping out of the bed.

7

Suspended weightlessly in midair, she sat naked, exposed to derision, on one of the pans of a huge scale. On the pan below, grinning at her with a cold confidence, sat a glass heavy with booze. Any further question was devoid of importance, her attempts to go on futile, her disgust with Doru's drinking pervasive. She could touch her inner chaos.

Think of something in the shower. I never get ideas in the shower. Perhaps in my sleep, but those I forget. I have to find an honorable solution. Why honorable and by whose standards?

A tiff erupted from the jumble of feelings.

"I could light your breath." She was loudly angry.

"Pretend it's your favorite perfume," he mocked her.

"Doru. This is serious."

"Nora. You seriously piss me off."

After removing themselves from each other's company for a while he called. "Hello, how have you been?"

"Living."

"With whom?"

"What's this? Are you obsessed, obnoxious, stupid, or all of the above?" she snapped.

"Forget it . . . that's not why I called . . ." He asked her opinion about a new anticholinergic drug. As if he didn't know all about it. He was manufacturing it. *Poor excuse,* Nora thought. Should he return some books to her? he went on. Anything would've been more subtle; she expected him to do a better job.

He showed up without the books. He thought he had them in the attaché case, he said.

"If you want to talk, go right ahead, no excuse is necessary. We're friends, aren't we?" Nora said.

"I was wondering what brought about this abrupt end?"

"Abrupt? Cumulative, perhaps." She was eager to talk, soon to be sorry. "Our ups and downs were getting out of hand . . . I can't tolerate your drinking any more . . . I often stepped on your nerves . . . I want a lover who is always pleasant . . . with whom I can always be pleasant . . . You disappear lately without warning, like saying something is wrong with me . . . Oh, no? . . . It isn't me? You're so generous. Let's leave it at that."

Her dread of longing for Doru slowly subsided in the following weeks.

Work was enjoyable and the load light. Not midsummer yet, the air was stale in the office, despite the open windows over the little flower bed with a wooden bench.

"This kind of weather slows me down," Rodica grumbled covering a yawn with her hand. "I wish I were at a beach somewhere."

Nora slapped her forehead in a gesture of recollection. "Thanks for reminding me."

She dialed an interior number.

"Is Comrade Davidescu there? . . . Yes, it's she . . . Sure I can hold . . . *Servus,* Liviu, how are you?"

The chief-engineer was fine and couldn't be happier to use any excuse to get away from his office despite Nora's apologies that she really didn't want to be too much of a nuisance. In minutes he showed up at the infirmary door. In his effusive way, he bestowed two kisses on each of the three women's cheeks, then sat down sprawling his legs wide, and slammed down his palms on his knees. "Now tell me, sweetheart," he said to Nora. "What can I do for you?"

"After years of not taking advantage of the battalions of auto-mechanics swarming around this place, now I need one."

"Something wrong or just maintenance?"

"You know, I put my stethoscope on the hood and didn't hear a heartbeat. You think it's dead?" Nora put on a clownish grin.

"Making fun of me, huh? I'll show you," he said and reached for the phone. "Is Tibor there? . . . No . . . Just tell him I'm coming." Then he told Nora. "Come on, let's walk over to the shop. It's too nice outside to sit in here." He put his arm around Nora's waist.

Liviu treating her with such intimacy bothered Nora only to the extent that people knew they were not related. On the other hand Liviu's friendship with Paul was known, as well as his outgoing exuberant personality towards everyone. They walked all the way to the taxi shops with his arm around her.

Earnest sandcastle planning and building kept all the children at the water's edge. The waves splashed them as they crouched low, scooping up the wet sand for their growing architectural masterpieces. White cotton sun hats floated over the keeps of the castles like clouds on a windless sky. They were cheerful days. Nora was content to acknowledge the sun's mending effect on her bones, back and moods. The mixed company and the passing of the time did the better part of the job.

Around the promontory of the sand bluff, the quaint nudist beach was dignified and respected, with the exception of the Bulgarian border patrols peering shamelessly through their binoculars at the sun worshipers. There, any erotic digression was discretely secluded in the craters some dug for themselves in the sand, big enough to spread a blanket under the overhang of the bluff. Nora hoped that discretion would bring those people out there at times other than the customary family hours.

The children never commented on the naked people, until one day Daniel stopped startled. "Mama, is that a chocolate statue?" He pointed to a woman smeared all over with mud, soaking in the sun with arms spread, palms to the sky.

"No dear. She thinks the mud will cure her aching joints," Nora explained.

"How do you know her joints ache?"

"I'm only guessing. Some people believe that."

"Do you believe that?"

"I guess if I'd hurt, I'd try anything to feel better. Like my back. You know when I ask you to walk on my back?" she said.

"I think you're joking. She's a statue." He positioned himself to emulate the woman's posture. Nora hoped the woman would not notice.

The sun painted the horizon in an orange glow. Nora and the children packed the car for a day trip to a beach campground where the Geras, practically Paul's and Nora's best friends, were roughing it, for contrast with their urban life in the capital.

Between spreading suntan oil on each other, preparing lunch, watching the four children, Magda and Dennis updated Nora. Their situation was desperate. They had applied for an emigration visa about two years before. Magda had lost her job. As an *undesirable element unfaithful to the motherland and to the Communist Party,* she couldn't be trusted to teach future engineers at the Polytechnic Institute. She had been demoted before she *could undermine any minds with rotten capitalist ideas.* Temporary jobs from then on were her lot.

"I've narrowly escaped prison," Dennis said when Magda finished.

"What?" Nora was shocked.

"Didn't you happen to wonder how I got a job so easily after I dared to apply to leave the country from the envied position of Senior Research Chemist at Lenuta?" he asked rhetorically. The common diminutive for any Elena, used with an unusually defiant inflection, meant nobody else than Ceauşescu's wife, omnipotent director of Romania's only chemical research institution.

"One of her foul plays?" Nora asked.

"Listen how far her claws reach." Dennis told the whole story. What he'd meant by an easy-to-get job was a position in a chemical factory where unspeakably hazardous conditions reigned, where exposure to fumes much above the allowed levels was the least of the occupational hazards. All reports were fudged. On paper, the place appeared to be as immaculate as a pharmacy. When someone got sick, he was denied the advantage of claiming an occupational disease. No such thing without occupational hazards. Hospitals were instructed to change the discharge diagnoses for such patients. So, when Dennis was hospitalized with the diagnosis of asthma after a few weeks of work, he found out the hard way that he was not supposed to make it. Lenuta got angry that Dennis, ungrateful for the privilege of working at *her* institution, had not paid yet for the affront with his life. Not long after, to everyone's surprise, new imported machinery, paid for in hard currency, arrived from Germany. The factory has been requesting it for years. Never receiving a word about the possibility of ever getting it, suddenly, there it was. It was installed at the testing division. Dennis, recently out of the hospital, was transferred there *to protect* his frail health. Dennis was known to be as healthy as a young lion, that is, until Lenuta planned to have him killed.

"Finally, a wonderful job, right?" Dennis sneered. After a few months of bliss, during the night shift—Dennis's shift that month—the new, expensive Western technology exploded, nearly killing him. He was accused of sabotage and arrested. It was close to a miracle that he managed to get away. Without access to the factory, he had a hard job, but managed to demonstrate that he couldn't be implicated, unless he was a determined suicidal madman. He was not interested in finding out who had been paid to commit the sabotage, and time it to Dennis's shift. "Now," he said, "we're waiting for an exit visa. Any place that would accept us."

"What do you mean *any* place?" Nora was ignorant of the Gera family's last six months. One did not talk about things like that on the phone. Weather, vacation, kids. That's all that their tapped phones could be trusted with.

"Every time we got a rejection we've re-applied to another country. At this point, we don't even know whether the application to Venezuela or the one to Australia is active," Magda said.

Nora, deep in her thoughts, kept poking a pickle on her tin plate. "Not much use crying over spilled milk . . . but if we didn't return in '69 from Belgium, Paul would be on dialysis, and the kids would probably already be there with us courtesy of the International Red Cross, and so forth," she sighed.

"Think future, not past," Dennis said.

"All right." Nora followed a line of thoughts that became a noose around her neck along the years. "Why defection couldn't fit into Paul's concept is not that difficult to understand. Intellectually. Emotionally, for me it was never easy to passively accept that we were stuck. And to see the children's future go up in smoke. The decision I'll have to ultimately make alone won't be easier."

"Positive thinking should simplify the process," Dennis said.

"What would I do as a single parent, if they would do to me what they did to you?"

"You didn't work with *her*," he said.

"Neither did Magda," Nora said.

"True, but I was on the teaching faculty. They could not let me poison the innocent minds of the Communist youth with some warped formulas."

"All right," Nora said. "They can send me to some godforsaken country district. What would my kids do there?"

"There's no easy way," Dennis said.

"Perhaps defecting comes easy to some," Nora said pensively. "Not to me. They wouldn't even give me a shitty tourist passport. I couldn't cross the border officially with my children." Nora was blissfully ignorant of what she was to experience in the not so distant future. "Some people flee. I couldn't hide in a refrigerator truck with two children."

Back home, refreshed and ready to embark on a road to normalcy, Nora returned to work, holiday over, half the summer still ahead. A new, sometimes excessive verve drove her from morning until evening.

The kids exhausted Adel who, by the afternoon, was ready to hand them over to their mother. Grateful for every bit of shopping Adel could do for them, Nora still had to procure certain items in short supply. There was a line at the Aprozar—the ignominious chain of moldy produce stores—one couldn't pass without estimating the length of the queue against the few crates of skinny chickens, disgusting in their scrawny, bluish half-plucked state. Hoping to get to the counter before the merchandise would be sold out, Sonya would be left behind in the queue. Nora would proceed looking for another store to plant the protesting Daniel, until she would come back with two rolls of toilet paper, if lucky, to collect Daniel with his half pack of butter. Then, they would share the spoils of an hour or two of waiting in lines with Manci, who was not able to shop for herself.

Other days Nora would drop Sonya at one gym, stay with Daniel at another for an hour, go back for Sonya, perhaps get to a movie if there was anything else showing than the newest agricultural romance between two zealous Communist youths. For some reason even the Russian fairy tales, like the *Snow Maiden* of good old days, and grand epic films, like *Alexander Nevsky,* had gone out of favor with the Romanian government. Not talking about the joys of the black and white TV. *Flipper,* or the *Avengers,* or *The Saint* by the early 1970s were definitely classified as *personae non gratae* of the TV programs. Their morality was no longer fit to be seen behind the Iron Curtain.

Nora's mind and body welcomed utter exhaustion. Not the drilling, painful heaviness between her shoulder blades that sometimes not even a night's rest could alleviate. That ache itself could be taken for exhaustion. She often wondered which was the case.

New prospects opened when Varvara, the Mann's last live-in maid showed up one day with her new husband. She had left to marry—as all Nora's previous maids had done—something she was indeed proud of, something she considered a certificate of good behavior given to her by the string of maidens. The open and cheerful young woman came back from time to time to visit. Now they came with a suggestion. "We'd like to have Soni and Dani with us for the rest of the summer," Varvara said. "The village is full of children, they'd have a good time."

"Wow! That's awfully nice of you." Nora was pleased.

They agreed on a month. Both Sonya and Daniel instantly threw themselves in Varvara's lap like purring kittens.

Marişel, a village nestled in a narrow valley, about an hour and a half's drive from Cluj was a sight deserving an artist's palette. Climbing along steep, stony streets from terrace to cultivated terrace to forested hillsides, it seemed like an ideal playground for the many children spending their vacation with relatives, getting a healthy alpine bronze tan and breathing the aroma of resin and freshly-cut hay into their city lungs.

A large log cabin with several rooms on one side of the yard, a spacious kitchen-dining room with a large brick hearth on the other side, and the entire family welcomed Nora and the kids. Stable and pigsty in the back, a path to the latrine and the corn field behind. Tucked far away from urban scarcity.

Saturday afternoons, Nora joined them until Monday, when she would take off at dawn and drive directly to work amongst the dewy hills and meadows, with the call of wildflowers Nora could never resist. Cornelia and Rodica were the pleased recipients of two of the three bouquets Nora had picked and now placed in a small mason jar in the office.

The third Thursday evening Varavara called. "Madame Doctor, I think Dani has mumps."

It took mere hours, and Nora set eyes on Daniel, a pitiful sight, slumped on top of the overstuffed straw mattress on the high bed. A little scared hamster. Varvara was crying for guilt. She needed more consoling than the medical attention Dani required. "It's not your fault, it could happen anywhere."

Soon, Adel contemplated the trio. "Pumpkins, don't worry. Adel is here for you. If Hitler didn't kill me, mumps won't." She couldn't remember whether she had had the disease.

Balancing work duties and the situation at home like a juggler, Nora lived in dread of failing through a slip of attention. Exactly three weeks after Daniel took ill, when Adel was already dragging with exhaustion, Sonya got sick. She missed the school opening and could barely round up enough energy to be envious of Daniel starting kindergarten.

Like clockwork, three weeks after Sonya's boisterous energy had succumbed to illness, and now that she was recovering, Nora's cheeks swelled up, painful and hard as rocks, barely letting her open a slit of a mouth to take in some fluids.

"*Nyuszi,* I'm still worried for you. I hope you didn't get it." Nora's words to Adel squeezed passed her tight jaws with difficulty.

"I told you. Don't worry, *Kis Hörcsög Nyuszi,*" Adel said calling her a Little-Hamster-Bunny.

Alone with Sonya in the evenings, after Adel moved headquarters back to her place with Daniel, Sonya became her mother's little nurse.

By the end of the first week, Nora couldn't stand on her feet. Not only was she weak, but dizzy to the extreme. When alone during the day, she crawled to the bathroom on all fours. *I'm not lightheaded, this is not weak-dizzyness. I've lost my balance. That's it.*

"Bubi," she told her physician friend on the phone, "you won't believe this." She described the symptoms of inner ear involvement.

"You're right. It's labyrinthitis," he concluded when he came to see Nora. "I've seen only one other case like this during my entire career in Infectious Diseases. I think you should be admitted."

Nora refused and chose to go on cortisone at home.

Recovery challenged Nora's not-so-outstanding patience. October came. The inventory of that year so far added up to an oppressive list. She couldn't wait to write it off.

Not inclined to meditation, not talented in relaxation, alone in the apartment, she tried to detach herself from the past and absorb the tranquillity of the clicking radiators, the warm air imperceptibly flapping the lace curtains, the remoteness of the whooshing trams in the street. She reached for her journal.

- I'm a discouraged creature. I've got the reverse Midas touch. Everything I touch turns to shit.
- If each adversity I survive makes me wiser, I should be a genius by now. Can I ever learn anything?
- I'm making supernatural efforts to regain some kind of balance in my life. Emotional, not only labyrinthic. Doru is too nice and helpful, the bastard snake. Nora, beware! No going back!
- I wish that gray matter would cover some of my organs other than my brain. I could use some on my ovaries.

She could've added for self-edification, 'Little do I know.'

8

A year's worth of paper work—or rather not worth the time, as no mandatory chore ever is—mostly shuffling around papers, Nora regarded as a refuge for her mind. The paper she eventually wrote proved that professional drivers have more, and worse, backaches, a larger ratio of herniated discs—the infamous pinched nerve—than the general population; that riding and driving vehicles with unkind suspension was harmful for human backs. "Isn't that a monumental revelation?" she scuffed at the idea but had no better one and she had to write a paper.

Much to her surprise, her retrospective and prospective study with the double blind approach was accepted for presentation at a national conference of general practitioners, no place else than her native town, a good three hours drive away. Amongst others, she boasted to Doru.

"With whom do you conference?"

"It's not a who. It's a lot of people."

"Oh! One man is not good enough for you any more?"

"How can you be so vulgar? You're pathetic. We've sung our swan-song months ago," Nora said with gusto.

"How many times did you say that? We're growing an entire farm of swans," he laughed sardonically.

"Don't remind me, you snake." She accompanied the remark with that kind of tender smile that the most stony-hearted could not resist. It certainly changed any derogatory word she might have used to a term of endearment.

Nora read her paper. That nobody laughed, Nora attributed to the fact that the entire two days of presentations could have been a burlesque. Participants pretended to listen and learn. Stuck in the rut of ceaselessly building the house-of-cards of Communism, was not a laughing matter. The awareness of how deplorably backward they were, as compared with medicine in the Western world, was beyond joking.

Without pretenses, they got together after the program for a meager lunch, dinner or cocktails. They discussed what was of more interest and impact: what lay ahead; what they could say and to whom, and mostly what couldn't be said; how they could keep a straight face and preserve their dignity. After all, they lived in the country of Caragiale, the Romanian Molière, the great humorist playwright, quoted left and right, whose words were a shield against accusations of disloyalty. His outlook on his own nation and its individuals exposed worthlessness, corruption and other social spices and vices, that would endure not only until Romanians, but as long as humanity existed.

Anxious how her stratagem would work, the conversation around the table punctuated by crude jokes, became, at one point, a mere distant background hum for Nora. After dinner she would go to the hotel . . . She wouldn't be alone . . .

Nora never shied away from noticing an attractive man for purely aesthetic reasons, but that was as far from wanting to sleep with any as wanting to make love to a painting or statue.

Virgil didn't drop from the sky. Occasional lingering gazes, light flirting, Nora had dismissed jokingly. It began at parents' meetings at school, as Virgil took up the habit of squeezing into the same bench with her. Once he had brought up the subject and said it had been going on for years. Nora neither admitted nor denied that as a fact, though she was convinced that he was exaggerating for effect. What the heck. Innocent exchange of pleasantries with anyone had always been a good antidote to an insipid meeting.

"Sure, we could be friends," she answered his question. Somewhere in the back of her mind, conflicts swirled. *Is he recruiting me? Is this flirting a cheap façade?*

He had corrected her then, "I feel we *are* friends."

"Well, if you consider that we have children in the same class, and now your grip, the least to say on *my company*—"

"By the way, how do you feel about that?"

She couldn't tell him that no matter who was in charge of the Transportation Authority, she couldn't care less, and she could only hope that she would never have anything to do with a legalized spy even if he called himself a friend of hers. "I feel that you are beating around the bush." She was aware that, indeed, she herself was doing just that.

"Is this an invitation to be more open?"

"I don't think I'm ready to hear you."

"I can wait. I'm very tenacious." He looked down at her grinning.

"I have no doubt about that." She couldn't discard it for a fact that for a State Security Officer the qualification of being *tenacious* was a euphemism. "I wish you were that subtle."

"Quite honestly, coming to *your* company, as you put it, had to do with wanting to be a little closer to you," he said without a discernible effort to sound candid.

What a fraud. "That's what you call closer to someone?" She asked truly stunned questioning whether this should frighten or flatter her, provided she could believe one single word.

"I was given the choice, and I took it."

"That sounds more like it. Forgive me for questioning the meaning of your words," she said.

"Save yourself the trouble. I don't need to lie."

"I believe you. Do *I* need to?" she intended the question as an attempt to sound him, not that she hoped that it was possible.

"You don't. Besides, I don't think you could."

He was quite correct in evaluating her, and that pleased her the least. She hoped, on the other hand, that her instincts didn't abandon her. The man either did not conform to the stereotype of what he publicly was, or he was the ultimate con man. Strangely enough, she couldn't ever work up a true aversion towards him.

Nora started to react to Virgil's *musicality.* In Vera's bird language it meant sexually high powered. Virgil's entire body laughed, not only his light olive-complexioned meaty oval face, which beamed with delight. Like someone who earned the right to enjoy himself and cared not at all about anything else. Mere appearance? She didn't want to know. Anything would have been presumptuous; she knew nothing more about him than what was obvious to the eye. If she were to pick a man for an after-Doru rebound relationship, she wouldn't have picked him for his cadre file. Imprudence was exciting.

Despite her delicate frame and average height, Nora never felt fragile. A gymnast during her school days she felt strong and agile. Yet, walking by Virgil in the echoing school hallways and along the alleys of their housing development lined by young shadeless trees, she felt frail. Her gymnastics teammates, of course very muscular, were not as tall as Virgil, as gymnasts generally aren't. Then, she had never looked at her teammates as males. They were pals. Virgil's mass was his prevailing feature, complemented by his deep and husky voice.

"We can't let any opportunity go to waste," he had said. "I never disregard my desires. What about you?"

"Look," she responded not looking at him. *Aren't you pompous? And besides, if someone's being used in this relationship, it should be you. Should I have any fears?* The spoken words did not betray her. "What's it to you to stick around and be a good sport?"

"At your order." With a mischievous twinkle in his eye, he gave her a mock military salute.

Yes, Virgil could manage the trip. That was of no surprise. Nora had no doubts that there had been no misreading of signals.

From the lobby of the new Hotel Dacia, where Nora and Virgil shook hands in a businesslike manner, they went for a walk. The yellowing weeping willows streaming over the path along the bank of the river provided a kitsch-like setting. The situation was so foreign to Nora that it seemed easy to look at it as an outsider. By the time they took the elevator to Nora's room, all verbal preambles were left behind.

Virgil started to undress without any fuss. Nora felt like a spectator at the unveiling of a masterpiece. The only blemish on his body was the untanned pale area of a bathing suit, which she found quite sexy. His hairless skin, tight over athletic, textbook muscles helped warm things up, so she too started to unbutton. He stopped her with a silently sketched gesture, as if promising he would be the one to take care of that. They stood studying each other, she still fully dressed, gazing at her statuesque nude companion. *As they all are, statues, built aesthetically harmless with their undersized penises.*

Somehow resigned to have gotten herself into a time-wasting situation, somewhat embarrassed not to have given him the benefit of doubt, she passively awaited the statue's approach. She put her hesitant hands on the back of his thighs. His skin was smooth and soft. Soft, all right, could be the working motto. The statue curled strong arms around her. His touch called forth the right urges. She was not sure whether she could afford them. A touch of sadness she needed not recall. It seemed a sacrilege to bring Paul's memory back that way. Such thoughts weighed on her eyelids. When she opened her eyes, there was another man undressing her.

Suddenly she erupted in an uncontrollable laughter.

Neither the possibility of a shameful effect on Virgil, nor his cool, almost threatening, question, "You aren't laughing at me, are you?" could stop her.

"Can I tell you later?" she asked.

"Don't worry, you can tell me now." He sounded sarcastic.

"It's a long story." She tried to repress her fright.

"Make it as long as you wish." He was coolly superior.

"We had a terribly dirty old Anatomy professor. His only pleasure in life at that point was to be vulgar and to abuse and embarrass students. He picked pretty girls for his games. So, at least I was safe—"

"Fishing for compliments—" His sarcasm was gone.

"All right, it's not about that. He asked Gabi, a real sexy one, 'Tell me which is the organ that can expand up to twenty times its resting size?' The result was predictable, Gabi blushed up to her ears. 'Let me help you out. It starts with a P,' the old bastard said. Gabi was ready to cry. The rest of us held our breath in solidarity. 'Well, miss, you are an optimist. I was expecting you to tell me that it's the pupil of the eye.'"

"Aren't you glad your optimism is honored?" Virgil said, proud as a rooster.

The discipline of a man able to control to the last inch, so to speak, everything around and everything about himself, impressed Nora as she soon realized her reactions were a precise result of his will. She had to convince herself that she wasn't frightened.

She drove home next day not thinking for a single moment of the past or of the future, just registering the miles as they ran backwards along the road in the company of the slender tall poplars.

Nora was sure that her mother's prodding gaze could not arouse her suspicion. The escapade was not part of her life. Only emotional things the daughter couldn't keep from the mother.

"No need for a ride, you rest, *Nyuszikám*" Adel said. "I need a walk."

"*Édes Nyuszikám,* thanks for the two days." Nora helped her Sweet-Bunnykin with her coat, kissed her on both cheeks, and closed the door behind her with a grateful sigh. The evening was tranquil, both children were engrossed in the new toys.

Virgil's presence was intermittent, but insistent. On an exceptional weekday, they were to meet the first time at her place. Citizens throughout the city were herded into the streets to cheer the visiting Ceauşescu. Work, school, life itself was suspended. A holiday spoiled. Virgil counted on getting off duty early—from his assigned position in the security cordon—and spending some time with Nora.

"Is two o'clock still fine?" He called Nora at one o'clock to confirm that the speech was over at the recently finished sports dome and he was on his way by foot from the other end of the city. On a day like that, all public transportation citywide was halted; buses parked across streets served as barricades. School children and workers pretended to be a sea of cheering citizens bathing in Ceausescu's wisdom, the same they couldn't escape hearing on the radio and television every evening.

At 2:30 Nora started to wonder what happened. Virgil's punctuality matched that of a Swiss watch. Two o'clock wouldn't be 1:55 or 2:05. Around three the doorbell rang. Virgil stumbled into the hall almost knocking Nora off her feet. His staggering steps took him into the kitchen, while she assessed the situation and her limited physical abilities against the drunk wavering hunk. *God! He can't possibly think of any funny business.* She felt sick to her stomach when realizing that she should've always been frightened of him. Never did she fear Doru no matter how inebriated he was. She had leaped out of the fire into the frying pan.

How could she get rid of him as soon as possible? Forever. After all, his self-control was not universal. With these thoughts, Nora urged him verbally to turn around. She wouldn't dare touch him. Instead, he slumped over in a chair. It was a position she could handle more easily. He looked less overwhelming.

Her tendency to be active in moments of resignation and despair—let physical activity take over where brain fails!—took her to the stove to make a strong coffee. She made him drink it. She failed in her endeavor to make him stand up. Finally, he was standing and leaning on the table with both hands, swaying, his face devoid of any expression. His breath reeked of alcohol. How he got to the sink she was not sure, but she started to splash his face with cold water, while thanking him greatly for not throwing up. *Miracle, only that I can't expect it to last.* She used the improbable short interval when he appeared receptive to verbal input to show him to the door. She called the elevator, nudged him in, shut the door and gave it a fist, as if putting a seal on it. From the window she saw him walk away from the building in an almost straight line. The coffee and the cold water were still working.

Next morning he dropped by Nora's office. They stepped outside.

"Please, forgive me," he said.

She had to be a total hypocrite—which she couldn't be even with the danger of raising a menace against herself—to pretend that it was nothing. Touched by terrifying thoughts, trying to guess his expression and meaning, she could not be totally candid either and tell him how disgusted she was.

"Tell me honestly, did you have to show up in that condition?"

"Believe me, I didn't realize I was that bad. I only knew that I promised I would come and I never break a promise. We did our job around the Chief, then our group was off duty. We all dropped by a friend's apartment on the way back and I couldn't get off the hook," he said matter of factly.

"Well comrade, good for you." *What am I saying?* She was instantly terrified for the derogatory use of the address, but there was no echo. He didn't even look in her eyes, as if saying, how do you dare, or something like that. Her palms started to sweat.

"I don't even like to drink. That's why I was so bad. I'm not used to drinking any significant amount in such a short time. I could count on my fingers how many times I was drunk in my life."

Difficult for her to believe. Was this episode putting a dent on his ego or was he trying for a break? Making himself disgusting was as good a way as any? That was fine with her, as she wanted no part of him, sober or not.

"What can I tell you?" She clenched her teeth. She had to come up with something neutral. Consoling. Something to show that she wouldn't mock a law enforcement officer. "I hope you liked my coffee."

He could not remember the coffee or the cold water, but, well-mannered, he thanked her anyway and laughed. Then went on with a deadly serious tone. "Did you hear what happened?"

"When?" She thought of a personal problem.

"The sports dome collapsed this morning," he said as if talking about a new movie. Now he was looking straight into Nora's eyes.

"What do you mean?" She felt her skin creep.

"The dome." He turned his hands palm up with his fingers spread and nodded. "The new dome? Yesterday it was packed with ten thousand people. Including me. Clapping every minute," he added with emphasis, suggesting vibrations by shaking his fists.

"Oh, dear. Do you think—?"

"I don't think anything and you shouldn't either. Or ask, for that matter. Or comment on the news. *This one* has to be in the papers," he said sententiously.

Despite his patronizing tone, it was the first time during the whole conversation that she felt secure. After all, he admitted that the press published nothing but a bunch of censured items, he confided in her, he expressed a personal opinion that condemned the official policy. He trusted her. Or was he above being susceptible to possible charges from such a nonentity, a simple mortal, as a company physician? She still didn't want to have anything to do with him on a personal basis and she didn't feel in control. She was hoping not to get into a situation that would provoke or oppose him. She dreaded the thought of repercussions. Abusing his position just a little, he could have put her in the most unpleasant situation, if he wished to maintain a relationship she had already severed in her mind.

A wet snow accumulated overnight. Cars were sloshing and skidding in the dark. Street lights were dulled by the curtain of falling sleet. Headlights were useless, as if hitting an opaque wall. Nora drove as if immersed in black soup.

She started the countdown of that horrible year.

The early morning work meetings at the Policlinic, though more to the point than Party meetings, couldn't elicit Nora's enthusiasm. All routine was upside down, everybody in the family had to be mobilized, kids displaced.

She stopped at the light at the corner of the Greek-Orthodox Cathedral. Her feet firmly planted on the clutch and brake, she was waiting attentively for the light to change when she was jolted, her hands slid off the steering wheel and ended up leaning on the dash board. She looked up and what she saw in the rear view mirror was a truck parked in her Skoda's rear-engine bay. Jumping out of the car was a result of pure animal instinct. Reasoning had no time to set in. The truck driver was not too slow himself after he turned off his engine. No explosion followed. Nora was thankful that in the cautious slow-moving traffic that she was not run over as she stepped back from the two fused cars.

Phone calls. Pressure. She was supposed to understand the poor truck driver. Big family, nice man, and more irrelevancies. So, she did. Good friend Laci vouched for the poor devil. Enraged though she was, she didn't have the guts to send Laci with his acquaintance driver to hell. Whose interest his licensed friend was serving became obvious too late, a month after she carelessly agreed to let the driver and his pals fix her car, so it would cost him less.

At that point she was busy alleviating the painful muscle contracture secondary to the whiplash. A new phase had begun gripping her in a never-ending string of mental, emotional and physical misery.

"Only for the evening," Vera said. "My friend is coming tomorrow. Sorry, he has priority."

Nora was lying in agony on the floor with a hard roll under her neck. She had not felt so much in need of spilling her guts since she was a teenager. Vera sat cross-legged next to her.

"I need to be tough with myself to cancel my hardship—" Nora said.

"Now, wait." Vera interrupted. "Can we make some sense here?"

"I'm not superstitious, and except for the temporary period of depression last spring, I don't think I lack the inner resources. So, tell me, what's going on with me?"

"You need to sort things out. Throw out the coincidental events, and then it doesn't look so bad," Vera said.

"All right. Let's lay aside that the three of us got the mumps. Coincidence. That's taken care off. This car accident is definitely coincidental. Morning meeting, slush, an idiot running into me. So, that doesn't count. *Pure* coincidence. Oh, by the way. My rebound is over." Nora arranged the roll under her neck in an attempt to maximize distraction and avoid extraneous explanations.

"How come? All cured?"

"Yeah, for sure. He showed up drunk and I dumped him."

"I'll have to make the selections for you from now on. You're a total klutz," added Vera, who herself was hanging onto a doomed relationship, the friend she had mentioned earlier. Wonderful guy, a perfect kinship of souls, "musical," and much more. Only a minor disturbing detail: married, apparently not unhappily, living in Bucharest. All that crossed Nora's mind when she said, "Blind leading the blind."

As an answer, Vera rounded up a pen and paper and they started to draw up the profile of the person who would fit the bill of *the be-all and end-all* of their future search. Their "Ten Commandments" as they started to call their list of specifications was not identical for the two of them. Nora's looked like this:

1. Intelligent
2. Personality: kind, cheerful, honest, amusing
3. Compatible temperament ("musical")

4. Pleasant appearance
5. Common interests, taste
6. Single but settled (to exclude any material interest)
7. Age - slightly younger (if possible)
8. Not marriage minded
9. Should not wear long johns
10. Should not snore

"Now, let's be serious," Nora said contemplating the piece of paper. "What man with at least six of these requirements, I'm trying to be reasonable here, would not already be pulling in the yoke of a marriage or some other significant relationship? Huh? And if there are any within my reach, how many dream of a widow with two children?"

Nora felt as if Adel's words had come true. A jinx, rather than a motherly blessing: "Your family should provide enough entertainment." Did she really know about symmetry? A balanced proportion of duties, needs and pleasures. Maybe she used to, but life had erased that part of her.

Inertia, enough by itself, let alone the neck pain, gave Nora ample time to think. An opportunity to put matters on hold, or rather snap on a chastity belt she could throw the key away herself. Duties and needs for now. Hope for the moment when her future would reveal itself. Until her neck would listen to commands, until she would get her car back from the repair, until . . . until . . . not everything was but a mirage. Was her past a mirage too?

9

Tibor threw on his leather jacket. Winter had made its entrance with a bluster of snow flurries. He responded right away to Cornelia's call and walked to the infirmary. He leaned against the wall in the packed waiting room until the door of the office opened, and Cornelia called him in.

"Nice to see you back, Doc," he told Nora who returned to work recently after several weeks of sick leave. She was seated, unusually pale and it seemed to him, not in the best of moods.

"Good day Tibor." She put her pen down and got up from the desk smiling. They shook hands.

This must be a private thing, he thought, and couldn't help noticing that the wings of the white coat, as they flailed open when the Doc stepped out from behind the desk, revealed her unusually thin waist marked by a large-buckle black patent belt. He raised his eyes as fast as he could, hoping that his gaze did not linger long enough to be noticed.

"Thank you for coming by," she said. "I have to apologize, but we are so busy, I couldn't come to the shop to ask you to look at my car."

"No problem," he said. "I wanted to talk to you about it anyway, remember?"

"Yes," she nodded. "Only that this summer and fall evaporated like camphor."

Starting to work on the Skoda, Tibor recalled his visit to the Doc's apartment that summer. His mind went back to his conversation with little Daniel. *Such a beautiful child.* He felt warm around his heart and wished he could see the boy again.

Tibor was absolutely aware of where he was going during lunch time. No, he didn't think he was out of his mind when soon he found himself in a toy store. He couldn't remember the last time he bought a toy. He was rubbing his chin. *Well, I can't go wrong with a car. A truck? No. I would like a race car for myself, but instead I'll buy one for the boy.*

"May I see the one with that broad crocodile nose?" He turned it belly up and was delighted to see a 16 cylinder, deceitfully real looking, reproduction of a formula. Made in Czechoslovakia. He fell in love with the little contraption. *How am I going to do this?*

The arrangement was different now. He had offered, and Nora had agreed to take his car. He would drive her repaired car to her place where they would swap cars.

"Doc, your car is ready, I'm on my way." He felt that his words were unnatural, as he was not quite sure how the idea about the gift came upon him, and even less sure how he was going to pull it off.

"Thanks. I'll be in the parking lot in ten minutes."

"Thank you," he said, and realized the idiocy of his gratitude. After all, was he shier than he thought, or was it that he was venturing on strange turf?

He sped, so did his pulse. She was not there, so he found something to do on the engine. He stuck his head there like an ostrich in the sand.

"Hello, that must be you," she said to his behind.

He straightened. "Good evening," he said and swiftly stuck his head back under the hood. "You're all set, it was not even as bad as I feared," he shouted.

"That sounds good." She stood patiently near him.

"Could you do me a favor?" He continued to busy himself, looking up, head turned towards her. "If you don't mind, would you give something to Dani?"

"To Dani?"

He straightened up again, went around the car and took out the box. "It's a gift."

Surprised, she could only repeat. "A gift for Daniel?"

"A little race car," he said holding the large box.

"Tibor, that's fine, but then I'll have to buy *you* a toy too."

"Why not? Can I ask for a real race car?" Suddenly, as if the sky changed, he felt liberated.

"You'll get the first formula running around on Romanian roads," she said. Both laughed. "But now, come up, please, and give it to him personally."

"I'm in my work clothes."

"How noble."

He didn't have a clue what the Doc meant. His raised eyebrows said it without words.

"Work ennobles, doesn't it?" She said and turned around, took the keys out of the ignition, and walked ahead of him to the building.

He followed her at some distance. Rubbing his forehead, he pushed his beret back, then snatched it off altogether and stuffed it into his overall pocket. The Doc was wearing a knitted sweater, quite tight, and the slacks were not much looser either over her hips. *Wow! No, I refuse to admit. What? That she got hips? So what? Every woman got hips. More or less like these. And this undulating gait! I only wanted to be nice to the little chap. Last time he looked as if he could use a lot of affection. An 'affectionate' race car, sure, from a mechanic who can explain it to him. That's good. How does this fit in with noticing her huggable hips?*

Getting into his car an hour later, turning on the ignition, his state of mind was as foreign to him as a faraway jungle. Not that he had no idea how the hour flew away so fast—playing with the boy, having coffee with the Doc, but he was baffled how come his car did not take off flying.

A few days later, at home, Tibor was reminded how much he loathed his uncle Elemer. He was sitting soused at their kitchen table.

"Hey," he called to Tibor. "How ar'ya wastin' ya time lately?"

"The best way I can." Tibor tried to sneak out of the kitchen as fast as he could and let Elemer pester his sister.

"If you did what I'm about to make you do—"

"Elemer, don't bother," Tibor cut him off.

"Have ya ever been paid to have fun?"

This sounded stupid, even if half as dirty as it sounded. Tibor was at the door.

"You square head," Elemer yelled. "What's wrong with driving some people around?"

"I'll give you a phone book," Tibor yelled back. "Call a cab."

"No need to be so rude, Tibi," his mother said. "Can't you at least listen?"

Nothing good for me could come out of this if Mother insists, that's for sure. With an expression of, 'Why am I wasting my time?' he sat down. To his surprise, he was offered the job of chauffeuring a family of four, neighbors of Elemer, to a far-away village for a wedding. Public transportation was too complicated and time consuming. Like the majority of people, the family did not own a car. An invitation and the overnight stay was included in the deal.

"So, whad'ya say?"

"Not impossible. I'd need a day off though, and that's money."

"So what? Your mother told me you fix the doctor's car, so, she'll give you sick leave."

"Yeah, right," Tibor said.

"Why not?" his mother asked.

"She's not the kind."

"Everyone's the kind," Elemer waved it off.

Tibor didn't intend to prove his uncle either right or wrong. He accepted the job tentatively.

The novelty of the country wedding turned out to be fun. Soon, Tibor came to be known as the ideal chauffeur for remote family affairs. On occasion Ibi would squeeze into the car and they would dance the night away in never-heard-of villages of Transylvania.

The heftier his savings, the more drunkard Uncle Elemer was redeemed in Tibor's eyes.

Part II

1

Unstoppable events ground Tibor into a wavering pulp, as he was unsure of what options and quirks were waiting to be dealt with. Another one each day, to be sure. The ripping feeling was still there gashing his insides. He was sure it was the worst tiff he had ever had with Ibolya. He struggled to see where he had failed in his promises. "Not happy with the two of us?" he had asked her. He couldn't accept her excuses for not taking a job, for postponing the wedding.

His newest dilemma was caused by a wooden barn for sale. Great for construction material. Except that the price was out of his reach. He had recently spent his savings on a secondhand, almost new car.

A loan was the only solution. His uncle, as always, was buying booze with his last *Lei.*

"Rodica, could you help me out with some change?" he asked.

"Forgot your lunch money? How much do you need?"

"5,000." He made a grimace, raised his shoulder, as if expecting to get hit over the head.

"You must be out of your mind."

He asked Cornelia. The two women couldn't put it together. Their arithmetic worked against him.

"You could ask Doctor Mann. What could happen? She could say no, that's all," Cornelia suggested.

The homework proved tough. The more likely it seemed that the doctor could spare the money, the more he felt a mistake looming. He didn't think the money matter was more private than showing her his bare butt, but it was not a professional thing. His money dilemma felt like a private matter. Nothing professional about it. It would involve the Doc in his private affairs. He felt uneasy and was helpless when her figure kept popping up in front of his eyes, not dressed in her tight sweater and slacks, but in a gauzy cloud of mystery. Asking her for a loan seemed absurd. Dishonest. Stupid. *Why? What's wrong with desiring a good looking woman. Me being engaged? One could say that.* What further confused Tibor was that he felt dishonest to the Doc, not to Ibolya.

Nora was bent over the daily reports covering the desk—forty patients, average day—legitimately tired. Spring flooded her senses. The moisture steaming from the rain-soaked earth, the erupting tender green everywhere, the sap rising in everything but the dead. Even if her own sap seemed to have clogged up her pump, she couldn't stop the sudden rushes welcoming the new brightness. Fleeting, disjointed emotions touched her like soft butterfly wings. She was glad not to be one of the completely dead.

"What can we do for you?" Pen held in midair, Nora looked up and scrutinized Tibor Rózsavölgyi standing in the open door. His name so appropriate for the season. Valley of the roses. He would make a better gardener with a straw hat than a mechanic in greasy overalls. More hues of her mood than reflections of her mind.

"May I wait till you finish?" His tone was apologetic.

Cornelia was chitchatting in the yard when they left. "How's it going?" she addressed Tibor.

"What's she talking about?" Nora sniffed a secret. "She thinks she knows everything. Better let her," she added, as they ambled on toward the street.

"I don't know what's better," he started off, pensively. "To goof or to be sorry?" He surprised Nora with an abstraction she didn't think he could make.

"You're too ambiguous." Her comment was an opening.

They looked at each other. Her eyes were probing, and detected a strange man walking by her. Perhaps it was the metallic spark in his eyes looking at her with a hypnotizing steadiness. She continued briskly, "Any special reason for your visit?"

"I wanted to ask you a favor. I'm not sure any more."

"This eludes me. Are you all right?"

"Yeah, yeah," he said absorbed. "Thank you, I'm fine."

They got to her car talking about commonplace things. "When you can figure things out, give me a call." She extended her hand for a handshake, but he bent over and kissed her hand by habit.

In the evening, Sonya called out, "Mom, it's the car doctor."

"I was waiting for your help, and you left me here high and dry," she said, holding the receiver between wet thumb and forefinger.

"Me too," he snickered.

"What did I do?" she asked puzzled.

"Just kidding. I've just dried off after a shower."

"I meant it. I hate to clean vegetables."

"Shoot. Now I've missed my only chance."

She welcomed his sarcasm.

He added, "How'd I guess you were serious?"

"I don't say things I don't mean. Usually," then she paused, for she had the odd realization that nothing was usual.

"Excuse me for calling this late." That's not what he really meant to say.

"It's not late. You could get on your white horse . . ." she envisioned him as a twentieth century knight in shining armor, ". . . and come over. Say, for half an hour."

While Nora tidied up the kitchen, helped the children with their evening routine, and answered a phone call briefly, Tibor followed them around, carrying on a smooth line of conversation. Nora tucked Sonya in for the night, while Daniel asked Tibor to read to him in the living room.

When all movement in the apartment had settled, it was mostly Tibor who talked about his diverse problems, mostly his dilemma about school. He squirmed occasionally in mild discomfort. He checked his watch several times. Exactly 30 minutes after he had arrived, he got up determined not to bring up his request.

"Did we talk about anything you really wanted?" She was genuinely puzzled by the whole situation.

"Perhaps next time," he paused. "Will there be a next time?"

"Call me," she told him at the door.

He couldn't do it. Clueless of how to overcome his inner conflict, he tossed around during the night and started out to the infirmary several times during the day. Finally, while crossing the empty waiting room, through the open door of the office, he overheard the Doc talking with Rodica about Sunday plans. He slowed down to hear more.

Nora and the children spread the picnic blanket in the middle of a clearing surrounded by elder bushes off the highest segment of the winding dirt road on Beech Hill. Unlike most Sundays, when they joined friends, today it was just the three of them. The smell of nectar made the air feel warmer. Sonya ran to size up the crop of budding blossoms on the tree-like elder bushes. The harvest, dried and placed in gauze bags, would make the base for the best sparkling fragrant drink lasting the whole winter. Daniel trailed after her from bush to bush. She pulled on branches, he monkeyed aimlessly with the lower ones.

"Beware the bees," Nora yelled. "Stay where I can see you."

Sitting cross-legged, Nora read the newspaper spread over her knees, occasionally lifting her gaze to check on the children. They were doing fine until, at one point, she saw only the bushes. Her eyes swept the fringe of the glade, her hands idle on the paper. They must be going around the thicket, she thought. She pushed the paper to the side, and got up lazily.

"Sonya! Dani! Where are you?" she called out projecting her voice through the funnel of her palms. "Sonya! Dani! Answer me!" Silence shifted to panic. She started to run as if jerked on a tether. Her eyes wandered back to the blanket. In half an hour her voice had climbed an octave, her running steps changed to an aimless staggering.

She ran up to a man who showed up at the top of the opposite grassy hill. He hadn't seen two kids, who might have looked lost. He joined Nora in her search.

After another endless half an hour, out of the blue, Sonya and Daniel emerged from the bushes. A sniffling Sonya dragged a reluctant and sobbing Daniel. Their accumulated fear poured out in a torrent of words and tears. Sonya knew where they were and how to get back, when they went around a small swamp behind the elder bushes. That's when Daniel bolted away, refusing to listen to Sonya, who didn't want to let him out of her sight. Sonya's truncated sentences, delivered amidst a staccato of sobs, brought the picture alive. Eventually they had both admitted that they were lost. They met a single tourist during their more than an hour of wandering. Sonya had asked where Salicea Road was with the big elder trees. The person pointed and left. Nora felt she could ring that irresponsible adult's neck.

Her body's self-defense mechanism against anxiety, stress, argument, or danger was to sink into extreme exhaustion and irresistible sleepiness. She felt now as if she was fighting off general anesthesia. However, two circumstances called for immediate attention. She had to make the best of the incident. Sonya didn't let go of her little brother and she knew what to ask. So, mother commended daughter with measure. And something else as well.

"Smart kids. Not for disappearing." She tapped their bottoms in jest. "But for staying together and asking for help. That you didn't get any is not your fault. But, what would you have done if you couldn't find me?" she asked them.

"We decided we'd go out to the road and ask someone in which direction the city is and start walking," Sonya answered.

"Would you have hitchhiked?" Nora asked her.

"Hum . . . We thought you would be around with the car."

"That's good."

They packed up. Nora moved as if dragging herself through mud. The second she was ready to turn the key in the ignition, a car pulled up, and Tibor, pencil behind his ear, a slip of paper hanging from his lips, leaned close to the open passenger window.

"This is my second time around," he said. He had been driving around looking for the people who belonged with Nora's car parked on the roadside, and had just decided to leave a note on her windshield.

"What are you doing here, anyway?"

"I was looking for you."

Like a vertical caravan of loaded mules, they moved slowly up the eight flights of stairs thinking less than kindly of the broken elevator. Tibor squeezed under his arm the Sunday *Torch*.

The overwhelming stress of finally presenting Nora with his request made him quiet. Up in the apartment he felt relieved. As if he had arrived somewhere.

Having dumped the picnic stuff in the kitchen, Nora observed how Sonya dragged Tibor by the hand, who in turn held Daniel's hand, the three heading to the kids' room. Instead of the usual superhuman effort to control two rambunctious mustangs back from the meadow, of the hysterical rush to put food on the table, now she got through unpacking, preparing coffee and a snack in a matter of a few quiet minutes. She raised her head and perked her ears in disbelief. Calm rained in the apartment. She tiptoed through the living room. The three sat on the floor, the children competing in showing off their toys. It seemed to Nora sacrilegious to disturb the idyll, but it was for a good cause. "Anyone for cookies and coffee?"

The children quietly settled down, munching cookies, holding their cups of milk, watching Flipper on the black and white TV. Sipping their coffee in the kitchen, there was expectation in the air when Tibor pointed out to Nora the ad in the paper.

“What would you do with it?” Nora thought of the idea as strange.

“Build an extension. Or a chalet somewhere, so I’d have my own place, at least for the weekends, if they wouldn’t allow me to build in the city.”

“Interesting. Would you like to hear a chalet story?”

“Any time.”

“A few years ago, maybe in 1968, I ran into a colleague at a meeting. A country physician . . .” she said, pronouncing the words as if starting to read a fairy tale. “. . . told me about this village mayor, with avant-guard capitalist blood flowing in his peasant veins. He got the idea to let city folks build chalets on village land. Paul didn’t want to get involved. When he was on one of his frequent business trips, I arranged to meet the mayor there. I took the bus. What roads! We walked around to see whether I’d like a plot. You know why the mayor came up with his idea?” Tibor shook his head, not taking his gaze off her for a second, as if in a trance. “In the valley just over the hilltop, the village ends where the works of a large damn started. You must have heard of the hydro-energetic dam at Tarniţa.”

“Sure. It’s still not finished,” he said, suddenly animated. “Did you buy a plot?”

“He was not selling. The land is people’s property. He was attracting business. The town is a dream. I chose a plot on a slope, below the hilltop, protected from the winds,” she sighed. “Clumps of spruce grow all around it. Guess what else.”

“You built a chalet.”

“Not so fast,” Nora motioned gently, and smiled. “There was a spring bubbling up at one of the rocky outcrops under the trees,” she continued, rolling her eyes as if savoring the spring water. “I could capture it for indoor plumbing. No need to drill for a well or pump the water.”

“Too nice to be true.”

“Your guess is right.” She pulled her lips tight. “Nothing came of it. Poor Paul got very sick.”

“I’m sorry.”

“No need to be sorry. Just memories. You don’t mind me telling you such stories, do you?”

“It’s a pleasure to listen to you.”

“Well, thanks. But back to your construction material.”

He finally told her.

“I’ll loan you the difference,” she offered casually.

"That's the favor I wanted to ask you." He was stunned how she anticipated what he wanted. "I could sell my car," he added swiftly, ready to withdraw.

"That's not a bad idea," she said with sarcasm. *But that's not why you're here, my friend.*

"Is my car so bad?" he feigned offense. They laughed at the thought of his old Moskvitch, a Russian car, as delicate as a tank and shaped like one. "It's more than you think."

"How much?"

"Four thousand Lei."

"All right," she said without blinking. Her monthly salary as a general practitioner at the highest ranking was three thousand Lei.

"Just like that? You trust me?"

"I haven't considered that aspect yet," she said and enjoyed immensely laughing with him. At him.

"You know, I've had so many disappointments," he said with the sudden sadness of a painful confession. "I can't trust people anymore," he added.

"Don't worry, I won't give you counterfeit money." Nora felt the roller-coaster quality of his moods and chose to cut the line leading too close to his feelings.

"That's exactly what I was afraid of," he picked up the lighter tone.

When time came to put the children to bed, he took his leave.

She tossed, she tried to read, she dropped the book. *What is my role here? Why am I preoccupied at all? What is the role I'd prefer? Friend, banker? Buy the chalet stuff together. That's the stupidest of all. Ah! Does he hope to sow a seed of financial independence with my help or through me? Am I being conned? Why would I build anything—nobody had mentioned anything like that—with an employee, a mechanic, whom I know only by being his company physician. True, an especially friendly employee, always of great help, surprisingly pleasant company as it turns out. What happened to the kids tonight? He hypnotized them. Wait! How do all these fit in the picture?*

She sat up startled in the dark. She couldn't deny it, even if she tried—but she didn't—she had stepped across the threshold of a fantasy. A torrent tumbled and took her on a crazy ride. She tried to keep away the images of an inauguration at the new chalet, just the two of them, she and Tibor, lying on a bearskin on the floor in front of a crackling fire. *Crazy!*

He only wants to borrow money. Is he a perfect con man? He's playing with my feelings. What feelings? Be real. Who needs another rebound relationship? One was more than enough. I'm cured. I can't assume what's with him. Isn't he getting married? Am I attracted to this man? The pounding lust left no doubts.

Tibor fell pray to daydreams, erotic daydreams about Nora and the chalet he wished they could share. She appeared satiny transparent like the clear water of a mountain lake, that couldn't cool his body overheated by excitement. At the point of no return, not concerned with blowing his financial goal, he dialed her number.

When the phone rang, Nora pulled away from the ringing unit as if she'd been attacked.

"I forgot to apologize for staying so late," he began, then realized how stupid it was to pretend that she wouldn't sense all the fretting that led to that call.

"Now it's later than when you left late," she teased. She hoped her mocking tone came out friendly enough and did not reveal her own inner turmoil. "But that's not why you're calling, is it?"

"No," he said without a hint of protest.

She waited.

"No . . ." his voice sounded insecure.

She knew exactly what she wanted to hear. And what she wanted to say. But she couldn't. She squeezed the blanket in her fist and pressed it against her mouth. Instead of two words, 'Come back,' ready to erupt, she took a deep breath, and said with a serenity ingrained in her by social hypocrisy, "Perhaps you'll tell me some day." She hoped that he wouldn't have the audacity to tell her right away. She was not ready. Neither was he.

There were not many instances when Tibor would analyze himself. Holding Ibolya in a desperate hug, when she announced that her parents were taking her for a week to Hungary as a graduation present, was not such a moment. "Let's get married without a wedding," he said.

"What a crazy idea," she said peeling out of his arms.

"Ibi? Did you say Hungary?" he said, as if waking up in a cold shower.

"Yes. Why?"

"When did you get your passport?" He felt lightheaded.

"Don't you remember? I told you," she said with a tone overly eager to convince.

"What did I say?" Tibor squinted.

"Hum . . . You said . . . I don't remember—"

"Neither do I. Knowing myself, I would've said something like, 'Could I go along?'"

"Neah. We're visiting relatives," she said. He couldn't help thinking of what position his bride's family would give him.

Tibor was sure he had never heard of her plan. One didn't decide overnight on a trip abroad. Any border crossing needed a tourist visa that could not be obtained, under any circumstances, in less than weeks, if not months. He blamed her parents.

Of all the places around the Transylvanian plateau where water finds its way to surface as marvelous mineral springs, Nora was charmed forever by Felix Spas in her very early years. Among the few memories that survived the war years, a soothing one was that of her father demonstrating to her how hot those springs were, right where they erupted from the depth of the earth into a rocky pool that lay under a cloud of steam even in the summer. They had actually eaten an egg that they had boiled in that very pool. Those were the real memorable times. Years later, for she couldn't tell how or when it started, it became a custom of hers, observed with almost the piety of a pilgrimage, to take a trip every year to Felix, where she would dedicate the weekend, or if possible longer, to soaking in the outdoor pools ringed by ancient oak trees. Often it crossed her mind, especially when trying to rid herself of her backache, to go for a couple of weeks to *take the waters,* along with the crowds who worshipped their miraculous power.

It was that time of the year, and hoping for a perfect weekend, they started on the three hours' drive to Oradea. Nora felt exuberant and talkative. She held the children's attention with old stories. The best way to keep her own mind away from the present.

The sudden wind picking up drowned out the happy splashing and screaming as people ran for shelter. The thunderstorm came unannounced. The feeling of safety the car offered didn't last long. The windshield wiper wouldn't budge, so Nora had to get out in the whipping rain and jiggle the wipers. She was drenched to the skin in three seconds, not any smarter as to why was the washer was stuck.

She drove nervously, peering between the rivulets running down the windshield. At an auto shop she was told she would need a new motor on Monday morning. No auto-parts stores were open Saturday afternoon. She was furious that neither the promise of a tip, nor her smiles, produced any result. She would miss work on Monday or drive home in a downpour. The inanity of the sudden need to ask for Tibor's opinion surged against Nora's refusal to admit her real motivation.

After dinner at her friend's home where they were staying, lying on the cot, the whole apartment calm, Nora listened to the rain pattering on the window. Hypnotized, she found herself at the phone in the hall.

"Tibor?"

"Nora? You caught me half way out the door," he answered.

"In a rush?"

"Not at all," he lied.

She needed the safety of the distance to ask what was drilling in her mind for a week. "Why did you call me last Sunday night?" she whispered, and leaned to the wall for support.

Pinned down by her undisguised preoccupation with him, he had to sit down in a state of shock. His rush to meet Ibi retreated into a blind spot. He had no shield against his own lust. "We had been up there together, on top of that mountain of yours," he said, as if recounting actual events.

"You were not alone." She said beyond pretending.

Is she giving me the signal? Leaning on the little phone table, he held his head. It was up to him at this point. He was searching for the right answer when he heard, with relief, Nora's skillful digression.

It was easier for her to go on. She didn't doubt that shock and not evasion was the reason for his silence. "I called you because . . . I need your opinion." Melodrama out of the way, she spoke about the car.

"Suppose your wiper needs a motor," he said. "I could bring one to Oradea and fix your car there."

Thoroughly gratified, she laughed uncontrollably at his outrageous suggestion.

"On the other hand, a June rain won't last, and you might not need a wiper," he said.

"But if it won't stop?" she insisted.

"The windshield wipers don't have as great a role as we attribute them." He continued his lecture. "In heavy rain, you won't see clearly when you start out. By the time you reach forty per hour, the water is a smooth film on the windshield. After such torrential downpours the roads are as clean as my palm. On a dirty road it would be a different story."

"That's halfway reassuring," she said. "I'm a maniac windshield cleaner."

"So, do you want me to run over?"

"Would it be terrible if I accepted?"

"Yes, but I'd enjoy it."

"Well, thanks, no. I'll manage."

"Be careful."

"Yes, *mother!*"

Tibor's confusion having cleared, there was nothing else in the world that could alleviate his craving more than to pace the street—for more than an hour by the time darkness fell—at some distance from Nora's building, on a route from where he could see both the parking lot and Nora's windows. He was not preparing a speech. He was not thinking of his commitments. He was not even daydreaming any more. There was no other place he could be that evening.

"I'm calling from Mercur," he announced, holding the receiver as if his life depended on it.

Nora melted like a piece of butter in a warm dish. "Come right up." From the kitchen window Nora thought she could discern a silhouette moving away from the public phone at the shopping center across the road.

In minutes they were holding hands as if trying to keep from hugging. Hands palm to palm, first only fingertips touching, then their fingers clutched fiercely.

"I want to ask you . . ." he couldn't finish.

"Go ahead." She waited through a long pause. "Yes?"

"I'm afraid," he said.

She was too. The magic was slipping away and she hadn't had the chance to see whether there was anything there.

"Let's go away together," he blurted out.

In the safety of the dark hall, where he couldn't see her blush, her words came out harshly. "Like on a rebound trip?" She didn't really want to know his answer, just as she didn't want to turn on the light in the hall. She knew only that she had no reason to run any place, no reason to hide. His reasons? She refused to mix them with the tangle of her own feelings and premonitions. Obvious to her were the long hours he must have spent thinking up that silly request. She could no longer think of anything that could justify their belonging together. Anything between them seemed more impossible than irresistible.

"Somewhere more real than that mountain top." His voice, hoarse with excitement, was the plain and touching reality. Another wave of magic sprinkled over her body. Crackling fire, touch of the bearskin rug on her naked body, exchanged caresses. She had no intention of naming or defining, accepting or rejecting, approving or scrutinizing. She rested her forehead on his chest, their hands still clutching. "It's not possible." She meant, 'I don't want to.'

He felt like a child caught stealing cookies from a forbidden jar.

The incantation broke. Their hands let go. She walked into the living room and sat on the divan. He followed and sat in the facing armchair. The children were asleep in their room.

"I don't need to hide and you don't need to be associated with a woman with two kids. You need your freedom."

"These circumstances don't count now." His determined gaze made her feel vulnerable.

I must clip his flapping wings taking him right into my life. An earlier suspicion painfully worked its way back. *Rules, come'on, Ten Commandments, come'on,* she invoked. The protecting list flew out the window with a whoosh of a wily bird taking away this man's suspected driving interests.

"We went to see a movie yesterday—"

"Now, that's naughty," she cut him off with emphasis, poking her cheek with an index finger. "You go to the movies one evening with your bride, then you'd spend the next with me, huh?" She couldn't decide whether she was hearing honest or stupid talk, but considered both.

"Yeah, one could say that." He struggled not to sound out of place, while very well aware he was out of *his* place. "Splendid cinematography, touching story. She wanted to walk out. I asked her, 'Is there something you'd like better? 'Nothin', she said."

Life is tough all over. Nora couldn't help gloating over the piece of information. She was also glad to learn that Tibor could appreciate something like cinematography. "You're marrying her, aren't you?" Nora said not minding her obvious hypocrisy. *This conversation is most unsubtle. The past few nights my fantasy carried me away. I have to clip my own wings now.*

"I gave her an ultimatum until this summer." Tibor didn't see any reason to hedge. His arrogance called for honesty. "A year since I proposed. I can't be a louse. I'll wait. But, I'd have an awfully hard time with a positive answer."

"And why's that, may I ask?"

"May I be allowed not to answer that just now?"

"It sounds like you have a grave reason," she conceded, almost succumbing to the temptation to insist.

"I couldn't imagine . . ." he paused.

"What?" Nora was intrigued.

"That we'd talk about anything else than cars or my health. I was afraid that, well . . ." he looked her straight in the eyes. "I considered the possibility that you were leading me on . . . when you invited me over that evening . . . to clean vegetables." She felt an overpowering self-confidence in his self-deprecating smile, but he was not finished. "And, well . . . I was afraid that I'd cave in to physical attraction." No one could be more candid. He was pleased with himself.

She, on the other hand, was musing how her invitation for a visit turned into his off-the-wall suggestion, and now this. Strange equation. She disregarded his possible disappointment leaving him without an answer when she spoke, "Well, let's retire, each to our own thoughts." She got up, calling an end to the evening.

The hardship of the two shifts was a blessing. Sweat streaming, dust rising, roof tiles falling, curses flying non-stop. With the help of two high school pals, Tibor anticipated that the demolition and the transfer of the material to his own backyard would be done in five days. They scratched their heads at every unforeseen difficulty. They agreed that the growing pile of loose lumber was likely to be stolen overnight, piece by piece. They figured they should draw a metal binding around the stack and affix it with lumber staples.

Next day Tibor was driving slowly with the large roll of metal strips sticking out of the open trunk, when he suddenly had to blink as if seeing an apparition. He stepped on the brakes. Ibolya's father, supposedly in Hungary, carrying a netbag of groceries? Tibor got out and approached his future father-in-law with anguish. "How was your trip?" Tibor inquired.

"Not bad, not bad," the man said and moved his torso as if suffering from back pain. "The driving was too much for my old bones. My wife can't drive."

"I keep telling Ibi to learn—"

"That wouldn't have helped now, would it?"

Tibor's knees gave him a message as they started to go from under him. He suddenly had an ego to protect and his shameful ignorance to hide. *Had Ibi stayed over? Will she return by train? Where the hell is she anyway?* "How is she?" he asked the old man.

"How should I know?

I'll be damned. I can't let him know that I have no idea where my lovely bride is. She was obviously not holding onto her mother's skirt. "Oh, it's Sunday, isn't it?" he queried, and then added, as if searching through his memory, "What time is her train coming?"

"I haven't got the foggiest. There aren't that many trains from Prague," the man said.

Back in his car, hitting the steering wheel angrily, amidst curses, Tibor found no relief. He left the car at the curb and ran to his room. He sank his hands in his hair and pulled at it, letting it go only to bang his fists against the wall. A sobbing cry shook his entire body. Bitter tears rolled down his face. He was sitting slumped over with his face in his hands, dejected, trying to make some sense of it all, when his friends entered his room, looking for him to start work.

"Is someone dead?" one of them asked.

"Yes." Tibor lifted his drenched face to the ceiling and slapped the wall once more on his way out.

"Sorry," they said.

"Don't be. It's something, not somebody. Let's go."

Even if Tibor would've known himself better he couldn't have named his current state. Blocked. Disconnected. Too hurt to feel the pain of being erased.

For the lack of a better solution, the three men joined together in declaring women the scum of the earth for eternity. None of them was, at that point, committed or under any moral obligation to praise any particular individual of the deceitful *species*.

The last part of the demolition was to take up all day Sunday. Lying in the dark, fingers crossed under his head, sleeping was far from coming to Tibor's rescue. *Let's face it. I've been at a watershed spilling from both sides before Ibi vanished from the world of decent people. Like I felt it coming. I actually might have some built-in defense mechanism. Never thought of it. No, she didn't act based on a vibe she picked up from me the last days before she left. She had been preparing that trip for months. Why else did she postpone the wedding? What was so important about that trip? Do I really want to know? To satisfy my curiosity? And would I believe whatever she'd say?*

His line of thought was inevitably brewing a renewed, intense, surge of desire. As unreasonable as his lust for Nora first seemed, it quickly ripened into an achievable fantasy. A deep breath raised his chest. *I had the nerve to invite her . . . Oops! Am I being unfair? That's what Ibi did. Went away. Yeah. For more than a week. Abroad. Preparing in secret. I meant maybe a motel. Well, perhaps something more stylish. When was that the equivalent of going away for a week and postponing . . . What? A disaster! I escaped being sucked in again. Thank you, Ibi. Perhaps my luck is turning. Maybe this is the price of experience . . . Where was I? Yes. Despite my nerve, Nora didn't throw me out.*

The knock at his door left no time to keep Nora behind his closed eyelids.

"Guys! If you want this heap of crap you can have it for half the price," Tibor offered. "Why the fuck would I build as much as a latrine?" He spat on the ground in disgust.

"That's more like you, old chap," one friend said. "You sound better. You gone to the girlies last night?"

"Ya bet," Tibor said winking.

"Good for you."

"I wouldn't know yet," he said and furiously tugged at beams—the heavier the better—all day.

2

At the end of the week, with year-end shows at Sonya's school and Daniel's kindergarten behind, Nora's bones ached for rest. Running all Sunday was not the idea.

While washing her hands in Adel's bathroom she stuck out her tongue at the mirror and grimaced in disbelief. How far—or how close, she wished she could say—was that image from a glamorous *femme á trente?* It was her 36th birthday. Earlier, at Beech Hill, the fresh air, the dewy meadows, the forest trails had freed Nora's long-time dormant enthusiasm. They rolled on the grassy slopes laughing, the kids on top of her provocatively waiting for their mother to tickle them away.

At Adel's they had to settle down. Arthur's presence was not conducive to boisterous play. At best, he played a round of instructional chess with the pair of youngsters. Adel was ready to serve dinner. The table was dressed in festive damask and set with fine china. Mouth watering aromas wafted around. Nora was praying that Daniel wouldn't start whining with some excuse: 'Why isn't the table round?' or 'I can't see the food unless you draw the curtains.' All deadly serious grounds for not eating. Marvel of marvels, like clockwork, all were sitting, and a happy Adel, her freckles and eyes lit up with excitement, could serve the large oval platter piled high with stuffed grape leaves with a well deserved pomp. A green mountain surrounded by a sea of tasty, sour cream-loaded sauce.

The conversational main course—vacation-time arrangements—was tougher to chew than the tender little stuffed bundles. Who is going to sleep, eat and play where, when, how and why, though the two apartments were only a ten minutes' walk away.

Nora told the children, "Look, Adel's nice enough to cook us dinners during the week. She needs to rest on the weekends." Then, she addressed her mother, "How does that sound to you?"

"They can also sleep here if they behave," Adel said.

"If I don't listen, means I can go home?" Daniel blew the offer in one logical remark. He liked to sleep at home. Nora hid her face. *Give the kid free hand to misbehave so he can have what he wants. What will I do with you, kid?* Adel smiled at her smart grandson with indulgence. An agreement was made by the time Adel's masterpiece—the decorated hazelnut torte—claimed everyone's undivided attention.

Half a town away, Tibor and his pals finished work. They were gulping down beer at the corner pub. After two beers, heroically bearing the others' mockery that he was drinking like a girl, sitting in his tank top encrusted with the dust of demolition, sweaty hair matted under a bandanna, Tibor couldn't steer his mind away from Nora, but he didn't feel courageous enough yet. He thought it somewhat improper under the circumstances to express his desire in an impatient way. Making subtle preambles was a skill he never thought he'd need.

Washing the dishes brought Adel and Nora together for a little heart-to-heart chat when the telephone rang.

"It's for you, Nora," Arthur called. "Someone, Tibor."

Nora took the receiver with genuine surprise.

"Am I disturbing?" he asked with a hesitating voice.

"Not at all, we've finished dinner."

"I wanted to give you the report." He feigned an official tone.

"Good job," her lips said, as an unforeseen surge blurred her eyes taking over her mind. A confounded hammering palpitation made her fingertips pulse on the receiver. A wave of lust erupted through all her pores.

"I'm very pleased," he said. She listened to the long seconds of silence and heard his sigh, "and . . . tired."

"How tired?" she rushed to ask.

He had no chance to dwell on her question for fear of losing his words, subtle or not, washed away in a sudden tide of satisfying deduction. The silent echo in the receiver told him that his unspoken words were heard. He was sure he understood hers. "I couldn't drive. Had some beer with the guys." Silence again. "But I feel like I could walk to the end of the universe."

To Nora, his words were her own thoughts she couldn't phrase. Doubts and worries about taking charge vanished. "I'll pick you up."

She took her leave with kisses on everyone's cheeks. In a rush of euphoria even Arthur got a peck instead of the usual handshake. "I'll see you tomorrow after work. Be good and don't upset Adel, please," she told the children. In her butterfly-patterned, light-blue sun-dress, light-footed, almost flying down the steps, she felt like a butterfly herself.

It was under the stream of the hot shower that Tibor worked up some confidence that felt more like the state of mind and anticipation he usually enjoyed in such moments. Then, he caught himself preparing with renewed anxiety, trying to come up with some elegant excuse justifying his call. *Should I use perfume?* He pondered while shaving. *I'll be damned, she knows me for what I am. I'll just be myself.*

She drove through a miraculous dream world, rehashing the conversation in her mind. *This can't be the end of my search for the few words that could tell more than hours of futile tête-à-tête shooting too many words at each other's gray matter.* She shook her sun-streaked long hair as her body protested the uninvited mental image of another man, Egon, a good man, a desirable, courteous, intelligent and handsome man, a colleague whose support and compassion meant so much at those critical times, who had tried for a while, but couldn't stir one molecule of her hormones.

Tibor was pacing the street under the row of trimmed acacia trees, their crowns like a row of cheerful green balloons. His wet hair combed back, hands in the pockets of dark slacks, checkered short-sleeved shirt, polished leather sandals over dark socks. She pulled to the curb in front of the small family house.

Not a single word did they exchange after the brief greetings as if they were on a secret mission. There was only the hum of the engine. He didn't ask, and she didn't tell him where they were going. They wanted to go to the same place, be in the same place. Doubt was not their preoccupation. Nora feared that unnecessary words or even turning to look at him in the confined space of the car would cause a melt down. She pulled the parking brake. Opening the door, she feared, might let the electrifying bond, the carnal heat, spill out and dissipate, leaving her more alone than ever.

It was still before the space at large could dilute their tiny sphere, doors still closed, that he took her hand and kissed it. From deep inside him, words came forth, that otherwise no coercing could ever pluck past his lips. Should Tibor have doubted their meaning, he might have recognized a warning. But Tibor had no doubts whatsoever that he would love Nora to the entire extent of a new passion. "I love you, Nora," he whispered.

"Tibor!" She did not reciprocate the statement, but turned to him saying, "What a birthday gift."

"Oh? Happy birthday." He relaxed in a smile. He pulled her close for a kiss well in excess of a birthday greeting.

They joked and laughed on the way up on the account of the elevator—working, for a change—as if cooperating with their rush.

They were in no rush, but slow in mutually exploring and conquering every inch of each other, sprinkling their way from the entrance door to the living room with his shirt, her dress, his sandals, her bras, his pants. Socks. Underwear.

The choreography of unbound desire left Nora gasping for breath, uttering mere syllables falling short of meaning, craving for his next move that elicited manifold unknown reactions that seized her entire being, her soul.

The unsuspected feel of her shape beyond the image of the maddening hips of his dreams filled Tibor with more than the extreme desire to possess Nora with his entire body.

Held in his firm hands, her back touched the soft velvet of the day bed. In the middle of what by any standards was mere foreplay, she discovered a totally new pleasure. Beyond her imagination, not disclosed by any of the most passionate words she'd ever read, an apotheosis of ecstasy that she would learn soon was but the beginning of what she would come to experience.

Never-ending waves saturated Nora with deep warmth from scalp to toes, from fingertips to the roots of her teeth and everything in between. The sound of a violin, coming from inside her, rang in her ears. A violin that had waited to be strung and played, now filled her with intensely passionate sounds she never heard before. She, Nora Mann, thirty-six, mother of two, gained a new bewitched definition, dimension and certainly function.

Tibor's moment of disbelief passed rapidly as the realization came that Nora responded to his embrace more powerfully than any woman at the end of a full menu of love-making. He kept enjoying the way her on-going orgasm hugged him inside her. Tuned to each other as they were, nature couldn't have been more generous.

She abandoned herself in the hot waves that rose to her head.

Tibor's urges abated in a bliss of self-control that he gratefully and expectantly enjoyed now, more than ever, in Nora's appreciative and cooperative company, for as long as a wild call didn't make him stir. "Do you want me to be careful?" he asked.

"I'm not on the pill or anything, and I despise condoms," she said with candor.

"Don't worry."

She didn't. She usually did in a nervous, unpleasant way. She didn't even question why she was so carefree and content with Tibor's choice, however he chose to take care of her.

All inhibitions, all his prior time limitations and deadlines, all her unanswered list of questions retreated into a profoundly soothing and confident togetherness.

The silence seemed to have lasted forever. A perfect extension of the nonplused, mystified state in which Nora had been immersed. She wouldn't have noticed or cared if she drowned in a flood, or if an earthquake had swallowed her. She held him tight in tired arms.

She wanted that moment to be her eternity.

They shared silently the sentiment that there was nothing left in the world to search for.

The warm puddle pressed into her belly button fused them with a feeling of belonging. His voice, a husky whisper—a mere echo of his thoughts—was blowing a balmy breeze in her hair, the antithesis of appearance, pretenses and considerations of weeks, while trying to give a definition to what they were feeling. Suppress, suppress, no more.

"We were made for each other." He meant it without a hind thought.

Her answer broke out despite her. A sobbing cry she couldn't control, hidden in the curve of his neck. She cried for the sadness of realization of what she had missed all her life, the sweet tears of joy celebrating her good fortune to have found it at last. Her tears soaked his lips, trickled down her temples. Her own reaction to the intensity of limitless pleasure was overwhelming. It was not her usual ambiguous reaction to pleasure that had always questioned, 'Shouldn't there be more to this?'

"Please, don't go away. Ever," she finally said. She hardly opened her eyes. Clothes scattered on the floor never looked so good.

Tibor had no intention of even budging, let alone going anywhere.

He didn't need to turn on his side to sleep or smoke. He was present, interested, ready to talk, laugh and touch. Late in the night Nora made an omelet. Tibor found his way around the kitchen and set a pretty table for their first meal together. He didn't drink his glass of wine to the bottom. Nora marveled at every little minutia of the whole new experience called Tibor.

3

A dreamy Tibor tried to pay attention to the work expected of him, while nuts and bolts took up animated meanings. Rare fleeting instances of curiosity brought Ibolya briefly into a secondary focus. Did she arrive at all? Had her father told her about their chance meeting? *I refuse to analyze. It's beside the point.*

All morning he agonized over whether he should drop by the infirmary, only to realize that he couldn't stay away. With every step his pulse got faster. He couldn't recall such anxiety on planning his previous approaches to Nora. Instead of feeling more intimate, an obscure fear took him in a disquieting squeeze. There was much more at stake. Something he didn't want to—or couldn't afford?—to lose. Will she play the cold fish? They had parted only a few hours before, barely able to peel away from each other's arms, and now, walking the distance to the small building of the medical office in the company's front courtyard, he was skeptical.

"Come in," Nora called out as soon as she noticed him outside the open door. She had to take a furtive deep breath to control her accelerating pulse and the warm wave spreading through her body.

He tried to shore up a neutral tone. The exchange of commonplaces in the office flew over his head like escaped balloons. He smiled, or nodded—at wrong moments, as he was not aware of the exact meaning of the conversation—caught up with the images a few hours back in Nora's bed. Composed—at the price of a superhuman effort—he finally asked Nora whether she would have a minute.

"Cornelia," Nora said, taking her white coat off, "I'll be back in an hour. When Rodica comes in she should start seeing the first patient. All right?"

"No problem," Cornelia said, and looked oddly at the two departing and walking close to each other.

Tibor could barely resist the force pulling him towards Nora. Beyond the company gate they took each other's hand. He turned around spying. By the time he leaned over, her face was turned to him in anticipation. She didn't peek around. Her walk and smile were carefree, as her sunny mood left no place for any shadows. Without realizing it, the social restraints she usually wouldn't ignore, had dissolved.

"Let's go to the corner of Văcăraşti Street to the *Sana* place, if that would be all right with you," she suggested. It was the dairy shop named after Nora's favorite buttermilk drink.

"Sure."

They took their orders—he didn't let her pay—and in gentlemanly fashion, he carried the plate, she took the soup bowls, rolls and cups of Sana from the plate, and placed them on a small table in the back.

"First things first," she said, as they sat down and he again felt his heart skipping expecting the worst. "If," she went on, "*if* we go anywhere together in the future, and being here illustrates better than any words that we might, this is the last time that I let you pay. I didn't want to make a fuss to attract attention. Fifty, fifty."

"Can I invite you ever?"

"Sure you can. Where are we going?" Her smile showed her bright teeth, her eyes all but disappeared in the narrow slits under her long eyelashes. With a coquettish gesture she smoothed her hair behind her ears.

"Ladies first. You invite me," Tibor said.

"Didn't I yesterday?" She said with a most seductive smile.

He nodded in defeat and cleared his throat. "Would it be acceptable if I invited you to the same place today?" They both burst out in a ringing laughter that escalated again and again as their eyes met.

If he had had the chance of a lull in the conversation—they were too busy being amused at themselves—he could have answered without a trace of hesitation that he had never tasted such carefree happiness since he had grown up. Like the creamy, sweet and tangy Sana: fresh, light, filling and stirring the appetite for more. As Tibor dipped his spoon, Nora's gaze followed his hand, then she looked straight in his eyes. Now her eyes looked light hazel, ringed by gold. His appeared moss green. They ate from each other's spoons crossed over the table.

Tuesday after work Tibor couldn't get away from his mother simply by saying he wouldn't be sleeping at home, because he was not even having dinner at home any more, and besides, she was trying to tell him something. He wouldn't listen until he got out of the shower and was ready to leave.

"All right," he finally said, grabbing a small pale-green summer apple from the dish on the kitchen table, tossing it up in the air and, with a wide cheerful motion, closing his fist over it in midair. "What was that you were saying?"

"Ibi called last night," his mother said.

"Oh?" He raised his eyebrows.

"What's going on?

"What did she have to say?"

"She wanted to talk to you, of course." Her voice shot up into high the register with the exclamation.

"I bet she did." His face showed all the disdain that bubbled up like a bad heartburn.

"You can't keep me in the dark and expect me to take your phone calls."

"Be an angel and tell her to buzz off—" fortunately, he thought, his mother interrupted him and made him realize that he cannot pass messages like that. His mother *was* in total darkness. Ibi was his fiancée as far as she knew. "I'm sorry, Mom," he answered, and in a rare manifestation of affection, or rather in apology, kissed his mother's forehead.

"Did you have a fight?" she asked her son, returning his unexpected tenderness with a softer voice.

"Mother, some day I'll tell you. Now just take my word for it, the case is closed. I'm not getting married. Tell her not to keep calling because I won't be here. I'll call her," he said and left.

Tibor had no particular fixation on the possibility that Nora would invite him to move in. The idea crossed his mind like a night owl stealing away with a barely audible whoosh along a dark forest trail. The Wednesday incident tilted his state of mind in that direction.

Tibor stepped out into the street after his brief daily hygienic foray at home before going to Nora for the night. Ibolya stormed him in front of the gate.

"What do you think you are doing ignoring me?" she screamed.

"Keep it down, Ibolya—"

Instead she raised her voice, "How can you—"

"There is nothing to get excited about. Nothing's left between us," he said with a calm that so surprisingly gave him the additional upper-hand he was looking for. Indifference. *I'm not even mad at her. I simply don't care. Thanks, Nora.*

"You can't do this to me because I took a little vacation with the girls—"

"Save your breath—"

"What? You don't believe me?" she cried with sobs.

"Look, sweetheart," he said walking to his car. "I don't have time for this." She followed him and started to tug on his shirtsleeve. "By the way, where's your engagement ring?" he asked.

"At home."

"Then, you can keep it."

"Whad'ya mean?"

"We aren't engaged any more, that's what I mean."

"Please Tibor, forgive me. I didn't realize that you were so touchy. I went with classmates—"

"Huh? Now they are not girls any more—

"Girl classmates—

"Yeah? That's why you lied to me that you were going with your parents to Hungary, as if going to Prague with your class was a crime. That's why you postponed the wedding, to see whether he's better?"

"Tibor, I love you—"

"Sure. Meaning he was not better."

Her crying reached a climax. He felt sorry for her, but satisfied that he had let it out of his system.

"Get into the car," he ordered her. He drove off without another word while she didn't stop sobbing. In front of the florist shop next to the National Theater he pulled over to the curb. "Goodbye, Ibi. This is close enough to your house—"

"Tibi, please—

"Please don't call me. I won't be at home." He got out and went to open her door. "And don't even think of calling me at work." She stepped out and stretched her arms towards Tibor's neck. He withdrew with a grimace of disgust and held her for a second by her wrists. Then he turned on his heels and went into the shop. She followed, escalating the scene.

"Maybe we should ask the lady what would she like?" the florist obsequiously asked Tibor.

"It's not for her. She's my sister and she's a little upset, so don't mind her," he said. "A dozen of those big red roses, please."

She kept sobbing at the window and followed him out of the store.

"Please, can we talk?" she asked, more timid.

"Ibolya!" While trying to stay calm, he started to get irritated. "Can't you see I have a date?"

Head spinning, blood pulsing in her whole body at the slightest thought of their nights, Nora slowly started to distinguish her new image. Arms that had been tossing around like two aimlessly searching and weary question marks, could finally hold her other half in a passionate embrace. She needed to get accustomed to living in her recast mold.

The fusion revived her as her blazing passion grew. Not a passion that she could name or measure in her old terms that had evolved along a rocky road to self-expression and acceptable compromise. A passion that annihilated all her prior personal life, her ways of experiencing sex—and love, too—without any options for amendments of the past. A passion that made her past look like a succession of surrogate satisfactions she had forced into shapes and means of sustenance.

As material attentions somehow escaped Nora's preoccupation, the more she was surprised seeing the bouquet of red roses walk through the door ahead of Tibor.

"Oh, they're beautiful. Thank you." She gave him a brief askew kiss holding the bouquet to the side. "We have to play with the cards on the table," she added.

"Let's pick up where we left it off this morning," he answered, pulling her close, holding her shoulders. He found it difficult to keep lust behind a dam of words. Words denying the past that he buried without regret or anger. His past couldn't touch him any more. He didn't want to talk about it.

"Could you be serious for five minutes?" Nora insisted.

"I can't imagine anything more serious than making love to you," he said, and meant it.

She resumed later. "We have to put ourselves on hold," she said with less certainty. She was dying to hear his thoughts. No response. "You're going to marry Ibi."

"This week has been addictive," he said. "I can't think of anything else but the two of us. How can you?"

"How can you not?" Nora was genuinely astounded.

He never spoke the words she was waiting for. It was beyond her grasp whether they were unspoken or missing.

Instead, he spoke with a passion she thought he could express only in acts. "Can't you see? Feel? Nori . . . I love you . . . I'm mad about you."

"Tibor, I love you too. This is insane," she laughed. "You wanted to go away together? How about to a loony bin!"

Finally, involved in a relationship that needed no banning to dark alleys, Nora felt like a teenager ready to climb the church spire and shout for all to hear: I'm in love, I'm loved, it's wonderful!

Nora discarded most people's consternation with an amused shrug. But Adel's, she couldn't. Her mother's disapproval also brought the benefit of a definition of Tibor that Nora was looking for: the opposite of Paul. Exact and total opposite. A definition of the situation she got herself into was simpler: A love affair. Mutual? She believed so. Though not his case at the beginning, she admitted. Paradoxically, ignorance worked like a shield for Nora.

"What's in your mind?" Adel asked when Nora came up with her two-week vacation plans.

"A week of hiking," Nora said. That it would be the four of them, with Tibor, was gasoline on the fire, so it went unspoken. "Then Sonya will go to camp. During that time if you would agree to have Daniel, I would like to go with Tibor to the seashore."

"So soon?"

"It's summer. When else?" A pause coincided with Adel forgetting her jaw fallen. "Why don't you want to meet him? See for yourself that he's a decent person."

"You're blind. Same as with your marriage. Without my endorsement, and look what happened. You're irresponsible."

Nora changed the subject before the confrontation could escalate.

Nora's hunter-green Skoda bounced off the asphalt. The road started to climb in steep serpentines. The forested slopes of the valley, like rich folds of a green velvet curtain, drew closer with every turn. The purity of the deep blue sky with bright cumulus clouds cast in artistic disarray was disturbed only by the clouds of dust that hovered around the slow-moving car. Then, the dust faded with torpor in the distance. They left behind the grinding sound of the wheels laboring over ruts of rock-hard dried mud.

The campground was high on the mountain, deep in the shady pine forest. They stopped at the manager's hut, and walked past a small dining room, which would fill in the evenings with the aroma of hot soup. The floorboards creaked.

The approaching evening infused the group with anxiety as if it had to present an unrehearsed performance. They unfurled the brown roll of the borrowed tent, dumping the bag of aluminum posts and cleats with great clatter. After an hour of raising tent poles, driving pegs into the ground, zipping open the tent flaps—in the hope of getting rid of the musty smell—figuring out a place for their equipment, and hiding Daniel's birthday gifts, they discovered that the promised four-person tent had barely enough room for two cots on the sides and two narrow air mattresses in the middle.

The children, cavorted back and forth between the tent and car, loaded with towels, books and hiking gear ready for some inaugural program. They threw themselves howling on top of Nora, who was stretched out trying out the mattresses. The ensuing wrestling match was quickly adjudicated by the self-styled and only available umpire, Tibor. And the winner was: Daniel! Sonya understood—to Nora's surprise it did not take too much hushed talk between her and Tibor—the value of generosity.

"I want a prize," Daniel declared triumphantly.

"It has to be something we have here," Nora advised him.

"I want to be a pasha. I'll sit and watch you make dinner." He momentarily illustrated what he meant by sitting down cross-legged at the opening of the tent.

The next day's activities were a prelude to the festive menu that Nora had planned for Daniel's birthday. Marked trails through dark forest and sunny glades led from slopes covered with thorny raspberry patches, to pits where a few late fragrant wild strawberries could be found by the lucky ones, to shady moss-covered clearings where *chanterelles* glowed like golden chalices. Everybody was at their happiest in their role as gatherers.

Back at the campsite, Tibor and the children followed the chef's orders. All the chopping and braising, mixing and beating, peeling and pouring went into the mushroom *paprikas,* a tasty thick-sauce stew of mushrooms with boiled potatoes, followed by a picture-perfect mound of hard, pink raspberry mousse with five slender candles atop. The flames played in the gentle breeze. Daniel's eyes sparkled at the gift of the little red harmonica Nora presented him. He patted with a coy smile the chain of dandelion rings Sonya made, now crowning his shaved head—his customary summer hair-do. He unpacked Tibor's gift, a lumber truck, and was instantly off to load it with the spoils of the forest.

After driving Sonya to a sleep-away camp for two weeks and setting up Daniel at Adel's for a ten day stay, Nora and Tibor left the world of snooping eyes and meddling advice behind. The metamorphosis to self-styled honeymooners came easy. They welcomed the rising sun as they drove amongst the rolling hills and wheat fields of Transylvania marked by villages, some of them forbidding, walled, well-to-do fortress-like Saxon towns. By lunch time they reached the darker and steeper pine-covered foothills of the Eastern Carpathian mountain range, drove attentively over the Oituz pass amid craggy, starker vistas along rushing rivers. Descending the slopes toward Moldova with its villages crying poverty, the plains opened to shimmering heat. The hundreds of kilometers seemed to flow by quickly, eased by the shared driving. The warm wind, swirling through the lowered windows, was a different kind of experience, not the endless two days of usually hellish hot torture that Nora was used to when driving alone with the children. The car ferry waiting at the Danube was like icing on the cake.

Before the sun set, they turned the key in the door of one half of a villa in Venus, one of the seashore's *astronomical* villages. The little building featured Mediterranean-style architecture, complete with private patios, like outdoor rooms without windows, open only to the sky and the gentle late-summer sun. The ultimate aphrodisiac. There were no crowds at the end of the season, as western tourists, whom the Romanian government had in mind when those seashore villages were built, became a vanishing species even in high season. The vertiginous decline in the quality of services drove them away to the Bulgarian seashore, a hundred kilometers to the south. To have sunk beneath the Bulgarians' level was the ultimate irony that bothered not a few citizens.

Moaning, Nora lay on the bed facing the verdant patio. She looked languidly through the open door at Tibor sitting in the worn-out lounge chair reading her book, Manchester's *Death of a President.* He had finished the only one that Nora had picked for him, Remarque's *All Quiet on the Western Front,* during long hand-holding hours on the beach, to Nora's greatest satisfaction. Both his reading and the hand holding, as it were. Despite the great discomfort caused by her honeymoon cystitis, she was musing how her day-long whining did not damage Tibor's sunny mood. She had spent the day slumbering between cramps. Now, noticing that Nora was awake, he moved a chair near the bed, and still holding the book in one hand, started to gently rub her neck and back. She groaned some more.

"You bring to my mind Axel Munthe."

"Who?"

"Don't you know the Swedish physician-masseur-writer?" Nora teased.

"Does he know me?"

"Yes, he mentions you on page 356."

"See?" He put the book in his lap. "You have a famous lover." He took a nibble at her shoulder.

"This might be just the right thing—"

"The bite or the lover?"

"*Tibikém,*" she said affectionately, and turned on her side facing him. "I'm not joking. Listen."

"I'm all ears."

"How'd you like to join the medical profession?"

"That's not even a good joke."

"Not as a physician. You are much too old for that—"

"And far too stupid, don't forget."

"Thanks for such good opinion about doctors. I, for one, am not that smart." She waved him to silence. "It takes a lot of work and maybe some memory. Logic too, all right. With average intelligence and common sense one can do a good enough job. The key is in the vocational motivation. But, that's not what I'm talking about. What do you know about Physical Therapy?"

"As a medical profession for me?"

"Yes. It doesn't necessarily go hand-in-hand with massage. By rule, PTs are not masseurs."

"So, how did you get this idea?"

"I guess it was an instant association in my mind. Your talent could be converted into a skill and your desire to get out of the auto shop could be accomplished by . . . and I can't think of anything else, because that's all I know, medicine." She moaned with pleasure, as he didn't stop rubbing the back of her neck. "On the other hand, you've never mentioned an engineering degree . . . or anything else you would rather do."

"No, I never mentioned anything because I know the length of my nose, thank you, or if you still don't believe it, the capacity of my brain. That of a thimble—"

"More lazy than stupid—"

"Go jump in the lake." His bantering tone did a poor job hiding his irritation with her teasing.

THE END was written all over. The end of a week of sensory fireworks out of the sharp contrast of light and shade of the deserted nudist beach; of the throbbing desire melting into the sand; of the leaves stuck on her nose and nipples as sunblock; of the carefree wandering; of dancing away the nights in vulnerable decadence.

Tibor drove a couple of hours. The first time she took over, still running from the rising sun, silence set in. A scratchy feeling bubbled in her throat reminding her of the need for some closing move, for a barrier to burgeoning nostalgia, for strength to combat any shared plans. How is he going to marry after going away for the summer, was a question as acute as a knife stuck right into the middle of her brain. Could he? *Will* he?

"Some summer adventure this was," she murmured, pursing her lips.

"Are you sure?" he turned a sad face to her.

"Of what?"

"The adventure part."

"I'm in the dark." In her wildest dreams, she didn't expect what followed.

"Nora. Would you marry me?"

Nora lifted her gaze to the rear-view mirror with apparent coolness, stepped on the brake and pulled off the road. "Is this as simple as me saying *yes?*" she asked perplexed.

"I don't think so."

"See. Tibi, please look at me. We can't leave this very spot without talking this over."

"We are free, we are in love with each other, I can feel for the first time in my life that happiness is in my reach. I have no doubts that we'd make each other happy."

"We should be damn sure about the big picture first. What we want, what we have, what we're willing to give up," she said. It sounded like a well thought out list.

"You swept me off my feet. I've lost my compass."

"We're in the same boat at sea . . . without a compass." They smiled bitterly.

"It has been less than two months. Can you believe it?" he said, with nothing else in his mind or heart than the warmth of love.

"I'm lost in you."

"You are lost in a good place. Don't worry."

"I wish. I'm complicated. I take everything too seriously. I need to go over every possibility and impossibility." She paused. *Then, long-live instinct anyway!* She didn't say that.

"Maybe it's time for you to have a less complicated life. With me, with your children . . . and ours." From a lofty exuberance, his voice plunged to a lower register as if mentioning the impossible.

Not again, Nora was begging herself. *I can't suspect him again. He's too simple to be doubted.* "That's what I was afraid of." She confirmed the prohibitive meaning of his proposal, and her resistance to having more children.

There was never anything wrong in the way they had communicated since the beginning of their relationship. But now the satisfaction of perfect communication was cancelled out by the chasm it could not bridge.

"Do you think we can find a better place than the roadside to discuss this?" He was not ready to jump into the chasm.

"Sure. You want to drive?" There was resignation in the fleeting hug as they crossed behind the car to change sides.

4

Long shadows crosshatched the street. Tibor pulled the brake. Softly, his car rolled into the parking spot. Nora looked at him from the corner of her eye. *Good try. Postpone the moment, old boy.* An implacable march drowned out the elegy of passionately roaring and tenderly whispered love songs. Songs choked by reasoning. Songs to be banished.

Nibbles of the summer's leftovers that Nora found delicious, were bitter for Tibor. "I'd share your load and you refuse my only dream," he said.

They were lying in the grass. She sat up, picked up a cookie, looked at the frolicking children, friends playing cards. *I have no obsessions like him. Unless my consuming desire is one. The fear that without his touch my flesh would fall off my bones like overcooked meat.* She rolled a minuscule crumb between her thumb and finger.

He sat up chewing a blade of grass.

She walked around in circles. "How much am I worth to you, without giving you a child?" She didn't want an answer.

He didn't see it that way, but there was no other way.

She had fought for her children and now she could be happy only knowing them happy. "I should know how strong is your want." She couldn't elicit as much as a faint nod from Tibor. "Could you see me pushing around a big belly?" She tried to pass the issue with joking.

"It would pass." He remained deadly serious.

"I'm afraid." Now, she meant it.

He came to life. "I can't argue with that, of course."

Nora and Adel brewed in a caustic brine boiling over with poisonous remarks more and more often.

"Your behavior is an affront to me and the whole town," Adel started the attack one day.

Nora instantly exploded. "I crap on the whole town. I owe the town nothing. What did it ever do for me? Your town is but a horde of gossiping old hags. What did I do against *you?*"

"What happened to your standards? A man comes along and picks you like a maid in the market. Think of—"

"He wants to get married. I can't promise you when. It's not up to me. If he doesn't get married, will that also be my fault?"

"I'm not talking about *his* future. Break up, right now!" Adel ordered.

"Contrary to your belief, Mother, I always consider what you tell me. But, there's a limit. It's *my* life. I'll decide with who I'll sleep. I'm a mature woman—"

"He's trying to catch you." Adel wouldn't stop.

"Catch who? Am I the catch? He is not—" Nora was crushed. Not because Adel could have been right. "We got carried away. We could've sent the kids out at least," Nora said with resignation." Adel suddenly froze. Sonya and Daniel were staring. "Well, sooner or later they'll have to learn about life."

"Is Adel upset about Tibor?" Sonya asked during their walk home.

"It's not only about him. We have to be honest with a parent, so we can look them straight in the eye. Same with strangers. You should never be ashamed of honesty."

"I'm honest," Sonya said with the serenity of innocence.

"That's great. We also should listen to other people's reasons. Maybe you don't understand why I'm asking . . . but I'd like to know what you think," she took a deep breath. "Did you feel neglected because I went out, like to play bridge, or away with Tibor?"

"I don't think so," Sonya said. Her frown expressed her earnest in answering the question.

"I'm the head of our family, but I won't ever make a decision which wouldn't please you . . . Dani is too young, I can't ask him now—"

"Try me," Daniel said with pride.

"All right. I'll always discuss everything with both of you first. Will you too tell me what's on your minds and what happens to you? And we'll hear each other out. And try to help each other."

"You know, Mama? We like Tibi," Sonya said faster than Daniel could answer. "Maybe not as much as you," she looked cock-eyed at her mother whose turn was to be awestruck by how Sonya anticipated her with unexpected maturity. "He's fun."

"A lot of fun," Daniel added.

"It means a lot to me to know what you think. When I know more, I'll tell you. All right?"

Sonya yelled, "All right," dashing in front of Daniel as soon as they turned into their alley. They were off for the usual race to see who would get to the seesaw first.

Nora treated her children as equals. She didn't know any better. She couldn't forge fairy tales to make the facts of life look better or any different from reality.

It was during the dinner, the four of them crowded around the table in the kitchen, that Nora noticed Tibor's starry eyes. "Nori, I went to the university today . . . to inquire . . . about registering for a junior program . . . My brains won't last through a full four-year program . . . They were very helpful . . . I mentioned what I have in mind," he said under one breath.

"And what's that?"

"What you'd suggested at the seashore."

"Physical therapy?

"Yes."

"That's wonderful, Tibi. I'm so happy," she expressed her excitement with two smacking kisses on his cheeks.

"They said I could take a special program if I have . . . a related job." He spread his fingers to emphasize his uncertainty.

Sonya and Daniel slid off their chairs and took their plates to the sink. Tibor followed suit. "Realize, this is a no-win situation," he said.

"Why?"

"Time—"

"How long would it take you?"

"If I work very hard, they said, two years, just like day school," Tibor said. "But, I have to know what kind of degree I need."

"Tibi," Nora said with a broad smile. "The professor of Balneology—"

"Sorry, I feel so handicapped," Tibor said annoyed. "I don't know what that means."

"That's all right. I wouldn't know what the different nuts and bolts are for in a car."

"Thanks. So, what's that word?"

"Balneology? It is the discipline covering the therapeutic use of baths and bathing, mainly the use of natural mineral waters—"

"Now, wait a minute—"

"You wait, I'm not finished." She waved him to silence. "In this setting, meaning this department, which happens to occupy a quarter of the largest medical school building, the modern one, you know? . . ."

He nodded.

". . . they don't only bathe people. They do that too . . . The name is misleading. They deal with muscular and joint diseases. It is basically a rheumatology division. You must know that word in view of your father's arthritis." Nora paused. Tibor kept nodding. "The boss is a superb specialist and an adorable man." She winked at him. "If it weren't for you, and if he wasn't happily married, I would ask him to marry me."

"Swell. Where do I fit in?"

"You tell me," she said with the authority of a schoolteacher.

"You'll tell this competitor of mine that you love him, but while he thinks about it, you want a job for your lover."

"Nora!" Tibor came running to the car, where Nora was waiting in a state of reverie listening to some dance music on the portable radio. "The die is cast," he said.

"Tell me all about it."

"He wants me to take Physics, Electricity, Math and Human Anatomy. The rest? He doesn't care. Whatever it takes to get a junior degree. And, hear this. Once I complete the first year, he would give me a job as a PT in-training." Tibor rubbed his forehead. "I bet the salary won't be a quarter of what I earn now."

"Probably not. What else?"

"Well, when I finish college, I'd still have to do another year of training."

"Sure," she said. "Puiu is doing his best, isn't he?"

"You know why?"

"Because you're great."

"Yeah, sure." Tibor waved her off. "It's for your sake. He said, as long as you vouched for me—apparently you did, didn't you?"

"No, bozo." She laughed. "I told him you are a moron."

"Then, apparently he likes the truth. Thanks, Nori."

"You're welcome. Now, don't you dare bring shame on my poor old head," she said and spanked his knee. "Go on, what else?" she asked, as she turned the ignition on.

"If I leave this shitty job which more than pays for rent and, let's say, I can't manage to finish school—"

"Do you plan to finish school?" she interjected quite abruptly.

"Sure," Tibor answered startled.

"Then, you'll finish school," she concluded.

During the fall Tibor was away most weekends, taking advantage of the seasonal epidemics of weddings, when his chauffeur-deluxe services were in high demand.

Carried on the wings of his own contentment, he practically burst into Nora's apartment one evening, presenting the happiest smile Nora had ever seen on his face. "I hate to owe money," he yelled. "Thanks again." He handed over a wad of bills to Nora.

"I'd totally forgotten," Nora said.

"Naughty. You should've told me you did." It was Nora's favorite thing to do with Tibor. Laugh together. Or rather, the second.

They settled in the car, satisfied with the success of their procurement foray into the countryside. Calling, now and then, on old connections from her country physician period, Nora managed to fill the gaps left by the empty grocery stores. The car rolled with a purr, as if content with the baskets of produce and crates of farm fresh eggs filling the trunk.

"Let's go for a little jaunt," Tibor said, sitting at the wheel.

"Great idea." Nora, who could never resist the seduction of a stroll in the open, or the prospect of picking wild flowers, now at their second annual burst of color, agreed. "Remember my chalet?" she asked dreamily.

"How could I forget?"

Of course, she realized. *Their* chalet that made them tick at the start of their romance. "That would be too far, but . . ." she pointed at the upcoming intersection, ". . . in less than half an hour we'll hit glorious valleys in that direction."

The car bounced on the gravel. Tibor pulled off the road. They stretched out on the grass in the middle of a small clearing ringed by trees gilded by the setting sun. The chirping of birds and chirring of crickets filled the warm silence. Threads of wild flowers with shy colorful eyes were powerless as Nora and Tibor rolled toward each other, prey to themselves.

Her primitive animal instinct, a sudden deep-seated need to bond forever, kept him prisoner against his will. "I love you, Tibi. I want you. All of you."

"Nori, my dear." A suspecting gaze said more than his words. "You'd regret it and hate me for ever."

"I could never hate you. I want your child." It was Nora's heart talking, not her mind. The height of passion is no place for reflection. Her irresistible desire was not a result of reasoning. Her previous refusal to have his child had not been a result of any rationale either. Both her selfless passion now, and her blind premonition then, were as compelling as life itself. Not a skin-deep infatuation, but an all-absorbing craving to make him happy.

Love fused them on the bed of crushed flowers. She looked at the trees above, bending left and right, nodding right and wrong, strong and weak, present and future. Their arms crossed over her chest. His happiness was complete. More than he could bear, and beyond understanding. His lips lingered on her shoulder, her forehead, her lips. Whispered words of love. They lay there, at the crossroads of total emotional and physical belonging, in total disregard of the world. Blessed by the sky above.

The Chicken Coop conference—as they came to call her folly and his hopeful surrender—left Nora in a state of emotional levitation. Hoping for neither the success nor the failure of their two particular reproductive cells to have a shot at deciding their future, she brought the word 'fatalism' into play. Fatalism that she generally regarded as the ultimate example of universal disclaimer. She never thought that saying something like, *I had nothing to do with this, it was fate,* could be an escape from responsibility. For her current state, she made a slight adjustment, a slightly more productive, or rather reproductive interpretation of the idea. For all practical purposes she had decided that she would not change her Chicken Coop mind-set. She would not have an abortion. Fatalism glossed over her inconsistency for the time being.

Nothing of consequence happened in Nora's pelvis. She couldn't tell whether she was happy or not. She was busy screaming every half an hour, and every time about something else. The buttons didn't fit the buttonholes, the knife cut her finger not the bread, the milk boiled over on the stove. It was not her fault. It was the hostility of the buttons, the knife, the milk. Her hands trembled in frustration. Then, the overdue floodgate opened. She could think without the strain of guesswork of the true nature of her sylvan folly. Firstly, it was an indication that passion could blur the mind. Until then, Nora would have vehemently protested that it could happen to her. Now, she regarded the Chicken Coop Conference as a flagrant example of temporary insanity. The realization put a painful spasm in her stomach. The chasm was widening.

The nicknames they had bestowed on each other—Mamatzi and Tatatzi—intimating the possibility of becoming parents together, would endure regardless of the fact that nothing momentous happened at a cellular level.

Tibor's disappointment turned everything with its shady side into full view. A sudden ill disposition toward Nora made him feel debased, for his mind refused the idea that she had not done anything to rid herself of his child. He was torn between the lack of comforting future prospects and present temptations.

In this mood, after the children had gone to sleep, Nora and Tibor settled to watch *Un Homme et Une Femme,* A Man and A Woman, the universally acclaimed French movie that finally made it to Romanian television. They sat motionless, merely squeezed hands, exchanged furtive glances. After the screen went dark they sunk into a depressed state and an embrace soaked in tears. The protagonists' emotional ordeal, painful memories and yearning for each other resonated in Nora's and Tibor's own insecurities. A chance for life; so easy to miss. As if there were no tomorrow, and as though frigid claws were ripping them apart in that very place and on that very evening, they clung to each other in silence.

"Don't tell me when it's the last time. I'd die in your arms. When you must, just leave me," Nora whispered.

The next day, and for years to come, she found herself humming the movie's haunting melody. Sorrowful foreplay to an impossible future.

It was with apprehensive expectation that Nora was thinking of Adel's return from a western European trip, her stomach a hatchery of fluttering butterflies.

She hung up, reassured that Sonya was all right, alone with her homework and lunch. One more hour, one more phone call to check on her, and she would be off to school. One more week. Tuesday, Rozsika was cleaning and washing; Thursday, Bertha was cooking and ironing; Nora herself would take one day off; the anxiety of knowing that Sonya was alone until one o'clock was too much for her nerves.

Two more days like this without supervision. *This day, thanks goodness, is almost over.*

Nora was writing a prescription when Cornelia called her, "Madame Doctor, Sonya on the phone."

"Mama, please don't be upset," Sonya whined.

Whatever happened can't be too bad. She is on the phone. That logic couldn't stop Nora's knees from getting jittery. "What happened?"

"I wanted to iron my pioneer scarf."

"You're not allowed to use the iron." Nora felt the words resonating in a void. "Or any electric appliance. Don't you know that?" Nora had the definite feeling that she was talking to the wall. "Sonya?"

"It fell," Sonya said mumbling.

"What fell?" Nora asked, envisioning the iron on the top of the cupboard in the kitchen.

"Everything," she started to cry. "Mama, I'm afraid."

"Are you hurt?"

"A little," Sonya sniffled.

"Are you bleeding?"

"I think so."

"Where?"

"My head."

"Your neck, your arms?"

"I don't know."

"Sonya, listen." She was sure an ambulance wouldn't get there faster than herself. "Lie down on the bed and press your hand where you're bleeding. I'll be there in ten minutes. Are you listening?"

"Yes, Mama."

Opening the door to the apartment caused a scraping sound. Nora stepped onto a layer of crunchy glass and china shards covering the floor in the hall. The light coming from the open living room door fell on what she recognized to be pieces of the everyday china and glasses, contained in the top portion of the cupboard. The tide of shards and objects was coming from the kitchen where the layer was thicker.

"Mama, I'm here." A voice, thinned by fear, reached Nora from the living room.

Sonya was pale. Her lips trembled. Her fingers were pressed against her temple. She had a few small abrasions around the hairline, halfway down her face and her elbows. Her abdomen was normal to Nora's examining fingers. Finished being a physician, the mother felt relieved but dizzy. "Don't worry, sweetheart," she said. "Now tell me what happened."

The wreckage in the kitchen illustrated vividly Sonya's story. She had pulled a chair up to the sink that was next to the cupboard. Climbing from one to the other she ended up standing with the right foot on the edge of the sink and the left on the ledge of the lower portion of the cupboard. The ten-year old could still not reach the iron. Stretching wasn't enough, so she held onto the top of the cabinet to gain leverage. A little more pull, a little more stretch, a lot of cracking noise and the brackets holding together the back of the two portions pulled out the screws. The upper part toppled, the doors opened, the dishes and the iron crashed to the floor. Sonya apparently remained planted on the sink for the critical instant, then tumbled down gradually onto the chair and floor.

"See why you are not allowed to do certain things?" Nora wondered what convincing power her mild words could have. "Sonya, please, always ask me first." Nora deemed more scolding unnecessary.

"Yes, Mama," Sonya muttered into her mother's lap.

Nora hoped that the reckless girl had learned her lesson. Small bandages in place, Nora sick to her stomach at the thought of what could've happened with less luck, they hugged.

Harvest time came and brought colorful mounds of produce to the otherwise dismal farmers' market. The socialist system tried, and nearly managed, to choke agriculture to death. It was one of the few occasions a year when cooperatives as well as individual farmers brought to the city market a substantial quantity of produce.

Winter was a time to starve unless one canned and preserved, stashed and hung. Bunches of grapes hung from ceiling racks would—with any luck—become raisin-like delicacies. With less luck they would mold and rot.

In the company of the portable radio on the windowsill and the sunshine pouring through the open balcony door, Nora moved around in the rhythm of the dance music between the piles of apples and pears, tomatoes, cucumbers and potatoes. The sensation of the hot nights at the seashore invaded her with a pure erotic nostalgia. As if moved by her evocative power, Tibor showed up.

He dove into the core of his fixation. "I tortured myself for nights." He was looking now at the apple he kept tossing from hand to hand. "When lucid, you show no intention of wanting to start a family with me." He stopped for a questioning look. Nora remained silent, so he went on. "I cannot give up . . . You wouldn't have any burden after you carried . . . I would take charge of everything in my ability. Everything. You wouldn't even have to change a diaper if you wouldn't want to. There's no other alternative."

Nora's words—if she could find any—would have been stopped in the scratchy narrows of her throat. She started to fret and feverishly look around for diversion. She turned off the radio. She felt worse. She took an onion and started to chop it with fury with no cooking in mind. It worked. Her tears that started to pour were nothing more than the onion-effect. "Tibi." She bit her lower lip. Then she collected herself and cleared her throat. "Why do I have this sudden inkling, that resuming the child theme is the result of some tangible events I know nothing about?" When he tried to talk she waved. "You suddenly want to get out without losing face. You bring up a subject on which you're sure we can't agree." She couldn't blame the onions anymore. They make no one sob.

Tibor blamed Nora for ruining his standards, for being a hard act to follow. She saw no compliment in his diatribe. He spoke of his selfish concerns about going back out in the single's world.

"Have you tried?" she asked.

"Let's say I had," he said. "And failed."

"Oh! You selfish cheat. My heart is breaking." She paused. "Don't expect me to ask you more." *Nora, be vulgar, that should be analgesic.*

"I can't but follow my instincts." He broke her line of thought.

"You're absurd. That's the only way you can prove your virility? That's what your ego asks you to do? It's primitive."

"I didn't expect this Nora. On the other hand, yes. Not the way you mean it. A man can have instincts too. I want to hear someone call me 'father'."

She had no moral ground to argue with that, since he had been fair not arguing with her premonitions about pregnancy.

"I'm sorry." She couldn't keep up the apache behavior. "I'm afraid you'll mess up your life again. At least do it with some innovation." She put on an outlandish grin. He wasn't receptive to grim humor. "All right," she said on a more serious note. "As long as we're not right for each other—"

With a gesture of outrage he snapped, yelling, "We're not right for each other? Isn't the problem that we're perfect together?"

"Obviously that's not enough." She angrily wiped away her tears. The rest, as far as she was concerned, was background noise until she heard him say, "Are you going to look for someone with two kids? So the balance will be perfect? Your kids will grow up, go away—"

"Thank you for warning me and reminding me of the need for balance." She didn't mean it sarcastically.

"It sounds like you gave up on your life."

"That's how *you* were when we started. I can learn." She was afraid that the bitterness that seeped into her, was there to endure.

5

Unwritten rules of social hypocrisy require one to hide misery. Nora did just that. Her aloof carriage, however, collapsed like a house of cards whenever crossing Tibor's path. The more she struggled for a neutral deportment, the more craving exuded through her pores. Staying friends took an enormous toll.

Tibor rang the doorbell while letting himself in. Sonya, in flowery pajamas, ran to the hall. Daniel, faking to drink his milk, sat at the kitchen table. Nora, with a blue and white-striped apron tied around her waist, was cleaning up. Tibor, still in his overalls, came to take the empty gasoline canisters.

Gasoline pumps closed down one after the other. The ones open sold only at certain hours. Stealing gasoline was the only way to keep a car running. Gasoline from trucks, buses and taxis was siphoned out and the stolen treasure sold at black market prices. It took Tibor a long time to get into the ring, and Nora even longer to accept such goods.

Not the only shortage, just another one added to the long list getting longer, that became the way of life. Nora also added Tibor to her private list of vanishing goods. The feeble consolation that sooner or later she would get over him only hurt more. Love was pure agony.

He walked out to the balcony. Nora followed. Canisters in hand he asked, "May I stay a few minutes?"

"Sure. Any time." She added with a bitter smile, "Almost any time." It had never been mentioned that he should return her key. "Let's go in. It's chilly," she trembled though it was a balmy autumn evening.

"I'm going insane." He grabbed Nora with an abruptness she was neither prepared for nor used to. Words would have done a better job than the kiss she tried to resist. "I can't live without you." He didn't think of Nora's side of the story. Just his dread of going back to point zero and being stuck there.

"It will pass," she managed to say, her palms on his chest, but not pushing him away.

Words gushed forth from his thoughts uncensored. "Don't laugh . . . I'm afraid I'll think of you even—"

"Pig," Nora snapped.

"Please, let's go for another Chicken Coop—"

"You're out of your mind." Her harsh tone subsided into a nervous laugh. *He's stupid, after all.* She went on gloomily, "Only another moment of temporary insanity would let haphazard dictate my life."

He left without another word.

Around midnight he filled the tank in Nora's car, went upstairs, tiptoed through the kitchen filled with the sweet aroma of cooking, returned the canisters to the balcony and placed Nora's car keys on the table. All doors in the apartment were open. Three people slept in the cozy warm silence. Tibor opened the refrigerator, took out a rolled and filled paper-thin crêpe, and ate it in two bites, licking his lips smeared with the apricot jam. His stealing steps took him to the small room. He bent over and kissed the hair on the back of her head.

Sitting in his car he thought of Nora shivering on the balcony. The only thing that could stop the shivers going down *his* back was sneaking back into bed with Nora.

He drove home.

Tibor was surprised that he could return so easily to his old haunts; fit right into his pre-Nora shoes. The disco lights blurred his pretended detachment. The rhythms took care of the rest. Misguided craving of body blurring mind, misplaced vision of future aching in his bones. Obsession of a missed fulfillment.

He offered himself as an object to someone else's wish for the evening. When the woman's strokes that commanded his renewed interest seemed lewd, it was only his disgust that stirred. It was not her fault. He apologized, got out of the bed, dressed and left.

After weeks of tension, fabricated smiles, the ring of the phone was a strident dagger Nora would rather disregard. Tibor's voice was calm, as if asking for the time of the day, "Guess where I'm calling from?"

"Downstairs." She tried a lighthearted tone as well.

"Right again. I got my hair cut and went to the dentist." He was sounding whether Nora was amenable to an ice breaking.

"Did he enjoy looking at your perfect teeth?"

"Yeah. I'm perfect." Only arrogance could stop him from begging. He called because he missed her, not really knowing what he wanted.

"And utterly modest." While dying to talk about the suspended impasse, Nora was now startled. Both the hope that he would help her get over him by not showing up, and the hunch that he hoped for the same to work for him, evaporated.

"I've never apologized," he said as if it were yesterday that they lashed out at each other.

"Oh, forget it. Neither did I. You have your life and I have mine. We owe each other nothing." A pang bounced back and forth between her heart and brain. *Why is he torturing me?*

"I don't have a life, for one." He didn't mind revealing his loneliness.

"You want to talk?" *Damn ego, what are you protecting me from?* "Come'on up," she said.

"I love you," he said, standing in the door and reaching for Nora, a few minutes later.

"Hum?" She mumbled on the way into the living room.

"I love you very much," he repeated. His words had a candid resonance.

"Hum." Her bedazzled gaze analyzed his expression without reciprocating his words. "Is this for goodbye?"

"No. For hello. Withdrawal hurts, damn it." He sat down on the sofa. "I'm going to bust. I can't study. I can't sleep. I only pray that the cars I fix won't turn into piles of parts in the gutter."

"So? What can we do about it, Tatatzi?" she shushed herself. "Excuse me, I mean, Tibor."

"Badgering you might help. Do you think I'm stupid, Mamatzi?"

You don't have to know everything. I'm telling you too much anyway. "It's a pity we can't synchronize the fallout. You're over it, I'm not. I'm over it, you're not. A seesaw."

"Don't give me this song and dance. You clown." The robust term of endearment definitely meant he felt steady in the saddle. She hated that kind of flick on her nose.

Evenings, when Tibor dropped by, followed in serene succession for weeks. He spent time with the children in exhausting play, pouring over them, brimming with exuberance. It was an exchange of energy, something Nora wished she could offer. A single parent's predicament.

"You've told me several times that my car is starting to look really bad underneath—" Nora said one evening.

"Yeah, the rust-proofing didn't help."

"I'll have to get rid of it. Six years old and—"

"It's not the years or the make. Skodas can last twenty. It's the crash you had. Sell it before another winter."

"I'm glad you agree. I'll put in an ad."

"You'll sign up for a new one, won't you? I can't see you buying a used car."

"I have a problem." She noticed his surprised look. "It's not the money. I love my Skoda and it's difficult to get one since we started to make Dacias." Her concern about the domestic cars, two models of Renault built in Romania, was well-justified. They were not up to par with good Czech Skodas, East German Wartburgs, or even the heavy Russian Moskwitch.

"If you want my opinion, go for what you like. Don't worry how long it takes. You can use my car meanwhile. We'll manage."

"That's very nice of you." She wanted to go and stand between his knees. Hug him. She didn't. "I like your car when you're in it," she confessed. The expectation, and later actually using Tibor's car, felt like vicarious togetherness.

For long hours, after the children would go to sleep, they would share their daily problems. Tibor's need to nurture the personal ties between them found an outlet, Nora thought, when one evening, he started to tell her the tale of his marriage. It was not premeditated; it expressed his troubling feeling of being misunderstood.

"I don't know whether you know things from my past . . . it's like a rock on my heart, or more like an indelible stain on my soul—"

"Are you sure you want to talk about this?"

"I need to . . . if you're willing to listen."

"Tell me then."

He took a deep breath. "In our family people do things without thinking. My mother . . . I doubt she can really think . . . she . . . at least, in the past, did what she, by herself, felt was right. Who knows maybe she didn't even care, whether it was right . . . things her way . . . and guess what? She slapped me around. Not literally . . . but worse . . ."

They looked at each other as if their life depended on the next words.

"I was twenty . . . I had my license . . . I was proud of it . . . my father was getting worse with arthritis . . . he couldn't climb the ladder any more . . . Mother was the breadwinner . . . and me . . . I don't really know whether I'm a good son or not . . . I don't think I am . . . because . . . because I can't love my mother." He raised an imploring look at Nora. "Nora, believe me, I want to . . . I don't feel whole not loving my mother.

I wasn't like this, but after what she'd done to me . . . I can't . . . I can't forgive her . . . forget being Catholic . . . I can't . . ."

She subdued her curiosity. Consideration took priority.

He put his elbows on the table. "I never disregarded the respect I owed my parents. I never brought a girl there. So, I went out a lot. My mother objected, then she started to fume and threaten to throw me out if I didn't behave. How did I misbehave? No drinking. You know me. No gambling. Only dancing. And girls . . ."

They exchanged mocking smiles.

"I turned almost all my earnings over," Tibor went on dryly. "It didn't bother me, really. Until mother made me feel like I was a depraved scum that she couldn't tolerate in her pure home. I thought she was right. I started to loathe myself but couldn't change. It was bad." He clenched his chin and mouth with one hand. He paused reexamining his doubts.

"I found out later, much too late, that in cahoots with a neighbor . . . but that's another story . . . a woman I knew only too well, I mean we knew each other . . . oh, forget it, what the hell . . . I got laid at fourteen by this woman . . . So . . . this girl . . . a niece of hers from the country moved in with her. Just down the block from our house. The girl was beautiful, that's true. Nineteen, I guess. My mother took her up as an apprentice. Teaching her to sew. Kati, that was her name, spent lots of time in our house. No way to ignore her. I was stupidly innocent. Then, Mother started," Tibor feigned an affected tone, "'Why don't you take Kati out to dance? She would love to go.' So, I invited her. It hadn't crossed her mind to go to dance, she said . . . She couldn't dance for her life. Just sat there, timid and beautiful. I tried to teach her. She was stiff as a board. But beautiful and modest. I had to take her home early. Mother was in seventh heaven. She had her sonny boy sleeping in his bed early."

Tibor threw up his arms as if saying, 'Big deal.'

"What else happened . . . between Kati and I, totally escapes me . . . so I can't tell you, not that I don't want to, but I don't remember how it came to proposing. I was twenty-one, she was twenty . . . We had the wedding in the country at her parents . . . well-to-do farmers . . . No honeymoon . . . stayed there a few days. Of course I desired her. I probably thought I was in love. I'm sure that in my ignorance I was looking forward to married life. Was she? It doesn't matter. Poor soul, she probably never found out." Tibor cleared his throat.

Nora was uncomfortable. "You want me to guess?"

"Don't bother. What would you say? That she was not a virgin? People make a big deal about it. If all else works out who cares? But don't ask me. I went just one degree beyond the innocent kisses we had been exchanging before the wedding and she got into a crying and kicking fit. I tried to console her to the best of my ability. I was in no rush. We returned home. She moved in . . . to my room . . . I moved onto the floor . . . she wouldn't sleep in the same bed with me. I didn't want to alienate her. You know, I'm a good sleeper. I was working over-time, most of the time so exhausted . . . intentionally . . . what was waiting for me at home?" Tibor got up and paced for a while. "It was weeks before I realized . . . strange things were happening during the night. I woke up, she was not in bed. I looked around. I found her in the street, crouching under the window, holding a pillow to her ear as if listening to Radio Free Europe. I thought at first she was crying, but no. She had an empty stare . . . mumbling to herself . . . to the pillow? . . . I tried to take her inside. She started to whack me with the pillow, then go at my face with her fingernails. No sound came out of her. It was ghostly. I carried her in my arms to our room. She ran to the kitchen, yanked open a drawer, and took a big knife."

"Was she insane?" Nora didn't mean the derogatory interjection, and was immediately sorry.

"Wait. Calm words didn't touch her. Her eyes spewed fire. Fending against a crazy blow, I managed to disarm her. I yelled out to my parents. Now Kati slumped, empty gaze again . . . That's not what made that scene unforgettable. You wonder what can be more shocking? My mother. All she had to say was, 'Be nice to her,' as if I hadn't been . . . for months . . . as if she knew something I didn't. I swear I felt that . . . for a split of a second . . . she knew what to do. We took Kati to the hospital. By ambulance. The whole street watched me carrying my bride to the ambulance. Her aunt watched as if saying, 'Sooner or later it had to happen.' What? I found out . . . it was not the first time she needed electroshock. Schizophrenia. Diagnosed at seventeen. Everyone knew but I. How do you think I felt?"

"Angry? Desperate? Cheated? Sorry?"

"Ashamed that I can't be just sorry and compassionate. I had no idea what to do. She came home . . . More talkative than ever, smiling a lot . . . you wouldn't tell something was wrong with her. I didn't dare touch her. Whether she wanted me or not at that point, maybe . . . but she had no idea how to . . . how should I say it? . . . how to be a woman. She was only a bunch of bungled nerves, a pretty doll. Poor Kati. But she was my wife, she was beautiful, there in the room with me. Not in acts, but in words, I tried to gain her trust . . . in another month she got as far as letting me hold her close without quivering in fear like a piece of aspic . . . Don't even think of it . . . I was convinced that all it takes is patience . . . she might get the idea that I could hurt her . . . which of course . . . anyway . . . it was peace . . . You will say this is really odious, but to make sure that I wouldn't make a mistake of impatience, I slept with one of my old girlfriends once in a while . . . My mother was still not the object of my anger. In hope . . . I guess . . . that patience would be the answer to everything. The doctors were saying that she shows . . . you know . . . medically speaking, signs of lasting improvement. How do you call that?"

"Remission," Nora helped out.

"That's right. Remission. Excuse me for saying this, but what do doctors know?"

"It's sad that you had to find out this way." Nora thought more in terms of, *Welcome to the club,* still obsessed by failing to help her own husband.

"You didn't think I'm the type to wonder what dreams are, did you?"

"Not much."

"Well, I'm an expert. One dream story of an hour, or a day, or a century, takes a fraction of a second to happen in one's brain."

"I agree. Your proof?"

"It was the French Revolution. I was some big shot, my arms were tied to my back, the crowds were yelling, 'Kill him, kill him.' My clothes were hanging in rags, as it happens in many of my dreams. I always wear rags. They dragged me up the scaffold to the guillotine—"

"Oh my God," Nora exclaimed, jumping up from her seat. "Your scar," she said putting her arms around Tibor's neck, hugging him and holding his head to her breast. Her tears fell on his hair. His hands on her back went limp. Nora returned to her chair.

"I won't ever know . . . the knife touching my neck, the dream . . . the shock of waking to her mad face hovering over me . . . maybe nothing would've . . . if I haven't jumped . . . slash . . ." he made a suggestive move with his hand. "Or, was I lucky jolting away from the knife? It doesn't matter. I can't stop asking this question for . . . well, almost thirteen years now."

"I can't tell you it's crazy to torture yourself. I have no right to say that."

"But it is . . . She was back in the hospital. Institutionalized. Then my mother broke down and admitted that she knew that Kati had a problem. My *own* mother used me as a possible cure for Kati? A guinea pig. Or used her to stop me from living my life. Whatever. All was plotted. Nobody asked for my opinion. I ran as far as I could . . . I wasn't interested in my mother's apology. I moved out before the annulment of our unconsummated marriage was pronounced . . . That's it. As if nothing happened, right?" Tibor sighed, his gaze lost in the distance.

The air in the apartment was still with heavy expectation. The traffic had dwindled to the occasional whoosh of the trolley rushing by in the street. The children were asleep, even the neighbors had settled down. It was later than usual.

Nora leaned back wondering whether telling her the story was premeditated on Tibor's part. Overwhelmed by her idle love, she didn't mind.

He felt relieved to have finally shared the memory his ordeal with the only person he could respect and love.

They carried their teacups to the sink. They stood there for a fraction of a second too long to be able to step away.

Now and then, Nora had likened her effort to wean herself from Tibor to walking a tightrope over a rushing, boulder-strewn stream. She wondered what was better: doing the weaning together, or in total deprivation of each other's cordial presence.

He simply followed an irresistible call and cashed in on their pledge to stay friends. He was there. The stress of work and school were enough of a hardship. He could no longer endure the total withdrawal from Nora on top of everything. It felt good to come after school to play, eat and talk. But that evening he caved in.

"What is this?" she asked now, suddenly enclosed in his loose embrace, ready to withdraw at any sign of her disapproval.

"Nothing new," he said without thinking. "Only the old stuff we both hate." He made no association between just having told Nora the story of his past misery and dipping again into a pool of present bliss.

Previous attempts to write off the romance faded. Nora realized how brief a moment is when one could choose to go both ways. How fast the momentum disappears leaving one without choices. Without a will of her own, she couldn't reject his embrace.

"Tibi," she muttered her lament. "You fool. You hold the key to my dark closet. Open it. Let me go."

"I opened it. I'm here to rescue you." He said with a touch of mockery.

Six months earlier, she had experienced passionate love for the first time in her life. At the opposite end of the scale of that fulminating infatuation was the astonishing awakening to a new meaning of her feelings.

Next day, at work, she felt like tossing the charts into corners and screaming in despair. She saw clearly. Living o*n borrowed time. Rescue me from the dark closet, my ass. Rescuing whom? It kills me. He is and he is not. Damn his priorities and his lust. Mine too. Would I be better without him? Maybe. Damn no!*

Still baffled by Tibor's renewed and unlikely presence, Nora was breaking eggs and slicing smoked sausage for Sunday breakfast. Roaring laughter came from the living room. She sneaked up to the door. Tibor was holding the roller of the typewriter high up, hindered in his endeavor to fix it by both kids hanging onto his arms like frantic bats, pulling on his sleeves, laughing hysterically.

Later, Nora sat down to try out the typewriter. 'Dear Sir, I'm undergoing a total overhaul; we shall adopt a proper behavior. Stop,' she wrote, not realizing how prescient she was.

Tibor took her place at the machine. 'I promise a proper behavior. Stop,' he wrote.

Then Nora typed, 'Namely?'

Tibor typed, 'Three steps distance.'

Is this what I meant? Her heart sank. She went to the bedroom to get dressed and to hide her long face. He followed. At a three-steps distance, as promised. "You're so good-looking," he said.

"Can you see better from a distance?" She wanted to sound droll.

"I see you're upset with me," he said, and not only the words but his dictating tone was new.

"Are you telling me I *should* be upset?"

"I'm leaving." He stood stiffly.

There was no question in her mind, he didn't mean that morning. Her arms hung limp, a blouse she didn't have time to put on fell out of her hand. She marveled whether his embrace was already a hallucination.

"I'd like to think you have someone else. Tibor, give me a justification for losing you." Her voice broke. *A reason that could dwarf this madness. I'm back in my dark closet. I'm madly in love and humiliated. You use me. That's for reasoning. How about chemistry? A ferocious enzyme that burns everything in me. I should pour in some neutralizing juice.* "Tibi, lie to me!" she cried.

6

Only a substantial distraction could keep her sane. *Remove myself from his magnetic field. Travel. To the West. Learn first-hand information. From where and whom, and what exactly, I'm not sure. Start a new life, somewhere at a friendly, Communism and Tiborism-free destination.*

The first step—getting the infamous "formular," application blank, took two weeks of queuing in the street in front of the Militia. She eventually filed for France. She considered taking Sonya, a good, adventurous, interested travel companion. But the question, whether that would reduce her chances to be granted a passport, was legitimate. Leaving two children at home was more proof that she wouldn't defect.

One detail that was reassuring gave Nora hope that she would obtain a passport. The minimum hundred dollars in hard currency was deposited in her name, courtesy of her Australian Uncle Zoltan, in the one and only Romanian National Bank for exclusive use for travel. It was a *sine qua non.* Hard currency was not available to private citizens. Proof of friends who would put up the pennyless Romanian tourist, was also a helpful asset. There was nothing else she could do but wait.

"Should I suffer or cheer?" Nora asked while helping Magda, the hostess for that evening's bridge party, arrange bite-size sandwiches on trays.

"I bet it's Tibor again," said Vera, her back to Nora as she was taking out glasses from a cupboard.

"What do you think, it's my boss?"

"The two of you over-complicate things. Life is not black and white. You have to make allowances for shades of grey," said Magda.

"Now it's grey. I'm not sure what he's up to and my will is flushed down the toilet." Nora lowered her voice as if letting them in on a big secret. "He'll be here."

"Say so." Magda was ready to give her blessing.

Around noon, Tibor had called at the office after not showing up all week following one of his long weekends of practicing being out-of-town.

"Yes, of course you can come by," Nora had answered. "I'd never stop anyone from coming to my office."

He had come to offer her a ride back home that evening. She'd accepted without as much as a blink. Her willpower flew out through a shutter that blinked open and swiftly shut closed as soon as Tibor showed up. That fleeting instant of choice! Now she sat at the table, her wondering mind trying to make as little damage to the bidding as possible, happy whenever she could be the dummy.

Tibor came at eight. Magda welcomed him with big snapping kisses. Tibor was interested in kibitzing. To learn the tricks, he said, and cashed in with no little pride the ovation for his pun. Though not willing to read about it, or rather not having time after school and work, he started to understand the game.

He felt safe from Nora's curiosity about his doings of the past few weeks—not that he didn't wonder why she never stuck her nose into his affairs, but she never did, even when they had been together.

She pigeonholed his absences with other inconsistent entanglements of their past and present. What the mechanism of his friendly returns and of her accepting him was, posed the trickier question. Tibor defined it as the void away from Nora. Nora called it being desperately in love. Beyond ego.

His hand reposed on her back. The touch of his fingers gave her shivers she could barely repress. There was a lustful glow around them.

They left around midnight. In the crunchy cold Tibor opened the engine bay and took the fan belt off to allow the engine to warm up faster. He passed the ignition key to Nora. Having a drink or two left no doubts in Nora's mind that he was not planning on driving.

"Where should I take you, sir?" she asked mockingly.

"To Unirii, driver." His crooked smile was brazen as he named Nora's address.

Nora let free all her craving accumulated during the evening. They kissed with a consuming passion.

Tibor said from the blue, "I felt like a little stupid boy amongst them." It was not him, it was his complexes talking. He never took part in any conversation other than about cars. Everyone accommodated him. Feri recounted his funny drink-and-drive stories with an engaging humor, Bebe always had some car problem, so he used Tibor's expertise. His presence had no restrictive effect on the company's mood as far as Nora could tell.

"Everyone had a good time," she said.

"I felt uptight."

"You fooled me. You looked comfortable. Lofty conversation is not a *sine qua non*—"

"What on earth does that mean?"

"It's a Latin idiom."

"What's an idiom?"

"Oh, stop it. Should I tell you what that means?"

"Go ahead," he said laughing and slapping his knees.

"*Par example,*" Nora mocked him with a French accent. "What you are to me," she started to laugh too.

"How did the Latins know what *I* am to *you*?"

"They were always bozos on earth."

"All right, tell me."

"Basically it means something indispensable."

Tibor took her gloved hand off the steering wheel and kissed it. "Thank you. Now, can you imagine how would I look saying *sine qua non*? You are giving me such a hard time," he complained.

"Pushing you to use your brain?"

"Yes."

"What's it for, if not to use?"

Weeks passed and Nora was not called to the Militia. Finally, a postcard came with a date.

"Your request to travel to France has been rejected," an officer told her.

"May I ask the reason?"

"*We* are asking the questions here, not you," he said.

"As a loyal citizen I have the right to know why I have been denied a visa. What is the objection as to my conduct." She was wondering how she got the strange idea.

"Who said there is any objection?"

"Well, I take it I've not earned the government's trust. I haven't done anything to have the trust withheld from me."

"There's nothing you or I could do."

Nora could never make peace with the idea that she was a prisoner.

Winter decorated the windows with frost-ferns. The city skating rink at the bottom of the hill opened. In the warm-up barrack people screwed the skates onto their boots, then hung the keys on a string around their necks. Outside, skaters of all sizes stumbled. Feet were stiff at the start of the season. Children with wobbling ankles hustled along the wooden planks to the ice.

The magic of the Waldteufel waltzes moved people around, children shrieked, chasing after each other and falling in piles.

"I had no idea you were so good," she told Tibor, who now concentrated on marking neat figures on the ice.

Nothing alluded to the turmoil in his mind that threw him out of bed that morning and made him offer the Manns his company.

Nora picked up with ease a few movements she was always yearning to flaunt and was never quite able to muster. Tibor proved to be a serious and good instructor.

For days Tibor had been reconsidering the essentials in his outlook. A new profession was the remote goal. But he couldn't live *now* in his goals, just as he couldn't enjoy a future back rub, as Nora had mocked him once while enjoying one, and at the same time complaining bitterly about the future. Unrewarding escapades made it clearer than the daylight that he was not able, or willing, to settle for surrogates. He was in love with someone who accepted him as he was. Whatever he did, he was losing, one way or the other.

Was his reproductive instinct a subterfuge to keep him out of Nora's life? Or Nora of his? He had no answer. Nora? She was an open book. She was not making ego trips about being in love. He had no doubts she would stick by him. Easily. If he gave up his demand.

Ruddy cheeks full of pep, the kids were fooling around with the growing pile of clothes strewn on the floor of the entrance hall. In a few twirls of sheer energy, Nora had the coffee maker going, milk on the stove, plates and cups on the table. Barefoot, Daniel and Sonya threw themselves down on chairs, grabbed cookies, and buried their faces in the steaming hot chocolate.

Nora took the carved wooden tray with two ceramic cups to the small room. Armchair and ottoman facing, Tibor's feet at Nora's sides, hers in his lap, they reached for their espressos. They measured each other in silence.

"I won't start from point zero," Tibor said. Nora raised her eyebrows in genuine surprise. "Let's have a clean breast of it."

"It's too early for a New Year's resolution, mister."

"Look, this is what I have to say. Let's assume we both equally desire each other. We could stay friends, just like before, I mean lovers . . ." he sipped the coffee, ". . . and handle our social lives separately."

"And then?" Nora was cautious about leaving the protecting domain of silence from where she tried to observe Tibor as an outsider. As if the humiliation of accepting Tibor's returns whenever he felt the itch, was outside her.

"Well, that's all there is," he said kissing her feet.

"I propose another clause, then. Absolute honesty about changes, even a rudimentary intent with a third person."

"That's a deal," Tibor replied putting his hands with palms facing up in Nora's lap. She put her hands into his to seal the contract. He hoped that she couldn't detect his guilt, and was glad she hadn't mentioned backtracking to clear the slate.

Nora leaned back and let a strange warmth, as temporary as she was sure it was, banish her tormenting abandonment. Tibor was there, at once strong, yet gentle, rough, yet kind.

The prospect of getting together with an old friend from high school lured Nora to the city of Brasov. Lia was returning to Romania to see her parents. Though not her first visit since her emigration to Germany, it was the first time Nora would see her after many years.

The five hours' train ride lulled Nora into youthful reverie. An old image popped up: The two of them as part of the gymnastics team to represent their city at the Youth Olympiads, a boastful term for the modest inter-city competition. Shivers ran down her back. They won't have much time for old memories. She was gazing through the soot-streaked window at the running landscape blurred by fog and speed.

Nora imagined Lia's aquiline nose, her poise exuding limitless energy, open features alive with laughter and frank language, her yells skipping over the skating rink as she pulled Nora along to meet some new boys. Big mouth. As conservative in conduct as Nora herself.

Nora was not happy about making the trip while Adel was away for her yearly spa treatment with Arthur. The resentment she started to feel for Adel's boyfriend disturbed her. Her natural inclination to find justification for others' behavior—even in her own disfavor—didn't seem to work with the old man. She couldn't fault herself for his displeasure with Adel's little family. Nora had no idea why, unless out of jealousy he was looking for alleviation in alienation.

Lia's streamlined hairdo, sophisticated make-up, sumptuous perfume, designer coat, high-heeled tight boots left Nora agape. "Is this really you?"

"It's me all right. You don't like how I look?"

"You look fabulous." Nora saw herself drab in her checkered wool coat compared to her spiffy friend.

"Be serious, Nori. You haven't changed. In the best sense. You don't need all this fuss I need as status symbol. It's business. I stick out here like a sore thumb, I know."

The two young women picked up the mood right from where they left it a decade earlier. When Nora hugged Lia's mother there was a round of hysterical laughter as Mrs. Popescu kept turning Nora around to look at her from all sides. "My God. Just like that evening when I took you girls to rent costumes from the theater for the ball. Remember? *Hansel* and *Gretel.*"

Nora nodded with a bittersweet smile.

"You have two children?" Lia's mother went on. "You must have plucked them from the cabbage patch. Still a little girl yourself."

"*You* are wonderful," Nora returned the compliments when she could get a word in sideways.

Before dinner, Nora made her promised phone call. "Hi, Sonya. How's everything? . . . Great, sweetheart . . . Dani too? . . . That's wonderful . . . When? . . . Tomorrow . . . Of course it's all right . . . Sure, put him on . . . Hello, Dani . . . I always knew you could do it . . . All right, you'll tell me the entire story when I get back . . . Tomorrow, honey . . . Sure. Let me talk to Tibi . . ." She covered the receiver as Lia was badgering her. "My boyfriend," she said over the back of her hand. "Hello, Tatatzi, how's baby sitting? . . . Well, I am glad to hear it . . . Perhaps you guys don't even need me any more . . . Good, do so. I miss you too and thank you . . . All right, sweet dreams and have fun at the movies tomorrow . . . Love you too."

Married to an ethnic German had saved Lia the ordeal of mandatory encampment when they arrived in Germany. They only heard of the hardship of the others who spent long months up to a year there, courtesy of the government. The search for jobs; getting used to enormous government and church taxes; sky high rents, Lia was saying, were difficulties that sounded ludicrous, irrelevant stumbling blocks to a standard of living unimaginable in Romania. Complete financial independence. One earns as much as one wants, Lia said.

Nora's turn came. "Your parents must keep you informed about what's going on here, don't they?"

"Yes, but your perspective must be different," Lia said.

"Well. Look at me as a horse harnessed to a cart. The pulling never discouraged me, but it gets harder and harder. Not because of the load. Because of the road. I'm mired."

"Nora, you were born to be a racehorse. What's this?"

"So, that's what my problem is? I knew something was wrong." Their laughter, mostly Nora's, was sardonic.

She talked about her professional ambitions wrecked in the shallows of the murky socialist medical system. No opportunities for a specialty. She could've been happy with either of her two favorite specialties. Endocrinology or radiology. Graduating in the top five percent of her medical school class, skills, connections acquired during the residency program, nothing helped. Those colleagues who one by one—not many—returned to take positions in the academy, were as good, some better than she was, Nora admitted. On the other hand, doctors with questionable skills, if not downright meritless, appeared in positions she couldn't dream of. Positions never published, circumventing the possibility of any competition. Nora saw clearly. She was no big shot's cousin or mistress. Her Jewishness? At that time, when still young and ambitious, she hadn't thought about that. Now, things were changing.

"The one miserable company physician position I competed for—successfully—was the only one available the year I was pregnant with Sonya. I was at the end of my rope, very pregnant, four hours' bus ride away from home and a sick husband."

Lia nodded from time to time.

"No way out, only ground down into the dust of the daily scut work of field medicine. My struggle to keep afloat is small change, my professional status barely average, my attempts to make an inch of difference smiled at as cute or bothersome. I can't shrug off that I'll always be a company doctor. It pisses me off. Enough of this."

"How's your family?" Lia asked.

"My mother has a boyfriend. He sets her against me. Yet she's a great help. Only gets a nervous breakdown once in a blue moon. So do I. My children? I won't be able to do a fraction of what I'd like to. I feed them, dress them, send them to school. Then what? With those basics fulfilled, not easily the way things are going, I would hit the bottom soon. I'll tell you more about education. First things first. Food. I'm not good at procuring through bribes and connections. It's the degrading daily drill of queuing up and often returning with empty hands or with a bag of sprouted potatoes and half rotten onions from Aprozar."

"God! I forgot about those grey and moldy vegetable stores," Lia exclaimed.

"I have to depend on more cunning people who know the ropes. Otherwise adieu sugar, meat, eggs, almost everything. Not talking about toilet paper. A depressive-obsessive-humiliating state. Then, there is the 'You roll my log, I'll roll yours.' An avalanche of illicit services I can't avoid any more. I feel debased."

"Mother tells me," Lia added, "it's like a fixation that rots her brain, takes up the room that normally should be devoted to better purposes."

"She's right. It's by design, so people don't have time or energy to think. I'm angry and disgusted when I catch myself thrilled for obtaining a chunk of meat. The disappearance of the bread from the bakery makes me lose my mind and hate the peasants. They come to the city during the night on their clattering horse-drawn carts and line up at the bakery, buy up the bread and take it to the villages, where they should make their own. They would knead the dough and start a fire in the hearth, but what for? They don't have the grain to make the flour. That grain is taken by the government and shipped to the Soviet Union under the title of war reparations. What's left is not enough."

"Still war reparations?"

"Still. Collected in multiples. It follows the same path as our uranium, clothing and who knows what else. They send us vacuum cleaners. Not bad ones, to tell the truth. Meat is sold for hard currency to Italy. Young farmers leave the villages, and crowd into the already congested cities to fuel the Communist industrial machine, instead of growing grain and baking fresh steaming breads. Nobody works the fields anymore. There is no reward in it. The wonderful white breads, fluffy crescents, rolls and brioches that you must remember used to fill the bakeries with their aroma, became a collective drooling memory of the many empty mouths. It's pathetic." Lia nodded. "Let me tell you a joke:

> Rumor that sugar will arrive makes people queue up at four o'clock in the morning in front of the grocery store. The manager comes out at seven and says there won't be enough sugar for everybody; the Jews should leave. The Jews leave. In another hour he comes out and says: 'I got a phone call. There won't be enough sugar for everyone. The men should leave.' The men leave. Around eleven the

manager sends away the women, except the old ones over seventy and the pregnant ones. At one o'clock, when all the remaining women are exhausted from standing in line, the manager comes out and says: 'I got a phone call. There will be no sugar today in this store. You can all leave, no reason to wait.' A disgruntled old woman says to the pregnant one next to her, 'See, it's the same old story again. The Jews always get the best deal.'"

"Yeah. Typical," Lia was laughing with bitterness. "I just realized the advantage of not being a minority any more. Jews? In Germany they isolate themselves or keep it a secret. It's common knowledge. Everybody coming from Romania is suspected. Most counteract by becoming conspicuous Christians. I don't care much about religion, yet, what do you think we do? We go to church."

"Hum. I don't care about religion one way or another myself. I care about education. After the war, universal education was the noblest objective of the system. It has changed its face beyond recognition."

"We benefited from the good period then, didn't we?" Lia asked.

"Exactly. While our generation was not a victim of discrimination, my children are sure to experience much worse times. It feels as if a vise is tightening around us. Now discrimination in education is becoming just another tool of the new oppression. The dictatorship screams, 'Democracy for all' while it indoctrinates people with slogans of non-existent achievements and impossible goals. There's discrimination based on principles having nothing to do with merit. Without meritocracy personal merit has no value. Quotas started to be proposed for entry to high school. Not only universities. Children of intellectuals, like physicians, are not favored. Children of ethnic minorities, like Jews, Germans, Hungarians, Gypsies are not favored. There is nothing left, but lost prospects with nothing on the horizon." Nora made a hopeless gesture. "I'm too young to stomach this heap of rubbish. I'm getting sick of myself for tolerating this system like a sheep."

"May I ask something?"

"Anything."

"Are you considering emigration seriously?"

"Before giving you the answer, I have to tell you something else. Please understand, it's the first time I'm putting it in words, bear with me. What sharpened my general outlook is . . . I'm in love like never in my life—"

"Great."

"Unfortunately, it's not . . . No, it's not that," Nora answered Lia's questioning gesture. "It *is* mutual, only our philosophy is incompatible. He has complexes of inferiority, though it doesn't bother me . . . I think . . . I don't want another child, a fact that he can't accept. What it comes down to is that *he* doesn't want *me* for a life partner. And I . . . please, don't laugh at me . . . I can't breathe the same air with him knowing he'll be with someone else . . . It kills me . . . I have to get away as far as possible."

"Then, emigration *is* the answer to everything."

"That's right. Basically the idea was always there . . . dormant. I don't expect it to be easy. The fruits of success would be the sweeter."

A spark of joy lit Nora's eyes as she noticed the threesome holding hands on the train platform. In a second, pain washed away the mirage in a film of tears.

"Mama," Daniel kept bouncing excitedly. "I made it to the top of the *espalier!*"

"Yes, dear, I was very happy yesterday when you told me. I'm very proud of you."

"The instructor asked if I was afraid."

"You were not, I gather," Nora said.

"N-o-p-e—" Daniel said with little conviction.

"Mama, we—" Sonya tried to interrupt.

"Wait Sonya, let Dani finish."

"He said he'd catch me if I fell. I told him that if he wouldn't that's why the mattress is there, isn't it?" he said all in one breath. "But you know how I fooled the instructor? I told him I wasn't afraid as a kish-kish-boom-boosh, Hah! He'll never know that I was really afraid."

"That's a good one." Nora held up a palm, Dani hit it with a resounding whack.

"Mama, Tibi didn't take us to the movie," Sonya said.

Nora turned and saw Sonya giggling, hand on her mouth. "What's this all about?"

"We went instead to the opera," Tibor said.

"Oh, come'on, quick," Nora said in disbelief. "Let me hear the truth."

"We saw the story of *Decebal* at the puppet theater," Dani announced loudly, as if he was a courageous Dac warrior fighting the Romans.

"Tibor," Nora exclaimed. "That's remarkably patriotic."

"Stop it. It was really nice."

"I'm so glad," Nora patted his hand on the wheel.

7

Manci called Nora at the office, her hoarse voice more muffled than usual. "I'm lying on the floor. I think I broke my hip."

"My dear," Manci said half an hour later, still lying on the floor, when Nora got there. "Everything I wouldn't have wished on my worst enemy happened to me. What did I do wrong? I love you all, Nori dear, but I don't want to live any more. This is my last wish."

Nora's heart sank in helplessness. In the ambulance, she held her mother-in-law's wrinkled hand. "We love you, you know that. You'll be fine." She felt her words falling short of the target and meaningless.

The telephone awoke Nora around three o'clock in the morning. It was the professor of orthopedics, also Manci's lifelong friend. "Nora dear," he said. "The hospital called me. Our dear Manci expired thirty minutes ago. Most likely of a massive fat embolism."

Nora could not temper her impotent rage. The simplicity of the end, the end of everything and start of nothing. A blob of fat detached from the fracture site, traveling in her blood stream carrying out Manci's decision to die. Her elegant demise was awesome.

Another unexpected late phone call came from Bucharest. It was Dennis Gera. "What's up?" Nora asked still sleepy.

"We are."

"Wow." Nora, suddenly bright awake, pressed her hand to her chest, happy for her friends but anguished to lose them.

Forced to look back and ahead at the same time to re-examine her perception of herself and the world around her, recurring thoughts cut deeper now that she was about to lose her best friends. Nora reached for her journal, then dropped it like a hot potato. No thoughts about emigration could be recorded. To whom could she talk? Nobody could be burdened, not talking about trust. Adel wouldn't spill the beans, but it might hurt her. Nora could not hold her imagination at bay. A totally sterile fantasy. Snippets of aborted conversation with Tibor resurfaced. Could she assume what was in his mind based on his attitude? Assuming was not her favorite choice of arriving at a conclusion.

The Geras arrived for a round of goodbyes. The three adults took a walk around the block. The apartment was not a place they would talk. Not in view of the microphone hidden in the chandelier Paul had discovered many years back. Nora felt protected between Magda, athletic-going-on-heavy, her face reflecting the honest directness she was known for, and Dennis, with his proud and statuesque poise, the spit image of a Roman senator minus the toga.

"After three-and-a-half years of barely surviving, now you've hit the jackpot," Nora said, stunned, when she found out that the Geras had been approved to leave Romania destined for the United States.

"It's a lottery, you know. After every rejection, we had to re-file, and every time we requested another destination," Dennis said laughing.

"Maybe the Americans want you," Nora said teasing.

"You bet. They can't wait to deposit a smacker on my cheek. Cross your fingers for us."

Nora was not sure what Dennis meant, but she said, "Fingers and toes. I still can't believe that I won't see you again."

At the playground the two women sat down on a bench, as Dennis crouched in front of Nora.

"Listen, you stupid little girl," he took her hands. "What's taking you so long to make a decision?"

"I'm afraid of possible reprisals," Nora said, feeling guilty for withholding part of the truth about her delaying.

"You can't get anything without running a risk," Magda said. "Look at us."

"I know and I admire you," Nora said.

"Now really listen. I'll let you know as soon as I find out how things could be fixed."

"Dennis." Nora tapped his hand. "I'm truly grateful," she went on overcome by emotion. The prospective of a single parent adventuring into, who knows what, seemed less agonizing with such friends. "I know I can count on you. It's just that right now—"

"Say no more. I understand," Magda said. "She was a blessed creature. Are you free now? Your mother?"

"She'd kick me out of the country flying."

"Any other reason?" Magda asked.

"Well, a mixture of extreme emotional contradictions which I'm in the process of sorting out."

"Don't let it be too late. You know, the older you are . . . the older you are," Dennis said and gave Nora an encouraging smile.

"I'll wait in the car," Tibor said pulling up to the wrought iron gate of the cemetery.

"I'd like you to come in." It was the only place Nora felt safe to have a secretive and vital conversation.

"Thank you." He followed her in silence.

They were sitting on the bench facing the tombstone Nora had designed, where she used to sit with Manci, not in silence, but talking freely, like two friends. Now, there was a fresh mound and a plain wooden sign next to Paul's grave. The asparagus fern was in bloom, flowing in a torrent of fresh green from the pot on the ledge; the Vinca filling the stone frame around Paul's grave glistened with morning dew.

Sitting next to Tibor, and yet so far from him, Nora was beyond crying. Nora's eyes were dry, her voice steady. "Nobody knows this, Tibi, except my mother. In a way, there's nothing to know. As we talk, it's a mere intention. This is as much a statement as it is a question to you. I don't expect your answer now and the details are irrelevant. Statement: I'll try to emigrate with the children. Question: Would you join me?"

Instead of an answer, he reached in his jacket pocket, and put on his sunglasses. After a pregnant pause he said, "I'm not surprised. I wish I could help." That included himself. Nora's venture threw him back to point zero and that's all he saw, that's all he could comprehend, that's why he put on his glasses, so Nora wouldn't see he was about to cry. Nora regarded emigration, both for her and for him, as giving life another chance. He could see it for her. Not for himself.

"Issue our passports." Her lightness was a façade that couldn't hide the tears pooling in her eyes, ready to spill on her face. She was suspicious that she would leave with him forever a part of her that was good, and afraid of having not that many good parts to dole out.

At the other end of the diagonal of the city, they arrived at the tiny, one-gate airport. A silent hug said more than a thousand words.

The build-up of uncertainty that went with the process was in distinct conflict with Nora's vital decision. The ignorance brought on by the system and the inability to communicate openly with the Geras in an understandable fashion almost drove Nora out of her mind. The inevitable inner perplexity was demolishing her bit by bit. The only way to shed some light on the procedure ahead of her was to contact David, a friend of the Geras in Bucharest, a cynic whose lectures were the best preparation Nora could get. She learned that there was no precedent, no published rules on which to rely. Everybody's case was singular, treated differently and unpredictably, as if nobody had ever addressed such requests to the government before. Everyone had to walk their own calvary. The sporadic shared personal experience one came by was practically worthless.

Shortly after her return home, Nora requested an approval at the Post Office to schedule a call abroad. When the time came, she lined up and waited four hours for a connection. She had plenty of time to digest the information—also from David—regarding the most-favored-nation clause that the Romanian government was dying to obtain from the United States. This was what gave hopes to people like her who rushed to draw on it. Later she was to learn how the list where their names were recorded really worked.

When she was connected with Dennis, they both chirped in *birdese* for the pleasure of the unauthorized ears—probably tapes—bugging the line. Finally Nora understood, at least she hoped she did, Dennis's statement that they had seeded their garden and that there was no weather so adverse that it would stop the crop next year. It meant that something had been done to make Nora's journey successful. Her name was on Senator Henry "Scoop" Jackson's list, she would learn later. With the tone of a marginal gossip, Nora conveyed Mary Magdalene's—her own pseudonym—final decision to buy her children some kites, and hoped that Dennis didn't forget what that meant.

The pseudonym soon became futile, when she stated openly her intention at the Militia. In the queue trailing around the block, people with tired faces waited for the gate to open and to be admitted one by one into the bare, prison-like courtyard. Despite published hours for interviews, Nora was turned away from the entrance booth, being told that the numbers for that day had already been distributed.

The lucky day finally came when Nora was escorted beyond the booth. After another hopeful hour or so, she sat in front of a wooden-faced officer in a Kafkaesque office.

"Why did you request this interview?"

"I would like to file the papers to leave the country on a permanent basis with my two children."

"Why?"

"This is the place where I lost my husband three years ago. I've been trying to recover. I can't. I have to try a new life." Not a single lie, she mused.

"Where do you plan to emigrate?"

It sounded so promising. He was sitting with a pen in his hand, ready to take notes or perhaps scribble some symbol of an open semaphore.

"To the Unites States of America." Nora tried to eliminate any hesitation from her erratic voice, as if that would matter.

"What kind of relatives do you have there?"

"Uh, I have cousins." Her voice tapered to a thin thread of sound like being choked. She had hoped to file the papers before they would ask such questions. Now, suddenly, family unification with cousins didn't sound too convincing.

"Any first degree relatives?"

"I have close friends. More supportive than any relatives."

"If you don't have first-degree relatives it is not family reunification, and you cannot file." It sounded final.

"I have to live my life irrelevant of relatives."

"I have nothing else to add," he said and rang a bell.

"I have an uncle in—"

"Not a first-degree relative. Where? In America?"

"No . . ."

"We are talking about America. Isn't that what you said?"

"Yes . . ."

"Your allocated time is over."

"I would like to ask—"

"There's nothing to ask." He got up from his chair and came around the table. He looked ominous. He grabbed her sleeve and pushed her towards the door. When he opened the door he released the sleeve, so it would look from the outside as if she was leaving on her own will.

It was a clear warning. Physical intimidation was not out of the question as a response to anything that provoked the interviewer's dissatisfaction. She was frightened and alone, with no outlet for her tension and fear. To confide in the children was too risky, though it was not only her own need she had to curb. She had to start preparing them.

Nora knew she had cut the branch from under her feet. Now she had to jump. She had to be dauntless. The only way to prove it was not to miss one single hearing day.

When long lost Uncle Zoltan had resurfaced from Australia a few years earlier, Nora took to the robust, garrulous and intelligent man she found both funny and exotic. Now, on his second visit, Nora would, with good reason, find him generous as well.

"*Eretz,*" he said. His brush-like mustache decorating a square face topped by cropped graying hair was the perfect source for his always opinionated, but nevertheless congenial, talk. "They can't refuse you emigrating to Israel. Don't postpone indefinitely for no certain better alternative. I'll help," he said, as if there was nothing simpler, when Nora presented him with her emigration plight.

In Bucharest, he found a money channel that bartered people for hard currency. A British subject, formerly Romanian, was the go-between the Romanian government and residents of capitalist countries who were willing to extract relatives from Romania. Zoltan was ready to pay the ten thousand dollars for his niece and her children. Nora's jaw dropped. A week later, and just before Zoltan was ready to take the plane back to the capital, the news of the go-between's sudden death saved the generous uncle's money.

Nora called David. She got a second crash course in the art of how to misstate her purpose. Also known, to lie. For starters she needed an interview at the Israeli Embassy.

The leafy street of embassies and the string of booths with armed police impressed Nora beyond intimidation. Drenched in cold sweat, she stepped over the threshold of the friendly territory. She didn't think she was afraid. Ashamed, yes. Standing in the middle of the entry hall in front of an elegant carved desk, she wished she could sink beneath the marble floor rather than tell a lie to the people there; as she had been advised that this was her only chance. She felt faint. They gave her water and encouraged her. There was nothing to fear; the building was not bugged, they said. They did not doubt Nora; they believed her that her friends had made arrangements in America to assure her exit from Romania.

That was good, they said, and promised their support. "There are some formalities. Fill out a form and wait for clearance from us to go to the police."

Facing the officer seated at the bare desk in the small room she declared, "I am Jewish and I want to emigrate to Israel with my two children." Repressing her trepidation she forced upon herself an impolite demeanor. "I came for forms." She felt like a daredevil simply by dropping her usual polite manners. An unknown nerve vibrated behind her lips, now reduced to an obstinate line.

The officer scribbled away. He put up no resistance.

After nightmares of clawing at unseen faces, blood dripping down her forearms, prostrating herself in front of policemen, having her ribs stepped upon, Nora told her jovial director the next day, "Gigi. Sit down. I've decided to emigrate to Israel."

"How is it possible, Nora? Did I wrong you?" he teased.

"Of course. It's all your fault." She felt like giving him a kiss for making it so easy. "I have to ask you to go through a routine you're familiar with. Honestly, I'm not. I imagine you have to kick me out," she said.

"There are only two things, Nora," he said. "You'll have to be excluded from the Party and demoted from your job. The Party part is not up to me. Don't worry, nobody that ungrateful to think of leaving our motherland is a desirable member. You can count on a green light there. As far as demoting you, I'm not happy to do it."

"Gigi, I understand. Please don't apologize. You've always been wonderful to me."

"Thank you, it wasn't difficult. You never gave me a problem."

"Am I making up now?"

"You certainly are. Anyway, I cannot say that the position you're holding is a shitty one, that it isn't worth the paperwork to transfer you. It's one of the best positions in the category and everybody knows it. I cannot leave you there."

"Bad boy! You're apologizing. If I may suggest . . . I'd gladly go back to the Brick Factory—" Nora's idea of going back to her first city job located in a decrepit village-like suburb would have satisfied the most bloodthirsty Party official.

"That's easy," he said this time.

"Are you serious? You don't have to put me at the disposition of the region to be sent and buried in mud?"

They hugged, he patted her back with his big hands and whispered in her ear, "Good luck Nori."

The following week Nora was the star at the Party's base organization meeting, just like when they voted for her fourteen years before, in the village where she was the buggy-doctor. Only in reverse.

The room was full of bored people, as absenteeism was political suicide. Attendance was a mere waste of time. Two hundred members faced the equally bored seven on the presidium. The two or three people selected to sit with the delegates from different superior levels considered the honor more like a punishment. Sitting in the rows still offered some chance for fun. Jokes were passed, people could gossip or mock the system. Cautiously. Statistically, every fourth person in the country was a *Securitate* informer. Nobody really cared. The power of the authority was blunted by overuse, and after all, even informers liked fun.

Jokes were delivered in whispers with lips pulled to the side, eyes fixed on the dais—blowing out the loud, authority-defying laughs through one's nose, possibly in a handkerchief. A colleague told Nora the latest joke to prime her for her Communist execution:

> The Ceauşescus are getting ready for bed. The telephone rings, as it has for a few nights. Elena answers and after a few seconds of listening she flushes and hangs up. Nicu hears and asks what's the matter. She is embarrassed to tell him. After umpteen nights of the same, he has to know what's going on. "A man keeps asking me if I've got a cunt," she says. "Miserable bastard," he snorts. "There is only one way to get rid of this idiot. Next time when he calls tell him that you do," he advises his darling wife. So, next evening the telephone rings, and when the same question is asked of Elena, she snaps, "Yes, of course I do, you miserable bastard." The voice goes on, "Then, why don't you tell your Nicu to screw you and leave the country alone."

The agenda plowed ahead. There was a five minutes' reading of Ceauşescu's latest published genius. Then the Worker of the Month was named. An employee from ancillary services.

Nora's exclusion, the highlight of the evening, was left for dessert. Her request was read aloud. She was called to stand by the side of the committee and face the membership, so designated speakers could vilify her while seeing what the new traitor looked like. She got up. Someone pulled her sleeve. "Take me with you," a voice said.

"Forgive me for not saying anything at this meeting. What I would like to say I can't," another colleague whispered in haste.

"Plug your ears," Sabina, a former classmate, said, "I have to speak up, they asked me. They'll be sorry."

"Sabina, be serious. You have to kick me out. Otherwise I can't leave," Nora whispered in haste squeezing her way out of the row.

"Don't worry." Sabina slapped Nora's behind.

She was ready for the stoning. The brief pause following the request for comments seemed as if it would never end. The buzz words had to be enunciated, so they could enact the exclusion on well-documented grounds. Nora didn't want to be liked. Not there. Not then.

Sabina stood up all flushed. "I know Doctor Mann since 1954 . . ." she talked slowly with a nostalgic drawl, ". . . since we both came to register for medical school. It was my fortune to be her colleague. Well, some things change, and they don't. What will change after Nora leaves is that . . . well, it will be one good person less to work with . . . I'm sure *she'll* miss us. It's not what we expected of her. My opinion is that she should be excluded."

A man rose looking around nervously. Nora knew him from other meetings. He was a janitor.

"Comrade Mann is doing an awful act," he said. "She forgot what the Party did for her. She kicks into everything we value." He could not see the faces of the membership. People started to bury their faces in their hands, some were shaken by laughter, some seemed simply embarrassed. He went on. "She got free education. She took a place from others more deserving. Like my son who didn't have a place in medical school because unfaithful elements . . ." he stopped for a moment and looked at the secretary's hand which was fluttering over the table, palm down, as if urging the speaker to sit down. "Yes, I propose Doctor Mann be excluded from our organization as an undesirable element."

The vote was unanimous. One step closer to freedom.

At the beginning of November, four months after her first *successful* audience at the Militia, she was handed the application forms. The family was labeled as *goers.*

"Nora Mann, company physician at the Brick Factory," the director, said. "Doina will take your position." Doina was Nora's counterpart at the brick factory.

Nora intended to make an objective and realistic acknowledgment.

She didn't get to open her mouth. Doina spoke. "On paper only, Nora." Nora was not sure she understood. She didn't dare assume she did. Doina went on. "I can't do it to you. I'd better not take the job. Gigi's an angel. He's willing to take the risk and not displace you. This way you'll have me pray for your passport too."

It was both easy and difficult to thank them, but whatever Nora managed to say was between tears. They hugged and Nora hoped her two wonderful colleagues were aware of their unique generosity and their place in her heart. "If it means anything to you, guys, you'll be on my honor roll forever," she said.

Enjoying the preferential treatment on the local level without strings attached, roused flattering thoughts, and filled Nora with the warmth of being liked.

Most notifications from police were not only unfavorable, but also unduly late, sometimes coerced after months of supplicating, and often heavy with some obscurely threatening rejection. Nora was constantly tense, like living with a continuous consuming heartburn. Envelopes were said to be an especially bad sign. Nora's pulse made a habit of hammering in her throat whenever she approached the squeaky little metal door of her mailbox. *Let it be a blue postcard.* Why blue? The gossip had been that the various colors *might* be some code. That proved to be a blind hope unsubstantiated by statistics.

Then gossip spread that passport approvals started to be delivered in a *manna-shower-like* fashion by messenger. The shock soon turned to jubilation when the cause of the sudden rush cleared. The Police was in turn policed. Deadline was approaching in the most-favored nation clause negotiation. Avoiding delays became more stringent than holding the *goers* in the vise. The Romanian government was suddenly eager to let people go, who until then had been held back against their will.

It had also been known that more rejections were better than no news at all. Not enough activity with one's application proved that they didn't take the petitioner seriously. Nora now responded promptly to the second rejection, just like on the first occasion. In a frenzy she traveled to Bucharest, where she paced for hours in a cold high ceilinged lobby, waiting for another, probably just as grueling, interview to re-state her determination.

The government building was appropriately unmarked as to which ministry it belonged. It was known to be a part of the Ministry of Interior.

Same octopus, different tentacle. Who cared? Just get in, get out, and make the point officially.

The room was on the ground floor. Petitioners never got farther into the innards of government. A small, bare desk and two chairs would have made the narrow room drab even under better circumstances. The last time, the high ranking *Securitate* officer didn't invite Nora to sit. Anything to deliberately humiliate a person stripped of any means to preserve her dignity. Pleading, trying to warm up an iceberg, being polite in front of the exposed face of the monster whom she would rather curse and, whose eyes she would rather rip out.

"Comrade Mann . . ." *Stupid way to address someone like me,* Nora thought . . ."the decision to deny you exit on a permanent basis . . ." *Bozo, you didn't let me go on any basis twice before!* ". . . is final."

"Comrade Colonel . . ." *Choke on your camaraderie.* "It might sound unavailing, but my decision to leave the country on a permanent basis is also final."

"You are one person against—"

"I'm not talking numbers of people needed to make a decision. I'm ready to overcome obstacles."

She was a shaking piece of aspic barely able to drag herself out of the dreary room.

Nora and the children returned from a week's vacation in the Western Carpathian Mountains. Scouring for mushrooms and berries, hiking and snooping for rabbits had been somehow therapeutic for her frazzled nerves.

With the envelope that Adel handed her with the mail Nora felt a negative energy invading her. A heaviness sank into her stomach as if she had swallowed river stones. She took a deep noisy breath then forcefully blew out the air pressing a hand on her chest. "Shit." Adel looked taken aback. "Sorry. Not you," Nora added. She hugged her mother. "A week of delay won't make a difference."

Next day, Nora prepared the kids for the first day of the new school year, went to the office, ran to get a round trip ticket to the capital, typed another petition, entrusted Cornelia and Rodica with the office, and paid a visit to the cemetery for momentary comfort and fortitude.

She had no new words or ideas. Whom was she kidding, she wondered. Just rub it in. She climbed the already known concrete steps under the red star high above the entrance.

Echoes of restless steps criss-crossed the dim hall. She shivered. Her feet were cold in the rain-soaked boots, her stomach felt heavy with the lumps of insecurity.

"Have a seat, Doctor Mann," the smiling handsome officer said motioning elegantly to a chair.

No wooden face and curt attitude? Doctor? What's this? She sat on the edge of the chair wondering whether she was dealing with a novice not properly trained to handle the lowlife unfaithful to the motherland, or . . . Nora noticed his rank of State Security Brigadier General. She was sure it was the first time she saw one up close. She hoped that the interview with a high ranking officer was not designed to deal with tough cases. Like final rejections likely to trigger scenes of desperation. Maybe he was bored with his daily routine, whatever that might have been, and he wanted to have some fun, get a kick out of mistreating people striving for personal liberty.

"What brings you here, Doctor Mann?"

"The same as the previous two occasions. To ask for the reason why—"

"Do you insist?" he interrupted without sounding rude.

Nora was confused. Her sensors registered an accommodating, lightness. A polished, subtle humor out of place.

"Of course, I'd rather go home and pack." She looked him straight in his eyes but couldn't catch his gaze. He was turning the pages of her file. "I came to restate my determination to obtain approval for an exit visa. Please take this petition. It explains my position."

The papers she held over the desk magnified the tremor of her hand. He put his fingers against her hand. "It's not necessary," he said, and gently pushed.

"At least I'd feel I accomplished something by leaving it with you." She had to be polite with that man. "It is very unpleasant to hold these papers like this," she begged him with an attempted smile.

"When you'll hold different papers, you won't think it was *that* unpleasant." Playing with Nora's words, his charade was accompanied by a look saying, I cannot tell you more, big shot that I am, I have to give you the official treatment. Have hope.

Nora reluctantly put away the papers and stood up before the officer could indicate the end of the interview. "You convinced me. Thank you for your words." She wanted also to soften her attitude, perhaps say words of illicit understanding, acutely hopeful that the hidden microphone was insensitive to kindness. No one outside that room needed to know that this man could be kind. He got up and held out his hand. Not a gesture of official treatment either.

"Good luck," he said very close to her in a whisper.

Nora felt like flying, sure that they would be on their way soon. The officer's encouragement was unmistakable. She said so at home and all she got was, "You fool. He tricked you. He managed to turn you away without taking your petition." It didn't feel right. She might be a pathetic fool, a hundred times cheated out of even her personal intuition.

The following week Nora got a green postcard. Never green before. Not much text. Her eyes blurred, her stomach heaved in a panic that wouldn't ebb.

She went to work and could barely hide her excitement. "Cornelia, I have to leave early today. I have to go to the Militia."

"I know."

Nora's chin fell. "What do you know?"

"Probably more than you."

"I know you well enough. If you said you know more than I, you intend to share it with me. Am I right?"

"This is a chance for me to redeem myself." She cracked her knuckles. "But you understand I'm not authorized to tell you." She was the wife of a police officer.

"My God. Are you sure?"

"Yes. They have it."

Nora started to cry on Cornelia's shoulder.

"I have to confess that I knew every time you took a day off for an emergency that you went to Bucharest for a hearing. You understand. No harm done. I had to tell them, as if they couldn't find out."

"Cornelia, I wish I could always have a shadow like you." *Of course they could find out, but this way they wouldn't miss any move.*

8

Nora stepped on the treadmill of a nerve wracking red tape, the only road leading to the coveted passport. When she finally set eyes on it, her universe was invaded once more by a vicious power against which she was defenseless. A dubious blotchy brown color, with its meager twelve pages, the little booklet fell way short of impressive—not because of the bold text in faded gold on the front cover: The Socialist Republic of Romania, or because of the title: *Passport for persons without citizenship,* under a smudgy, megalomaniac, national coat of arms. No. When she decided to renounce her citizenship, she did it convinced that it was for a good reason. Namely: cut all ties. Now she was levitating over a dark bottomless pit that would prove in the future to be a quite befitting premonition. Instead, what hit her like a punch in her chest was the date of issue inside the cover: *September 3, 1974. What?* The Ministry of Interior, the *Division of Passports, Record of Foreigners and Supervision of Border Passages,* she read, *approved and stamped my passport on the same date they mailed the third rejection? The godless bastards! Instead of sending me a notification that my passport has been approved, they delivered a last kick in my ribs.* The charade that the General had played at the hearing, secretly chuckling at her humiliation, now made Nora feel like a mouse dangled in the teeth of a vicious cat. The confidence in her intuition no longer felt rewarding.

People's reaction to her imminent departure was just as shocking. Adel calmed down, tolerating the "aberration," as she had qualified Tibor, who on the other hand became a renewed perplexed and panic-stricken omnipresence. The children were jumping out of their skin expecting around-the-clock excitement.

A self-styled pillar, Nora shrugged off exhaustion. With moods oscillating from impulsive decisions to endless ruminations, she eventually discarded the string of reasons, bursting in remarks, which oddly enough provoked lots of laughter. The air around her vibrated non-stop.

She had never been in a stampede, but that's how it must feel, she thought, the way she was running and being run over in the operation of uprooting, preparing for the road and the new life beyond the forbidding cliff of the unknown. She saw everything through a distorted magnifying lens held in trembling hands. Priorities were garbled. Objects grew by a value factor she had never imagined they could possess. People gained new fictitious qualities. Irascibility, restlessness and the oppressive quality of shrinking time brought a blend of pride and benevolence to her attitude. *Misplaced and condescending feelings, arguably my real feelings right now.*

Events took off, started to rev up and buck like an old rusty engine yanked out of a dingy hangar.

The day had been an obstacle race. Every service had to be cancelled during a scheduled visit from the authorities. Teams of officials came to perform the bureaucratic hocus-pocus with sullen faces and outstretched palms. The telephone company had to send a man to "cut" the wires; the power company's representative came to record and disable the electric meter; the gas company had to recheck the meter, which had already been sealed since other officials disconnected it when she had sold the stove.

"Ma'am, I have to bring up the rest of the team and tools, so we can check the lines," the gas man said after he showed up two hours late.

"Isn't everything in perfect shape?" Nora chanced an expert opinion and ostentatiously reached in her bulging pocket. Expecting several teams, she was well prepared. She pulled out a bunch of bills and put it in his outstretched palm. "I'm sure you're competent enough without your buddies and tools."

Pocket flat by the end of all the "formalities," Nora could go in person to the City Hall to confirm the appointment for the next day. A city agent had to release them from tenanthood. Stage one on the road to freedom, despite all its slime, it didn't fail to impart the satisfying feeling that she wouldn't ever have to do it again.

Nora sighed for she knew it was no escape. "Nyuszikám, let me catch my breath. I couldn't swallow a thing right now . . . I'll eat later . . . I'm sure you made some goodies for the party."

"You won't eat till the guests come?"

Nora shrugged and went around placing pecks on everyone's cheeks. Daniel was building a house of cards—how appropriate, Nora thought—too busy to look up. Sonya was peacefully storing her collection of paper napkins in a shoebox with quiet concentration. She intended it as a goodbye present to a good friend.

Nora was unaware how Sonya and Daniel really felt about emigration. Discussions usually got mired in the shallows of the tangible facts of material life. Feeling like a horse with blinders, Nora was busy pulling relentlessly—she had embraced the metaphor since she had visited Lia—suppressing the curiosity to find out what everyone really thought.

Over the years, when friends had left, Nora had traveled to bid them farewell, shedding many a farewell tear on railroad platforms. Others came on their tours of farewell, just as Paul went to them when he felt his end nearing. Nora wanted no train station farewell. In an hour, the afternoon before the day of their departure, friends she'd invited would show up at Adel's.

A quiet threesome sat on the bedroom floor, Tibor demonstrating to Sonya and Daniel the little magnetic and other miniature toys the children received as farewell presents. There was sadness in Nora's eyes, and mist in Tibor's, as his big hands handled the small objects, as the children, full of understanding of the adults' grief, let him play, let him explain something they most likely knew better.

Rows of suitcases with stuff piled high were gaping behind them.

"Mama, I want to fly on a big plane. How big do you think the plane is?" Daniel asked.

"I don't know, maybe 200 seats. Big enough?"

"I think so."

"Will we go to school in Israel?" Sonya asked.

"What's the hurry?" Nora was trying to avoid the truth. "I know you love school, but *that* much?"

"Well, I like to goof off too . . . like now." Sonya admitted.

Nora tucked them in for the night. "We'll go now. I'll be in my dungeon. For any emergency call the Popescus across the hall," Nora instructed Adel.

"Will you be scared in the dark?" Daniel yelled.

"I have a flashlight," Nora responded returning to the bedroom and pointing the beam at him. He covered his eyes with both hands.

Tibor drove Nora to her apartment. "Dani's question was legitimate, you know. Let me sleep here with you." He couldn't stand knowing she would be alone. Nora was to sleep on a mattress on the bare floor to avert a burglary, a common occurrence in places where people had left their packed belongings. This never happened though when someone was present. Nora planned to walk around with the flashlight in the apartment, letting any curious eyes see that it was not deserted.

"Square-headed-devil. Nope." She enjoyed contradicting him and showed him the funniest face in her repertoire.

"Will you give me a good reason why not? You pig-headed-darling."

"Something I told you two years ago." With a questioning look, she waited for him to guess.

He scrutinized her. "That I should never leave you?"

"Too late for that buddy, isn't it?"

"Tell me again."

"It's plenty what you do for me. Plus, you said you'll work half a day in the morning."

"Somehow that doesn't seem to be your reason."

"It's not."

"What then?"

"Two years ago . . . almost to date, as I think of it . . . I told you . . . I would die in your arms . . . if I knew it was the last time . . . This could be it. You wanna hug a stiff?"

"We can skip the last time in Bucharest."

"See? That would make tonight the last." She tweaked the back of his hand. "Now go. I'll be at your house around ten with the truck."

The echoes of Nora's steps bounced off the bare walls as she ambled absent-mindedly from room to room. Visions of limitless future opportunities emerged in her fantasy like soft wet clay figures in the hands of an artist. In a wave of breezy disposition, Nora swirled between the silent wooden crates. She set the alarm clock for six.

She lay on the mattress. The room was warm. The ghostly wooden shipping cases in the empty apartment lost their obsessive power. She felt free of their sad austerity. When she heard a knock at the door, she realized that the suspicious noise she had disregarded a few seconds ago had been a timid knock. She sat up, grabbed the flashlight, turned it on, then switched it off fast. She sneaked to the door and leaned to the peep-hole. The landing was pitch dark. Her pulse beat in her throat. She prepared: *if someone would force the door, and the neighbors wouldn't hear or wouldn't care, I'd cower behind the door, then sneak out when the burglar steps in.* At the next knock she felt the vibration on her nose. She pushed a hand to her chest as if trying to keep her jumping heart in.

Her name was called gently. *God! Is that good or bad? Should I pretend I didn't hear? He knows I can hear a loud knock through the earplugs. He might have seen the light through the keyhole anyway.* "*Tibikém!* Why did you have to do this?" she said, opening the door.

"Let me think of something."

"You sneak."

"Now, shush. Let's go to sleep. We have to get up early." He undressed to underwear, pulled a sleeping bag and a tiny cushion from his duffle, laid it down alongside the mattress, got in and turned his back to Nora who was sitting cross-legged, mesmerized.

"Would you please turn off the flashlight?" he said.

She crawled under her blanket. "Thank you, love. Can I kiss you?"

"Sure, queen-of-square-heads." He didn't budge. She climbed halfway over him, her head upside-down, she looked at his face. She turned his head to reach his lips and kissed him softly. Kissed again his inert lips.

The truck was half-full with what Nora doubted could save them from neediness in their new life. As soon as she was across the border, she would be penniless anyway. She found the sight of the pitiful load disgusting. That everybody was doing the same, was of little consolation. She took the maximum allowed household items, all new, documented by receipts. Anything one owned had to be left behind. Her belongings somehow gained in value when Tibor offered to escort the truck to the Customs House in Bucharest. He had refused to listen to Nora's objection. He was going and that was that. She had suspected, and she was not far from the truth, that Tibor needed to make a last sacrifice, and needed an excuse to be there to show them off.

Daniel and Sonya were asleep in the upper berths of the two adjoining compartments in the lulling accelerating rhythm of the Orient Express. Nora lay in one of the compartments separated from the other by a shared tiny, but tastefully panelled and outfitted bathroom. A true little luxury gem of comfort on wheels. They kept the doors open.

Closed tight, her eyelids failed to bring sleep to Nora's brain, which was working at breakneck speed as if recapitulating material the night before an exam. Except that now it was firing into a vacuum, without a goal. How could she recapitulate everything by morning? The answers got lost amongst subjects not even strangely associated.

Does the place where one sleeps make the person? Like clothes. Not beyond appearance. You are what you eat. Ridiculous! Nora compared sleeping on the bare floor a night before, guarding her pitiful belongings, like peasants guarding their watermelon patches sleeping in sheds in the middle of the fields. Today the luxury sleeper car. Tomorrow? A hotel. And after that? A wave of shivers shook her. Homeless, with two children unsuspecting that their mother was dragging them into the unknown.

Her disposition cleared as the recent memory of relinquishing the apartment popped in her mind. A burlesque. The city clerk showed up on time. The usual sullen face. He checked the doors, walls, parquet strips and all items of people's property. Nothing missing. He nodded. Everything in tiptop condition. He couldn't know that the way Nora felt about the years spent in that apartment, she should have left the place in shambles, just as her life was at that point. Maybe with a few gilded spots on the walls, for the few bright moments, here and there. She wouldn't create problems and clashes. Any little irregularity could have interfered with their departure. No one knew for sure what could make officials object. If they didn't like the amount of *baksheesh* they wouldn't have any scruples finding something objectionable to put in their report. So, behaving, doing nothing which a city clerk, a customs officer, or a train conductor wouldn't like was one's best bet. Just be modest, quiet, tip well, take your passport and disappear. The clerk had locked the door and ceremoniously applied a huge red wax seal next to the door handle. She walked away feeling light and almost free.

She held her wrist to the night-light and looked at her watch. Almost midnight. She pushed the pillow out of the way, to the wall, and stretched out in a yoga resting position, relaxing her muscles one by one. Her mind didn't obey. Went on firing. She had not been sad at the cemetery. Three generations of women sat on the bench facing Paul's grave. Daniel had collected stones to put on the graves. She had left money at the Jewish community office. She would miss the routine of taking care of Paul's and Manci's graves. She would miss the spiritual balm that somehow permeated her while tending to it. Strange. Were they so spiritually nurturing to each other during their troubled marriage? She was not thinking of Paul's incurable illness, but their relationship. How many ways could one look at a marriage? At least two, if one doesn't count the children.

What was the question? Sleeping arrangements in Bucharest. Nora moved. She turned on her side but couldn't sleep.

9

An opaque frigid mist hung over Bucharest like a gray wet blanket. The early November wind was so mean that a few degrees colder and one could have thought it was January, and the merciless *Crivat* was blowing its icy breath from the frozen lungs of Siberia. Nora stomped her feet in the deserted street, pulled the fur collar around her chin already buried in the angora scarf. Employees walked passed her to the gate punching in their time cards.

Her nerves were tightropes. All the contortions and expenditures for tipping various officials would go to waste unless her truck was first at the gate. And it was nowhere to be seen. She fought visions of what could have happened since Tibor confirmed his arrival the night before. *Is he lying in the gutter, gagged, hands tied to his back?*

As her truck turned the corner and drove right through the opening cargo gate, Nora shook an angry fist in jest to a laughing Tibor. Never late, just last minute. Last second.

Cases unloaded, truck, driver and Tibor gone, Nora looked around the cavernous warehouse. The echoes of the heavy cases being dropped to the cement floor were painfully deafening. She felt like Jonah in the belly of a *hostile* whale. No matter how prepared she was—a preparedness based on hearsay—the suspense, the burden of accumulated rumors, made the waiting oppressive. One wouldn't know whether the assigned customs officer was bribable, or a square head following orders.

Everybody tried to smuggle prohibited items. Not only valuables but items like personal letters, too many family photographs, the smallest object made of any precious metal, far from being worth-while jewelry, were prohibited from being taken out of the country. Anything could happen: you could be stripped of those emotional or worldly valuables or your passport; be fined or thrown into jail; have your bribe accepted and be allowed to leave in peace. Sometimes the customs would hold back objects in exchange for a receipt. A proven relative, a Romanian citizen, would have to go through a maze of red tape to recover them in an impossibly short time before the objects disappeared in some official's deep pocket. The method was a euphemism for confiscation.

Written material hidden amongst one's belongings, made customs officials flip their lids, with severe consequences for the venturer. A poet once tried to smuggle out his own manuscripts. He ended up in jail, his family on the street dependent on the compassion of relatives and friends. They eventually left years after he had waited in prison for a trial. He was never tried. There were rumors that he was released—out of the prison and out of the country—after his name appeared on Senator Scoop-Jackson's list. The senator was working on tightening the requirements whereby Romania would qualify for the clause of the most favored nation. The list worked as a tool for reinforcing human rights in Romania. Nora hadn't paid more attention to that particular information other than filing it in the "fearful anxiety" drawer of her mind. Lacking important information, she couldn't guess her own situation that her name and her children's were now on the same list. One couldn't dream up a more flagrant breach of human rights than the case of that poet. He and his family had to be basically lifted out of their ordeal. That was the worst case Nora heard about.

Silver, if found—usually swaddled in clothes—was shared with the customs officer. If he was reasonable and modest. Otherwise he would make a big fuss and the emigrant would swear ignorance. A two-way joggle of meaningless charade.

As Nora was opening the heavy padlocks of the largest case she noticed a young customs officer standing behind her, and saying, "May I help you with that, *Doamnă?*" Being addressed politely, Lady, when she expected a brute, instantly handicapped her and blew her vigilance away. It almost put her at ease in the illusion of dealing with a gentleman, who instantly bent over to help her out.

The officer dug into the material proof of her little family's existence as if he had detectors for fingers. "What's this?" He pulled out one of the large photo albums.

"Family pictures," Nora answered, with a painful knot starting to bloat in her stomach, like a dollop of rising dough.

"How do I know you haven't photographed prohibited military or industrial objectives?"

It flashed through Nora's mind that on one outing with the children's school they went to a dam with a power plant. Not a military installation, nevertheless surrounded by big signs: "Prohibited to photograph!" An ubiquitous sign of the Communist paranoia. She had taken group pictures, and as far as she remembered, no prohibitive signs were included, but she couldn't be sure. She was terrified of the odds, and barely managed to sound cheerful as she said invitingly, "You can look at my kids."

"Is this the only album? You know you are allowed to take only a hundred loose photos." He delivered the official line with a suddenly wooden face.

That's when Nora sunk her hand in her pocket. Trembling, she pulled out a wad of bills. She was aware of her hesitating gesture and expression, which probably was very familiar to the officer, for it was a matter of a fraction of a second that the wad disappeared in his pocket with a swift, barely noticeable movement of his hand worthy of Houdini.

"Excuse me." He turned away and headed to the office booth, his fist in his pocket, holding a tip equal to a month of a physician's salary.

Rivers of cold sweat ran down Nora's spine. She felt nauseated and light-headed. Now, the *nice, polite* officer would bring out his boss and they would take her for interrogation. She already heard her own voice calling Adel and Tibor at the hotel telling them to go back to Cluj with the kids, because she was going to jail for trying to bribe an official. She didn't have time to picture the prison. The officer returned with a big, radiant smile on his face. *The bastard!* Nora sank her fingernails into the flesh of her palm, *he went to count the money.*

Occasional questions from him about the nature of some ambiguous objects were obviously meant to point out that he knew there must be more money available and he was not planning on letting Nora get away with it. With the art work Nora had packed—mostly paintings—he was out of luck. She produced the official approval from the National Treasury, as was required. Not that she cared any more about the money. He could have it all. She thought of the joke circulating that qualified Romanian money as inadequate even for toilet paper. Too rough. As long as he was accommodating and she could take her innocent little memorabilia, it seemed like money well spent. On opening the cases in Israel, she would realize the true nature of the officer's attitude, when an antique clock and a Texas Instruments calculator would be missing.

Calculators in Romania belonged in the same category with oranges, chocolate, coffee, car radios and antennas, deodorant, and other achievements of the western technology of decadence, lightyears ahead of the Eastern Communist austerity. Special stores—stocked well enough so people would drool from the smell of coffee and cocoa just passing them—sold merchandise for hard currency only. No Romanian citizen was allowed to hold foreign currency, under penalty of law. The customers were the few Westerners who visited and bought goods for their local relatives. There was also a small group of citizens Nora unknowingly joined when she had applied for an Israeli visa. She became a recipient of financial aid, which she really did not need, but it was channelled to her anyway. At the Israeli Consulate, she had been told that it came from a *cousin* in Eilat, a name pulled from the hat that she had never heard of, simply because he didn't exist. The channeling worked two ways, and the *cousin* would prove to be not a selfless one.

Nora had taken her good American dollars, backed by a diplomatic receipt, to the currency store. Not a lot of money, but enough to make Nora feel privileged. She and her family could have managed very well without the calculator, the sturdy German bicycles, the car antenna for Tibor. The coffee, chocolate and citrus fruits were a more meaningful story. That was the calculator the customs officer stole.

At the hotel, they were sitting around on the beds in the girls' room, the kids, cross-legged, played cards. Adel, quite convincingly acted relaxed sat at one end, while Nora was told them about her adventure at customs. Tibor was catching up on lost sleep in the boys' room. Adel was the only one with her own private room.

Nora was racking her brain to think of some diversion that would appeal to the three generations on hand, some interlude of memorable redeeming value suited for her sentimental mood. The need for dinner was in sharp conflict with the imminent feeling that she could implode any minute. Her heart ached with the eroding feeling of the finality of things, but her brain couldn't disregard her utilitarian bent.

Dinner. Something memorable? In Bucharest? In the middle of the food shortage of 1974? She couldn't remember ever going out any other place in Bucharest than to outdoor grills which served *mititei,* the flavorful and juicy Romanian grilled garlic sausage and *must dulce,* the freshly pressed, barely fermented, cider-like grape juice.

A mischievous smile of sudden recollection. A piece of conversation, inconsequential at the time, she had had at the seashore years before. It came back to her together with the cradling feeling of the warm mud packs that greatly helped her pains and aches. Now she exclaimed. "I know of a place."

She flipped open the phone book. There it was: The Black Sea Restaurant. Perfect for a farewell dinner. Remembering the name of the maitre d' came as a real gift of the memory. Hoping he was still there, she asked for Grigore. He came to the phone.

"I'm an old friend of Comrade B . . . ," Nora gave the name of the Attorney General of Oltenia, who was a regular at The Black Sea whenever in business in the capital, and who was no one else than sweet Nelu, nicknamed by Sonya as *Mielu,* the Lamb, that could top any misnomer for the insistent, romance hungry, skirt-chaser comrade, and the last but not the least, a Richard Burton look-alike.

"It's always my pleasure to be of assistance to Comrade B . . . ," Grigore said, confirming *Mielu's* description of him as a man with the slickest manners and the biggest tips in Bucharest. "When would you like to come in?"

"Tonight," Nora said.

"Quite a short notice, but I'll see what I can do . . ." he said, with a well punctuated pause, waiting for her to interrupt.

"I *am* sorry for causing such trouble . . . You know, my time is very limited, but my *appreciation* of your service won't be," Nora hurried to fill in the pause, reassuring him of what he obviously wanted to hear—before he would lift a finger—that not only the Attorney General was generous, but his friend was as well. Grigore didn't have to know that in 24 hours she would be joining the hordes of *rotten capitalists* outside his and Mister Attorney's protective Iron Curtain.

They looked like a happy family. A respectable youngish couple. Her hair—as everything had to be practical was cut short for the road—was combed coquettishly to the side. A perky slender figure. Dark mink collar of the silver-grey wool suit drawn gracefully tight around her long neck, knee-high brown leather boots, brown leather bag hanging on a long strap from her shoulder. His light hair shone with the drops of drizzling rain. At every step his unbuttoned trench coat flailed showing the grey suit they had picked out together a couple of years ago. Nora soaked up his looks. She wished he looked awful, as if that would have made a difference deep in her heart. Sister and brother, proper in their woolen coats and hats, held hands as they walked passed the door nudged by Tibor, like little lambs led by a friendly shepherd dog. The grandmother a model of pride—arm-in-arm with the young woman, her mane of silver hair sparkled—approved with barely noticeable nods, the lackeys lined beyond the entrance.

They were escorted to an indoor garden balcony, which Nora was sure had not seen common mortals like them for many years. Three waiters hovered over, sleazily underscoring the special services they performed for the "special" guests' sole pleasure. *Thank you, Mr. Attorney General.* Tibor's funny face made it more difficult for Nora to control her explosive laugher.

Nora ordered caviar and sturgeon steak. Her senses were titillated. The debauchery, should she have needed to live on her earnings, would have been criminal. But now, it was all to be thrown out in style. At usual restaurants a hungry visitor would've been happy with, a *ciorba,* a warm, strongly seasoned sour soup, and perhaps a main course of mostly side dishes piled around a trace of poor quality meat. This restaurant was the archetype of favoritism, where only the very top could afford or would dare to even try to get a table. Nora was thrilled by the affront she had orchestrated.

The kids were up to par with the grown-ups enjoying the chilled mounds of fresh grey Black Sea caviar. Nora couldn't stop smiling with mischief and pride. Not all the education was lost. She was ebullient. The feeling didn't last. Daniel started to push around the plate the bite-size pieces of sturgeon steak that Nora had cut up for him, each piece worth its weight in gold. Sonya was eating after she first cut then sampled with suspicion. "This is better than fried chicken," she said, comparing the fish with her favorite food, home-made fried chicken, the only kind known to them. She understood the humor of the situation and giggled her way through dinner.

"Dani," Nora insisted. "Try it. This is a very special fish." He speared the tiniest piece on his fork and bit off half of it carefully sinking his teeth in and keeping his trembling lips from touching the food. He turned it over in his mouth, looked at his mother with imploring eyes, and bulging cheeks, then spat out the semi-liquid mouthful in the middle of his plate. The waiter politely turned his back.

"It's not that good," Daniel said with tears in his eyes.

A cold cruel morning came. Checking out of the hotel bore the gloom of checking out of all past life.

They called two taxis. "Boys and girls," Tibor called out as Nora tried to deal with a sudden teenage desire to be alone with him in the back of a cab. They both laughed at what felt like a shared wish.

"Only bird language, please," Nora whispered in Adel's ear when the moment came. "We can practice right now."

There was not much more to say than what had been said hundreds of times before. Silent tears rolled even on Adel's face, which was by itself an epiphany. "Don't worry, we'll all be fine," Nora said.

How defeated Tibor felt by the only words that came to his mind: *Don't go.* How unreasonable all his past subterfuges seemed, how crushed he felt by losing Nora, how worthless the existence ahead seemed. His tears said it all. The long restrained hug gave plenty of opportunity for his tears to trickle down Nora's face like hot glue.

"I love you," she whispered in his ear. "Do me a favor, be happy."

"Always favors, huh? Good luck, my love."

"Good luck," she kissed his neck. "Please, go before my mother gets a heart attack." Nora let go of him, briskly turned around and grabbed the kids' hands. Bent under the heavy side bag, she pushed ahead as if put to the yoke. Halfway turned around, Sonya and Daniel walked next to her and waved.

Part III

1

The loud drone of the Russian Tupolev Jetliner could not cover the storm in Nora's mind. As much as she would have liked their first flight to be a cheerful experience, Sonya and Daniel would have to find out that their mother was a liar.

She was reaching for a straw of truth to save her from drowning in dishonor. She had been an instrument of an oppressive regime forcing her to lie to her children and letting them build a false illusion. Now she had to let them down. One way or another.

"Children," she said pulling them close with her arms around their shoulders. "I have to tell you something very important." She took a deep breath. "We couldn't talk freely in Romania—"

"Someone you didn't want could hear, right?" Sonya jumped to this conclusion, with eagerness pouring from her eyes.

"Yes, dear," Nora was relieved and hoped that, after all, her fear was not justified and she would not have to say what she detested the most, that she couldn't have told them for she couldn't trust them. She didn't *distrust* them, she only had to keep in mind the undeniable facts of their inexperience.

"We're going to try to leave Israel." She waited.

"Isn't that where we're going?" Daniel asked.

"This plane is taking us to Israel," Nora said. "But after that, we'll try to arrange to go to the United States."

"Then, why did we have to learn Hebrew?" Sonya had a practical mind.

"As a precaution, so we won't be totally ignorant while we wait, because we won't have the benefit of a free live-in language school. What they call *Ulpan.*" Nora told them half the truth. That she was not sure about the success of her plan was another matter.

"I'm glad we did," Daniel nodded, lips pulled in like a little old wise man. "It's an interesting language."

"Why don't we stay in Israel?" Sonya asked.

Nora welcomed her question. Answering it readied her for the official questions she expected in a few hours.

"Because I love you," she said and squeezed their bony shoulders. "The only way I can love you is to protect you from something I know could be a threat. There are enough dangers in the world I cannot predict and I cannot protect you from."

"Like what?"

"Like being drafted in the army."

"In America we don't have to go to the army?" Daniel asked.

"Not unless there would be a world war."

Spending some time with the frugal, tasteless snack, courtesy of Tarom Airline, and trying to keep up with their own imaginations that soared higher and faster than the plane, they arrived in Lod.

As they descended from the plane looming over the hot tarmac, their life shrunk to a *microdot* in the invisible vastness of the vibrating hot air. They entered a long hall, with a ceiling rising into the sky amongst steel beams, that echoed with a symphony of hushed whispers as background to shouted commands in the nebulous blend of gloomy corners and sharp floodlights.

Officials sat at a long table behind stacks of files. The table was so long that the man at the other end looked like a tiny mouse. By the time she got to the middle—Sonya and Daniel standing glued to her knees—a hundred questions later, she felt she had been washed ashore an inhospitable rocky beach of bureaucracy.

After all the newcomers had left, a clerk told Nora, "Your choice, our terms. No free school, no free housing, and of course, no transportation. If you don't plan to stay in this country you will have to come up with the money you owe the state of Israel. Then we'll supply you, as fast as we can, with an exit visa. You understand? . . . Hah? . . . Oh'ho? You have no money to go anywhere? You wouldn't need money for a long time if you went to the *Ulpan*."

As she pictured trudging thirst stricken across the desert, a soldier was led to Nora. He handed her a note from someone called Rachel: "I have some money for you. Please answer through this messenger." "*What money? I haven't got any money. Who are you?*" A second note from Rachel said, "You could have. You have friends, don't worry."

Men at the long table prepared papers. "What's this I have to sign? I don't understand Hebrew. Oh. The back is in English? I wouldn't understand that either, sorry, thank you." With a condescending smile she was assured, "You're signing to pay your debts. The money from your cousin in Eilat." Her chin fell. "But, I have no cousin . . . I didn't ask for anyone's money. Why should I pay back?" She became what could easily be seen as slightly belligerent. "We'll give it to someone who will appreciate it, someone who will not want to leave this country—" That sounded fair enough. "How much money are we talking about? . . . What? Three thousand dollars?"

The messenger came back. "An old man outside, who looks like he might keel over dead any minute, said he's your uncle."

"Must be Uncle Bandi. He never answered my letter."

Nora felt as if she had been dumped from a conveyor belt that processed her into ground meat. The tall pillars echoed silent cries in the cavernous hall: 'Come back when you have money, eat dirt till you have money, have your kids suckle you.' *What? I'm an old woman.* 'Yeah? Then, you figure it out.' *I, I, yes, I . . . will. Every day somebody must go off the walls here. Nothing new to these wooden faces. Today it was us.*

The lights went out. They followed the shafts of light to a large hall with an endless flat iron snake. It was eerily quiet. A small red light flickered over three bulky pinkish-yellow suitcases, like some dead pigs lying along the wall.

"Mama, look, our luggage," Sonya's scream resonated in the empty hall.

The *dead pigs* were heavy as if filled with stones. They started to drag the stubborn pigs squealing unhappily, one by one, toward the exit. They all started to laugh and laughter made the load lighter.

At the curb a blue-eyed skeleton of a man smiled at them shyly, arms held out to take them in. A strange woman rattled off a few words in Hungarian, "Take a taxi and go to the Tel-Aviv Hilton, ask for your room." She handed Nora an envelope and ran away, her voice fading in the revving up of hurried cars. Nora's hand froze in midair like a statue's. Money and a decrepit old man. An almost forgotten brother, of a father she couldn't remember, hugged them.

Is this all a practical joke? This Rachel woman, the money, the hotel. Hilton? What dump could that be?

Bandi, with Daniel in his lap, sat next to the driver and tried to talk to Nora. She could barely hear him as she labored to keep one suitcase from squashing her at every turn, while Sonya wouldn't stop giggling sitting on top of it. "You could stay with me in Haifa," Bandi was saying.

"How about your family?"

"They left me," he said.

That was a burdensome piece of news, three minutes into the taxi ride and renewed family ties. He had recently left the hospital and was recovering from major surgery—it sounded like gastrectomy to Nora—when his wife and children left the country.

The site of the lush dark-green citrus orchards that defied the arid ground from which they sprouted, would in any other situation have earned Nora's undivided attention and admiration. But soon the modern fantasy-like suburbs of the city, nightmarishly simplified from place-to-place, replaced the green emblems of the human conquering nature. The car turned into the circular drive and she saw the dark high rise of the luxury Hilton. She wished it *was* the dump she feared. *I'll be everyone's laughing stock here.*

The practical joke was not the hotel but her passport. At least that's what all the clerks must have thought knocking each other over behind the reception counter to see a Romanian passport in the Hilton. They looked at it like at a white crow. A miracle! Its ugly brown color unavoidably evoked excrement in Nora's mind—*Quite suitable for what it is!*—and embarrassed her. While the spectacle was going on, Nora became aware of some uproar in the lobby, only to see that her children were not standing behind her any more, well-behaved and waiting for things to happen to them. They were off, making things happen. They could be located by their screams and laughs as they chased each other in their tight corduroy pants, jumping like colts in a meadow, around leather armchairs and elegant guests who didn't seem to mind. Nora turned back to the registration counter, waiting for things to happen, gathering strength for times when she would have to make those things happen.

Eating places lined the innards of the hotel. They passed an elaborate door with an impressive menu displayed on a polished lectern. Nora peered at the price list that made her heart sink and her money shrink. Insecurity punched her with a pasty fist. Who was her benefactor? This Larry—friend of friends and harbinger of the free world—who didn't mention the money she would have in the moment of need, when visiting her in Romania and introducing himself as the "cousin-sponsor?" Spending a loan carelessly was not her style. But waiting for answers was not an answer for their empty stomachs.

In the street the sound of the Mediterranean waves lapping at the shores of the Promised Land was magnetic. Enveloped in the shroud of the night, the waves and sand had to wait. Friday evening. A few street lights punched white milky cones in the deserted darkness. They started a hungry search along *Rechov* Disengoff, *the* avenue of the capital. Everything shut tight as a drum. No hope for food. The kids dragged along by Nora's side like sad, starved puppies drained of their youthful energy. Suddenly a heavenly perfume of cooking. They followed the compass of their noses afraid of becoming mere victims of an olfactory mirage. Then, they noticed the crowd under an awning of a building's entrance. They drew closer. Little balls bounced merrily in sizzling oil releasing an irresistible aroma of exotic spices. Stainless steel bins full of fresh sliced vegetables were sending out their own enticing call. Olive-skinned people were standing, talking loudly and taking sloppy bites bending over split slices of little round filled flat breads.

Nora pointed to everything. She held out some money for the man to take as much as he wanted to charge, and hoped that what he took was right. She didn't know the bills. They joined the crowd with their *pitas* loaded with *falafel, salad, tomatoes, sauerkraut* and everything that could fit and more. Their ultimately happy stomachs greeted the new acquaintance, the falafel. Coca-Cola, the legendary Coke!—they had not seen much of it in Romania—washed down the feast.

The plane from New York had arrived. Larry would appear any second. Nora had nothing of the feeling of support he imparted back in Cluj when he came as a messenger from Dennis and Magda.

In Larry's bear hug Nora felt suffocated by question marks. Commonplace chat formed an immense surf that separated them. His confident extrovert personality was contagious though, and much more manifest than on the unfamiliar territory of a Communist country where an American could not be prudent enough.

"We'll dine here." Larry announced later. "You put on something for a festive dinner, dear."

In the full regalia of behind-the-Iron Curtain elegance, freshly pulled from the bowels of the yellow luggage, the three Manns examined themselves in the mirror.

"Did you grow overnight?" Nora looked at Sonya who now at eleven stood above her shoulder, and seemed to have already grown out of her new dress. Daniel pushed his beautiful head into Nora's armpit.

"You look very pretty, Mama," Sonya looked at Nora adoringly.

"Whatever you want you can't have," Nora laughed, so did the children, who knew her jokes. "Presentable, I'd say," she admitted, smoothing out the skirt of the custom made dark earth-colored paisley dress that left her knees uncovered. Not quite a mini. She wiggled her toes, uncomfortable in the pumps with the two-inch heels. Too high.

Larry led them to the restaurant with the forbidding polished lectern. He ordered champagne, raised his glass to toast a new life, to the questions to be asked and answered openly.

"Your best old friends are my best new friends," Larry opened the conversation by mentioning Dennis and Magda. "I gave you the affidavit with no second thoughts . . . it was obvious that I wasn't taking any risks sponsoring you . . . but a month ago in Cluj . . . when I saw you . . ." he hesitated. "Let me be frank. Dennis and Magda's description doesn't do you justice . . . I'm here for you, I'd like to always be." He held out his hands across the table towards Nora. She hesitantly offered one hand.

Her chair precariously levitated over a gaping depth of misunderstanding. "I'm lost," she said. "It may sound unfair . . . I feel hindered while you made this trip to be here for support."

"That's right. You should feel privileged." His broad smile was full of self-satisfaction.

"Perhaps. But you know everything about me while I'm in the dark . . . The only light here is the one from your eyes . . . and that's a problem . . . they are honest . . . I'm in a most vulnerable state, I have enormous doubts . . . mainly because you're here. This is beyond—"

"Nothing is beyond what I'm not only willing, but *will* do."

It's difficult to refuse honesty . . . but . . . please, don't make me feel controlled by material obligations. Perhaps my need for independence is overgrown, but this is the story of my life. I cannot start a new life with my wings cut off. Any material help from you or Dennis will be a loan . . . Do I have to elaborate on this to a free spirit like you?"

"Accept one courtesy. Be my guest at the hotel." He took out a little box from his pocket. "This is a souvenir and my view of life." Nora looked at the long gold chain and read the triangular pendent: *Live, Love, Laugh.*

"It's so sweet of you. Thank you." She actually held back tears while she showed the gift to the children. "But the rest, like this hotel business? True, I wouldn't have stayed here on my own . . . I cannot bank on the remote outlook that I'll be able to pay back one day . . . I don't even know whether *you* can afford it, but, I guess, that's not my business. Thank you."

"Nora, officially I'm on business. Rachel's a good friend of my wife."

Nora couldn't help uttering an, "Oy-vay!"

The days of Camelot over, Nora moved in with the abandoned uncle. The *sherut* took them and the three sickly-yellow stuffed suitcases through the sudden slanted downpour whipped up by a vicious wind. It came and went abruptly like a dream.

Bandi's address could've read "Hell at the seashore in Haifa," as they were soon to find out. The sight of the modern apartment buildings mirroring in the wet pavement was refreshing and filled Nora with hope. Inside Bandi's apartment was almost empty. Cockroaches, dead of starvation, lay along the kitchen walls. There was a torn box with some nondescript food and a small carton of milk in an old refrigerator, a rusty gas stove and a table on which to eat, provided someone scrubbed off the layer of crud and put food on it.

The dangling windows creaked. The wind, free to roam over the rough waters whistled amongst the buildings and didn't evoke the Mediterranean breezes Nora expected. Worn-out bare mattresses on rickety metal frames in two bedrooms, and some makeshift furniture under a thick layer of dust in the living room, were unsuccessful at making the place look inhabited.

Nora and the children walked to the window. The view of the glittering magnificent Haifa Bay was wasted on them. The wind swept the deserted beach, the sea gulls screeched, the gray clouds ran across the sky to catch happier eyes.

When they woke up to the angry banging on the door, all the emotional satisfaction of the mutual services between uncle and niece shriveled to a visceral fear. The wild looking creditors, Bandi said, were Arabs. They sounded determined to take the door down and claim whatever was theirs. Bandi must have said something convincing. After some argument they left.

"Bandi, what's going on, for God's sake?"

"Well . . ." He made Nora believe that the creditors' claims were not realistic, the only place he was protected was the hospital, his only consolation for leaving his stomach there.

"How much money do you owe?"

"A few hundred dollars would placate them." He was evasive.

"Look. Would two hundred be enough?"

"It would help. I'll give it back to you as soon as I can." His soft voice weakened by ailment was inspiring nothing but doubt.

Paying for part of her uncle's debts bought peace for the week during which Nora cleaned up the apartment, put her own linen on the beds, stocked the refrigerator, cooked and made the acquaintance of the family from Romania living across the hall. Their children, Sonya's and Daniel's age, were going to school, while hers, were combing the wintery beach, reminding Nora of their own outcast condition.

One morning, the resumed banging drove Nora to actually pray. A most rare occasion, when Nora addressed the subject of her agnostic beliefs. She didn't care for their meager property that might have pacified the raging creditors for another week. She only wanted to get out of there alive. Sonya and Daniel clung to her as Nora pushed their trembling bodies down and under the bed.

Nora called the only source for advice she knew, Irene, an old friend of Adel's living in Haifa, whom they had visited the week before.

They had never been on the Carmel. The bus left behind one hairpin turn after the other. They passed the dazzling cupola of the Bahai Temple. From the bus terminal they followed the directions along the streets lined with modern high rise buildings.

The clean one bedroom apartment, obtained with Irene's help, was complete with scarce but functional furnishings, bath, kitchen with gas stove, utility balcony with washer and clotheslines loaded with familiar wooden pins, and to top everything, a leisure balcony off the living room overlooking the steep rocky slope of the Carmel. This time Nora absorbed with unbridled delight the view of one of the most beautiful city panoramas she would ever encounter.

No more wind rattling the broken window shutters like bells of doom in the sleepless nights, no more sick uncles and ferocious creditors. Soon Nora could take a deep breath, open *Merck's Manual* and *Harrison's Internal Medicine,* put her legs up on the balcony railing, look at the blue horizon and start studying. Their basic needs took up less and less of Nora's time as Sonya, blooming under the pressure of multiple responsibilities, took charge. She dealt with her own precocious maturity as if it were a thought-provoking fun game, an attitude she would carry all her life with a natural buoyancy. She found it fun to deal with the old man at the *makolet,* the grocery store two blocks away, who always gave the two children something extra when they were shopping alone. The school textbooks came out of the luggage, and Sonya set up her own and Daniel's schedule. She was both pupil and teacher, a strict one at that, whom Daniel had no choice but to respect, which he did, for there was no playing unless the homework was perfect. And it always was.

The day came when the Israeli government acknowledged that the $3,000 that Nora had deposited in the account of the *Sochnut,* the Jewish Agency, covered the state's expenses to take them out of Romania and consequently granted the three of them exit visas. It took another week to find out that they were just as trapped as ever, only at a different level. They were free to leave but had no place to go. No country would accept them. Nora could change her mind and stay where they were as free citizens in their own land. She reached out and inquired using all connections she could round up.

"You'll get a job as soon as you show proficiency in Hebrew," a colleague told Nora. "It's not going to be a real job. There are no real jobs for physicians. You'll have to pay back the salary you'll get."

"What? More debt? When will a job be a normal one?"

"Who knows?"

The "fake" general practitioner's salary, more a government loan, the real possibility that the children would grow right into front line uniforms, the climate—meteorological as it was—did not look appealing. To pursue the ultimate goal to immigrate to the United States, they had to get out of Israel. She couldn't see the way. How the tacit agreement between the two countries worked, Nora had no way of knowing. She knew she couldn't apply in Israel for an immigration visa to the States.

She made a habit of running to a street corner before daybreak, taking a *sherut* to Tel-Aviv, and lining up at various wrought iron gates of foreign consulates for hours in the company of other pitifully hopeless individuals pulling their coats tight around their shivering bodies. No consulate would deem a passport stating "no citizenship" worth stamping with their visa. "Just few days, I beg you," she pleaded. France, no. "Organization and friends will help, please," she begged next time. Switzerland, no. Italy, no. Belgium, no. France, no again. The Italians were at least polite and willing to nod to what she tried to say about the widow with two children and no money to wait forever. Then she realized they didn't understand her, but as they were never in a rush, they listened.

In another attempt, Nora pressed the children between her and the window at the Italian consulate, the only place where she didn't feel totally ignored and humiliated. "We travel very difficult. We ask for transit visa, please."

"Not good now," the woman at the window matched Nora's poor English. "No work now. Vacation. *Melio per voi si ritorna dopo Natale . . . Eh?* She went on in Italian when she saw that Nora didn't object. *Il melio dopo capodanno . . . Prego . . . Capisci?"*

Nora's language mind shifted into gear. *Natale* as in born or birthplace? Not mine I bet. Birth, born, now, in December . . . *Ecco.* Jesus! It's Christmas time! A week away and they don't work? *Capodanno,* the head of the year . . . *They won't work until after New Year? God! Whatever! They have it easy.*

The Italians obliged, granting the Manns a week-long transit visa under penalty of deportation. A quick and nervous phone call to Dennis followed. "What can I do there in seven days?"

"Go," Dennis said. "HIAS will take you under their aegis in Rome."

"Don't go sooner than in two weeks," Larry said next day.

"Why?"

"I'll be there, waiting for you."

"Larry, that's not necessary. I can manage—"

"Say no more, I'll be there—"

"Larry, it's very difficult to do this on the phone—

"That's why I'm coming."

"Larry," Nora almost screamed. "This doesn't mean I don't appreciate what you've done for us," she took a deep breath, already eaten by guilt. "If you don't listen I won't even tell you when we're flying." *That's terrible of me. But it's my life and he has to listen and understand. Even if he were free I wouldn't walk from the airport to the altar. I'm not going to America to marry or get led by the nose. Sorry, Larry. You probably don't deserve this, but I really hope you're not in love.* Silence. "Larry? Are you there?"

"Yes, I'm here." His sigh weighed down the receiver in Nora's hand. "My little Nori, other people would be happy to get more help. But you are not like other people. Perhaps you shouldn't know that either."

2

What is immigration? Sort of a hopscotch on a universal scale. You jump on each square—a country—one at a time, precariously standing on one foot in a fleeting state of balance you can't retain for long.

The Italian *square* was the Manns second square to jump onto, introducing itself as the Leonardo da Vinci Airport in Fiumicino. An awesome venue of marble and chrome glitter.

They stepped out of the terminal. The fragrant Mediterranean air was most welcoming. Flower bouquets were waived by an excited and vociferous crowd as people ran into each other's arms and spoke with joy of a land of love.

The Manns arsenal for the battle ahead was a sheet of paper with addresses and detailed public transportation instructions featured meticulously in Dennis's last letter. Paper arrows to shoot from a non-existent fortress.

The only decrepit building on the entire stretch of modern high rise buildings housed Nora's hope to save them from being deported in a week's time. The clunker of the old elevator cage took them to a high floor where the Hebrew Immigrant Aid Society operated from a maze of dark offices and hallways lined with benches.

Russian emigrés filled the available sitting space. Not a single smiling face to encourage Nora that this was a place where she wanted to be. From the school-Russian she had been exposed to—and resisted for years—Nora could understand shreds of conversation. *Ostia camp . . . killed . . . two . . . five months waiting . . . afraid . . . apartment too expensive . . . want to work . . . crazy . . .* She wanted to find out more. Her rusty Russian and the embryonic English, sprouting in everyone's desire, more than a serviceable knowledge, established communication.

Walking in from the street with their own travel documents did not bring anyone at HIAS to even acknowledge their presence for hours. People usually came there herded in groups by a leader.

"You have American sponsor?" Nora realized the question was addressed to her.

"Yes, in New York," she turned to the young man.

"I no sponsor," he said. "HIAS has sponsor for no sponsor people. No New York. Atlanta. Jewish there."

Sounds like complete service. What she was expecting from this generous organization was much less. Merely what the American immigration rules required of her. A recognized forum to file the papers. And perhaps show her the ropes, provide some assistance while they waited, advice at arrival, peers along the way to whom she could talk. Now it was time to do things in an informed fashion. She felt she could finally relax.

"How did you get here?" was the first thing the bottle-red, heavily-made-up woman wanted to know when they were finally called into an office.

"From Bucharest we *flyed* to Tel-Aviv. Today from there to Rome." That's not how she wanted to say it but that was always the case. Nora was not always sure what was wrong with the words she spoke, but sure that something was.

"You came from *Eretz?*"

"From *Romania* and *Eretz.* My visa not allowed to come by train from Romania here." She knew that some people managed to get to their destination of choice, but she couldn't know how they'd done it, because even if they wanted to tell her, nothing could penetrate the Iron Curtain's sound and censorship barrier.

"HIAS doesn't support people who choose not to stay in Israel." The officer stripped down her English to Nora's understanding which not only enervated her, but the condescending and cold lecturing tone hurt her almost to tears.

"No place to go. We *are* here," Nora said.

"That's unfortunate but not my fault." The woman said, shuffling papers which Nora saw were not even hers, which were lying untouched.

"I have Italian visa for seven days—"

"Try another agency, I can't help you—"

"I am Jewish . . . with two children, need you only arrange paper for immigration to America." Nora waited for some acknowledgment of her words, even if not the request. "*Advices.*"

"That's not our business here. Our support has to go to people who—"

"I am physician, "favored profession," I will get visa by fast INS rules—"

"Doctor Mann, I'm afraid you'll have to manage on your own." The woman got up as if she had finished dinner, not as if she was sending three people out in the street.

Later when it became clear to Nora that most of her Russian competitors of the same communion decided to turn away from Israel in Vienna, where they arrived by train equipped with a visa for Israel just like her, she shook her fists in rage for the injustice that had befallen her family.

Would it make a difference if she had heard only one kind word? Starting a new life, making vital decisions, started with the problem of where to put their heads down on this cruel first night of the rest of their lives. Nora broke out in a sobbing cry on the sidewalk. The children walked obediently in front of her holding hands.

Nora took out Dennis's letter again. She peered at it as if figuring out a coded map to hidden treasures. International Rescue Committee was listed next.

The over an hour long tram ride through Rome, and the changing scenery from old stone to fresh green-trimmed modern boulevards failed to cheer them up. *It's not fair to be so miserable and hopeless in the midst of such loveliness,* Nora thought, contemplating Rome in the jangle of the tram.

Unannounced again, walking in from the street with her stomach heaving in fear, not really master of basic introductory phrases in English, every sentence Nora uttered past the entrance door she had to put together in her mind word by word in Romanian. Complete and proper sentences. They passed her lips in spurts, like a pulsed fountain of fragmentary and incorrect sentences in English.

The thin, dark typist-clerk in the front room, an old spinster type woman, seated in the middle of the light-flooded room, looked at Nora over her half-frame glasses, and patiently listened with her hands resting on the keyboard of her typewriter.

"You need to speak to our director, Doctor Radivan." The woman invited them to the row of plain wooden chairs lined along the wall. Next to a tall plant in the corner two men were bent over a small table filling out forms. They looked up and smiled at Nora.

There seemed barely time enough for the secretary to close the door to the inner office, certainly not enough to tell whoever was inside everything Nora had told her, when the door opened again in full swing.

Nora stood up and shook the sturdy hand of the husky man with salt-and-pepper crew-cut hair. He showed all his teeth in a wide smile. "I'm Radivan. You are welcome and please feel at home. If you have any worries, please don't. You understand me?"

"Perfect. I can think now I know English." Nora suddenly lightened up and the fact that her words failed to quite express the sudden surge of enthusiasm and feeling of security, stopped bothering her. The man's tone managed to dissipate her dismal mood lifting her from the dumps.

"But of course you do," he told her, as if evaluating Nora's English fluency was their most important goal.

"My name is Nora Mann. These are my children, Sonya and Daniel."

Soon they were sitting in front of Radivan's desk, at ease, as if they were at a friendly reunion. He listened to her answers to his questions. Then carefully weighing the words, his searching glance attempted to ensure that there was no misunderstanding in Nora's eyes, he went on. "The most important thing is that you understand that you are preparing to join a world totally new to you. Others have done it. Most of them succeeded. I know people. I dare say I have no doubts about you. You *will* understand, you *will* make your *own* decisions, and you *will* succeed. I will do my best to help you understand the system, but *I cannot* make decisions for you. You were a member of the Communist Party in Romania. You can either tell this to Immigration or you can deny it. They may reject your application based on this single fact, or they can disregard it. If you lie, they will let you in, but they can deport you at any future time, if they find out that you had lied. You have to make the decision that is right for you."

"I will."

"Whatever we can do for you ends as soon as you arrive in the States. Your sponsor will take over from there. Our support does not extend to the settling in process. Here you will have from us around two hundred dollars a month to live on. IRC does not expect you to repay that."

"How long does it *takes* to obtain approval?"

"An average of four to five months."

"What I do first?"

"You have to write a few explanatory notes in your own words. We'll help. Every single word is just as important as the entire application. Miss Luca will explain everything to you," Radivan said, standing in front of his secretary's desk. They shook hands and he retired.

Nora nodded, acknowledging the order of priorities as Miss Luca explained to her the papers she was pulling out one by one from a folder. The *pensione* where they would stay for three days, courtesy of the agency—time deemed necessary to complete the US Immigration forms—was a few corners away. The medical clearance they would have to submit to, was also to be done during those three days. Miss Luca took out a little book, flipped it open and made a phone call. In two minutes they had their appointment at an unknown hospital. The free English school was an unexpected icing on the cake. There Nora would meet again the people she had seen at the HIAS office.

"Worry about one thing at a time. Now it's time to worry about your papers. Don't think of how to get your luggage from the airport," Miss Luca said as Nora had expressed her concern about their suitcases. "Or where you want to move to, until after you have filed your application."

Nora held the folder as if it were a treasure. A gift extended with utmost grace. The greatest gift of humanity she had ever, or would ever, receive.

She was to get familiar with the requirements, look up words in her dictionary and come back the next day with a list of questions she would need to clarify before filling the forms. She was never too good living by checklists. A responsible spontaneity was her credo. Now she felt her judgment restored to an operative state, not unlike the direct road so clearly pointed out to her.

"This money will buy you food for three days."

"Thank you Miss Luca." Nora took the small envelope as well.

The knapsacks—bulging with the bare necessities—seemed decidedly lighter as soon as their destination became a real address. A welcoming and comforting place for that, the *Pensione Piccolo Parioli,* where they had no problem communicating in the newly discovered Romanian-Italian pidgin. There was not much to talk about; the IRC voucher would have gotten them the room without a spoken word. But Nora needed to open up and pour her bubbling exuberance over the receptionist.

The small room was crammed with three beds, a yellow desk and two scuffed chairs. Not much space left for the otherwise wonderful floor tiles to show. A sink in the corner was the only plumbing. Shared bathroom and toilet at the end of a corridor with windows overlooking a flower-filled inner courtyard.

"This room is very small," Sonya made a funny face.

Well justified observation. "It's cozy. We'll have to find out what two hundred dollars can buy to see whether we can do better."

"Is the money here dollars?" Daniel asked.

"No, Dani," Nora said. "It's the Italian Lira, but the agency is American so they pay the support in dollars. We'll have to exchange the money like we did in Israel."

"Is the school American too?"

"I don't know, but it very well may be. I don't even know where it is. We'll have to get ourselves oriented."

"I'm hungry."

"Me too."

The busy boulevard around the corner was a different picture than the shut-down dark Disengoff of their first evening in Tel-Aviv. Following the receptionist's directions, they found the square bustling with shoppers and diners, bicyclists and honking cars, lined with opened frontage stores and products overflowing the sidewalks. Everywhere flowers seemed to be growing out of the asphalt. "Cucumbers? It's February."

"Look, Mama," Sonya called. "That man's changing the signs."

Nora looked at the man bedecked in a white and green striped apron that made him look like he had come from an operetta set, replacing the price cards. "We're in luck. Tomorrow these things won't sell. We learned something. We can shop cheaper late in the day."

"When are we eating?" That was one hungry Daniel. *This question was worth the trip. I shouldn't say a word.* "What do you guys think of bread and cheese and ham and milk?"

"And oranges," Sonya added.

"Great. We'll feast in the room, and before going to sleep we'll look at the papers."

"Yes, yes!" Sonya was caught up in the outpouring of her own enthusiasm. Daniel started to jump up and down as if offered a round of Monopoly then he suddenly changed gears and said, "I want my race cars."

"You have your new Testa Rosa," Nora advised him.

"I want *all* my cars," he insisted.

All his toys were locked away in the airport. Nora looked around for a toy store. She would have done anything to save the evening. *In my next life I shall remember never to travel without toys,* Nora thought and sighed. "Dani, you'll be so busy helping unpack while I do the papers with Sonya. How's that?" His grimace meant meager consolation, while Nora hoped he'd be tired enough to just go to sleep.

"That's it. They want to catch people lying." The forms with their redundant questions felt like instruments of cross-examination. The papers spread out on the tiny desk seemed more daunting than unclear. Every question called for an explanation. Each a separate headache in its own way.

"Mom, what's prostitution?" While Nora thought of an answer she was faced with the next question, "Mom, what's violation of law?"

"If you understand all the rest you're ahead of me." Nora feared this evasive answer wouldn't satisfy her daughter.

"I understand registration . . . and registrant . . . and following . . . and . . . Mom, what's prostitution?"

Ecco! "When a person makes a living by going out with people."

"Like a gigolo?"

"How on earth did you learn that word?"

"Is it a bad word?" Sonya evidently was proud of her knowledge.

"Not really. It might mean that a man dances for money."

"That's all?" Sonya looked disappointed as if she wasted energy on something not worth her while.

"It might mean also that he is paid for living with a rich woman."

"Like cooking for her?"

Nora had the feeling that Sonya knew and was testing her mother's frankness. "No, not cooking. Having sex. Same for prostitution."

"Why do the Americans want to know that?"

"I don't know. Americans must think of themselves as very proper. A prostitute is not considered proper." She did not go on explaining out loud her thoughts about crimes of all sorts plaguing America. As far as she knew, more crime than in most other countries. She had even flirted with the idea of trying Canada. Somehow she had the feeling that Canada was indeed more "proper." What had stopped her thinking along those lines was the fact that the friends Adel had made there, and to whom she had written to ask for information, had never answered.

"They also ask you about the Communist Party."

"We knew they would. That's tougher to answer because it's a 'yes.' For every 'yes' we'll have to write a whole big story."

"Can we write it tomorrow?" Sonya yawned.

"Of course, sweetheart. Go to sleep now." Nora kissed the sleeping Daniel, and tucked in Sonya. "Let's count the corners so we won't have bad dreams," she said.

"You believe that?"

"Not really, but it's fun."

"Do we count that zigzag there?" Sonya pointed to a column.

"Why not?"

"That makes six. We are sleeping in a hexagon," she exclaimed. "Aren't we?"

"You're a smart little girl. Sort of a hexagon. Sweet dreams now," Nora kissed Sonya's cheeks, then her two hands as she peeled the skinny arms from around her neck. She peeked out through the parted drapes to the deserted and quiet street. Her heart was the only sound she heard sing, like a bird just freed from its cage. She walked back to the desk, propped her elbows, rested her head on her hands and took a deep breath.

Sonya and Daniel reached up to the hands of a handsome Alitalia flight attendant—whose eyes, as green as dewy moss, did not escape Nora's attention, for all the world looking like Rossano Brazzi's identical twin—who was giving out plastic toys to all the children. The attendant reached over Nora, who was sitting in an aisle seat. His perfume hit Nora's senses beyond her smell. In her fantasy, that took off before the plane did, he was following her with no objection. Daydreaming made for a most pleasant flight, a subliminal self-indulgence that easily subdued the predictable anxiety of the very special flight.

In this mood of reverie, even the memory of the vital events of the three months spent in Rome, took up a curiously light texture, like the daydream taking the handsome steward her way.

Though rehashing all the circuitous events was not Nora's intention, eroding doubts returned again. The rental of the modern studio in Trastevere—way beyond her means—popped into her mind. Was the sunny mood, the time saved by not commuting, the ease of their chosen Roman lifestyle a good investment in their future? This was yet to be seen. Did she do it for safety reasons? The drunkards from the disco across the street could only wake her up now and then, but they couldn't pass the concierge. *How pretentious!* Convenient walking distance to the school; to Standa, the department store *cum* supermarket which the children figured out to their own and their mother's complete satisfaction; to the fun square around the Santa Maria de Trastevere, the old church a stone's throw away from the American movie theater. True, the *Sting* had a questionable educational value—though good fun to look at Paul Newman and Robert Redford—but the children liked it. If she doubted before that she would ever bet on a horse, she was certain after the movie that she wouldn't. Ever. They loved the freshly cut coconut pulp chilled in pots of crushed ice by the tram station. And walking up to the Giannicolo, not too far either, the immense terrace, the kids looking through the telescope at Rome's vast panorama accented by spires and cupolas. She remembered with pride that the children wanted to go back to the Vatican Museum for more. On Sunday of course. No charge. A tinge of guilt again for feeling better about Rome than Haifa or Tel-Aviv. There she had lived immersed in a numbing single-minded obsession, with neither desire nor energy to see or do anything; she was sorry now to have missed the chance.

The notes she had made for her interview at the American Consulate were in her carry-on bag. At the time, she was perhaps unduly inhibited even by the address. Via Veneto sounded so pompous. How childish. She smiled at the thought with the superiority of a winner. Everything went so well. So gratifying, the way she had delivered her memorized speech the three of them had put together with such care and labor. Even Daniel, contributed. What was that he had said? Nora tried to remember. Yes. He had asked how old Paul was when he died. She had mentioned that at the interview, amongst other facts to support her reason for joining the Communist Party. The American consular officer let her tell the story in her own words. She hadn't taken an interpreter, as many others did. She wanted to prove her proficiency in the English language, though terrified to bloody sweat that she wouldn't understand their questions or would forget her lines. They had listened with compassion to her sad story of why she had to join. They didn't rush her. She had explained how as a top student, she was requested several times to enter the party, but she had managed to decline. Her personal conviction was contradictory to the party politics. While colleagues who were party members by the time of the graduation obtained jobs in the university medical center, she preferred to keep her principles and work as a country doctor. She had explained in simple words and short sentences that "country" in Romania meant traveling on dirt roads, hurtling in a crowded bus, the possibility of going home once a week for one day. She had recounted the husband's waning health, shortened life expectancy, need for care, the approaching baby. Kindly, the consul had joined in her affectionate smile directed at Sonya.

She was aware as she squirmed in the seat with such limited leg room that she could barely cross, or uncross her legs, that the way she had expressed herself then was not correct. *The officialities let me know that leave the job is forbidden and punished and get another in the city is possible only if I join the party,* she had said. The consul appeared to assent. He looked at Nora as if saying that's what I would've done. She had also said something like to hell with the principles, they had lost their value.

The sick husband's death eight years later, grief, young children, agony of not being able to mend her life, the realization, that took years, that she needed to overhaul her entire life, all came through in her plain words.

What more rewarding zenith for Nora, on the road toward re-settling, than being issued an immigration visa in record time? And nothing more natural for her than being proud of her convincing power, of her decision to be open and honest, of her choice to go to a country whose representatives understand human misery so well.

After the less-than-exciting airline lunch, and after she surprised the children with the new toys she had bought in secret—a new Matchbox car, a Ferrari Testa Rosa for Daniel, and a few discs of American tourist attractions for Sonya's Viewmaster—Nora tried to take a nap. Sleep eluded her. One subject needed rehashing. Larry. Nora suffered from terminal inexperience with love letters. She had never been away from her men. Not exceeding an afternoon. Not beyond the extent of 'Gone to gym with the kids, be back by dinner.' The sweet Hallmark cards pouring from Larry opened a new world of industrialized sentimentalism Nora had not imagined. Her own letters to him were more like diaries and yearnings for something brighter—she had to balance his syrupy confessions, respond, react, didn't she?—these proved addictive for Larry, who kept asking for more. In English. Nora took the challenge. Letters became a team effort at Nora's end. Sonya and Dani took turns looking up English words in their dictionaries; Nora wrote and all of them suggested topics. Different ones for Larry, for Dennis and Magda, and more intimate ones for Adel and Tibor. They were writing during practically all their spare time. She thought of the three of them bent over their own concentration reflecting in the round glass table of the sitting area of their small studio. *Quite idyllic that was.*

She had been far from unburdened at other moments, like that strange event at the ORT school. A clerk had entered the classroom one day to deliver a message. Everybody was expected in the conference room to listen to Mr. So-and-so's lecture. Guesses along the dim hallway about the subject elicited some derision, some hope. Was the talk going to answer the most ardent questions on everybody's mind? How were they going to be welcomed in New York? Would specially skilled people be offered jobs? As what? Belly-dancers? That's special enough. Laughing with grim humor, they entered the already packed room. On the podium, the director was chatting with a tall, handsome and equally handsomely dressed man. Soon the director turned to the audience and introduced the delegate from the United Jewish Appeal headquarters. Nora turned up the English receivers in her ears. The deep baritone of Mr. So-an'-so wafted overhead and bounced back as Nora refused to absorb what she was hearing. She sensed the sound waves ricocheting off the lecturer, who, oblivious, kept sending back the sound bites at ever increasing volume. As if cranked up by his own speech, he spoke faster and faster. He soon lost his audience in need of small pauses to mentally translate. Understanding the New York prattle was still far in the audience's future. What they heard before So-and-so lost them was already too much. Their place as Jews was in Israel; it was expected of them to make alliah, he had said. They were needed in Israel. It was not too late. Perhaps they had had no chance to think about it . . . *He thinks I've just randomly drifted here not having anything better to do!* Nora had thought.

Not so much the increasing rate of his speech, but rather her own intention of asking a question, her waking feistiness of having a debate with the speaker, had turned Nora's hearing off. Her pulse sped up even as she relived the scene in her mind as she sat in the plane.

She had made a decision about ten minutes into the talk. If the man would not remove his hands thrust deep in his pant pockets, jacket wings pushed back, and would not stop swelling his chest with pride, would not . . . He hadn't. At least one hand, she had bargained with herself. A subterfuge to avoid confrontation. She wished he would show some respect for the audience and save her the humiliation of exhibiting her poor English in public. It didn't cross Nora's mind that across the ocean and the three hundred years of assimilation into a new world, the gesture of talking to someone with hands in one's pocket, carried much less insolence than in the old world's social code. Anyhow, a speaker should be humble in front of his listeners, she had argued in her mind; this one was a boor, unsuited to give a talk of any kind. She had been irritated enough to express her discontent with his mere presence, not talking about his out of place message. She had been told more than enough what to do, where and how to live. She was not in Rome, waiting for the American immigration visa, to be told she was doing the wrong thing, that she was abusing her rights, that she was in the wrong place. The man stopped talking, the time for questions came. Nora's palms turned clammy, her throat constricted. She was horribly nervous but raised a hand and got up to speak. She asked Mr. So-and-so where he lived. Somethingville, New Jersey, was the startled answer, accompanied by a condescending smile. Hands still in his pockets, he didn't realize he was talking to a truly offended lady. Are you Jewish? *If you don't know by now that you're up against a big-mouth, you're a dense cocky peacock,* Nora remembered thinking at the time. She'd poured out rhetorical questions to which she was not expecting any answer. The more cranked up her anger, the calmer her speech became, with the words more properly stressed. She recalled exactly what she'd said. *"I can't know why I would be more help in Israel than you, for example. By birth you and I have the same right to choose what we want to do in life. I know I never wanted to do anything bad. I don't know about you."* She let her peers laugh at will. *"But I know that so far where I lived they took my right from me, I had to fight very hard to get out and now I . . ."* she knew she wanted the word "exercise," but it wouldn't come to her. So she said, *"practice my human right."* The man took one hand out of his pocket. Nora smiled, *Too late.* He gestured to stop her. She was not curious what he had to say, but politely, just to teach him, she acknowledged his gesture with a little sarcastic grin and a hand gracefully waving back at him. *"Yes, sir, you answer this last thing I want to say, please."* He let his hand drop apparently losing his confidence to stick it back into his pocket. Did he realize what brought this upon him? His disrespect to people sorely in need of some respect.

Nora had cleared her throat, she didn't want to be misunderstood. *"I don't know as much as you about government problems, but I am convinced that the Jews of Israel and America, more than any in the Diaspora, need each other. They can't exist without each other. I am sure for me will not be easier in America than in Israel. I didn't choose to go to America because it's easier. I made a choice. People who can help others are good. If you want to help us that's good. I would like to be help, not need help. My dream is to help others later see their dreams, not tell them what to do."*

Mister had attempted a few feeble words of excuse after he managed to break through the applause Nora elicited from her noisily excited peers. He addressed people's backs as they were leaving the room. Nora had not been pleased when the director called her back. It became obvious that Mister wanted to introduce himself personally. Without qualms she used her professional title.

"I couldn't agree more with what you've said, Doctor Mann. What my organization does for Jews anywhere cannot be matched by any other organization. What I was trying to convey was the idea. The principle. Some people might be confused. A straight talk might help open their minds—"

"Except that this is the wrong moment and place, sir. People already decided when they are so far on the road."

The director interfered. "Nora, I'd like to ask you to join us at the dinner Mister So-and-so invited us to."

Flattered, perhaps for the wrong reason and aware of it, Nora declined. "I wouldn't leave my children alone in the evening. Thank you."

The landing gear screeched. Nora's heart skipped. *At last!*

"What's that noise?" Dani's anxious question diverted Nora's attention from her palpitation, squeezing stomach and popping ears.

"Oh, that noise?" She shook her head as if trying to rid herself of unwelcome thoughts and concentrate on momentary priorities. "Don't worry," she said tugging on his seat belt. "They're getting ready the landing gear."

"What's that?"

I hope he won't ask me to draw it. "During the flight they pull in the wheels so they won't be damaged and they won't be in the way of the wind to slow the plane."

"How many wheels?"

"Three."

"Why does a plane have three wheels?"

"It has to do something with better balance—"

"Like a piano." Sonya said.

"Like anything with three legs. Now try to pay attention to the instructions."

Sonya craned her neck towards a window to no avail. From where they were seated, the sight of America eluded them. No chance for love at first sight, Nora thought with regret.

3

They stood stiffly in front of the booth, ready for the conversion from homeless emigrants to hopeful immigrants.

It took a few short minutes of the officer's time to check through loose-leaf folders. Fearful of missing the meaning of words—the hearsay that New Yorkers speak fast made it worse—Nora readied herself to answer. Following the bang of the seal she heard him say "O-m' to Am'ahr-ca," followed by the flashing of two snow white garlands of teeth framed by the man's fleshy smiling lips. In seconds, happy to process the sounds she couldn't first understand into the friendly "Welcome to America," she said "Thank you." The officer was already calling the next family, who like in a pantomime, stepped across the white line, passports held in trembling hands.

The entry seal to the United States of America canceled years of struggle and changed the worth of the ignoble document. Nora saw it as the symbol of her own worth.

An emotional incongruity materialized. The row of luggage carrousels, the milling of people bumping into each other, the many problems of arrival, the prospect of collecting and having to deal again with the vinyl pigs, all felt irrelevant to their being there. The only surreal relevancy seemed to be the world beyond the stainless steel customs counters and the wall-size frosted glass sliding door where the standards she always lived by would not apply. A transparent but confining curtain of never experienced fear lowered between her and the roped off waving crowds beyond the glass door. She felt her natural impetus—that she always captured with ease in critical moments—flee through the deceivingly flimsy curtain of fear she wouldn't have the strength to push aside.

Her soul was locked in a forlorn inertia as the children shrieked and, "They are here . . . Look Mama, Dennis and Magda . . . Larry, there, he's waving . . ."

They all hugged at the end of the cordoned exit. Nora held Magda as long as she could. The spasmodic sobbing cry she could not control felt disgraceful. Happy and desperate. Tibor had made her sob like that. Something she wanted so and could not keep. She hid her face, her thoughts, looked at the concrete covering the soil of America and wanted to go down on her knees and kiss it. She slouched in Magda's arms, who called out petrified, "Help."

Dennis grabbed and held Nora upright. Not the most helpful position to bring a fainting person back to consciousness. In seconds, head hanging, drenched in cold sweat, Nora realized what was happening and muttered, "Lay me down or I'll throw up all over you." The incentive worked, they laid her on the floor along the wall. Now she could force an apologizing grin between taking deep breaths to suppress the nausea associated with her rare episodes of fainting. *Sweet American ground, what a way to make your acquaintance.*

Larry's Buick closely followed Dennis's Chevy carrying most of the luggage. The choking humid heat hit them outside the terminal. The air smelled like boiled mildew.

"Mama, America is ugly." Daniel's words sounded irrevocable.

"You're right Dani," Larry said. "Our city fathers who built Queens didn't have a lot of imagination. The real America looks better."

"These houses are unfinished," Sonya joined in Daniel's assessment looking at the brick covered buildings.

"Oh! Wow!" was all that came out of Sonya later, awe struck along the span of the George Washington bridge into New Jersey. "Mama, I want to build bridges when I grow up," she said as soon as she could catch her breath between sighs.

Nora's imagination took off above the traffic going West on I-80. She didn't know yet where they were going to sleep that night, but it was clear that nothing would stop Sonya and Daniel from accomplishing their dreams, that America is as grand and beautiful as that bridge. They would see everything beyond it, the entire continent inch by inch.

The cars stopped in front of an apartment building that looked as if it had been imported from Queens. *I thought they'd bought a house.* Nora expected the most likely first stop to be at the Geras. She got out of the cradling soft leather seat and took a hard step down from her lofty visions.

"Where are we?" Asked Nora addressing no one in particular.

"We might as well tell her," Dennis said, looking at Larry. "We're in East Orange, you know we live in West Orange and Larry in Montclair next door. We rented you an apartment here for as long, or as short, as you will need it." He hushed Nora's questioning gesture. It isn't expensive. If you don't like it you can move out in a month. No penalty."

"This is more than we could've dreamed." Nora felt energized by a suddenly regained independence (worth more than bothering with the question of how much this would add to her accumulating debt) provided by her caring and thoughtful friends.

"Wait and see," Magda added heading to the door.

The carpeted narrow hotel style hallway with its stark walls silenced the little procession. Magda opened a door.

"It's a one bedroom with a convertible sofa here," said Magda, pointing it out in the tiny living room. "This is a kitchenette . . . this is a standard American apartment bathroom, just like in Romania plus a shower curtain—" Nora's eyes shifted from the buzzing air conditioner to the small television set on a trolley in the corner of the living room. The yellow wall-to-wall carpet had seen better days, while the kitchen cabinets were strikingly new. *They must be fixing things as they wear out.*

"I love shower curtains—" Sonya yelled.

"Wonderful," Magda went on. "Pros: it's close to us, they don't require a lease. We put up a month rent. You pay on a weekly basis. The tenants are professionals on temporary assignment in the area. Cons: no kids in the building, but we're not far, the town might come as a shock—"

"What do you mean?" Nora asked.

"It's not the safest, but during the day it's fine, I mean to go to the supermarket, we'll show you. Leisure walking? Not really. We'll do that around our house."

The men arrived with the suitcases. "Nora, come here," she called after the narrow space in the hall was cleared. "This will keep you from starving till you get around. She opened the stocked refrigerator. "Enjoy."

Nora hugged Magda. "You are the best."

"You can tell me *that* as often as you want. I need to hear it." It sounded like a complaint, but there was no opportunity to analyze. Nora was ready to console if she could.

The first weekend was a surprise, the sleepy newcomer threesome—Nora and the kids—landed in the big company gathered to welcome them at the Geras.

"Are you looking for work yet?" *Who might be this inquiring platinum blonde who assumes that I know her?* Nora thought, while trying to dispense answers everyone wanted to know before she even had the chance to think of herself. Before she could open her mouth to hem and haw, Magda was at her heel, "You girls are ahead of me. I was just about to introduce you to each other. Miriam, this is Nora, indirectly your protegee. Nora, this is Miriam, your sponsor's wife." Now the women shook hands good old European style and exchanged smiles. *I could be friends with this gal . . . not in a triangle, of course . . . Larry must be the ultimate liar . . . or this one here the best actress.* "Nice to finally meet you," she said. "I hope Larry's generosity didn't cause you any sleepless nights. As far as your question, I plan to spend Magda's savings until after my exams—"

"Well, of course, first things first. Your friends swear you couldn't possibly have problems with *any* exam. That's not something I ever heard said about me—"

"Aren't you too modest?" seemed a safe and nice thing to say to an ex-lover's wife. Nora considered a compliment might bring some details to light.

"Modesty is not my middle name. That's how Larry likes me," Miriam replied waving a hand with a flourish. "It's mutual. He's anything but modest and I love that in him. Modesty doesn't take you far," Miriam patted her heavy diamond trimmed gold pendant with a manicured and bejeweled hand, her ruby red curved fingernails voluptuously touching the skin in her deep cleavage.

"I'll take this as a first lesson in the New World," Nora said sliding her thumb along her short round finger nails. *It's clear, she isn't gainfully employed, she never was, she knew how to pick a husband, she never forgets her own needs, she might even be a good wife and mother and she wants to see me work as soon as possible to eliminate any possibility of cashing in on Larry's Affidavit. Magda, where are you. I need validation.*

"Very good," later Magda laughed hearing Nora's guesses. "Miri is a good mother. As far as wife, nothing that anyone could perceive as wrong, but of course we're all irked by her being the most successful in getting everything we others will never have and all that without doing much. I wish I could stop getting up at 5:30 and into my car by six and getting home in the dark more often than not . . . God, for two months only, please. The usual envy, you know."

"As a matter of fact I don't envy her . . . nothing personal, please, it's all right to be envious . . . I think I would get bored out of my head . . . besides, my nails don't grow, they break—"

"See, you're envious—"

"Aren't long red nails the only thing I need right now?"

Sitting in a diner "out West" overlooking some little body of water in the Delaware water gap, the small mid-week quiet crowd made Nora uncomfortable about wasting her time. The children were chasing around the small playground. They looked happy. Sonya stopped by a baby carriage. The grandmotherly woman put the paperback in her lap and started talking to Sonya.

"Larry, I need to talk to you—" Nora lifted the coffee mug and grimaced at the bitter taste.

"I have something to tell you too," he said.

She picked up a shaker. She stirred the coffee disregarding that it was gaining in viscosity. Absentminded, she sipped the thick concoction. No grimace could have expressed what a bad mixture the Parmesan cheese-coffee turned out to be. Not heeding the options lined up on the table—salt, pepper, sugar and grated cheese—she had generously cheesed her coffee. She ran to the bathroom to spit it out.

"Take that as an omen." Larry's laugh rang through the diner. "What you were about to say must be wrong."

"Listen." He sounded grave. "When we met for the first time in Cluj, when I visited, I brought out your jewelry and your diplomas, but that was not all." Nora's brows arched. "Adel gave me two envelopes for you. She made me promise I wouldn't mention them to you until you got here or made a final decision where to settle."

"What do they contain?"

"They are sealed and very flat. Probably some papers—"

"Where are they?"

"I have them here." Nora's heart skipped as Larry continued. "Adel gave me no indication what the envelopes contain . . . she was very firm that I shouldn't mention them until the right time . . . I suggest you don't open them here . . . Who knows it might be too shocking."

"I can't imagine . . ." Yes she could.

Her mind drifted away in time and space. Her parents . . . Maybe they are alive and they never wanted to hear of her . . . She craved to meet them and forgive them . . . Tell them that Adel did a good job raising her . . . that she would never abandon her children . . . that's crazy . . . abandon . . . Was Adel abandoned by her beloved husband too? . . . Easier to feel that way . . . They didn't want to live? . . . She couldn't make peace with herself abandoning Adel. Stubborn Adel, hiding behind her year-long horrible experience in a devastated Western Europe after the war . . . What kind of desperation brought her back the second time to Romania? Is Adel going to hold her responsible for that? Looking at the barely alive skeletons in the concentration camps . . . the liberated groups, the featureless sunken eyes . . . to match with the few childhood photos of a dainty young woman holding a big doll topped with a huge bow . . . that was her . . .

Larry pulled from his attaché case two similar white envelopes and handed them to Nora. They were addressed: "For my daughter."

Nora's tears welled up. "I don't know why I feel the worse ingrate . . ."

"Everybody for themselves, Nora." Larry put a hand over hers. "There was no way you could've convinced Adel to leave Romania. She told me so."

Nora's blurry eyes expressed gratitude. "Those people. . . . " She was not sure whether Larry had met Arthur and she herself was not sure what Arthur really meant to their family. Did he hold back Adel? Her hands rested on the envelopes. "Let's go."

Larry drove them home.

"Larry. . . . " She shuffled the envelopes intently. "Have you noticed these numbers?" She pointed to the accents on the letters 'á' which were shaped as a 1, respectively a 2. Without further delay Nora took a knife and opened number one. Took out a sheet of paper. "Larry, do you know German?"

While he read, she opened letter number two as she called out. "Sonya. Daniel. I want you here. Sit down. These letters are important for all of us."

One could touch the silence in the room. Nora's eyes opened wider and wider as she read on. "Oh, my God! She's incredible," she wiped her eyes. "I never imagined she can keep a secret . . ."

"Who?"

"Sonya. Daniel. Your grandmother Adel did something extraordinary . . ."

"Is she coming?"

"We'd like that very much, wouldn't we?

"When is she coming?"

"Kids, kids. Not so fast," Larry said and moved next to Nora on the sofa. "Look here," he pointed to the German typed text.

Vollmacht . . . Gezeichnete Adela. . . . , hiermit bevollmaechtige ich Frau Doctor Nora Mann, ueber mein Konto bei ihren Bank zu verfuegen.

"Authorization, regarding . . . bank account number . . . undersigned Adela Hermann I authorize Doctor Nora Mann to fully dispose with the entire amount of 15,000DM . . ." Larry looked up at Nora who sat with fallen chin.

She cleared her throat and started to read:

'Dear Nora, Sonya and Daniel,

Nora, I have been at times harsh in judging you. I hope I did not hurt you with words of disapproval. You are smart, you are different. I wish you all to be happy wherever you are.

My dears, I will not pretend that what I give you here is a little thing. It's my life. I had to deal with the Germans for this. I felt that I will die again. I couldn't avoid reliving the tortures of their hell. However, during the years when I was trying to find myself a place on this earth, I was successful in collecting reparations. The money is in a bank in Leingarten where I stayed with friends of friends I told you about. The address is in the other letter. Your name as a co-owner of the account is recorded at the bank. The bank book is in Budapest with our cousin Feri who's address you have. They will send it to you when you ask them. When you mail it in with a notarized signature to the bank in Leingarten you can have the money. Use it wisely. It's all yours. I don't need it. I don't want it. For me it's nothing. They couldn't pay for what they took from me with millions of dollars. No material goods could undo the wreck they made me. For you I hope it's a big help at this time.

Forgive me for not telling you about this at least before your departure. Maybe it would have given you some feeling of security. Perhaps too much. Not that I don't trust you. I know you are no spendthrift, but it would be only human to spend more if you know you have money.

With all my love, Your Mother Adel'

When Nora called her mother, words of gratitude to express the complexity of her feelings eluded her. Through tears and the knot in her throat, only the blabber of bird language acknowledged that the homing pigeon has arrived and carries back kisses.

It was quiet, except for Daniel's moans that came from the kitchen. It was his turn to wash the dishes. Sonya stood behind the couch. Her skinny fingers moved patiently rubbing Nora's scalp. Nora sat slouched, held her face in her palms and lamented. "I couldn't have forgotten . . . they never taught us genetics. These notions didn't exist during my med school years. Then I didn't keep up because there was no consistent source available. You know? The ignorance that they imposed on us is my main accusation against the Communist regime."

Sonya lifted two tufts of her mother's long hair. "I'll cut your hair."

"God no," Nora exclaimed suddenly animated by the threat. "I'll rather put it up in a bun."

"Like an old woman?"

"I *am* an old woman."

"A good looking old woman," Sonya said holding a brush and watching how the static raised her mother's hair.

"Mama told us there are no good looking old women or good children." Daniel yelled from the kitchen.

"That's a stupid saying," said Sonya. "We are the living proof. If anyone objects to this I'll come with the scissors."

Nora couldn't deny that they needed some color in their cheeks. The Geras took them to the local YMHA for what turned out to be more than a tan.

"Ruben," Magda stopped a gray-haired man in a business suit dodging the sunbathing crowd. They walked away talking.

"Nora," Magda returned all excited. "Sorry I didn't ask you whether you agree. Remember we mentioned it would be great for your kids to do something for the rest of the summer? We'll see Ruben tomorrow evening about camp."

"Who's Ruben? What camp?"

"The director of the "Y." Then Magda explained what sort of summer camps there are, how much they cost.

"It doesn't sound like that's for my pocket."

"I'm sure they'll give you a break."

"I'm not good at asking for favors, except from friends like you."

"Maybe you don't have to ask," she screwed up her eyes. "Do you have a problem accepting?"

Charity was offered as graciously as if Nora was doing them a favor. Politeness to a pauper like Nora was tenderly handled, to keep it as far as possible from being condescending. Nora paid the five dollars per child as a nominal fee. She ruminated over a hidden meaning of the term with not much success. Sonya and Daniel were whisked away to a "Y" camp in the Poconos for the next session starting the following week. Something to learn every time anyone around opened their mouths. *Poconos?* The map showed a scary distance of 100 Miles.

Nora was in a state of blissful abandonment sprinkled with fear that the unfamiliar camp condition would be too much of a strain for her unaccustomed children. A mental agitation—not a kind of inquisitive interest whether there was anything she might have missed preparing for an exam—a frightening intellectual emptiness seemed to have totally drained her brain. Exhausted, eyes burning, limbs numb, back aching, she would crumple on the bed trying to sleep a few hours, only to be tossed out of sleep by questions lighting up her synapses like light bulbs on a boiler room panel. Like a somnambulist, she would rise and follow the question to a text book lying somewhere next to the couch, or under the small desk in the unseemly company of scribbled sheets of paper, difficult to find with eyes that wouldn't open.

Then, sleep played hide and seek with her. She stretched in a basic Yoga position, closed her eyes, and focused on relaxing each muscle group as she knew them. Drop the jaw, shoulders flat to the floor, hands cupped symmetrically in a neutral position. In a few minutes the restful tingling appeared in her arms. *Couldn't move them if I wanted, but I don't want yet.* Felt a rejuvenated energy flowing through her brain, breast, limbs. *No, not that.* She was determined never to look for, or accept, a surrogate of the real thing. And the real thing *was* unattainable. The memory of Tibor impossible to match, therefore not to be craved for. The meaningless promise: Not to ever compare. Like any promise. The unadulterated memory was worth more than anything. *Poor Larry. Why? Poor me. Fortunately our little side trip was not important enough for him to put up any resistance in ending it.* Nora was happy that Larry accepted the status quo. She was not willing to start from the garbage can of adultery. What he was doing from now on about his mid-life crisis was none of her concerns. *There!* Fantasies of being in Tibor's arms had to take care of the needs of her private parts.

The crowd filing into the auditorium at St. Barnabas Hospital in Livingston New Jersey looked and sounded like it was descending directly from the Tower of Babel. All individuals visibly unhappy for not having reached the heaven of their dreams. *This must be the right way to it judging by the shear numbers of candidates.* The room was cool, overly so, Nora was happy for bringing a shawl and a jacket. Does it matter where she sat? Should she sit between two already seated people of her choice that didn't look like they might make distracting noises, would give her a headache with a perfume or body odor, would try to talk to her. She needed to be comfortable. Out of the question. She had never seen a multiple choice question examination sheet, short of the tests of the "Medical Examination Review Book - ECFMG" she was taking at home every week. Tantalizing sets of hundreds of questions. The fact that Sonya, randomly checking off the answers, consistently scored better than Nora, sweating out the bloody answers for hours, was not too comforting either.

Now here was the real thing.

She refused to spend money on any preparatory courses, let alone English courses, special ones offered for medical doctors at an upscale cost. She hadn't even practiced much with the 50 minute tapes emulating the real exam.

Language? She knew herself well enough. She would have to live with it for a while, then she would pass any test. She was not deaf, but she couldn't make out the questions from the tapes, no matter how many times she ran them on the borrowed cassette player.

She sat between two women, they smiled at each other. No one talked. The loud tapping on the microphone brought silence and froze the air. She blew warm air on her cold hands, she spread the shawl on her knees, she put on the jacket. "Attention, candidates." Nora was paying so much attention she had to make herself breathe, she was shivering and tense.

Booklets distributed, names recorded, pencil on the page, the clock was started for the first three and a half hours in which they had to answer 180 questions in Basic Sciences. Reading, thinking, head scratching, ceiling gazing, filling the tiny "A" oval with the pencil, erasing it and filling the tiny "C," marking on the side the next question with a totally mystifying meaning, leaving it for the end, as if she would ever have time to go back. These were all stages most of the questions demanded. Grossly 70 seconds per question, normally just enough for head scratching.

A short break was not more than a physiologic sprint to the bathroom.

Act Two. The instructions coming through the loud-speaker were clear. *Maybe it's a good omen, maybe I'll understand the tape.* It ran for the announced 50 minutes. There was practically no time to mark the correct interpretation of a run of sound bites, and she had to listen to the next question. Or statement. Often Nora couldn't tell them apart. At the end, she felt like tossing up the chair, the sheets, sending her sharp pencils as missiles to the dais and screaming for unfairness. Couldn't they pronounce the words with some consideration for the unaccustomed ears? Why should they? Patients in real life won't. One is proficient or one is not. Damn test. Nora filled hit-or-miss answers for questions that passed her like an express train.

Break. Another run to the bathroom in a pre-emptive move, a sip of water, a quick glance outside, a look up at the seven floors of the slick building and suppress the premature fantasy of being a resident there, back in the seat for the last stretch of 180 questions, this time to deal with in only 3 hours. *What do they think? By now we are warmed up? Oh! Well guys. And hello. This is my turf, everybody who I talked to said so. It looks like they were right.* The sight of the questions in clinical medicine that counted for two thirds of the score made Nora stretch her arms up as if waking up from a nightmare and realizing she was in a wonderful garden with her favorite flowers. *Now we are talking,* she almost laughed out loud. She only had to be careful not to misinterpret the tricky formulations and fill the right oval. No careless mistakes.

After about four thousand calories had blown up the chimney, burned up by her brain and fighting the chill, stiff and beat, she could barely get up from the chair. She folded the arm back, bent to lift her purse and could have cried. Except that she didn't care. No feelings, no regrets, no panic, just numbness.

The Babel came alive. Accents vaguely suggestive of English provided the sound track. Nora pretended not to hear the question of a neighbor. She felt bad being unsociable. Her mind processed this foreign behavior as a bad omen. *I did badly, I'm losing the ground from under my feet. What ground? I'm going over the deep end. I'm not going to take this again. It's offensive. It's subhuman. It's over, I shouldn't think back. Think ahead. I can't think. Period.*

Nora took the bus. She called Magda. "Don't take it personally, I'm going to unplug the phone. I'll call you."

"How did you do?"

"I have no idea, but I feel like my brain is going to liquefy if I don't get a good sleep. I'll take a Valium, just to make sure."

She threw herself on the bed, unwashed, unfed and lapsed in a deep sleep, barely able to place the empty soda bottle on the night table.

The clock showed four o'clock. *I've slept twenty hours?* Rarely did a hot shower caress so tenderly. Maybe at the sea shore a million years before, back from the beach, tasting each others salty lips, their hands lathering each other. She hugged herself crossing arms over her breasts, finger nails digging into her skin. She let the water run down her face and wash her hair back. She was dizzy. She stepped out, wrapped herself in a towel and sat at the small desk with dripping hair. She pushed the notes off the table and started to write.

> 'Dear Tatatzi, Remember our mountain top? I have no intention of driving you crazy. Not more than myself. It's sad to think that nothing will come of this but I WANT YOU HERE. I miss you so, I take my showers with you, I keep talking to your stupid coward head. What you do there you could do here better. I refuse to understand why are you so afraid. Of course it was not that. I'm so sorry we couldn't find a way. You be happy. Please. I'll give it my best try too. I have to. The kids deserve a happy family. I cannot be a whiny mother. I cannot cry all the time as I do right now. My flesh trembles at the thought of you. This sounds very narrow minded considering the immensity of my feelings which are far from involving only my body. I don't want to go on with this because I might be barking up the wrong tree. I wish it was true and you are getting on with your life. That doesn't mean you have to forget me. We can go on, and we will, I swear, without throwing away the past. Devil, devil, devil.
>
> My little devils are away at camp. Some people here were generous enough to take them without pay. Big help at these difficult times. I hope a day will come when I can be of help to others. For weeks before the exam I couldn't write. Time evaporated. You are the only one I'll tell this, don't even tell Adel. Why? Because I would be dreadfully embarrassed if I would turn out wrong. I didn't think of it yesterday when I dragged my tail away from the battle ground, meaning the amphitheater where we took the nine hour exam, but now, after twenty hours of comatose sleep I have the definite feeling that I passed. The shower I took with you rubbing my back helped to create this optimistic outlook.

What's next? I'll find a job. Anything.
How's work? Regards to Puiu.
Your Mamatzi'

She took another sheet of paper.

'Dear Mother, Well, here we are, apart for the last two weeks. Sonya and Daniel are in summer camp. It happened so fast I couldn't get a moment's break from running, arranging, packing, going on with the studying.

The examination that doesn't seem more than a physical torture now that it's over, is just that. Over. I can't tell you more for a few weeks. They take their time in letting you know what you can do with the rest of your life. I don't know whether I've told you, the so called "Training program" starts on July 1st. At least the majority of good programs. Some start on January 1st, but besides being difficult to find one, they are said not to be the best. What does this mean? That I am not interested in a program just because it's available. Snotty? Nothing new, right? Conceited me. I'll have to work something, anything—I don't mean to clean public toilets—to make a living. See? I'm not that snotty.

I had to knock my friends senseless to have them accept the repayment of the entire loan. I had to promise to tell them if I'd be in need. It's a great feeling to have had enough to open a bank account in my own name. Dear! Does it feel great? I'm sure NOT ONLY to me. There is God and she has freckles all over her fair body. I am looking forward to payroll checks and to start saving that fair God's MONEY even if I can do it a dollar at a time. God might be in need sometime, hopefully, soon and here. After I have the American license under my belt I'll be in the position to raise a strong voice to that God to support this quest. I hope she will hear my voice.

I wrote to both of you, you needn't share this letter with Tibi. My best regards to friends. I'm glad your blood pressure is behaving, don't forget to take your medicines. I'll send you the next dose on time. Write long letters full of nonsense, gossip and mostly yourselves. Anything, everything. Now I have plenty of time to read. Suddenly I got twelve free hours on hand each day.

Regards to Arthur, your loving daughter, Nora'

4

Nora felt like celebrating and brought up the idea of a party to Magda who said, "Invite Ruben and Judy."

Judy, as an official of the Red Cross district, had been instrumental in solving the Mann's medical needs immediately after arrival, something Nora couldn't have handled by herself in the absence of organizational support. Now, at the mention of strangers who had lifted heavy difficulties off her shoulders, Nora didn't have the nerve to extend a social invitation to them. How would "real" Americans accept lowering themselves to a greenhorn's simple gathering, celebrating not even the passing of an obstacle, but merely its possible happening?

Magda didn't agree. "People like to be acknowledged."

"Would you do the invitations for me?"

"Why? Are you mute?"

"I can't talk on the phone."

"Grow up and try."

"You're a natural," exclaimed Judy when she called Nora the day after her party to thank her. Assuming that Judy couldn't mean anything bad, Nora thanked her too. "We had a marvelous time, and those yummy and beautiful bite-size sandwiches! I'd like to invite you for next weekend to our house," Judy said.

Nora thought of those half strangers actually coming to her party as a sign of social acceptance, a thought reinforced now by Judy's invitation. Little did she know how about acceptance in the American society.

However, Nora's problem appeared to be the nature of the party she was invited to. "What exactly does a pool-side party mean?" Her dilemma grew as Magda shed more light on the event. "It's Judy's husband's unofficial retirement party. It's a big deal in town—"

"That's no place for me. I'll excuse myself—"

"That would be the stupidest thing you could do—

"She'll understand."

"*You better* understand. It's a chance. They know a lot of doctors.

Dummy. Aren't you looking for a job?" Magda accompanied her rebuke with appropriate gestures of mockery.

"Point taken. All right. What should I wear?"

"Not much. A sundress over a bathing suit. They expect you to honor their gorgeous pool with a dip. Take a change of dry underwear just in case they throw you out before you have a chance to dry."

"I'll behave. But I own very revealing bikinis only. You think it will be appropriate?"

"For you? You could get a job just by the looks of your belly button."

"That's not the kind of job I'm looking for. Though who knows? It might pay better than a medical residency."

Loose and semi-see-through dresses on women, unbuttoned shirts boasting a wide selection of hairless to furry men's chests, made Nora feel as if she stepped was walking around in a movie set. She forgot for a few fallen-chin minutes about the impression she was expected to make. Judy dragged her around, and graciously introduced her to people ambling about with frosted glasses in their hands, sitting cross-legged on cushioned iron benches under the willow weeping over a neat little rock garden. The pool, rimmed by the colorful ring of Italian tiles, reflected its placid blue.

"Dotty Eisen, my right hand at the Red Cross," Rachel said. "Nora Mann, the Gera's friend freshly off the boat." Smiles and laughs united people in a ring of undertones. "It must have been a luxury liner," and similar humorous comments made Nora blush.

Then Judy stopped in front of a burly man with a silver crew cut. "Dr. Harold Bont heads the research division at—" she stopped, "Why am I wasting my time? You tell her, Harry."

Nora walked the endless maze of corridors back to Professor Harold Bont's office, whom she was determined to think of as Burly.

"This is Doctor Nora Mann who will fill the spot on the grant payroll," Burly spoke puzzling words to Gill, the tall, horse-faced supervisor clacking around on awkwardly high heels.

What Burly had told Nora to that point threw no light on the job she would have to perform. She was not sure of anything else than that she would be a Microbiology technician, and that the job would bring her a weekly payroll check enough to live on until the next. She was practicing a new philosophy: take everything in stride; don't push for instant gratification, like understanding everything on the spot.

Moving happened like in a dream, almost effortlessly: looking a little bit for an apartment, quite pleasant; a little down-payment, using up her last pennies; a little packing, already a habit. Larry produced a van. Well timed detours took care of picking up the children from camp and buying a king size mattress for its added benefit of providing three independent beds for the price of one. Courtesy of friends, and friends of friends, thanks to the donated brick-a-brack and Nora's newly discovered gift for second hand interior decorating, the Forest Hills apartment became livable in a week. The three Manns luxuriated in the faded elegance. The children didn't object to sleeping on the box springs cushioned by a pile of blankets and, of course, Nora didn't complain about slumping onto the boxless mattress on the floor.

When all human ingredients were present, the mosaic of the microbiology research lab was quite colorful. Gill mostly hovered over the column of the incubator computer studying the endless data tape or sat sideways at her worktable, oblivious of her long legs blocking the only narrow passage to the computer. Kenny, the round faced young black man rolled around a clattering cart with towering stacks of cultures, glassware or computer paper, always ready to deliver a joke or a pun to any receptive ear. Shean, not as young as he would have liked to look, wore a bandanna over his long reddish-blond locks—a carry-over of his years of hippie experience. Rochelle filtered a mysterious gaze through long eyelashes that needed no mascara. Gill, Kenny, Shean and Rochelle were real Americans. This fact expunged Nora's first stomach-squeezing doubt whether she was committing herself to the salt mines for life. *It can't be that bad if real Americans worked here.* There were also three women at different stages of their personal venture into the American experience. More or less recent immigrants from around the globe, they were working on doing something better with their lives.

Painting Petri dishes in the research lab, Nora needed none of the communication skills that kept—so often and painfully—deserting her. Actually, she was more in luck than ever. Not for the opportunity to handle the stinky cultures of varieties of Serratia, Pseudomonas and Staphylococci from plain agar mediums to Kirbys, not for the rewards of nurturing them through days in the incubator then testing their sensitivity to antibiotics, known or experimental. Nora, as a simple practicing physician, never had close dealings with saprophyte bacteria in innocuous looking stacks of glass dishes with the odor of deadly decay, labeled, color coded and dated. The yeasty rot blooming in dots of the most varied colors on the glistening gelatinous surface were the purpose of all her toils. Nora got used to it, though not without a slight touch of returning fear. Would she ever get out of there?

Lyuba, who sat across the table from her, had been trying, and failing, the ECFMG. Had she given up? Was that lab to be her American experience after practicing Psychiatry in Russia for many years? *Why would I, Nora Mann, pass, when the other, a smart young woman, keeps failing?* Sashi Mehta's husband was already in a training program somewhere down South; she would leave as soon as they could find a job for her. Hopefully before she would give birth. Of course her English was great, she grew up bilingual in India. Nora wished she were Indian too. Then she might also have those beautiful intense dark eyes.

Nora's luck resided not only in getting the first payroll check exactly when she ran out of money, but in simply being in that lab, surrounded by English-speaking extroverts. In her ardent ambition to adjust, the desire to learn English fast and well was kindling to Nora's inner fire, though she would complain to the Geras, "English fluency feels like a huge stump of wood hard to crack." Her learning process—always in focus with annoying insistence and not always stimulating effect—was punctuated by linguistic blunders. "This makes no sense at all unless you got it with your mother's milk." Nora would vent her frustration about idioms and second meanings ready to jump at her, always at the wrong moment.

Painting and scraping Petri dishes all day long and pulling out miles of printout from the tight lips of the computer were not the most intellectually challenging activities. Outbursts of chat interrupted the dense boredom, usually as soon as Gill closed the door behind her. Every new subject would shift Nora's ears into gear, happy to catch a new word or phrase. Naturalization seeped into her blood word by word.

Some confusion was to be clarified in the meat department. Veal and calf were words Nora saw in the supermarket, but for budgetary reasons had not paid heed. She never desired things she could not afford. Nora asked whether the calf was a live animal. All confirmed. "When it's dead, it becomes veal," Kenny said. "Partly," Nora argued. "Does liver, brain and feet *stays* alive? Calf liver, brain. No?" Even her flimsy grammar abandoned her in the heat of an argument.

"It's the vernacular," Trudy, the young lady born in East Germany, said. "Same with the pig."

"Where's the logic?" Nora asked.

"Don't look for logic, just say it as we do, and you're gonna be fine," said Kenny who always proved Nora's most ambitious language teacher.

"What's 'gonna'?" Nora asked totally at a loss.

"It's *going to,*" he explained.

"So? What's going to gonna?"

"Gi'me a break," was an unmistakable signal that he was finished with Nora's education for that session.

"I feel like a *fucker,*" she said disappointed. Kenny gasped with a noisy breath and said, "That's not a word a lady uses."

Sashi's giggle rose from the other side of the table. She, of course, coming from the land of *fakirs,* realized what Nora meant. Ignorance was torture, like lying on a bed of nails. That the Hungarian pronunciation of the word comes the closest to what she had just said was her bad luck and the reason for sounding not at all lady-like.

Learning had to wait, until bent over the high slabs of the stone tables her lab mates' tolerance for her ignorance had time to regenerate. Then, Nora was ready with the next subject awaiting their input. Sex.

They found it hilarious that Nora was terrified of the prospect that some day her circumstances might change and she would find a lover.

"Good for you . . . what's to be afraid of?" asked Trudy.

"Yes, true," Nora hesitated. "What . . . if he . . . if he . . . speaks only English?" she blurted out.

They didn't mind teaching her some key words, mostly verbs, to help her look less lost at such happy times. But, on the other hand she was unanimously declared an ingrate, when she contested the rationale for using the verb "Come," in the respective context, when "Go" would be a much more obvious way to announce an exit.

"Forget it . . . you are too much . . . suit yourself, do it your way . . . good luck with your 'goin's'," said the chorus between bursts of laughter.

Nora switched to compliant assimilation. Whenever a sentence free of mistakes left her lips she felt the improvement taking her on a victorious flight with unbound leaps.

Nora had the disturbing hunch—a drilling pressure on her backside when Burly was around on his unpredictable rounds of inspection—that after all it had been her daring bikini that secured her first American job. Neither her language skills, nor her medical knowledge qualified her, she was respectively either under or overqualified for the menial work. She had not yet conceptualized the notion of cheap labor. But of course she was not the only one in that position, she was not even amongst the few foreign physicians who earned a living by being overqualified.

The confirmation of the suspicion of the merits of her bodily charms came when she met Burly in the coffee shop. He pulled up a chair and sat down, an act of definite irregularity judging by her lab mates' flabbergasted looks. There was an aura of discomfort sparing only Burly. He went on with his soliloquy. When they all got up, he kept talking to Nora and walking by her, steering her toward his office two floors away from Nora's lab in the basement. On the way, she admitted to liking classical music, but how it came to being invited to attend a New York Philharmonic concert—oh? missus was away, extra ticket, she couldn't quite fathom, she could only fidget trying to figure out how to decline firmly and politely. *Old goat!* As a response to Burly's poorly disguised barrage of flattery as he walked around his enormous desk, Nora jumped up startled. She was sure she could see her own image in his hazed-over eyes—as she appeared scantily dressed when introduced to him. The factual translation of his thought was the grabbing of her arm as she reached for the doorknob. What came to her mind to say—Pig!—was somehow out of the question despite the fact that it felt quite suitable. She ran downstairs, her pulse racing faster than her feet. The first impulse was to get away from it all riding the wave of her attacked sensitivities, but in minutes other points came into focus.

The following week, Gill was the one to convey the message, "Harold wants to see you in his office." She added with a wink, "Good luck and don't let him bully you around."

Sitting at his desk, Burly looked as if he had nothing else to do than wait for Nora. "I wanted to congratulate you for passing the medical portion of the ECFMG."

She was not flattered. *The man has buffalo hide for a face. What's wrong with congratulating me in the lab?* "Thank you," she said. She was embarrassed anyhow, like a diligent schoolgirl showing a less than satisfactory grade card. Failing the English test—despite her unusually high marks on the professional portion—was bad enough.

"I assume it will be some time until your next chance, so we can enjoy your presence for a while," he went on shamelessly and tactlessly digging into her fresh wound.

"I registered for a TOEFL in December. I missed the September session." Then she added for the sake of his baffled expression, "Sorry. The Test of English as a Foreign Language."

"What a pity," he clicked his tongue.

"I hope I'll still have time to find an internship for next July. If I pass the English, that is."

"That's a good half a year, isn't it?" It was something Mephistophelian in his voice. Not a single word of encouragement.

Bloated idiot. She was now wondering how long he was going to beat about the bush and what purposeful and effective text she could prepare to show him the straight path home to his wife and grandchildren. *Maybe I'm stupidly suspicious and the man is as innocent as a babe.* Next he mentioned that three months of outstanding work—*Transparent bull! Are my colonies growing with more gusto on the cultures I smudge or what? You old libidinous goat*—would entitle Nora to a raise. For a brief instant, Nora's suspicion vanished and some furniture for the children's room flashed in her mind. Then she realized that the emphasis was on the word: would. Would entitle . . . Nausea mixed with the fear of losing her job rose suddenly into her skull, but quickly gave way to an irresistible desire to humiliate him in exchange. Contained words came forth instead.

"I don't understand."

"If you doubt ask, as we say around here," he winked slyly. Now she really had to corner him.

"I ask."

"Are you free Thursday after work?"

"Thursday? Free?" She thought for a second. "The first Thursday I'll be free . . . is the one after the end of the world." His fallen cheek didn't satisfy her. Now she wanted to make everything absolutely clear. "I know that my work is good. Thank you." She turned on her heels. She was no longer watched. There was nothing left for him to watch.

"Gill," Nora asked. "Anybody gets raises here?"

"Are you asking me for a raise?"

"No," she smiled, "But I would not refuse *you.* I'm only curious . . . and confused."

"I think I know which way the wind's blowing," Gill said. "Don't feel less important, but all girls went through this. He's a monster. His wife should've divorced him long ago."

"He'll fire me, hah?"

"Don't worry. He can't."

"Why is he not fired, the pig?"

"Because he's too good at what he does."

So much for the analysis of Burly. Nora didn't take the case too seriously. Gill's down to earth approach helped.

The radio was always on in the morning for the pure benefit of her ears to get more accustomed to listening, with no special attention paid to the weather report. Nora had difficulty making out the exact meaning of the rattle on 1010 WINS. "*Wizard warning?*" She had no time to figure out a relevant meaning, only gave a marginal thought to "gusting," *they can't mean guts,* from the Canadian neighbors. The "50 Miles per hour" had a remote impact on her hurried morning preparations. The thermometer in the kitchen window, however, justified serious bundling, after she had arranged sandwiches in the front of the middle shelf of the refrigerator for the children. She checked whether the alarm clock was properly set for 6:30 and at exactly six o'clock she locked the door of the apartment behind her.

The F train came faster and was emptier than ever. The brisk run up the stairs and across Queens Boulevard in Jamaica rewarded Nora with a surprisingly empty bus. She relaxed on the bench when she heard the driver strike a conversation with the woman standing next to him. "You sure sweetheart get there before the whopper." Nora wondered what Burger King had to do with them. "They say we can expect over two feet." Was it snow they were talking about? Heavy flakes starting to swirl in the air veered Nora's thinking in that direction. But it looked lovely. Much nicer than the dry gray cold.

She got off the bus daydreaming and still excited by the beauty of the snowflakes. She might get a chance to go out with the kids in the evening. Well, no sled, no hill, but maybe snowballing. By the time she turned the first corner, she had to lean into the wind and pull her scarf across her face so she could breathe. She got to her basement lab much before 7:30, before anyone else. *Much* before anyone else. Like three days before. No sight of Judy, the department secretary, who was usually the first in her booth at the corner of the hallway. An eery feeling took hold of Nora. She was deliberating what to do when the phone rang in Judy's booth. She reached in. "Microbiology research," she said.

"Nora? What are you doing there?" Gill sounded surprised.

"I came to work. Judy is not here. I'm the only one."

"I guess Judy didn't reach you. She's calling from home to tell people not to go in. Don't you know there is a blizzard on the way?" Gill's usually calm voice conveyed haste.

"Oh? I think I heard people on the way—" *So, the wizard was a blizzard?* Nora put the words together.

Gill went on. "Listen. As long as you're there, I couldn't get out of my garage here in Westchester, someone has to move the cultures from the incubator to the refrigerator, otherwise we'll lose about two weeks of work and God knows what that could do the NASA grant deadline."

Nora had no idea she was being paid from NASA money. What did that mean anyway? "What do you want me to do?"

Gill named which shelves of cultures were the most important, approximately three floor-to-ceiling baker's shelves full of stacks of Petri dishes. "But, please, get out as soon as you can. I'm afraid the transportation will come to a standstill."

Do all that work and get out in time! Sure! Nora called the children. "Money is in the white desk's drawer; go fast, buy milk, bread, oranges, chicken, whatever you want. And don't spend more than ten dollars."

When her stomach started to growl, Nora took bites of her sandwich between runs. Finished. Out she was and fast. One floor above her lab she saw people from the Biochemistry lab setting up cots in the hallway.

"Ar'ya sleeping here?" she asked.

"Yup. You're not? Live walking distance?"

"No. I take the bus and subway." Nora was truly surprised at their interest in her.

"Not today, babe."

They were right. The bus stop was deserted as was the entire stretch of wide street as far as she could see. *I must be more stupid than everybody else.* The thought was quite disheartening, but it produced the right amount of spite to face the march ahead of her. Walking westward along Union Turnpike, against the gusts that stuck frozen needles into her face, was a gravity defying act; her body leaned at an acute angle to the sidewalk, reminding her that she was not supposed to lean that much without falling at the moment when the gust shifted. Along forested sections, the wind blew with mysterious bellowing whistles. Blinded, out of breath, toes getting cold and starting to hurt.

Occasionally a car passed her in muffled silence. She twisted her torso without stopping, looked back over her shoulder every few minutes, her arm swung up, independent of her own will. "Never hitchhike! If you can't cover a distance on your strong little legs, don't get started." She could hear herself lecturing the children at every opportunity.

The car stopped in the middle of the road. Did not pull to the curb. A man rolled down the passenger window. "We'll drive as far as we can. Can't tell how far," he yelled before she could say anything.

"Thanks," Nora said and got in the back seat.

"You want to get where?" the driver turned and asked Nora.

"Forest Hills."

"Well. Pray. We might even get you there."

"What's your destination?"

"University Hospital?" The interrogative tone of the answer seemed to express his doubt whether a stray person in Queens would know where that was.

"You must be physicians," she said.

"Are you a psychic?"

"Nope. Who else would do this to get to work?"

"Nice to meet someone to appreciate physicians' work ethic."

"If I can't who can?"

"Oh. You too?"

"Yeah. Just off the boat."

"Where from?"

"Romania."

"Oh, the land of Dracula?"

She didn't give them the regular: gi'me a break with your Hollywood stereotypes. Instead she stretched her upper lip with her two index fingers. "You didn't notice my fangs, did you?" They turned to look at her and laughed nodding.

The visibility was so poor, it was like looking through milk. The tires labored in the deepening snow.

"We might not make it," the driver said.

"Chicken," his friend taunted him.

"We'll leave the car near the subway."

"Finally you came to your senses. I was telling you that's our only choice." The radio was on. "Psst!" The driver shushed his friend. Nora couldn't make out the news but she understood that the Long Island Rail Road had suspended service on all branches. She was not interested but apparently her saviors were. "Well, good for you. It would've been a total waste to go for the train. Such primadonnas. Always the first to sign off."

"I bet there is not a damn spot to park in Queens . . . What could be the garage situation?—

"We'll figure out something."

"You wouldn't happen to know a garage?" the passenger turned to Nora.

"No, but you can try my street. It's close to the subway."

"Why is your street better than others?"

"I don't know. I think it's my natural hospitality. Besides, you would drive me home." She was pleased she could make them laugh. "Is it practical to live so far from your work when you have a choice?" Nora steered the conversation away from her selfish proposal.

"It's a matter of the life style one chooses."

Nora thought with more than a little discomfort at her own narrow window of choices. Was she prepared to negotiate her choices by looking at residency programs? Or at least planning to for the time being? Based on her belief that one never knew when some useful information could be had, she talked to anybody willing to lend a listening ear. So, she talked. "I'm thinking myself of getting out of the city for my children's sake—"

"See, that's a choice of life style. You'll make a good American, I bet," the passenger said. "Ben," he addressed his friend, "we are in Rego Park, have you noticed?"

That moment, like a good omen, near the grocery store on Queens Boulevard, she noticed Sonya and Daniel pulling the shopping cart. "Gentlemen, if you're so kind to dump me here, before my children can see me hitchhiking." Her saviors loved the prank. She pointed them to Booth and Saunder's Streets as possible parking opportunities.

"Good luck with your job hunting."

5

A sore point that persisted in Nora's habit of mind was a handicap, an imprint that the Communist information vacuum left on her. She felt uneasy with her poor ability to compile comprehensive information from the ocean of available sources. As if she had to cut through a dense forest aiming at one particular tree at the other end. Though aware that a beaten path must exist, she would fight her way through thorny undergrowth. Arrive, always arrive, find the tree, but with an excess of effort. Shortcuts, like some other people? Never.

Whatever she knew now, of ways and choices, was more doubtful in her mind than ever. *What else is there I can't find? I am probably missing the obvious.* She started to rely on personal connections.

Sitting in the breakfast nook in Joe's Manhattan apartment overlooking Central Park, Nora laid down her questions. "Now I have my license. Do I have a chance to train in this area?"

"Have you made up your CV?" Joe, the old time colleague asked.

Nora showed her friend her papers. "Look at it as if you were a program director."

"I plan to," Joe said and went on reading. Barbara put the hot pancakes, bacon and maple syrup on the table.

"Well done," Joe said. "Let's see. Here is this Eastern European graduate with all the credentials needed. Is she knowledgeable and hardworking enough to make up for her age?"

Nora felt her heart sink. "It is little I can do to improve that."

"They'll interview you only if you manage to hook them."

"Besides my irresistible face that will glow in the upper right corner on my application?"

"You are 36, right?"

"No Joe. I'm 40."

"Who said you have to be?"

"I can't lie. Besides. I cannot change my diploma. Graduated medical school at 19 or something like that?"

"Yeah. That's a problem. But you are a genius. You could have done it at 21. Accelerated program. That is very impressive around here, if anyone would care to get down to numbers."

"You're serious that I should lie about my age?"

"Uhum."

"And what do I do later? Let's say if I survive till retirement?"

"Later you can correct your 'mistake' as a typo."

By the time they cleared the table it was evident that Internal Medicine wouldn't be a good choice. Too little time for the children.

"Children? Sure. They kick their parents in their ass at the first opportunity?" Barbara chimed in from the kitchen.

"I don't believe that," Nora protested thinking of her children and how happy they looked spending time together at the neighborhood "Y," sitting at the TV together, trying to have as much fun as their favorite Brady Bunch characters, going after their business, bringing home great marks.

She got back to Joe after she'd tossed a few sleepless nights. "I always liked Radiology. I never had the opportunity, just as I never could become an Endocrinologist. Now, this one is out of question. It would take an entire Internal Medicine *plus* the specialty training. In that time, if I'm a good girl and get down on all fours to deal with Physics and Anatomy I always hated—"

"Now, wait a minute and make me understand," Joe said. "You said you like Radiology but hate what goes with it. How's that?"

"Let me give you an example," Nora said laughing. "I always loved *foie gras.* I could die for it. I equally, if not more, hated to see the geese being force fed. I could kill for that. See my quandary?"

"They have *foie gras* from geese that have not been force fed."

"Joe, my friend, you're from a land of *foie gras.* You know it's not the same."

"So? There's a difference."

"By the way, Joe. Do you know the joke about Moishe studying to become a Talmudist?"

"No, tell me."

"Moishe reads. To light the fire on Saturday and to commit adultery are equally bad crimes and call for similar penance. He scratches his head, then makes a note: I tried them both. What a difference!" She loved to collect people's approval when she got a joke or repartee right.

"It's the road which gives you problems not the destination, hah?"

"I can't even say I'm original."

"No. I haven't heard anyone who loved the residency, but there is no alternative."

"So what do you say about Radiology?"

"It's great if you can do it. I heard that the boards are very tough."

As days and weeks passed, Nora felt the familiar squeeze in her stomach as she waited for the mail. She could not put it in the back of her mind and go ahead with her life. Her steps sounded more resonant along the faux marble floor of the Forest Hills lobby than on the narrow cement staircase in Cluj. The mailbox she opened now with trembling hands was shinier than the one with the paint peeling off her old mailbox. Yet the anxiety was the same.

The letter came. Nice letterhead and courteous introduction. ". . . Your letter requesting acceptance in a Radiology training program without the required year of Internship, based on your prior experience had just missed the Board's Executive Committee meeting . . . Your request will be submitted for consideration at the next meeting in June . . ." she read.

"What does this exactly mean for us, Mama," Sonya asked when she told them of the bad news.

"Well. All programs start on July first. I have to start applying. Without the Board's approval I can't even think of Radiology. Then it's the extra year of training that I wanted to skip. Then we might have to move twice, depending on where I find positions." *I could've saved myself the humiliation.* Nora had not told the children about her demoralizing, now needless, interview.

They ate the dinner she brought in from the Fish and Chips shop across the boulevard quietly. Sonya surprised them with a vanilla pudding "á la box." Nora looked through tears of joy when Sonya put the individual little bowls decorated with Maraschino cherries on the table. Smoother and sweeter than anything in a gourmet restaurant.

Nora took a sleeping pill. She might have slept, like in a coma, as sometimes happened after severe stress, but she didn't want to take the risk of the other possible extreme: crying over her bad luck all night. Defeat and insomnia were a mixture harmful enough to render Nora *out of order* the following day.

Nora rode the subways to Brooklyn and Manhattan. She trotted along tree lined streets trying to disregard the warnings about their safety, or rather the lack of it.

It took her well over an hour to get to East Harlem; make her way through the milling crowd around the shabby city hospital entrance. Healthy looking teenagers and young adults were hanging out under the sign, Drug Rehabilitation Program. She waited there and at other just as rundown looking places throughout the city. Small rooms, department directors usually late for the interview, busy secretaries. Highly disheartening, if one had not much else to hang onto than appearances.

Nora's stomach contracted in more and more painful spasms as interviews came and went. She tried to imagine keeping their apartment, assuring the kids continuity in school, and commuting from Queens to Brooklyn or Manhattan. With the minimal rest she could hope to get the following year, after endless hours of work, she could barely picture herself standing in overcrowded subways in rush hour. It seemed to her like an act of self-persecution. Any energy left for the children? She was not a bottomless well of energy, though she acted as if she was.

"I have no choice but to buy a car," Nora told Marion. "And how I hate to put myself into debt again." The Marion of the Ritter couple, of which Max was a newly found childhood friend, was an extra bonus when they'd moved to Queens. Almost real Americans, as Nora thought of them, for they were naturalized in the deepest meaning of the word. Nora trusted Marion's opinions blindfolded.

"Don't look at a loan that way," Marion advised. "That's the way to acquire things. You can enjoy them while you save the money."

"I guess it's not the last thing I have to learn." Beyond the minimum balance, her savings and checking account was always under assault. Nora knew nothing about how credits and loans worked. Holding a credit card was not yet the subject of her daydreams. Her shyness to ask about money matters reached the range of a complex of inferiority. She was totally innocent about how to make herself financially trustworthy. She found out the hard way. From a store counter she took an American Express application and filled it so the signature stood in good faith as the small print said. Rejection was a rude awakening.

"You have to build your credit line," Marion told her.

Nora applied for a car loan at her bank. She learnt what collateral is. Certainly not her lean and lonely bank account, but her friends.

Shean, Nora's post-hippy lab mate, offered to help her. He crawled under the bellies of half-rusted Chevies advertised in mint condition; checked out rattling Buicks in remote driveways; then convinced Nora that a car dealer would be a better source.

Flying a magic carpet couldn't have been smoother or more thrilling than riding her new second hand '72 golden-brown Dodge Dart. A thrill short lived. During the car-buying campaign, Nora had developed a keen eye for parking spots around her block. Home with her new car, she looked at the curbside as if through the wrong end of binoculars. All spaces she used to see had shrunk to nothing.

Suddenly, she imagined driving home after a 36 hour shift, circling her neighborhood as she was doing right then for over half an hour. Finally, she squeezed in at a curb four blocks away. Commuting to Brooklyn or Manhattan lost, rather than gained, a dimension.

Nora rang the kids on the intercom. They ran downstairs excited. Nora understood their disappointment that an immediate joy ride was out of question on the grounds of parking problems. Instead she let them frolic inside, change places sliding over each other on the bench seat, sit at the steering wheel and fake drive, while she chased away the procession of drivers stopping and asking whether they were pulling out.

"Frodo," Daniel screamed while bouncing on the back seat.

"What?" Nora asked.

"Frodo is my favorite hobbit," he said. Nora remembered the Tolkien book he had been reading recently. "Brown and fuzzy."

"A fuzzy car!" Sonya exclaimed scornfully.

"Yes," he said as if nothing would be more natural. "He is precious and cuddly."

"You know what else is wrong?" Sonya went on. "Cars are shes."

Nora cut in. "I like Frodo. Sounds like a name for a good faithful friend. Let our car be a he."

Now Nora felt fully equipped to search up and down the suburban metropolitan area. Her energy bloomed with the spring thaw. New vitality drove her like a well-tuned engine. Like Frodo himself.

She had never driven by herself outside of Queens. Her New Jersey destination felt like the American wild West.

Engaging on the exit to the Brooklyn-Queens Expressway from the Grand Central Parkway was not rewarding as she had thought it would be by looking at the map. Busy traffic, trucks blasting past. The entity of claustrophobia passed her mind though she never thought of herself as a subject of such handicap. Anxiety stabbed Nora when the signs to the Williamsburg Bridge she planned to cross disappeared suddenly behind her. She took the left side exit as a personal affront. Should she stay in the fast left lane for the next exit she must take, no matter where it would take her? The middle suited her better with all its risk of missing the next exit.

A full circle of axle braking potholes finally let her off a right hand exit in a deserted street of faded commercial signs and half burned out warehouses. At the first traffic light she found herself in a different world. She needed to consult her map. Making the mandatory left, *whoops, that was a bridge on the right, wasn't it?* She couldn't tell which one. What was the wide thoroughfare she was traveling along? She looked up to the sky at the next stop, the sun was in front of her. South. By the fourth or fifth light, approaching and passing the imposing pyramid she recognized from her Manhattan wanderings as the Williamsburg Savings Bank building, she managed to make a right turn into a side street.

Nora landed in a bizarre setting: men wore long white garbs and skull caps, women were wrapped in large kerchiefs, stores poured their contents, despite the cold, onto the side walks, car wrecks blocked portions of the dirty street. Not one visible street sign. Not a spot to pull into. A fire hydrant. She couldn't see the corner from there. She tried to open her door. Couldn't. A car stopped blocking it. She pulled her door. The wild-looking man in the passenger seat raised his right hand, middle finger sticking up in an unmistakable gesture. They were telling her she didn't belong there, then disappeared.

A group of men turned the corner. Some in long burnouses, some sauntering along in worn out bomber jackets over garish shirts. She slid across the bench, rolled the window down. "Sir," she yelled when they passed her. An unbuttoned youth put his hands on the door, dark fingers and dirty fingernails gripped the light beige upholstery. "Ye'lone, babe?" Nora's heart skipped. What shall she do first? Roll up the window or slide back as quickly as she could and drive away? Too late. The man pulled the door lock and opened the door. Nora's thoughts froze, her heart seemed to have stopped. She could see herself between two hulks, one driving her car, the other's smelly hand covering her mouth. She could barely get air as it was, sitting still alone in the car. Suddenly, the man was yanked away from the door. Another took his place. "Ya' lost, doll?" he asked. Should she admit it or say she was waiting for her world champion wrestler brother? The most obvious question, Where am I? didn't seem the right thing to ask. "Would you be good to direct me to the bridge?" and suddenly she remembered it must be the Manhattan Bridge, the middle of the three lower Manhattan bridges. She couldn't have missed two. "The Manhattan Bridge," she added. *There. See? I'm not lost.* "No problem. Three lefts 'll be Flatbush. N' don't stop until you're out'a Brooklyn. N' lock your doors, doll." He pushed the lock down himself and shut the door, turned to the first man, shoved a fist under his nose, while that one waved mocking big fists around the other's face too. Both laughed. Nora wouldn't have wanted to hear their comments.

The bumper to bumper traffic across the bridge gave Nora the chance to bring her shaking knees and hands under control.

If a medical resident's schedule borders on the impossible, an interns' or PGY I, by the new terminology, is hell on earth. Beyond being alive to do the job, an intern's private life is negligible. No one pretended otherwise; everything was made quite clear by the end of the orientation day that gathered the new house staff in the hospital auditorium. Nothing more normal for a young doctor without a family than to work around the clock. But her? Nora stepped into the realm of an unfamiliar calendar. No distinguishing features. Only an endless succession of hours. How one could go on around the clock like this was unclear to her.

Cement walks criss-crossed the lawn that filled the space between the large U shaped row of old garden apartments. Children were running around like free mustangs, having arrived from all over the country and beyond, because a parent, or both, were working, or were just about to start at Lewisville Memorial Hospital. Others dragged around reluctant to make roots and meaningful friendships; nevertheless in need of buddies, they checked each other out, started to play. People carried their belongings up the narrow staircases.

Sonya, now going on thirteen, took charge of arranging most of their things in the narrow and dark kitchen. "Doing most of the cooking is my next project," she said. Most of the dining area, between the kitchen and the living room got curtained off to offer Daniel a small private space. The consensus about how to use the living room was easily reached. A leisure space where no one had to sleep. Sheer luxury. A small passageway at the end led to the one bathroom and two bedrooms, one smaller than the other. Nora took the other. The hospital building was hidden behind tall oaks, so Nora could forget about it when off duty.

The day when Nora reported for her first rotation on the second floor in the Blue Wing of the "Old Barn"—the nickname given to the brick building flaunting a tall and round Dutch style roof—marked the first time she set foot on an American hospital ward, as part of an American medical team, taking care of American patients, ready to learn the American way. Aware of her lost, terrified look, she tried to boast a more self-confident carriage: brand new stethoscope around her neck, shoulders pulled back; hands sunk in the pockets of her new crisp lab coat.

A tall and skinny junior resident, Bakhari, met her and her two fellow interns by the nurses' station. The four of them were all foreign graduates. The head nurse, Fairweather, the only person on the ward Nora could later relate to as a human being, proved to be an infallible nurse. She handed Bakhari stacks of patients' charts by room number. Nora got her assignment. Six patients.

"You have an hour, go over the charts, I'll take care of your duties. After that you're in business," he said as if just the day before he was not on the other side taking his junior's orders. *I hate his guts.* Nora thought of the accent on `your duties' and correctly suspected he wouldn't be of much help thereafter. The three interns exchanged furtive looks that assured Nora of their unconditional solidarity and unanimity of opinions.

"I need you to start a line in Room 10," Bakhari ordered as soon as Nora dumped the stack of practically unread charts.

So, which of my duties did he take care of? Nora stared at the I.V. cart. A new galaxy. It was ultimately tricky to get information without disclosing her ignorance. She needed to borrow time to prove—without making an ass of herself in the first half hour—that she was not a total fool. "You have a suggestion . . . for this particular—" she managed to ask her junior resident. "A butterfly will do," the junior said, already busy handling another naive question of another green intern.

Nora looked around at a loss. Nothing was flying. She pushed the I.V. cart into the room. Stuck a winged needle, *Ecco! a butterfly*—in the patient's ante-cubital fossa. Soon her first American I.V. line was running. Her sense of victory was short lived. To her misfortune she was not the only beginner involved in the heroic act. So was the patient, who thus would't ask for a board to keep his arm straight, or at least keep it straight without a board, or tell his diligent doctor not to use a butterfly in the elbow fold altogether. But no such luck. Between two novices, the entire contraption was compromised, the patient's arm swelled up infiltrated by the I.V. fluid. Fairweather came to her rescue quietly, as if nothing had happened.

She carried the letter from the Executive Committee of the American Board of Radiology in her coat's breast pocket. It had arrived a week after the internship started. Suddenly, she was declared eligible for a radiology training program without the introductory year of internship, a dispensation she earned based on her prior experience as a general practitioner in her old country. What was she to do with such generosity? She was offered a bonus year of life. Should she quit? The rent had to be paid. What rent? She would lose the hospital apartment. Move after just having unpacked a few weeks earlier?

A wasted year. Regression? Stagnation? Repetition? She tried to think whether she'd ever gone backwards before. Being a technician after being a doctor for fifteen years *was* regression. Or, rather an optimistic beginning of honest work.

Carrying the letter in her lab coat's breast pocket and fumbling with it every time she reached for a pen didn't advance her decision.

In the small room behind the nurses' station, Nora bent over sheets of papers arranged in sets. Three sets needed the last touches before taking their places in charts. The completed ones she had already passed to the nurse who was recording the orders in silence. An unlucky night with a record nobody wanted to beat: seven admissions. Nora was in worse shape that any of the patients she had admitted that night. She desperately needed to lie down on an empty bed. Four in the morning and the ER was still busy. *I could use a truck,* she told herself carrying the charts to morning report. Another 14 hours of work lay ahead, after the 18 behind, and she had not yet set foot in the on-call room to put her head on the bumpy hard pillow. She tried to imagine the children sleeping by themselves. The thought of running across the street, sneaking into the apartment and blowing a kiss on their cheeks, brought a comforting smile to her exhausted soul. An urge she had to repress.

Nora's junior resident, Richard's, impetuous and noisy entry abruptly brought Nora back to the poorly ventilated stuffy reality. Coming from the patient's room, where he reviewed a history and physical, he was holding a chart. He sat down opposite Nora, ready to write his note.

"Nora," he thundered. "Isn't this fascinating?" he asked.

She pressed her palms to her ears and gave him a desperate look. "Dick, nothing is at four in the morning. It was very much so 20 years ago when I did my first internship." There was no point hiding her exhaustion, not that she could have, but she refrained from speaking out loud the rest of her thought: When you merely grew out of your diapers. Richard was not guilty that she was born too early or came to this country too late. Or at all.

Dick appeared truly baffled by Nora's rebellion. He tried to cheer her up. He closed the door to the station and started to sing "La donna è mobile," in his professional quality baritone. Nora leaned back, her head hung in desperation over the back of the chair, her arms hanging limp at her sides and let out the moan of a tortured animal. She had to smile after all at the big kid teasing her with his singing. He wouldn't understand that the only thing she wanted was sleep.

There was no time or room to complain. When her tired fingers were too weak to hold a pen, she had to start intravenous lines with steady hands; when her knees were too shaky to stand at a bedside to give a reassuring answer to a patient's question she would rather have heard tomorrow, she had to run down to the blood bank for a new unit of packed cells; when her mind was blurry from lack of sleep she had to make prompt and correct decisions.

Frustrated and overwhelmed, she thought endlessly of the letter she intended to submit to the Director of Radiology at the hospital, but didn't have the guts. She had to at least get an interview. She had to help her children with their schedule; they were busier and in need of more attention. She had to squeeze out a few hours to go to the medical library. The window of opportunity had passed when she could ask questions right and left. Now she was supposed to know everything. All those wise faces probably didn't have to fight their way with a linguistic machete through the jungle of medical acronyms. *STAT.* The American obsession with abbreviating even the universally used Statim enraged Nora. Was the *ASAP* better? *What does it save to pronounce four syllables instead of six?*

Don't waste too much energy fighting, she kept pacifying herself, after she found out the meaning of one or another alphabetical curiosity of life saving importance. *Accept and assimilate. Play the game.* The first days clarified *the ASHD, CAD, HTN, CHF, LVH, RVH, VSD, ASD, PDA* and the likes. The *MVP* somehow fell through the cracks to torment her later. Mitral valve prolapse was not something she had learnt the first time around. Neither were *LVEF* or *Swann-Gantz.* Or *IHSS.* That one made her pull her hair for not having the slightest idea about which organ system it belonged to. In later years she would have the satisfaction of the entire term of Idiopathic Hypertrophic Subaortic Stenosis being discredited—surely by virtue of her cursing it out of existence—as it was swallowed by the general term of Hypertrophic Obstructive Cardiomyopathies. Wasn't HOCM so much prettier? Worthy of a Hudini. Until some cardiology researcher would manage to make a name for him or herself by changing it to some other un-memorizable combination of letters.

Her confidence was inversely proportional to the length of the list of terms to be clarified. With such problems to solve before she could go ahead with her work, wishing that days had at least 30 hours, Nora collapsed after an all nighter on-call.

She awoke on the bouncing stretcher. After the annoying employment physical she hoped not to see the Employees Health service ever again. A summary work-up declared her eligible for a day off. She looked at her watch; no reason to make plans, the precious day was almost over. At home she had merely time to rummage for a business card she vaguely remembered having stashed some place. Glad that she had not thrown it out, Nora made a phone call. "Look, I hate to be arrogant," she told the woman on the line. "If you can make it today you have a good chance. By tomorrow I might change my mind." She didn't specify that today was the day when she was terrified of dying and leaving her children without resources. Croaking in the middle of a night of strenuous work didn't look so threatening with a $100,000 life insurance policy in the drawer.

I'm too old. I'm not up to the challenge, Nora thought when she filed the Radiology Board's letter with other paper relics of mere emotional value in a weather beaten folder. After all, in New Jersey, she could practice General Medicine with one year of training. Isn't that what she was? A general practitioner. And damn good at it, she was confident.

Letting the idea of a new specialty rest gave Nora some peace of mind. More than that. Looking in the mirror, holding up a small round hand-held one behind her head, Nora was about to do what she used to. Give herself a hair cut.

"No." She screamed at herself. Sonya came into the bathroom asking, "Mom, did you call?"

"No. But tell me anyhow. Do I need a hair cut?"

"Oh, and how," Sonya said and pulled up swatches of her mother's hair in disgust. "Look at this."

"What?"

"You want me to do it?"

"I was thinking more of a professional hair cut."

"It's about time," Sonya concluded and was out of the bathroom.

The compliments Nora received on her trendy new look, a tapered short hairdo, chipped a little off the lump of her insecurities.

In December, Doctor Riley, the Chief-of-Medicine, presented Nora with a surprise rejection. It was an honor to hear from the chief personally, before the official notifications were out, that she was amongst the interns to be dumped from the program due to the pyramid system. Nora felt a great deal of kindness in how he protected her ego. "Do you have alternative plans if you wouldn't continue in our program?" That was a tactful man. He made her feel proud for deserving to be kicked out in private. The three letter dirty word: A-G-E was bouncing in front of Nora's eyes like pebbles ready to fly into her face. It came to a tactical moment to expose her self control for not bailing out of the program in favor of Radiology.

"I'm impressed," the director said. "I would be glad to help you along *those* lines. I hope you won't regret the year you've spent here."

Riley set her up for three interviews including the one with Doctor Wolffe two floors below.

She didn't dare think how wonderful it would be to be accepted and stay were she was. Only advantages and practically no drawbacks. How many times would that happen in one's lifetime? The race was on.

Opening the mailbox had become an act loaded with emotional conflict. It brought into focus the time and energy she didn't have to answer letters any more. Longer letters from friends irritated her. They selfishly demanded too much of her time. Short letters expressed lack of interest she considered offensive. To sever the old ties by not answering felt like ripping out her soul piece by piece. She was not fond of bills either. She was relieved when there was nothing but junk mail.

With such mixed feelings, Nora sifted through the mail and looked at the thick envelope of rough paper with Tibor's familiar handwriting. Nora wondered whether it contained photos.

She found the apartment door ajar. "Sonya, Dani, I'm home." Silence. "Hello there." Silence. She dumped the mail and her keys on the coffee table, and turned to the entrance door to hang her coat. "Dani, are you there?" Nothing. She peeked around Daniel's drawn curtain. His school bag was on the bed. Well, Nora thought, he's off playing.

Sonya stormed through the living room. "You need help?"

"Set the table."

"Where's the brat?"

Dusk gave in to darkness. Something was not right. Daniel wasn't back. Kids had quit playing. The two classmates whose phone numbers Nora had knew nothing. Sonya went to canvas the neighborhood only to return to check whether he had come home.

They drove around searching ominously quiet alleyways.

"This won't work," Nora said after they'd checked out the train station.

"Let's look at the hospital," Sonya said, but Daniel had not been spotted there either.

"The Y." The idea brought hope. A place he knew wouldn't be like he ran away, Nora thought.

In fifteen minutes, Nora turned into the Y parking lot almost hitting an exiting car. Her hands were shaking. Despite the shield of squeezed trembling lips, the words slipped out, "Why would he run away?"

"I haven't got the foggiest," Sonya said.

They headed to the illuminated entrance of the building. Sonya ran ahead. Leaning to the railing of the steps was a silhouette of a small person, his arms wrapped around his head, forehead resting on his knees. In a few seconds Nora realized it was Daniel as she heard Sonya, "What on earth are you doing here?"

Daniel lifted a tear-soaked face, ran down the three steps to the first tree, leaned his hands on its trunk, hung his head low between his arms and kicked the tree angrily.

Nora put an arm around his shoulder. "What's wrong? Is it the incident at the school? Talk to me, please." Nora felt like apologizing for her failure to act on his complaint of being bullied after school hours.

"You don't understand anything." He swung his arms in a wide arc pushing his mother away.

"Dani. I'm sorry. I'd like to understand. Please explain." He only shrugged.

A silent dinner followed a silent drive.

Until the Valium kicked in, Nora reflected on the story Daniel gave her days ago about being bullied at school by boys twice his size, kicked in the gutter, mocked. Looking at his clothes for proof, as in disbelief, was not the comfort a scared young boy expected from his mother. How she regretted. Tears oozed, her lips quivered. *What did I mean with those absurd, awkward questions? Should I insist? Should I talk to the principal?*

Couldn't she see the forest for the trees, the big picture for the current event, or was she losing the site of the one important tree in a forest of tasks exceeding her abilities? Other tasks were nothing but a heap of irrelevant details when her children were at stake. Work was not irrelevant. Passing more specialty exams was not irrelevant. Was daily living possible without the daily drudgery that sapped her strength? The children deserved more time, more patience, not the short peaks of her exuberance which they all enjoyed no doubt. Peaks that almost always would forecast flat periods when she would be drained of her prodigious energy. That's where her intention of making that phone call disappeared like a life giving trickle of water in the thirsty desert.

Days later, Nora pulled a bunch of envelopes from behind the coffee table. That's where it was? The overdue telephone bill. Tibor's letter came to light too. She split it open with a finger and read it in the car. A final good bye? The news failed to touch anything but strictly grey matter. There was a man sometimes, somewhere, who might have been a support in sorting out the troubles of a growing boy. Might have . . .

6

See one, Do one, Teach one. The phrase became Nora's *modus operandi.* In Radiology, she was thrown into what looked like water and she couldn't swim. The medium was foreign. During the first few weeks, an attending radiologist introduced the first year residents to the basic rules to save themselves from drowning. Tens and tens of rules. And miles of view boxes hung with films to be gawked at without the knowledge needed to actually read them. The *See one* phase. Sooner than she imagined, in mere weeks, Nora found herself in the *Do one* phase, much before she thought she was ready to handle the intimidating machine with components of obscure function. It wouldn't lock into place, it wouldn't release, the table would jerk, not slide, it would not expose because the tech left the door to the room ajar while chatting in the hallway, or the patient couldn't move. Help came from her fellow senior residents as part of their *Teach one* phase.

Then there was the daily list of terms unknown to her; she scribbled them on pieces of paper to look up later in the library. Physics, geometry, anatomy were enemy battalions attacking Napoleon style from all directions. Soon she was about to curse the day she thought of going into Radiology.

"I'm afraid I'm not doing as well as you guys do," Nora told the kids at dinner after they reported from their own battle fields.

"It's tougher than internship?" Daniel asked.

That sounded like pushing the right button. "Good question. It's relative."

"You did that, why couldn't you do this?" Sonya's logic took Nora further.

"You're both right. I need a strategy."

Nora was aware of the pattern of her waves of energy spurts alternating with slumps of vexing sluggishness. A pattern she could not escape. She couldn't plow on like a traction horse. At times she wondered whether it was lack of consistency, a self-defense mechanism against burn-out or . . . no, she really didn't think of herself as a manic-depressive.

Petit à petit l'oiseau fait son nid. The phrase of popular wisdom came to her, and even if it was French, wasn't that exactly what she was doing, building a nest? From scratch. Small but significant decisions were called for. Not a day should pass, when she, Doctor Nora Mann, the future Radiologist—*God it sounds good!*—whether at home or away, would not set her eyes on a textbook, journal, or some medical literature. Cover opened! An accumulation of knowledge by disciplined continuity, that should be the motto. She announced to the children. "You'll be my whip. I won't mind if you ask me everyday whether I learned something that day. This way we'll do it together."

Nora would always answer night calls at first ring. She would reach for the light switch and look at the clock. Now it was six and almost time to get up anyhow after an easy on call. *Thanks guys, for not calling earlier.* Crackling static and an indistinct female voice asked her to hold for the international operator. More crackles. Only extremely optimistic thoughts kept at bay the impending disaster that such an unexpected call could bring. A few seconds later Romanian syllables emerged from the noise. Years after the final farewell, she wished it was Tibor. Rascal! "Arthur? Is that you?" She screamed. Between lagging echoing sentences bouncing back and forth, Nora got the terrible news. Adel had been admitted last night. A stroke, coma, the worst prognosis, not likely to make it.

The children awakened by the yelling listened in silent consternation. "Are we going?" Sonya asked later between spoonfuls of cereal.

"My place should be at her side holding her hand." Nora dabbed her tears.

"Is she gonna die?" Daniel's question was the more painful as children are not supposed to understand death. He had learned about it much too early in his life.

"She's in bad shape. Max could get me a ticket." She thought it was strange that they'd received their Green Cards recently. "I don't think we shall all go. Can you take care of yourselves for a few days?"

"Don't worry. We'll be fine."

"I'll ask Sandy to stay with you." The kids knew the radiology technician, a single woman, whom Nora had befriended.

"Okay," Sonya said.

Nora called Adel's number late at night. Arthur had moved in soon after Nora left. It seemed the right thing for her lonely mother. They also got married, and soon she had transferred half of the apartment onto his name. Nora had taken the news with little emotion. She was to take a flight to Budapest the next day, hope to be granted a visa at the Romanian border, and drive to Cluj. Even if Adel was in a coma there was always hope she could emerge, at least partially, so she might find comfort in having Nora there. That was the idea.

Nora had no chance to tell any of that to Arthur. His voice came as if from beyond the grave. "My poor dear closed her eyes forever around midnight."

Nora's immense sadness and irreversible failure to redeem herself for all the anguish she had caused settled in forever. The happy times retreated and the desire to bring them back here in America . . . Arthur's voice interrupted the silence, "Can you hear me?" She had to answer. She never felt Arthur more alien. "When is the funeral?" Nora asked.

"Traditionally it should be tomorrow . . . we can postpone it, of course, if you want."

Three parents. All died in her absence. Remorse brought uncertain thoughts. Never suffered the burdens of an offspring's duties. She couldn't fix that by walking alongside with strangers as Adel's remains were taken to her grave. She'd left Adel with strangers. Parents and children have their own separate lives. How could it be illustrated more painfully? Nice to have met you. She cried while trying to talk. "Arthur," she said, "I'll let you lay her to rest. I'll always be with her in spirit."

"She was a very noble soul," he said.

"I thank you for all the happiness you brought into her wrecked life."

Returning from a conference in New York Nora turned the key carefully like a burglar. Put the chain on. The checkered curtain separating the dining area and providing Daniel his fake privacy was drawn. She moved through the dim living room lit from the light pole in front of the building. She navigated between amorphous piles, hostile bicycle horns sticking into the narrow passage between the coffee table and the wall unit. *It's all right. They are good kids. So, they're a little untidy,* Nora placated her first burst of anger. In her bedroom she undressed, put on a robe. Walked to the bathroom. The sink was smeared with lipstick, a pair of bloody socks was still soaking in a plastic basin, now more like rotting after days spent under the sink. She ran a bath.

She stepped into the tub, her skin responded with goose bumps to the water's embrace. She let out a sigh of satisfaction almost synchronous with a wild knock on the entrance door. Then the door was rattled. Then another angry rapping. Nora put the robe on her wet body and walked to Sonya's room. Opened the door. She was not in her bed.

Nora threw into Sonya's face her disregard of the explicit request not to stay out on the evenings when she herself was away. Though explanations were superfluous, she gave plenty anyway: Daniel alone, her much needed rest, enough to worry other times when Sonya would come home late. Sonya, self-confident, returned the favor by casting the blame on her mother for never hearing what she had to say. That was *exactly* the evening when she needed to go study for a math test with Sam.

"What's wrong with studying here?" Nora asked.

When Daniel offered his input, they realized he was awake. "*Me* is wrong here. They send me away. She can go away with that thug and never come back. Bitch."

"Daniel!" Nora yelled now disregarding the late hour. "What language is this?"

"Creep!" Sonya growled. "Mind your own business."

So much for sleep. How to make them understand? Hold back the little weekly allowance? Didn't they have their needs too while carrying more than their share? Nora hadn't even seen the laundry room they used in the next building. Sonya took care of that without being told. She also did a lot of the cooking. The dishes were always washed, that was Daniel's chore. The school work? Nora had been checking on them mostly to feel that she was doing her parental duty. They needed no nudging. Nothing to worry about in that department. But, they started to fight and now Daniel started to use foul language, none of which Nora considered inherent to growing up. What's happening to him? To them all? No, she couldn't take away the allowance. Then how could she send the message? She could cut it. *Right. One dollar instead of two?* When they both, especially Sonya, supplemented her modest *Two Guys* wardrobe from her allowance and own earnings to keep up—more or less—with her classmates. Never complained or demanded more than her mother could afford? However, occasions like that evening confirmed that the children were not ready to manage on their own for days.

Nora looked her proudest and best in her tailored aqua linen blazer over an off white dress even without high heels. Daniel was strutting in his new navy suit that Nora had bought him just weeks before for a Bar

Mitzvah ceremony. He looked up at his sister mesmerized; Sonya looked gorgeous. The blue eye shadow transformed her round grey eyes into azure pools, radiant for the occasion. Nora's dark crepe dress suited her perfectly. She took her seat in the front row of the auditorium, turned around and winked at Nora and Daniel sitting a few rows back. The speeches had started. Sonya was being inducted as a member in the National Honor Roll Society. A fringe benefit for all that work for the advanced placement classes she took.

"You can boast when we go to celebrate George's graduation from Princeton," Nora said after the ceremony, meaning the weekend invitation to friends living in Philadelphia.

"Why don't you brag for me? I'll stay home," Sonya said.

"It's in a month. Such long term plans?"

"Yeah." She started to laugh uncontrollably and hid her face.

"I can see you'll tell her," Daniel taunted his sister.

"Shut up." She slapped his chest with the back of a hand. He grabbed her diploma.

"What's all this about?" Nora asked Sonya.

"I'm planning . . ." Sonya couldn't stop giggling, ". . . to give up my virginity," she said with determination.

It was Sonya's turn to be astonished at the sight of her mother's face barely surprised and saying, "Any contraception and a partner in mind?"

"Are you done with your homework," Nora yelled across the lawn to Daniel bouncing the Badminton birdie.

"Am I ever not?" Completely true. Such a problem was history. Sonya passed her at the mail box running to the hospital dressed in a crisp pastel green uniform. She was such a happy senior; Nora could never have imagined that kids would be so carefree before going to college. The dinner shift was starting; Sonya took both her job distributing the trays on the wards and her earnings very seriously. A few days before, she had brought home from the framer her needle point based on a Gauguin painting, finished and framed. It was hanging in the living room. "On loan until I'll have my own home," she said when Nora expressed her admiration and suggested displaying it in the living room.

The mailbox was full. Nora shrugged at every piece of junk mail she dropped in the wastebasket. A large official envelop from Daniel's school. *It had been too tranquil lately, something was bound to happen, isn't it always the case? If it were anything good Dani would have trumpeted it.*

Hesitating, she opened it. A parchment colored diploma. Nora's eyes fell on The John Hopkins University heading. She never read any announcement or instruction sheet from the top, so she went right into the essence.

This is to certify that
Daniel Mann

She recalled the Saturday when she took Daniel to take the SAT, but totally forgot the background. Her eyes shifted back to the top of the diploma.

1979 Mathematics and Verbal Talent Search
conducted by the
Office of Talent Identification and Development

The small print showed that 15,000 seventh graders from seven states took the test on an experimental basis in cooperation with the Study of Mathematically Precocious Youth.

There was a congratulatory letter signed by the president of Drew University, in Madison, inviting Daniel Mann and his parents for an open house in view of having been selected to attend a college mathematics course based on his recently taken SAT.

"Daniel?" Nora yelled through the open window, her voice bouncy with joy.

Daniel, jumping around and running to hit the birdie yelled back without looking up. "I know and I'll take it."

There was no playing or bouncing the afternoon that Daniel got off the school bus with a long face. "I've told you that jerk, that slime Craig, he always picks on me—" He complained.

"Who's he?"

"You never listen." Daniel was angry.

"Chill it, and tell me again. I'm sorry if I forgot."

"An eighth grader stinkin' thug. I gave him a piece of my mind, so he hit me. First in my arm then in my belly. I hit him back, ha, ha, I got him."

"You kicked him." Daniel was usually not too successful with his fists, which gave him great frustration, but he could be quite swift with his feet. He used to run, which Nora didn't mind. Hearing that he defended himself made her happy as a lark.

"How'd'ya know?" Daniel was surprised.

"It sounds like self-defense, you are supposed to do your best. Good for you."

Sonya and Sam were in her room, door open, gesturing victory signs.

Daniel appeared pleased for the unexpected support, looked with loving eyes at his mother, but was still in a speculative feisty mood. "No matter what I do it's not good for me. If I don't fight back, they make fun of me. If I do, they hate me that I can defend myself. What do you think the teacher did? Nothing. He gave us these notes." He handed Nora a piece of paper. Next day the two belligerent parties were supposed to stay one hour after classes.

"Would you write a note that we have an appointment or something?" Daniel suddenly begged.

"That's the least. I want to get in touch with the teacher to ask for an explanation. I don't think you should be punished. It sounds like self-defense to me." She recalled the "Y." *He needs my support.* While writing the note she asked Daniel, hoping to break a predictable resistance. "Don't you think it would be nice to take some judo?" She was not wrong. The answer was a definite "No."

She stayed on track beating the hot iron. "You have something else in mind to develop some muscles?"

"Yeah. I'll wait for the testosterone to kick in."

Daniel never laughed at his own jokes. The others roared.

"Where is the answer from the teacher?" Nora asked Daniel next day. It was her turn to fume.

"Just another moron," he yelled. "He said, all right, let it be self-defense, you can go home, he didn't even finish reading your note and threw it in the garbage."

"I'm afraid—" she stopped herself short. Undermining the teacher's prestige, was a no-no. "Let's forget this. Look what I've made." She lifted the lid off the pots on the stove. Daniel peeked at the freshly breaded chicken breast and mashed potatoes.

"My favorite dinner!" He threw himself on the chair.

"Doctor Mann line two outside call Doctor Mann line two," the overhead page blared.

Nora was in the middle of a procedure. Wearing a lead apron, a thyroid shield and a giant lead glove, she operated the x-ray table. The patient lay in a contorted position with his head lowered, sipping barium through a straw. "Lori, please answer it," she asked the technician at the control panel behind the radiation divider.

"It's a Martin Ferber," the tech said.

Nora's eyebrows jumped. She put on a funny know-nothing grimace. With her hand engaged under the image intensifier, she pushed on the patient's stomach. "Would you ask, please, what's this about?"

"He says you'd seen him in the ER," Lori informed Nora.

"Well, let's see—" Nora, addressing now to no one, pulled back her hand, then raised her voice, "Hold your breath." She pushed a button, the exposure was accompanied by a loud click. She commanded, "You can breath now." She removed her left foot from the floor pedal. The cassette carrier moved noisily. She faced the image intensifying tower, gave the cassette carrier a flick with the right hand, grabbed the popping cassette with the left, a swift turn, an exchange of the exposed cassette for a fresh one from the cart, turn, push, flick, and in seconds she was back continuing the procedure. "Lori, take his number, please." She concentrated on the procedure.

Three more cases later Nora hung the lead apron on the wall rack. At the light from the view box she wrote the provisional report in the last patient's chart, walked through the room and thanked Lori for a good day's work. In the hallway she remembered the piece of paper in her coat pocket with the scribbled numbers—work and home—both 212 area code. Not a clue. She rubbed her chin as if the gesture could deliver her from her obfuscation.

"Zelda, may I use your phone for a long distance call?" Nora asked the director's secretary who put on a shocked expression at such an unorthodox request in a department where every penny had to be accounted for. "Not so long. Manhattan. And probably official anyhow. A former ER patient."

"I hope you're not being sued."

"We would've heard that from the administration." Nora dialed. "This is Doctor Mann at Lewisville Memorial in New Jersey. I'm returning a Mister Ferber's call."

"By the way," Zelda said while Nora was on hold, "He's from the *New York Times.* Called earlier. I did put his call through." Nora covered the mouthpiece with a hand. "Did he tell you why?"

"I wouldn't be surprised—"

"Yes, that's her," Nora answered and motioned to Zelda she was sorry for not being able to follow her.

The man refreshed Nora's memory without much difficulty. She could even attach a face to the name. And a hand. Yes, his thumb was fine, he answered her question. *Isn't that a relief. He was not a disgruntled patient trying to make trouble.*

She remembered now quite clearly. It had been a wonderful sunny summer weekend. After lunch she had been craving for a nap. Twenty minutes. The interdiction to leave the premises of the hospital during the day when on call, and being out of earshot of the blaring page system, seemed as justified to Nora as the infamous prohibition she'd never understood. But she was not the one to commit an infringement after she had lived with the rule for three years; not now when she was the one to enforce it as a Chief Resident. She had timed herself. It took longer to get down to the department from the on call suite than to run across the street from her apartment. Anyway, digestion claiming her blood supply away from her brain, she was sitting in the residents' room, more or less napping, more or less watching the TV hanging high on a wall bracket.

Nora noticed the technician's sorry face, apologetic, his head tilted as he leaned to the door frame, and waved a few small films and a paper slip at her. She gave the technician a grimace of disgust that made him laugh, took the package and flipped the films on the view box. "Kevin, I'll be right back. Tell me what happened," she had pointed to the TV as she got up. "I have to go look at this patient." She wanted to correlate a suspicious finding on the film with the point of tenderness. A common practice. She had walked over to the ER, found the patient and introduced herself before asking for permission to examine his hand. It was some kind of weekend sports accident. An untrained klutz, showing off and spraining his thumb in the process, she suspected, looking at the middle age man. The area of suspicion was not tender. The base of his thumb was. He had probably suffered a severe sprain that had reduced spontaneously. "I wanted to make sure you didn't suffer a wrist injury," she had added.

"Looking for a navicular problem?"

"Are you a health professional?" Nora raised her eyebrows, slightly annoyed by not being warned that the patient was peer or something of that sort, unless he was an impostor.

"No, I'm not," he'd said.

She had found his hazel eyes provocative, sparkling fresh and a total antidote to her flurry of irritation. "Just plain smart?" She counted on her almost infallible gift to detect an opportunity to joke without penalty.

"As much as two years of med school make one. On the other hand . . ." he paused as she laughed at his pun, "I injured that navicular as a teenager—"

"That explains the slight irregularity that worried me." She had noticed he was nodding with respect. "By the way, you never finished med school I gather."

"I exchanged the scalpel for the pen. Just as sharp, I assure you. I've pursued journalism."

So she remembered this Ferber guy. His eyes, his wit, being a sport about her arrogant mocking, perhaps a little out of place in her position. She recalled the fifty-something old man speaking very softly. A lingering memory of something intriguing, of an old timer, an unusual elegance that exuded not from the informal summer clothes, too impeccable for what they were—a striped polo shirt and light denim pants. Nimble conversation style. Definite sense of humor. She had put him to a test, hadn't she? Not that she would have intended to test him for anything beyond the location of tenderness in his wrist.

"I've been wondering for quite a while what your answer would be if I asked you to have lunch with me? Or dinner."

A journalist? An interview? Nora couldn't imagine on what subject. "May I ask about the nature of the meeting?"

"Totally social." His voice sounded confident.

Hers didn't when she plainly admitted. "This takes me by surprise."

"I would've liked to extend the invitation in person. I thought it might be too much of an imposition."

They agreed on Saturday.

Nora had indicated a modest Italian restaurant off Route 506 in Montclair. Classy address. But, first and foremost, she knew the exact directions. Also, midway. Perfect for the situation. She was planning to be a little late, a goal she could never achieve, always promising herself never to be on time again, when she would be the one to wait. *How weird that I should think of this now!* She paraphrased her thought.

To her greatest surprise the word "weird" turned up in Martin's first sentence as Nora held out her hand and rated favorably his strong and dry hand shake. A test of character, if not temperament, that Nora never failed to appreciate. Decisive first impression.

"Please, don't consider it weird or outlandish that I called you. It would be superfluous to say I have been thinking of you a lot since you set your sharp eyes on my x-ray," he said.

She intentionally disregarded the thinking part. She said, "Outlandish? No. But certainly not shy."

"At the school of journalism they offered a course: 'How to be shy 101.' I tried it. I dropped out to avoid failing."

"Have you ever taken a course on how to take rejection?"

"I didn't need one. I'm a natural. My call is my witness."

"Sorry to disappoint," she said without knowing why and feeling a little patronizing, perhaps, with a newly invented self-confidence.

Nothing more inductive for the conversation than being sunk in a resilient leatherette bench in a booth. A picture window to allow for a flash of evasive gaze while figuring a difficult question, like, "You aren't planning to write a column on the inhumane American medical training based on an interview with me."

With his elbows resting on the table's edge, fingers braided, Martin didn't hide his mounting interest as he listened to Nora's convoluted ways of answering his question about her future plans. "I'm finished here. I don't regret a minute of the four years. It was good for all of us, but I'm ready to move on. I mean ready, as in well equipped."

Imagining her future office with a tall narrow window opening over an inner courtyard appeared to Nora as a token of triumph over all the odds she was ready to leave behind. A sunlit azure pool where her river's agitated waters could finally calm down. Having to share the office took nothing away from its value. It was still a spot she could call her own in the world of American medical life. It felt good, positively worth talking about it to this Martin guy.

"You leave with the satisfaction of good training?"

"Yes. But not only that. I'm able to bend my warped Eastern European mentality to handling the quirks. Before, I used to be stupefied by every little detail. I'm not talking professionally. That too, to some extent. I mean socially. It's not my experience that makes me feel ready. What could I have learned living in a quaint town? But ready to face whatever comes my way. Does this make sense?"

"I'd call it boldness. Or rather courage."

"You're flattering me. I'm not good at taking compliments. I tend to analyze and look for grounds."

"I'll keep this in mind. You were mentioning your plans."

"Oh, yes. Before my *real* job starts I have to get the approval of a Coop board. By the way, I think the procedure isn't fair. What would they say if I asked to see the tenants? Maybe *I* don't like them. Maybe *I* don't want to live in the same building with them?"

"You expected through and through fairness?"

"Why not?" She smiled. Martin returned an admiring gaze and she was aware he reflected her engaging smile. "This apartment needs a lot of work. As-it-is means amongst other things some electric zigzags on the living room walls. What else? We have to pack. But I have a daughter—"

"Isn't she away?"

"No. She's going to college this fall. She made up her summer schedule so she can help us pack."

"She's a good daughter."

"Good is not the word. She's . . . well, both my kids are nothing short of wonderful. Even normal." They kept on smiling.

"How old are they?"

"Sonya is going on 18, and Daniel is a 13 pre-Bronx High School of Science."

"He can't be—"

"Of course not, but he's determined and that means he will get in. I trust him."

"Your kids have a good mother."

"I'm trying. Though my ways are debatable."

"Now you're fishing for compliments you said you have difficulty accepting."

"I prefer flexible to consistent." Another unapologetic glamorous smile elicited Martin's appreciative nod.

The hour and a half of Picasso at the Museum of Modern Art trailing at a snail's pace amid the wall to wall crowd worked up Nora's appetite both for dinner and for getting more personal. She hoped Martin was of the same mind.

"What are you looking for in a person?" Nora asked when seated in the sunken middle of the dazzling King Cole room at the St. Regis Hotel, trying to think of her own appearance as reassuringly elegant in her basic black, high-low heels, sparse and modest jewelry, contrasting with the mostly flashy every-other-woman. She lifted her Harvey's Bristol Cream on the rocks.

"Let me see," he held up his Martini. His cuff link glittered as the sleeve of his blue blazer pulled up. "I toast for a pattern—"

"Oh? I have one," Nora interjected with a teenage vivacity, put her glass down and started to count on her fingers. "The man of my dreams should be intelligent like Einstein, look like Gregory Peck, have a character like George Washington, be witty like Oscar Wilde—"

A spasmodic laughter took hold of them. Martin could barely speak. "This reminds me of one description of hell, where the Frenchman is the banker, the Englishman the cook, the Italian the mechanic, the German the policeman, the Swiss the lover. Or something like that."

Nora knew the joke, she laughed nevertheless. "But we're talking paradise where maximum one mismatch is allowed—"

"Such mixture of realism and idealism in you! I don't know what's the proportion—"

"Don't try to figure out. I can't," Nora said, then added, "So, what's wrong with you?" while the feeling of "you might be it" made its way from her heart to her brain by the time he asked teasingly, "For sitting here with you?"

She shook her head with the sudden realization that Martin's eyes resembled Tibor's the instant when he conveyed some flippant idea. "No . . . For not being married."

"I'm not the marrying type."

"You're not hedging. You wouldn't be a good radiologist."

"A journalist who hedges should have his head chopped off."

"Isn't that a bit radical?"

Intrigued, he rubbed his chin in jest. "OK, then shot. But to answer your question, I've held out, or rather, I've stayed wedded to my freedom through tough calls . . ."

"I didn't mean marriage. I ran into this problem myself. There are other ways of commitment—

"For example?"

"I don't know . . ." *I'm here and I like you.* She wished it could have been all right to just say that. The fact that she couldn't joke about the idea was a warning that she might believe it herself.

"Reason. As in motivation, decency, reality."

She exclaimed. "I like this. It sounds unconventional. On the other hand in the conventional sense, one of the most powerful moments in my personal life would've been spoiled, if not missed altogether, with any reasoning."

"A romantic moment, I assume."

"It doesn't have much relevance—" *Why not?* Nora thought when

Martin uttered a few unrelated prepositions followed by "I don't mean to prod . . ." Nora felt he was bursting with curiosity. She was right. He went on. "The way you mentioned that moment . . . Frankly?"

"What we say should be frank. What we don't, let's assume it can be ignored."

He nodded. "To illustrate that I can be spontaneous, if you accept it as an opposite of reasoning, I didn't mean envious. I meant jealous. Of your past."

"That's unreasonable enough that it calls for celebration," she raised her glass. "To unreasonable spontaneity."

"May I kiss you?"

Nora leaned over the table. She felt neither a deep physical response, nor was she displeased by the touch of his lips. She wondered whether Martin in his declared state of jealousy at her past was more attuned to react. She found Martin's mind to be the more exciting part of him, and was ready to be challenged and immersed in more main stream America, or rather, as Martin would have put it, into the undercurrents of his complex areas of interest.

By the end of the evening a garrulous Nora presented Martin with the essentials of her family's story and in turn listened with chin propped in cupped hands to him giving an account of what he called his unexciting life. A succession of well planned years at Princeton followed by a few short-lived jobs, an unstructured, freelance life since, reporting mostly on social issues, mainly in the New York metropolitan area. She was speculating where he intended the emphasis: the school, the structure, or the freedom.

7

Nora stood by the picture window in the living room of her new co-op apartment. The George Washington Bridge spanning the Hudson dominated the panorama. Anxiety and expectation ran neck to neck.

Tomorrow she'd drive over the Henry Hudson Memorial Bridge, under the GWB she had crossed so many times in past years. Down the West Side Highway, exit at 79th Street, into the hospital garage and hope for a spot. What would her thirteen year old do day after day, alone, with nobody to call by name?

Daniel was unpacking boxes in his small room—the dining area of the L-shaped living room—with its large window opening onto the terrace.

"I'm afraid you'll be bored," Nora said.

"Would'ya?"

"No. But I'd—"

"What?"

"Wouldn't catch me staying at home all summer," she said as Daniel nodded in disbelief. "I don't remember ever being bored in my life. Maybe it'd be fun to have the chance for once."

"I'll tell you all about it," Daniel said smartly.

She almost uttered the four-letter dirty word: camp. Her promise to Daniel not to ever mention it forced her to silence. The first postcards came from Sonya. Her elation was universal. The bunk, the counselors, the bed-wetter seven year old campers included, were all delightful. Nora read it ostentatiously loud. Daniel just as ostentatiously replied, "I knew she was weird."

No more than two weeks of arduous work and pretended cool confidence had passed. One morning, as soon as Nora set her Styrofoam cup of coffee before the viewer, she was paged to the Chair's office. She was known to call one or another radiologist for a consultation to her office. Nora shrugged off the idea. She couldn't have possibly achieved that status yet.

"Nora," Doctor Helen Smythe motioned to the leather bench she was already seated on. "Have you heard? Jeff had an accident."

"Oh, no. Is he bad?" Nora exclaimed truly concerned for her cross-sectional imaging colleague, a jovial person, and the only one present in that division, for Andy, the other one, was on vacation.

"Not in any danger. An uncomplicated pelvic fracture."

"What happened?"

"Believe it or not he was hit by a car in the supermarket parking lot. How prosaic. A water skiing accident would have suited him so much better." She raised a hand to magnanimously urging Nora not to respond to her cynical remark, a hallmark that didn't earn her much popularity. "Unfortunately, we have no fellow in body imaging. The senior resident is okay, but as the year had just started he's tied up with the novices. We can't afford any July catastrophes. It was my understanding that you came with a good all around training. I trust one can be well trained without a fellowship. You must have realized that was my philosophy when you came for the interview."

Deep breath, swallow her scruples, grab the opportunity. *Now or never.* "Helen, thank you for your faith in me. I trust I'll have no problems filling in." Nora could hardly contain her excitement. She couldn't let this chance go by.

Thinking of the renewed need to bury herself in textbooks, Nora told Daniel at dinner, "I know how you must have felt when I was going off the walls, neurotic, probably a little selfish, while preparing for the boards."

"I bet you don't," he said harshly.

The riposte caught Nora unprepared. She intended to express what she thought was mutual. Now it took great discipline not to run into her bedroom to cry. She swallowed hard. "I'm sorry, I wish I could have been a better mother."

"Forget it. Don't cry over spilled milk." He got up and stood by the window. "Mom, I need a hair cut."

Nora was jolted out of her first shock. Her boy was otherwise preoccupied. He outgrew his page look. If not in the width of his shoulders then in height. The Donny Osmond-as-idol period was over. His increasing need of privacy erased the moments when mother could observe the additions of time to her son's body. She was sure the pageboy hair style Daniel used to like and comb in front of the mirror—just about the only self-grooming he was doing spontaneously or otherwise—was not in accord any longer with his perception of himself.

Observing the visible signs of puberty filled Nora with a different satisfaction than when Sonya came of age. She remembered laughing when Sonya wrote from camp one of the past summers: I think I'm growing hair in my armpit. A daughter's puberty was something less enigmatic. A rerun. Nora was glad to think, that in Sonya's case with better results than her mother. Sonya grew into a young woman, beautiful and pleased with her own looks, without making a sport of admiring herself. Nora, without knowing, tried to compare the entire process—both internal and external manifestations—to Daniel. Correlate. Not finding much—if any—parallel, she was confounded, left behind by Daniel's aloofness. It came as his changing colors came, his skin tanned, his hair bleached in the poolside sun, his grey eyes lingered for longer and longer periods over the Palisades and the great bridge over the unruffled river carrying cruise and tug boats. His voice was most of the time grave. Nora would join him after work at the pool and find him more and more idle as the summer went by.

His unsettling melancholy gave way to bursts of anger, so hurting to the mother who expected more grown-up behavior from a son of Daniel's intelligence. She was scared. Was it the loss of the big brother back in Lewisville? How helpful the Trenton based branch had been. Should she call the local Big Brothers and Sisters of America? She hated to pass Daniel from hand to hand.

She called Daniel's big brother in New Jersey on Monday morning from the hospital. "John, please keep this conversation confidential."

"Anything wrong?"

"I hope not. It's only my ignorance about male puberty. I'm afraid Daniel's moods are going down the deep end."

"Oh, don't say that. He's such a smart and funny chap."

"Not around me. Not any more. The couple of months you haven't seen him . . . I think you'd be surprised. Not only in a positive way."

"What's he doing these days?"

"Not much. He's catching up with reading literature, he's helping me a lot fixing up the apartment. We're painting it all by ourselves. Window frames included. He even likes it and is good at it. Also, he spends a lot of time at the pool. I don't know whether that company is good for him. He's the youngest amongst 17–18 year olds and he dropped hints. He's not included. I'm afraid they are oversexed youth, condescending and rude to him. By the way, he was just thirteen. He had his Bar Mitzvah back in Lewisville. It went very well. I got him a small TV for his room. We took him out for dinner. Not exactly what a growing boy needs."

"You know what? My wife is going to visit her folks next weekend, I was to go but she'll understand. She likes Dani."

"John, you can't imagine how much I appreciate this." Nora was touched to tears.

"I'll pick him up. Can he stay for the whole weekend? We'll go hiking in the Poconos."

Nora was not sure how she felt about not seeing Martin for weeks, only that she was not burning with desire to fly into his arms. She felt no need to get physical. In its suppressed perception, her flesh refused to be awakened by anything less than an irresistible lust. *I'm such a snob,* she thought when she refused Martin's offer to pick her up. Her apartment was not presentable yet. She wouldn't have visitors. She needed the rug removed, she needed the paint job finished, she needed accents. She needed money.

She had no problem finding the Ginger Man on 64th street.

Martin stood in front of the restaurant dressed in a blue blazer, light slacks, crisp shirt and well-coordinated tie in a pink-beige geometrical pattern. Impeccable. His cheerful gaze framed by a new tan enhanced his silver temples and slightly raised wavy light hair. Almost a *pompadour.* He tilted his head and handed Nora a white rose.

"Thank you." She kissed him on the cheek.

She stepped ahead of him into the packed bar under the high pressed tin ceiling. Narrow steps in the corner carried running waiters up and down. "Interesting room," she remarked.

"It used to be the entrance of this building," Martin explained.

"And now the residents fly in by helicopter?"

"As a matter of fact I saw them scaling the facade."

In high spirits they sat at the small table in the loft as if suspended under the ceiling. The whole menu, the crunchy salad, the Veal Oscar with a perfect creamy sauce, fruit tarts and coffee, though perfect, was marginal to her feeling of well-being. She wished they didn't have to get up and go. She said so on the way to the concert. Martin put his arm around her shoulder and squeezed ever so lightly saying "Same here." She let her body mold to his side.

The post-modern setting of Avery-Fisher hall, a decorous venue to *Mostly Mozart* and its eclectic musical selections, seemed right for interlocked fingers on Nora's bare knee and a stimulant to shifting her mood to excited reverie.

All that uplifting mood plummeted, like a rock rolling down a mountain slope, right into an almost painful embarrassment. Her mistake felt pitiful beyond words when they found the garage she had pulled into that afternoon locked. Gently, but firmly, Martin convinced Nora that the idea of a taxi to Riverdale was silly when his car was less than twenty blocks away. An almost cheerful coziness set in as they walked to Riverside Drive. On Palisade Avenue, in front of her new home, Nora acted on impulse. "My garage spot is empty." She gestured to the compact row of cars along the curbs. In the elevator Nora rambled on. "You'll have a chance to compare the before and after. We're working our magic with Daniel."

"Like what?"

"Like painting it head to toe, Daniel removing the awful old rug, etc." With great pride Nora passed the paint cans stacked on a tarp next to the kitchen door. "This is the dining area, you could tell, right?"

"I'm glad that we had dinner if that's what you would've served."

They stood on the balcony holding drinks, looking at the garland of the great bridge's lights spanning the dark river. Their glasses clinked like a shy cue on the small cast iron table. Nora took Martin's hand and moved an arm around his neck. He kissed her, she responded. Now she knew she did.

"Marty, we don't have to play teenagers-under-a-gateway." Nora felt pleasantly dizzy.

"Any suggestion?"

"My bedroom?"

Nora found an approving mirror as Martin's eyes reflected a desired woman as she walked in from the bathroom wearing her only decent robe. Sexy was not on her mind when she had the practical, garish piece made years back. Aware of the flaw, she dropped it to the floor. They scrutinized each other as if they were texts to memorize. He stopped stripping.

"You look fabulous undressed," he said putting his hands around her waist.

"You don't approve of my dressing style?" She teased.

"There's a good time for everything," he said pulling her closer.

Her hands slid down his sides gently pushing down his white cotton briefs. He stepped out of them. She put her hands in his hair and let her skin enjoy the caress of his hands that were full of life.

She dropped the conversation in the pile with the clothes, too busy measuring up what she was getting into. Her mood sprung up too.

It was time to put an end to her celibacy. Dating service, which she had tried once, didn't work for her. She'd canceled after a few phone calls; once she was accused of cowardice for not grabbing the opportunity to get married, without seeing—or wanting to ever see for that matter—the promising scientist looking for a sucker with money, or at least prospects of it. Another caller, less crazed, with quite a glamorous voice, took her to the Metropolitan Opera for the first date. For the second, he took her to a Mexican restaurant and into bed with a heartburn, a suggestion of sex and a night-long snoring that cured her of meeting men for years.

Now the absence of burning hunger did not feel like a compromise, the playful mood seemed to come naturally to both. Martin's less than athletic, but well proportioned lean build made a lively playmate in a light sexual game. Nora wondered just for a passing instant, then she realized, it was better for the moment than anything she could've thought of.

What had been outlandish and embarrassing the night before, was now charming, even hilarious, short of the parking fee.

Nora welcomed Martin's invitation. From the turn of the century foyer with marble columns, they took the paneled unmanned elevator to the top floor. His door opened onto a smell of books that dominated the narrow room more than the dark mahogany desk or the Eames lounge chair or even the floor-to-ceiling bookcase itself. It was not as if she'd never seen a private library of this size, but she felt overwhelmed by what she might have omitted in measuring up Martin. From the window, she contemplated the leafy old crowns of Riverside Park.

The day was pleasantly warm. They went down to the park and settled on a bench in the shade.

"You said you'd tell me about your board exam one day," Martin opened the conversation.

"You want an account of this phenomenon called oral boards? Radiology residents tremble in fear and lose sleep over it for years. It's held once a year in Louisville Kentucky. A month after the derby."

"Any relation?"

"Both are races," she said. "Ours brings business after the horses are gone, I guess."

"You're on track," he said, bathing in Nora acknowledging his pun.

"Courtesy of Piedmont Airlines I found myself in front of the terminal looking for a bus to the Essex across from the airport. A case of you-can't-get-there-from-here. I lined up among good-looking young men, strangely enough, all soldiers. Some young women were in line too holding babies, small children clinging to their mothers' skirts. A soldier politely inquired. `Mam, you heading to Fort Knox?' That took care of my attempt to take a look at the country's gold deposit." It was her turn enjoying Martin laughing at her joke.

They walked under the trees.

With a luxury of details, she told the story of that unforgettable day; about the malice of some and the joviality of other examiners; she described the incredible mental effort required to sustain the rate and efficiency of one's thinking, and of the delivery of the observations along the ten half hour sessions.

"You like to talk about this. The result must have been favorable."

"Naturally it isn't fair to see the entire exercise as exhilarating through the *retro-spectoscope* of having passed it."

8

"Daniel, do your room already," Nora yelled as she wrapped in foil the tray piled with cold cuts, sliced peppers, cherry tomatoes and cubes of cheddar. She spun around, grabbed a large Coke from the storage closet, spun again and put it in the fridge. With yet another twirl she answered the door as Daniel was now doing his room.

"Mom, we're here," Sonya stepped in. She stood tanned, tall and straight as a pine as if the knapsack the size of an armchair was not on her back. She hugged her mother and stepped aside. Her long pony tail swayed. An endless Indian file entered the apartment. Nora searched in her mind for an amendment of the term *a couple* that Sonya had used when she mentioned bringing her five British friends home.

The question *How long* didn't seem polite, so she didn't ask. Daniel's displeasure burst through the thin layer of inhibition inherent to his age. "Where're they gonna sleep?"

"I'm sure you'll offer your room—"

"What's in it for me?" Daniel interrupted his sister, putting on a cocky pose.

"I'll take care of this." Nora wanted no international showdown.

Following endless thanks for the late evening snack in a Liverpoolese that left Nora in need of a translator, Daniel moved out of his room loaded with the bundle of his bed linen. He threw it on the floor in Nora's bedroom, with only a reasonable amount of opposition.

Friday, after work, they took to the road. The car rolled in the late summer sunshine amidst scattered flower trimmed villages, stolid correctional facilities packaged in spirals of barbed wires, dusty industrial towns, sprawling shopping malls, cheerful arrows pointing out touristic attractions. Pennsylvania. The euphoria of promises picked up the rhythm of the running tires on the concrete slabs.

The central lawn of Penn State campus was a colorful tapestry dotted with people saying goodbye, the student center, the HUB, a beating heart, the right angles of orderly streets and modern buildings, a still life of aspirations. A tearful Sonya appeared to be the embodiment of a scared little girl she certainly was not.

"Am I being punished or what?" Daniel yelled as a tired Nora stepped into the apartment, home from work. There was no hello to answer his mother; his knapsack lay thrown on the kitchen floor. He yanked the refrigerator door open, snatched a bottle of soda and drank.

"I hate when you do that," she said. The Coke splashed from the open bottle as Daniel slammed it on the counter. "What's the matter now?" she raised her voice.

"What's the matter? This school . . . this kindergarten . . . full of morons—"

"Who?" Nora knew in her heart both that her attempt at diversion was futile and that Daniel didn't belong to Junior PS 41, the neighborhood school *cum* daycare center, but she failed to prevail over the city bureaucracy to obtain an exemption for Daniel.

"Who? Everybody. There's not one person I can talk to—"

"Could you be more specific?"

Yes, he could, and spared no words in doing so. He showed Nora his class work. It looked awfully familiar from the previous year. "Dani, what do you expect after your college course at Drew?"

"So? What am I supposed to do for one whole fucking year—"

"Daniel, watch your tongue!" Nora was louder than she liked.

Daniel rephrased. "Wasting a whole year."

"Don't look at it that way," she said and probed her son's expression. Seeing only protest in his frown, she went on. "We could forge a report card, run to the Bronx High School of Science, tell the principal that we'd forgotten that you already went through eighth grade when we showed him your college credit from Drew—"

"Yeah, all you can do's make fun. *You* try it . . . babies bawling at the end of the hall—" Daniel was shouting by then.

"And you go to do my work, read films, teach the residents, consult, dictate and sign reports, hah?" Her voice was argumentative, while his eyes opened wide at being confronted with his own weapon. "Deal? I'll go back to school—" She held out a hand.

Daniel turned his back. "Yeah, sure," he mumbled as he dragged his knapsack into his room.

Life smoothed out like a river beyond rocky narrows. Mother and children followed separate currents under the placid surface. Daniel was loftily satisfied with the complex challenges of the Bronx HS of Science; Sonya radiated a liberated, reassured confidence in her new college student status. Nora was suspended between the pleasant spins in the eddy of intimacy with Martin and the main stream of her new professional life.

She started to refer to her relationship with Martin as *chronic intermittent.* Sonya, when it came to medical terminology, proved herself a chronic ignoramus. Frustrated, Nora couldn't find her own joke funny and explained, "As in receding and recurring symptoms or their treatment."

"What do you want to do about it?" Sonya asked.

Nora took a deep breath. "Okay. Is it satisfactory enough to leave it as it is, or does it offer grounds for working it into something more substantial, or . . ." she scratched her head, ". . . maybe it has no potential."

"For marriage?" Sonya asked.

"For long term commitment, call it marriage if you must."

"You know what I call it?" Sonya waited for Nora to guess then continued. "You're too sober. Do you really like him."

"The problem is that in my experience—"

"Don't brag, you have no idea what experience requires."

"Sonya," Nora revolted. "I hope neither do you."

"It's not about me. You could be classified a greenhorn—"

"You're not helping—"

"I'm trying."

Nothing could have filled Nora better with a sense of an achieved balance, a soothing family idyll, than the scene she was a part of that Sunday morning. The three of them sitting in the sunlit kitchen overlooking the changing fall colors of the Palisades was as good an illustration for all struggles conquered as anything else. A movie scene. Cut!

The affable conversation, was over. She expected Daniel to know better than to storm out before finishing the last mouthful of French toast. Meaningful topics, or commonplace, she didn't really care, as long as both men—Daniel trying to define himself, Martin trying to find a private life he supposed had the potential of making him happy—looked like they were enjoying each other's company. They enjoyed absurd subjects like: anti-matter in Garrison Keilor's humor, or melting of the polar ice cap and the space gained for water sports. Nora would gladly stay out and not spoil a budding rapport she saw as the key to her own dilemma about Martin. And now Daniel had to run in the middle of Martin's sentence. To play chess.

Nora saw herself as an open book for her children to read. A manual of how-tos as well as how-not-tos. How did her children perceive her? Did her children worry about how they were perceived? Or Martin? She felt as if her fair mood was flushed down the toilet. Like sometimes in the company of Martin's friends whom she found aloof, Nora felt that Martin regarded her as an accessory he could take or leave. The doubt that she would ever be accepted came upon her once in a while like a bad heartburn. Her doubts included Martin and what they were sharing. Commonplaces, caresses, well groomed smiles, a penchant for classical music and faraway places. Yes. He was there in her bed, getting amazingly better, with willingness and eagerness to follow her in blending their needs and desires. Distrust didn't bother her in that little square space. She refused to admit jealousy of a double life that he didn't hint at, but she couldn't stop suspecting.

It was not the intensity of their romance, it was not the erotic passion despite the almost instinctive working out of rough edges. It was the spicy mix of an undeniable sexual compatibility and intellectual kinship. A balanced recipe. *THE* balance? How would she know? Never been there. *When* then, if not in her fifth decade?

Onions sauteing, veal roasting, pudding steaming didn't claim Nora's undivided attention. Plenty left for day dreaming. Reality burst in when the phone rang.

"I got back this afternoon." Sweeter than she knew it, Martin's voice came as if refuting all the questions churning in the grinder of her mind. "Nori?"

"Yes?" She was puzzled. He had never used her nickname before.

As if explaining, he went on. "I did a great job, if I may say so myself . . . Would you forgive me if I were just a few minutes late for dinner?"

"That will make the timing perfect . . ."

As if the wind suddenly changed direction, suspicions—like dried leaves of a past season, until then stubbornly pasted against her by a chilly draft—were picked up and swept away by a new warm breeze. After two years of dating—she would rather say spending time together, for not having grown up with the term dating it had no other meaning to Nora than marking down occasions on a calendar—and a brief list of occasions when Martin had honored her with a flower or a similar token of attention, the dozen creamy white jumbo rosebuds he presented to her rendered Nora speechless.

"But Martin." She hugged the bouquet, almost forgetting she owed a kiss in exchange. "Wow. Am I glad I made a festive stuffed veal roast instead of ordering pizza."

Martin turned to Daniel emerging from his room. "Hello partner."

"Hello buddy," Daniel said with teenage theatricals. He looked at the roses Nora was arranging in a tall cobalt vase. "Why does that look like a bridal bouquet?" he asked.

Martin stepped behind Nora and cupped her shoulders in his hands. "Your son is very observant." He kissed the back of her head. "Could you see me as a groom?"

The topic of a legalized mutual commitment, had not yet entered their agenda. Now, what was this charade? What was Daniel doing? Marrying off his mother?

She turned to Martin. "Is this a rhetorical question?"

"Only in the best sense, as in *significant*," Martin remained serious.

"Well, just to avoid any misunderstanding, could you rephrase it?"

"Would you marry me Doctor Nora Mann?"

"Wait a minute," Daniel interfered. Actually he came between them, holding them apart with stretched arms. "Before you say something irrevocable, Mom." He looked provocatively from one to the other. "Mister Martin Ferber, are you aware that I come with the turf?"

That *was* rhetoric. Nothing was significant enough for Daniel to miss the opportunity of a prank. Especially verbal. Daniel looked pleased as the other two laughed.

Right after dinner, Daniel left for his usual alternate Friday Dungeons & Dragons game that lasted half the night in some Fieldstone home's basement. Martin sat sideways at the kitchen table, brandy glass in hand, watching Nora clean up. His job was done, he had rinsed the dishes and placed them in the dishwasher while Nora put away the leftovers.

Settled at the opposite ends of the couch, she pulled up her bent right leg and dangled her left leg over her right ankle. She held the short stem of her glass with cherry liquor between thumb and index finger, resting it on her knee. He looked relaxed, as if freed from a wrapping too tight, his legs crossed, his left arm over the soft back of the couch, the right holding his glass in midair as if posing for a painter.

"I was not avoiding an answer," Nora declared holding out her right hand, palm up. Martin let his hand slide off the back of the couch and rested it in Nora's. "You know me well enough by now. It won't surprise you that I will discuss your proposal with my children. You heard what Daniel said. He's talking from a high saddle."

"Meaning that a yes has to be endorsed?"

"That's right. It's a promise I'll keep."

Martin uncrossed his legs and slid closer on the slick leather. They put the glasses on the coffee table. A kiss sealed the dialogue and brought the romance back where it belonged. Then, he took his empty glass and refilled it at the small bar in the wall unit.

"I want you to know . . . the part of my work that called for all that travel . . . I've restructured it . . ." Nora found his hesitation uncharacteristic. ". . . so . . . it's less travel starting right away."

Nora was indulging her eyes on her two beautiful children. Their grey eyes gained intensity with maturity, light brown wavy hair framed their light complexion. One feminine, thin and round at the same time, one masculine with broad bony shoulders emerging at a rate of a size per month, it seemed, judging by the pile of clothes saved for charity. She took a deep breath.

"We went through much together, we can't ignore each other's opinions. This is about Martin."

"If I wouldn't like Marty would you still marry him?" Daniel took another chestnut-rum-ball from the little dish. Nora had made them as a token of welcome home. "Hum. Thank you Sonya for coming home," he added, talking with a full mouth.

"I'd concede to a serious objection . . ." she paused searching her children's faces. No expressions of worry. Both munched with angelic smiles of satisfaction. ". . . well substantiated." There was seriousness in their nodding. "It never came this close."

"Never?" "Sonya's stressed the question.

"Well," Nora suddenly found herself in the middle of the rushing stream of memories pushing through the floodgate Sonya had raised. She stayed afloat. "Not since you grew up and I can have your opinion."

"How much do *you* love him on a scale of ten being the top?" Sonya asked.

"This is not fair because . . ." Nora couldn't believe Sonya's cold blood. Her daughter, very young at the time when she was fighting her emotional battle, knew exactly what she was talking about. To quantify her affection for Marty? It had taken plenty to qualify it. She had gone through that scale, tested it from top to bottom and she was now very comfortable and safe in a high mid-scale. ". . . enough to wish to spend the rest of my life with him, to be responsible for each other's happiness—"

"I pity him. You'll drown him in your care—"

Nora didn't let Daniel finish. "That should be men's worst cross to bear that women take too much care of them. Your recommendation is TLC with measure?"

"Whatever," Daniel had a tic of impatience.

"Are you interested in each other's work?" Sonya asked.

"We don't analyze each other's workday, if that's what you mean, but certainly we are."

Sonya hesitated for a moment, then went on with her investigation, "How's sex?"

"You women are disgusting." Daniel got up and started to gesture angrily as if stirring the air in the room. "She's getting married so she won't have to go to the door when the burglars come to ask who the hell is trying to break in." The women turned their eyes to the ceiling.

"All right, point well taken little brother, but sex doesn't make anyone disgusting." Sonya's gesture suggested that his comment had been answered. "Let me put it this way. Is Martin like Tibor was?" Sonya continued her interrogation with eyes fixed on Nora.

Nora was wondering what her daughter *really* knew or thought. "I doubt whether he can fix a car," she said.

"I'll take that for a no. Is that good or bad?" Sonya carried on.

"What are you two talking about?" Daniel sounded irritated as always when at a loss.

"Mama's boyfriend in Romania. Before we left."

"How old was I?" Now it was a what-d'-ya expect face.

"How old? It was, what, nine years ago? Right Mama?"

"Right."

"I don't remember," Daniel said plainly and Sonya put him into his place with a curt gesture.

Nora pleaded, "I need to know—"

"All right," Daniel said. "Here you go. I think he is smart, I enjoy his company when he puts on his funny hat, I wish it was more often. I gave up teaching him chess, I have to give him credit though for trying to get into my good books, I also have to admit he tried harder than I ever did. Or will. He even took to potatoes. That's to your credit, mama."

Nora was listening with fallen jaw. Nothing escaped her boy. "Thank you. Is this an endorsement?"

Daniel nodded.

"It seems I'm missing a lot of fun around here."

"I wouldn't go that far," Daniel corrected Sonya. Nora looked now at Sonya.

"How many times did I meet him? Eight? Tops ten? I'd hate to see you unhappy, that's why all the questions." She put on a cute grimace of compassion, then perked up asking, "Where will I sleep when I come visit?"

"All right, let's vote," Daniel said. "I move that Mama marries Martin. Second?"

Excitement of planning, designing, creating, arranging was always food and drink to Nora's hands and mind. Life-giving milk and honey. Now she could bathe in it. Plan and dream all she wanted. She dreamed of a loft. A shell of walls, the more air between them the better. That was not Martin's choice. Rather than dealing with an architect, remodeling, building, he would sleep under a bridge on an old car seat, he had said.

"You haven't done anything to help the old lady reach Elysium, have you?" Nora was pulling Martin's leg as they rang the bell to meet Martin's deceased next door neighbor's rich heir.

"We didn't give each other a hard time. She was the sweetest thing you can imagine. And allow me to say, you needn't express condolences, we've gone through that."

"Hello, Bob," Martin responded to the greeting as the distinguished middle age man, a head taller than himself, motioned them in. Bob Karp patted Martin's shoulder while holding out and shaking Nora's hand. "Pleased to meet you Doctor Mann."

"Nora," she said with inviting emphasis. "My pleasure." Easy guy, she thought. Probably a tough bargaining partner. The apartment, which Nora expected to look like Miss Havisham's, was to supply a series of shocks in automatic rifle style. She realized that Martin held back all information and now it was obvious he had been pulling her leg in ultimate irony.

She tried her best to see past the museum-like collection of paintings and wall hangings—she itched to ask whether they were originals. Was that a Mary Cassat? And all those moderns! She must have lingered, she heard Bob answering her unasked questions by addressing Martin, "I don't want to move anything before Sotheby's comes to take a look. One can't present these works better than Mom managed to with her impeccable taste."

"She was certainly unique," Marty confirmed.

Nora tried to look behind the mesmerizing sight to see the bare walls; and the mahogany parquet with inlayed medallions of light essence wood; and the oak moldings around the dining room ceiling; and the black and white checkered tile in the kitchen. An endless array of old time quality. A wide spiral staircase rose from the floor oddly placed in one corner of the entrance hall. Suddenly Nora understood the reason, just as Bob Karp was pointing to the wall behind the steps. "This is the divider—" Bob must have noticed Nora's questioning look directed to Martin and that made him shift his eyes between the two in disbelief that Nora was ignorant of this detail, then went ahead, "—it was put up when Dad passed on. We, the children, were out of the house by then. I kept calling the apartment *house* all my life, you can see why, if you add Marty's part and another one on the other side of this portion that Mom kept for herself—"

"I see," Nora regained her composure. "They did a great job with the division as far as one can tell." Her feelings were wavering about Martin leaving her in the dark, but then she looked at the pleasure of the surprise, which no doubt Martin reserved for her.

They all climbed the spiral staircase to a white door and stepped out on the roof terrace that covered the entire original luxury apartment. The view of Fort Lee beyond the river, the remote buzz of the Henry Hudson parkway below and the early spring breeze defied the invisible pollution. Despite the rotting trellises, broken flower pots lying like corpses on their side—someone had the well-meaning of saving them from cracking in the winter freeze—Nora envisioned the potential to own the hanging gardens of Semiramis, which inevitably led to a more realistic thought. *I can't afford this. No broker fee. Big deal. That would lower the price by six percent. It's the ninety-four percent I'm worried about.* She was not versed in financial dealings. To be sure, she was quite handicapped.

"I'm glad you appreciate the wholeness of the apartment. This section is very spacious even though it consists of practically only one bedroom," Karp said.

They were sitting in Art Deco armchairs in front of the cold fireplace. Bob wheeled over the liqueur trolley. Nora could barely hold a smile behind twitching lips. *Nine years ago I stepped onto the soil of this city as a pauper with money counted in the negative. Three years ago I spent all my poor dead mother's savings and the little I could scrape together from my pay-roll-to-pay-roll living on an apartment suited to my means. And now I have the audacity to listen, to pretend, that I'm interested in buying this apartment?* Nora was not aware how much Karp knew about Martin's and her private financial arrangements.

"It all comes down to this. In the name of all these years, as if having a brother living next to mother . . . you have to know Nora that sometimes I couldn't escape being jealous of Martin . . . she adored him . . . this is the offer, Nora. For a sum of two hundred thousand dollars I would like you to have my mother's apartment. It would please me a great deal."

Nora could scream. Karp ruled out any debasing bargaining. It was almost condescending, but Nora could take such offense. The Sunday before, she had leafed through the New York Times and got an idea of prices. Without suspended gardens. Next year Bob would contribute a few hundred thousand less to his philanthropies. His offer could be qualified as one. He certainly did his good deed for the day, no, for the year, she thought, *I must have done something right in my life after all, for that matter it appears that Martin did.*

Karp was apparently enjoying the sight of his interlocutors deadpan faces. What was he asking the money for? The roof terrace?

Every morning on waking Nora had to think before moving a limb. Moving first she would have to struggle harder to remember the objectives she had set for herself the evening before. An unexplained aversion kept her from making check lists, as if writing down things, the paper would outweigh her own worth. How many points were on her imaginary list last night? Who were the people she had to talk to, where exactly did she need to show up? Work at that point, she had to admit, lost its appeal; it faded behind trivialities like apartments to be sold and purchased, preparing herself physically and spiritually to give up her singlehood. She never held onto it deliberately. Or chosen it as the particular state of being that suited her best. Was it her lot for so long because of her ability to manage? Proud of it? Maybe. Not without rebellion. Now it was again up to her abilities to change the *status quo.*

Her head clear by the time she got out of the shower, after the three minutes of hair drying and five seconds worth of make up, Nora was ready to go. She passed a half asleep Daniel staggering into the bathroom, took the elevator with neighbors she didn't know or wish to. She pulled out of the garage, and continued tidying up her thoughts while driving down the busy West Side Highway. Now that she reconstituted the seven items—she knew all along they had to be seven—she felt ready for the day.

"The deal on my apartment fell through." The deal on the Karp apartment was almost a *fait accompli.* Her sale gave her major headaches. A hint leaked to Bob that she was facing a major financial problem with the bargain he had offered her would have shattered her ego. Not selling the apartment shattered her bank account. Never did a money problem get so close to affecting her self-confidence. Not when she had none. Now it looked as if she wouldn't be able to keep Martin out of it. She felt embarrassed, then discarded the idea as an aberration. She recently got a handle on the quandary raised by the clauses of the prenuptial that Martin insisted on. It sounded so pompous to her, as long as she couldn't see in her future an excess of wealth anyone could've squabbled over. But then, Martin had outlined his view that favored a legal paper.

He had argued, "Our incomes will always be very different. Yours is predictable, mine is predictably lower and only on one occasion possibly higher. I mean if I manage to write a good book. It's not a basis for a life style. On the other hand you shouldn't be responsible for another person's future, that means I have to have my own provisions for an unmentionable and possibly hideous state. Remember statistics, and that doesn't even take in consideration that I am twelve years older."

"But Martin—"

"You're the doctor, I don't have to tell you."

"Well, in a way, true, you shouldn't be responsible *either* for my children's expenses."

"Now we're talking," he said calmly. There was not much room for ad-libbed solutions, there was no place for the amount of trust she had in her sense of fairness or devotion. She started to understand a social system that created little precedent. Was this kind of knowledge part of growing up in America? She was not jubilant. This phase of the marital arrangements fit as well with emotion or passion as onions with cappucino. True, difficult to imagine life without either.

"Apropos," she had said. "We'll go to the store, I'll pay for six eggs and you pay for the rest of the dozen?"

"Something like that," he conceded laughing. "I suggest that we keep a household account where we both deposit amounts matching the smaller of our incomes for the period. In my dry months my bank account will oblige," he added.

"And she who cooks doesn't wash dishes?" Nora asked.

"We'll be the most over-qualified dishwashers," Daniel had chimed in.

"How embarrassing, besides being unfair to your mother. Let me know when you feel like scrambled eggs for dinner, you won't regret, I promise," Martin said.

"Well, well. This exceeds any bride's dreams," she had said.

Now Nora and Martin agreed that, "The loan is a loan," as she concluded.

Never had moving been so much fun. Moving had never carried the connotation of arriving, not even when she unpacked for the first time on the American continent. Now the unpacked boxes failed to be the unsettling and ominous sign of fleeting hopes. The echoes of the rooms waiting to be filled with body heat and new furniture sounded like a silvery ring of carefree settling.

It was such a moment when Daniel raised a critical issue. "We're gonna go nuts. We'll need either a traffic center reminding where is whose and which room, a map or traffic signs—"

"Common son, you must be in shock. All this luxury went to your head. The apartment isn't that huge," Martin observed.

"Okay, what do you suggest, Dani?" Nora played his game suspecting he was in one of his naming moods.

"Thank you. I've been thinking. Martin's quarters are to the North—"

"That's good—"

"Just wait. It's too obvious. Mama's is to the South—"

"And yours is in the middle. How about Divider?"

"You have no imagination, man," Daniel argued.

After rounds of suggestions Daniel's idea was accepted as the most time saving for the words' brevity: Tops for Martin's and Bottoms for Nora's. Daniel's room, the formal and former dining room was to be *Donjon,* French accent and all. For reasons not completely obscure. A keep accessible only by special permit, including the cleaning lady.

9

I stalk an elegant Woman, who might be Marion, though more beautiful, follow spellbound by the Barbie doll legs and swaying hips. Aroused. Woman has an egg for head. No face. We cut through the bustle of an outdoor market. A frenzied mob ambushes us with wilted vegetables. I and Woman pick grey shapeless big leafed produce from the loaded tables. We don't ask or pay. We drag the large sheaf up wooden steps creaking under our feet to an ominous raw timber door. It opens into a luxurious living space we came to buy. A young woman dressed in a transparent frock is on her way out to do the sidewalks. In passing she tells me about workmen expected to fix the place. I listen but pay attention only to the male standing in the doorway. I am astonished by the sight of him. Alone and not alone. A raucous crowd pushes its way in from behind him, advancing forcibly, but without hostility, through a barrier of silence they force their way through. The co-owner of the place is amongst them. They keep coming and filling the space like liquid, leaving no air to breathe, they cling to my skin. Awash like a jellyfish in the tide under an old world rusty hospital bed, I have sex while in the midst of the hellish noise a policeman appears in the open door. He compassionately holds my arm, standing in the frame of the door, but I am under the bed. He asks, without uttering a word, whether I need help. I am a mute. With my free hand, I point to the crowd. He doesn't see it, or me, or me having a tremendous orgasm. I am at the door looking after the policeman descending a grand marble staircase. Resigned, I start to grab people one by one and throw them down the stairs, the wooden one that I had come up on. My arms thrash in the air.

Alone, full of fear, my skin crawls, my stomach heaves, my knees buckle. I look around for hiding people. Shadows fill corners, they mix with my fear like curdled mayonnaise as soon as I set eyes on them. I push the front door to the wall in utter anger. I go weak at the feel of hitting soft flesh. My hands press against the door, but all my strength cannot keep the door from forcing its way back, slowly, pushing and tipping me over. With a great power, not my own, I hold the door, also the wrists and the ankles of an immense male, though I am half of the size I really think I am. My knee is on his neck suffocating him. I observe him turning blue, when sufficiently so I throw him down the stairs as if he was a rag doll. He tumbles, wedges between the bars of the banister in a grotesque position, limbs sticking into the air like bizarre dry tree branches. He looks dead. He IS dead. I know and feel nothing. A sexless human, the co-owner of the loft, comes back with numerous Vogue-magazine-type elegant company. They sprawl all over the large loft from where I had just come out with the dead man, but now it resembles a Brazilian shanty town shack, only larger and with an upstairs reaching into the cloudless sky. People unpack. Police come and take me away in handcuffs. I can hear the co-owner's sarcastic cackle. The crowd cheers. "She didn't know that the guy behind the door was already dead. I left him dead. Same method. We have her framed."

The handcuffs burn my wrists. I reach for a shape that looks like the Woman who was not there all that time I needed her. Touching her burns my palms and she evaporates.

Nora woke with an eerie guilt that didn't leave her all morning. After almost three years of knowing Martin, Nora wondered whether she was looking forward to meeting Edith, his older sister. The rehearsal for her little-sister role had surreptitiously begun, she thought, when the same afternoon they stepped into the lobby of the Pierre.

"I'm so glad you like the tie I bought you." The willowy woman defying any age, with a huge hairdo defying any style, unless it was meant to double as a peach soufflé for four, took Martin's face between her bejeweled hands. He hugged her as if his limbs were bound in a suit too tight to allow a full range of motion.

A stocky man with a wisp of colorless hair combed over the shining zenith of his head, proud in his green blazer and matching plaid slacks took Nora's hand between both his. "A great pleasure to finally meet you dear, we heard so many wonderful things about you, and your children, we'll see them soon I trust," he jabbered using every second of the short interval before Edith would take over for the evening.

"The pleasure is all mine." Nora had no idea how short-lived the amusing feeling would be, but withheld her usual comment that whatever the rumor about her was, it couldn't be true.

A purr of pleasantries accompanied the group to the table, to their seats and candle flame that answered every word blown across the table with a nervous flicker.

"You must get the best interior decorator, my dear. That's what I was doing around New Year, or was it Thanksgiving Marty? When you came with that dame. Oh, it doesn't matter, that must have been before your time Nora dear." She followed with a theatrical cackle. "You should come, now *you* could stay with us, you would like what a tasteful job . . . Oh, but everything at its time, thank heavens, you came along, my prayers for my little brother have been answered . . ."

The rest was lost in a sleety fall of words that Nora didn't hear. The freeze in Martin's voice as he suddenly called for the sommelier and ordered a bottle of champagne, "To celebrate the lovely family reunion," failed to nip anyone's feelings around the table. Edith and her husband were deaf to that kind of undertone, Nora too occupied with the effort to move her fallen chin against gravity and regain the outward composure evaporating with her every fluttering blink.

The pearly sound of the champagne being poured was the first proof that the physical world had not disappeared. By the time the hand of a robot lifted her glass, a toast was ready. The robot registered a three way toast, "To health and happiness," around the table. It was her turn, with a sneer posing for a smile, to spit out the toast she had prepared in haste, "To Mr. Ferber's double life and the humiliation of Doctor Mann." She opened her mouth and uttered her universal, "L'Chaim," took one sip of the champagne, and picked up her salad fork.

Central Park was filled with the shadows of its ominous reputation. The drive across it was too short for Nora to shuffle around her thoughts into a logical list. Thoughts that had accumulated during dinner, and now were pyro-engraved on her brain feeling like crumpled wax paper. She was not ready to face a baffled Martin and to tell him she didn't trust him any more.

It usually took Nora three days to get over a hurt that rendered her mute. Words gained a gluey quality and wouldn't leave her chest. With the glob stuck behind her sternum—like adherent purulent phlegm that one could attempt to get rid of only at the expense of a deeply painful cough—she couldn't see herself sailing in a daze of happiness, towards a marriage ceremony at the end of those three days. She had to do her own mental thrashing and come up with a solution. Sound and fast.

They walked out of the garage in silence. Martin gently put his arm around her shoulder; she did not feel its weight; it seemed as if he was testing for acceptance. She expected him to try to divert the course of her thoughts. What could he have said? Perhaps some acrimonious comment at his sister's inanity? Or, looking her straight in the face, he could have said, "Never again will I cheat on you." Was he still? He didn't say anything and her instincts said he had ended his double life. Nevertheless, Nora felt as if under the weight of past offenses she had lost a few inches of her not-so-impressive height.

She felt an unexplained pity seeing him walk to Tops but turned around to retire to her old bed lying amongst unpacked boxes like a lost raft on an ocean of broken wreckage in Bottoms. The sound of music braided with the beam of light glided into the foyer from under Daniel's closed door like a beguiling apparition.

Nora discarded the idea of a hasty decision. She lay with hands clutched under her head, trying to press her thoughts into the organized pattern of the lines of the vertical blinds through which she was peering into a void. *Why would I agonize over the past? Didn't I suspect that he was having a side affair? When did that stop? I believe in my instincts. The roses after last Thanksgiving! That's when he twisted me around his finger. For two years out of our two and a half? Martin's potential for lying and mine of being cheated on are apparently limitless.*

Startled, she sat up, planted her elbows on her drawn knees and buried her face in the hem of her silk gown. *How can I hope to have a complete relationship with an Ivy Leager who sometimes has to down-translate his English to my level because of a language barrier, damn it. His and my sense of humor sometimes pass each other like express trains. I probably cannot even screw decently in English. And if I may ask myself, why should I? Chicken paprikas doesn't need to be Americanized. And he likes it. That's a very lopsided view. I don't like everything he says or does either. Don't I feel sometimes, even after sex, as good as it gets between us, that . . . what? . . . With hair streaming across her face, eyes closed she welcomes the murmur of the surf, the smell of the salty air, the sun-heated skin tight over strong muscles under her fingers. They slide down and kneel in the sand, their arms encircle each other. The tide kisses their legs and engulfs them little by little in the wet churning sand. They roll and pour hot sand on each other's naked bodies, they run around, their laughs plunge ahead of them into the waves. They find each other's pleasure under the overhanging cliff . . .*

Nora lifted a defiant blind gaze to the dark ceiling and got off the bed. She shook her head like a dog shaking its wet fur. The vision from the past wouldn't go away. Back in the bathroom she brushed her teeth. Just to do something. A wave of rage rose as she looked at her own image foaming at the mouth. *Sweetheart fucking left and right, I can't be bothered now with the question of my naïveté or vulgarity, let's face it, when does jealousy come to anything else, even if jealous of your lover's past as you said once, all right Nora, don't get carried away, and why not? How about staying good neighbors? Don't even have to cancel the party. Make it a house warming. Just cancel the appointment with the Justice of the Peace.*

Carried in the eye of a hurricane, tossed between a bold urge to get the crisis over with and the throbbing lust of the past, she followed the beam of light from her bedroom through the dark hallway. She pushed the chrome button lightly. It clicked. The new folding door opened between her and Martin's living rooms. The desk light fell on a large addressed white envelope with a crenelated green margin. The door to his bedroom was open, the window shades were up. He was sleeping facing the room, purring and puffing, wearing only a pajama bottom. His healthy complexion looked dark in the dimness in contrast to his silver temples fading into the white pillow. She knelt on the small throw rug. She lightly put her palms against the hair on his chest. He stirred. "Nora?"

"Yes, dear. I came to tell you something important. I've—"

"What's the time?"

"Shush." Her whisper was harsh. Her arms, freed from her will, slid over his shoulders pushing him onto his back.

He attempted to move his arms evidently unsuspecting that conventional love making was not the one in Nora's mind.

"Fucking me on the side, hah?" She hissed into his ear.

"But Nora—"

"Nora who? Oh, *that* Nora? She wouldn't talk like this . . . Nor would she do things like this . . ." He put his hands around her waist to pull her onto him. She briskly stood up, fists on her hips. He was not part of her game. Not yet. "Wait and see when I do it with two of you, but not like you did. The same time . . . You are just one of them . . . wait for your turn . . . if you feel like . . ."

In the morning Nora turned around under Martin's arm and threw a leg over his hip. "This can't get any better. Do we need to get married?" she murmured. The statement was a departure from the idea that brought her to his room during the night, but then she didn't expect her feelings for Martin to soar.

"Yes. I want to make sure I can keep you. You made me feel like I never felt before."

"Why squander energy like this unless to prove a principle?" she teased him.

"That's what a really terrific screw does to one's principles."

"*Au contraire.* That's what principles do for a good screw."

WE
Nora Mann and Martin Ferber

request the honor of your presence
at the interactive ceremony / reception
on the occasion of changing our marital status

Please
arrive at exactly
or as close as you can come to
6 o'clock in the afternoon
on
Saturday, May the 27th, this year of 1983
at
175/B Riverside Drive
Manhattan
Take the elevator as far as it goes

Dress code
We'll enjoy your choice, but keep in mind
that we plan to re-inaugurate the roof terrace
No other function follows, no scheduled departure time
(sleeping bags not provided)

RSVP at (212) 549-1097 by May the 14th

Sonya burst in giving off an aura of nurturing cheerfulness. Like always, after not seeing her daughter for a long time, and now it was the longest yet, the mother was overwhelmed. A long hug would have quenched Nora's shivers of admiration and worry, but Sonya had no time. She needed to storm the apartment right away.

"Is this all yours?" the young woman asked with genuine awe as if the number of rooms and their square feet could tell tales of her mother's battles and achievements. She considered every nook and corner just as important and interesting as the next. She leaned her wasp-slim waist and craned her long neck when she pushed a door open with a gentle hand. Nora walked along to collect every drop of light from her daughter's admiring eyes.

"For a while. Until you'll have it," Nora feigned a blasé tone though she was bursting with the eagerness to tell Sonya again, with the proper illustration this time, what they had talked over not once on the phone.

"Do you have to talk about that?

"It's the normal course of events, unless you make me disinherit you and let Dani have it all."

"I'm working on it."

"Oh, dear, what are you up to now?

Sonya stood in the door of Nora's bedroom with a piece of clothing thrown over her arm. Her discerning look threatened to pour an unbridled opinion over the couple standing next to the dresser loaded with florist's boxes. Nora, looking shapely and slender in a short and tight beige satin dress, was pinning a crimson rose boutonniere onto Martin's off-white blazer lapel. To her relief Sonya said, "Very chic."

"What exactly is your notion of chic?" Martin asked. "I need to know whether my ego should be flattered or shattered."

"Classy?" She waited. "A handsome couple."

"Mama," Daniel shouted coming into the room. "I grew out these slacks." He stood legs thrown wide, looking at his ankles showing under the cuffs.

"My God," Nora turned and started to pluck at the silver grey slacks of the suit they had bought not long ago for the occasion. "Could you let out one notch of your belt?"

"I can drop them all together, then they won't be short."

"There's no time to fix them, Dani," she said. "It'll have to do. Don't worry, you look great."

"How about me?" Sonya came back in a few minutes all dressed. She held out her hands palm up, as there was no answer. "What?"

"You are so beautiful," Nora said with genuine admiration and hands clapped together.

"You really like it?" Sonya looked relieved. A person with less self-confidence might have considered the underscoring of her nature given femininity a little out of place at her mother's wedding. She merely looked wonderful in the tight white dress with scattered colorful geometrical accents—what else for an engineer?—and a deep cleavage.

"I'm proud to acquire such a family," Martin said, and embraced the three Manns tenderly.

Part IV

1

Nora and the children could no longer be seen that frigid November afternoon in 1974 when Tibor turned around and walked away from them in the Bucharest airport, an arm around Adel's slight, but strong shoulders. Self-conscious of his face ravished by tears, he had to do his best to comfort the old lady. *I should let her console me.* He doubted though that Adel would have any inclination to console an undesirable ex-lover of the only daughter she had just lost.

He was not looking forward to the half day they had to spend in the wet city. Fantasies of a life beside a woman who thought of everything—not-the-least sleeper tickets for their return—taunted him. What eluded him at the moment was reality.

The gasoline shortage decimated the cab fleets throughout the country, but Tibor did not expect it in the capital. He didn't expect a lot of the shortages that lay ahead. The lack of a cab was the least of them, but right then, it was the most annoying.

Blowing his breath into the cold air, he looked at the puff of mist that took on features too well known. He shook his head to chase the vision. He almost missed the one cab that pulled into the stand, unaware how long he had been contemplating Nora's dissipating image.

In the dark glassy evening, Tibor and Adel moved soundlessly, like cartoons emerging from the fog, across the dark-yellow tiles of the station platform slick with condensation. A whistle slit the damp air like a knife. Peering out above scarves pulled up against the penetrating cold, they found the sleeper car.

He returned later from the exploratory foray along the train and suggested a visit to the dining car. Adel had a way of staring meaningfully, building Tibor's guilt. *I've earned this expression of disapproval.* He fidgeted in his chair, waiting for his soup.

"How's school?" Her question didn't dismiss the tension but hit Tibor with another wave of guilt.

"With a little luck I'll graduate next spring." *What does she really know? Were my grand achievements no longer important enough for Nora to mention them?*

"Congratulations," she said.

"Thanks," he continued, lacking a better subject. "I've left the company since we met."

"Really?"

"Nora never mentioned it to you?" He followed his question with a noisy breath between his teeth, as if trying to suck his words back. He couldn't suppress the need to talk about the part of himself that now, carved away, hurt like an amputated limb.

"She mentioned that she's not seeing you." Her lips stopped twitching, apparently pleased to bring Nora back into the conversation on her own terms.

There was a ripping sensation right around his heart. "They've demoted me from the taxi to the bus shop which means much worse working conditions for half the money. That, after they've refused to give me the exemption from mandatory overtime, so I could go to school. One who can't put in overtime is not fit for the taxi shop. Real bastards."

"Why would they give you an exemption?"

"Because that's the rule to encourage workers to further their education. Some would even get a small stipend. Not me," Tibor said and stopped short of mentioning the resentment that both Nora and he felt at the time. "For a little less I chose to concentrate on my career. I quit. I work at the Balneology now, full time."

"The hospital?"

"Yeah. Training on the job." *I won't tell her that Nora got me in there.* "With a little luck, I guess I need a lot of that stuff," he chuckled, "I'll get a physical therapist's diploma. Provided I can cram the Physics and Anatomy in my stupid head."

They finally smiled at each other. *Maybe she doesn't hate me. What would that mean to me? An extension of Nora's love?*

He checked the weekly schedule. *Hydrotherapy. That's good. Alternating with the wards? I could skip that,* Tibor thought while he put on a clean white tank top. The uniform made him too hot and he started a popular trend by not compromising. In the steamy room—the largest of all treatment rooms, with the deep lower extremity tin vans and the smaller ones for the arms lined up around the walls and the three oval full-length wooden tubs in their half-open compartments—he wouldn't wear the required high neck white piqué jacket.

"Don't be taken aback," he told the first patient who walked in on the arm of a nurse. This bath will feel cold. It's only cool."

"I don't like that," the old lady said in a surly voice.

"You'll change your mind, especially that I have a surprise in store," Tibor said, leading her behind the screen to undress. "I hope you're wearing a bathing suit."

"Yes, they got me one."

"Good." Tibor checked the water temperature, it had to be 27°C and wrote the patient's name and diagnosis on the first line of the work sheet. "Ready? Good. Now, jump."

"What do you—"

"Just kiddin', but in ten days, you will. I promise," he winked at her.

"You're sweet. Ar'you gonna do all my treatments?"

"Nope."

"Pity," she said and put one foot in the tub.

"How is it?"

"Not bad."

He helped her set her neck in the rest, and put her hands around the holds inside the tub. He sat on the bench at the foot end of the tub. "Now, here's the surprise," he said. "Did you know this is a bubble bath?"

"You kidding again?"

"Why would I? Here you go." He turned on the compressed air that started to bubble all around the wrinkled body and swollen legs marked by the blue serpents of varices and red patches of suffering tissue.

"Wow, I'd lie here all day."

"You'll change your mind. In a few minutes I'll start warming up the water."

"You wanna cook me?"

"No," he said. "You tell me when it's getting hot. And don't worry I won't let it go over 40°."

"What does this do?"

"It's called an ascending bath, because the temperature goes up. Both this and the bubbles massaging you gently will help your circulation, both in your legs and your heart."

"Well, I need all that."

By the time the lady's twenty minutes were up, three other patients took their places at different containers of water. The floor under the wooden lathwork got wet with rivulets of spilled water. Tibor loved the coziness and discreet echoes of that large room where he felt free to move, to joke and when not too busy, which was rarely, to sit with his notebook and study.

"Now, we'll wrap your arm to keep it warm," Tibor told a patient finishing his hydrotherapy session, while he rubbed his arm dry. "Please follow me to the next room."

"What's there?"

"Well, I cooked you, now they'll fry you," he joked.

"Do I have a choice?"

"I don't think so, but you'll love it. Maria, here is your next customer," he announced from the door letting the patient walk past him with his treatment slip in hand.

"Good to see you back." Tibor was running to the back door leading directly to the parking lot, hurrying to class, when he heard Puiu's voice, as Nora called the Professor.

"Mister Professor? Good evening. How did you know I was away?"

"Nora came by last week," he said in his kindly low voice. "Did everything go well?"

The awareness that Puiu might know everything left Tibor in utter confusion; an almost tear-jerking blend of shy pride and irrevocable loss. *Did she tell him about us? She shouldn't have. Now I have to live up to what's obviously expected of Nora's intimate friend. You certainly know how to keep me going, Mamatzi.* "She took off to warmer climates without a hitch."

"I hope she'll be fine," Puiu said warmly.

"She better be." *For both of us.* "Sorry, I have to run, I'm almost late for school. Good Bye."

The Professor released the group of medical students after rounds in the electro-therapy room. "Tibor, we need to talk."

"Yes, Professor." Turning his head, Tibor held the ultrasound transducer in midair over the patient's shoulder.

"In private," he said with a strict tone. "Viorel, would you mind taking over," he told the chief technician supervising Tibor and turned on his heels heading towards his office.

All Tibor could think of was Puiu's tone. He had never heard him so strict, or seen him so grave. *A complaint? A patient? The lady who's freshly done hair got wet? Or the amputee who said I hurt his missing limb while giving him passive exercise? The school? Nora left, now why should he keep me?*

"Please have a seat."

My last supper, Tibor thought sitting as he usually did, deep in the chair, legs crossed, elbows on the arm rests. Self conscious of his air of confidence and its probable demise in mere seconds, he stirred, then thought, *Come what may!* and settled back.

"Your supervisors gave you very good references . . " Puiu took a little too long to go on giving Tibor a chance to think of the praise as sweetening-of-the-pot.

"Thank you," Tibor butted in. *Why not collect this part before the rest will demolish me?*

Puiu scratched his forehead. "This is a little unorthodox, but I'd like to change your schedule. Naturally, if you agree."

Instead of saying something like, 'Whatever you say,' Tibor remained silent. *Why do I have to do something unusual?*

"Of course I will have to give you a test personally, to verify that you are finished with your basic training. If so, in the remaining time you'll take the minimum rotations downstairs. Most of your time will be spent with massage and bedside care." Puiu waited for Tibor's reaction.

Tibor squirmed. "If you think that that's my weakness I'll be glad to spend more time on massage," he said.

"Not at all," the Professor smiled. "It will be more like cultivating your forte."

"I wasn't aware that—"

"What? That massage is your forte, or that I am aware?"

"More or less both," Tibor said genuinely puzzled.

"Well, obviously Nora was aware."

Tibor bent his head and hid his blushing face in his hands, then shook his head in disbelief and looked straight into Puiu's eyes. "She's terrible."

"You think so?"

"Of course not." The confidential look they exchanged was two men's shared recognition of a person they esteemed on totally different grounds.

"So, what do you say?"

"I feel confident with all procedures, and well, thank you." Years later,

Tibor would think back to that very instant as the turning point that had shaped the rest of his life. "Massage is really what I like most," Tibor added, not minding the tremolo in his voice, "Maybe 'cause of Nora." He pinched his lips to suppress the twitching until they became pale, devoid of blood.

Flares of searching for an affair declined into stretches of vanishing desire. The longer he insisted on working out a relationship with various women, the more deeply etched was the certainty that it wouldn't happen. The dry factual letters he wrote to Nora felt false, but then, soaking them in tears was not a solution either.

Work was more and more a consolation as time went by. The motivation to make up for those wasted years in the pit under the bellies of the cars gave him strength. It animated every stroke, it graded the pressure of his fingers over the pains his patients said he lifted from their ailing bodies. The feedback of praise and his skills fed on each other to levels that could not be overlooked by his own ego, or by Puiu's watchful eyes, or as the word of mouth got around from sick room to sick room, by the patients who never failed to welcome him with a friendly smile. He was not insensitive to recognition. He reckoned it was a good springboard. The sour grapes of his personal dissatisfactions made the fruits of his assiduous work sweeter.

There was no celebration, he wished for none. Nora's congratulation was the best he could wish for. The achievement, the one supported by Puiu's recommendation, the full-time position of Physical Therapist at the Hospital for Neurological Disorders was the tangible reward.

His attempt to re-start moonlighting was motivated less by his need for money than the need for diversion.

Tibor arrived with his customers just before the ceremony around noon time. While the couple claimed each other's freedom, he took a walk. He pondered the probable outcome of the vows exchanged in front of an altar. The occasion reinforced his doubts about his own unrelenting and likely unattainable desire and his certainty that something was wrong with him.

As he ambled around the cemetery fence behind the church, down and back from the little creek, chewing on the blade of grass, he found himself at the front gate as people walked out of the church. He mused, the blade of grass still hanging from his lips, whether it was the spring or the long lapse since he had found any interest in the shapes of women's legs. Now he measured them up as they tottered in high heels along the crunchy gravel path.

Another gravel walk took Tibor, trailing the crowd, to the long table of plenty set up in a yard a few corners away. It seemed a hallucination to a city dweller. Farmers could still manage to put together a feast from their own backyards, from their own pig pens and chicken coops. Tibor was not shy to respond to the kind invitation of the hosts. Praise good old Uncle Elemer, he thought downing a shot of home-made plum brandy as he ambled across the courtyard flooded by the slanted rays of the afternoon sun to congratulate the young couple. In the middle of the milling crowd the bride and groom stood like the figurines on the cake waiting on a table under the roof of the veranda, displaying frozen smiles and robotic nods as if their heads were connected to their necks by wire. Tibor felt an insistent gaze fixing him from the peach cloud of the group of bridesmaids. He couldn't ignore the young lady he then saw separating from the group, as if a petal blown by wind had settled in front of him.

"You don't remember me, do you?" the petal spoke.

"I'm sorry." Tibor was uneasy. "Could you refresh my memory?"

"I hope this won't upset you." She looked truly preoccupied how to put it. "I was a classmate of Ibolya at the Teacher's Academy."

Ibolya? Amazing how she disappeared. His interest having done the same, Tibor realized he hadn't thought of Ibolya for years. "Well, of course." He dug in his visual memory and came up with nothing. Now he felt truly embarrassed offending such a lovely woman with his ignorance. "Did I ever know your name?" he asked.

"I . . . don't think so. Marika Szabo. But of course you *are* Tibor Rózsavölgyi if I'm not mistaken."

"I'm him, all right," he bent over, lifted her hand loaded with costume jewelry and kissed it. "May I get you a drink?"

He poured her a glass of the ruby red stuff she was pointing to. He poured himself another half a glass of plum brandy. They touched the thick glasses that didn't clink. "To your health," he said. "To yours and to an evening of fun." She bowed her head to sip the cherry liqueur but held her gaze fixed on his face. She was not short. Even so her eyes turned up sharply and boldly with a telling look. In the frame of her blonde locks—he couldn't tell whether from the bottle or not—her eyes looked dark hazel. A small wreath of paper flowers crowned her head. His instant assessment was: Not bad. "I'll drink to that, and in that case to a *per tu,*" he said and his mind skipped back four years when he drank *per tu* with Nora.

They linked their forearms and drank a sip from their own glasses. As he turned his face to deposit the required kiss on her cheek sealing the agreement to call each other by their first names, their lips brushed. He was sure it was not his intention. He was just as sure that it was not accidental either.

Her question came as no surprise to Tibor after they had danced together for hours. "Are you staying overnight?"

"I wouldn't leave now even if it was not for the agreement," he said with intended undertone.

"They put me up at some neighbors. A nice room at the back of the house," Maria said.

"Should I tell the host that I made my own arrangements?" He tried and managed to sound business like. Just in case. Shriveled by disuse, his ego was suddenly bright awake. He was not sure whether he needed to know more than that she lived in Cluj, commuted to teach, was almost thirty, and hoped to meet her right man some day. The way she molded her sturdy, well-made body to his, Tibor felt as if he was chosen to be the one.

"Don't you need your rest right now?" she asked. "You said you have been up since dawn, didn't you?"

Pushy, pushy. I'll show you rest. Didn't I rest for too long now? Tibor acknowledged the passing of a state of indifference that he was more aware of now looking back. If it was a temporary depression, it certainly was not his first, and who could guess the future? In the high spirits brought about by the rapid development of a situation he used to look forward to at such weddings, the last thing Tibor would do was meditate over the reasons for his past episodes of sexual disinterest.

She locked the door with the large iron key. At first, he thought that the overly enthusiastic woman was not exactly the sex partner of his dreams. *An unbroken filly on the pill. How close to thirty did she say she was? Sensuous she's not. But good raw material. She feels alright.*

Inexplicably, trying to sleep on the narrow bed, his memory evoked Nora, who came into his senses as perfect, despite the skin deep pleasure he obviously owed right then to Maria, asleep with her head on his shoulder. She smelled good. More perfumed than Nora ever was. Was that good? He could cry thinking of the promise: Do not compare.

"Yes, it's me," he said and raised his eyebrows. "No, I didn't forget you. I had a course to go to after work for two weeks."

He found nothing wrong with the ease with which she agreed to celebrate his confirmation on the job. She didn't claim to be busy. On the contrary, he found his own weighing of every little detail ultimately contrived.

He was caught up in a storm of questions feeding upon each other. Why did Maria tell him that she used to have a crush on him on their first date? A tardy first date, at that, after they had slept together, but still. Furthermore, that years back she had cheered at the news of him breaking up with Ibolya. A shy crush, she said, that she kept to herself. She had to give up hope of getting near him when she had found out his reasons. She had even heard that he had married that lady doctor.

Tibor couldn't cash in the compliment without a second thought. *Maria! Don't! Don't get into that. That's no one's business. You touch that subject and you'll turn to dust. If you have any sense stop right here.* He said nothing waiting for her to go on with her monologue. She didn't. Perhaps he could use this introduction to reap some benefits. Give Maria some education. *Why should I? I have no reason. Me calling her up might be enough reason. Now, is she digging into my past uninvited, coaxing me to feel sorry for calling her? No. As a matter of fact she stopped right there where I wanted her to stop. She might be sensitive enough.*

"Ibolya dug her own grave with her deceitfulness. I had suspected her." Tibor didn't blink over his half lie, but was pleased to send the message that he's not a guy easily deceived; his subtlety gave him a measure of satisfaction.

"She got what she deserved," replied Maria appearing good-natured enough not to consider being slighted by Tibor for not acknowledging her long-time crush on him. "I'm sure you heard, didn't you?"

"I hate to sound rude, but I never did and don't care." To underline his statement he flagged down the waiter. "Would you have a bottle of chilled sparkling wine."

"Oh. That's very nice." A flattered Tibor took her remark as a compliment.

Writing to Nora felt like the climax of a most satisfying evening.

'Dear Nora, Congratulate me. I was confirmed after 3 months of probation. I had no doubts. Conceited? Just realistic. The Chief PT is close to retirement (two years) and I think I have a chance . . .

Meanwhile I'll build some kind of device. It's simple, it would deliver passive motion to certain patients. Based on a timer and an adjustable sling/pulley system. Simple, gentle and efficient. Like me. Wouldn't you agree?

Now, sit down. I met this Maria. She comes from my past. I don't know whether this is good or bad. She knew about you, not from me, and respects my feelings. Whatever she knows it can't be more than a fraction of . . . don't you dare laugh. If she realizes that I still love you, what a perfect rival you are. Wouldn't you say she's smart? What do you women think of faithful men? I get a star for being faithful. Does this make sense?

You're moving again? Is that good for you? How do the children take all this? I know, I should shut up. I'm the same unimaginative coward.

Loving kisses, Tibor'

2

Still skeptical of his regained ability to take pleasure in togetherness, Tibor enjoyed Maria's company more than the plain necessity of a warm body. He hadn't found comfort, let alone satisfaction, in his attempts to live the life of a single man until he met Maria. Marika, Mari? Trying nicknames to fit. The twinge of being unfaithful to his deep feelings and the conscious comparing started to fade. The inability to let go, the fear of going mad, slowly subsided.

Tibor was mindful not to flaunt his past seashore experience, trying not to think of the itinerary as a re-tracing.

"You seem to know the place well," Maria said as they got their room key to the accommodation in Venus, the little resort town, Tibor's gauge for paradise since he had stayed there with Nora.

"I did my homework," Tibor answered with a wink. *Very observant, I must admit.* "I hope you'll like it." *What do they call it? A double blind? Some way of choosing a bride. Purely scientific, Hah, hah.* Then he laughed out loud, not without a tinge of sarcasm, when Maria found the closet too small for her clothes, the verdant patio too overgrown with hedges and the two street blocks too far from the sea.

Your crown is going to fall off walking to the water, Tibor thought, but instead he said, "I'll carry you there."

"Silly," she said. "I'm too heavy."

"Better than lightweight," Tibor used a pun and waited for the effect. Nothing. "You know what I mean?" He asked.

"Meaning . . . that's what you like?" she hesitated.

With her sense of humor, Tibor was just as glad to be misunderstood. "I meant you're important." He kissed her.

The sun was flirting with the horizon, the dark turquoise water lulled itself in lazy placidity sending its white caps to sleep. Under the cliff, they lapsed into their own thoughts. Tibor rolled over, arm around her chest, knee over her belly, kissed her on the neck and down her breasts. She took quick looks around. His hand slipped into her bikini. She pushed him away.

"You must be joking. Here?"

"Why not?

"Someone might see us."

"No one's around."

"Go jump in the lake."

"Nothing easier." Tibor smacked a kiss on her cheek, stood up, his erection stretching his bathing suit. For a fraction of a second, he considered asking her whether she would mind if he went skinny dipping, then at the thought of her negative answer, he said nothing. She could take it as a tit for tat if he stripped there. He was not in an argumentative mood.

He stood at the water's edge. Soft lazy waves caressed his ankles. *Mari should have accepted making love on the beach. Now I wouldn't take this swim with Nora. It's hopeless.* His limbs, then his body, then his imagination, cooled as he floated away. He pushed off, swimming faster and faster, farther and farther, closer and closer to the horizon sinking in the dusk. He turned around at the limits of his resistance.

The day before Christmas, the slush in the streets was nearly unmanageable. Heavy wet snow fell all night. Cars skidded all over the place. Maria's parents had arrived the evening before.

Tibor arrived with his parents at the City Hall. Their expression and silence was rather funereal. He couldn't totally ignore the intimated disapproval. Understanding his reasons, his bride had agreed to an informal affair; in exchange she was not denied the opportunity to display her wildest fantasies in putting together her outfit. He started to get used to pastel clouds of ruffles and ribbons. Underneath was a caring person who accepted nonc of his shy advice that less adornment would her firm roundness best.

Tibor and Maria exchanged vows, signed the registry, accepted the good wishes and congratulations and then treated the company to dinner at the new Belvedere Hotel's restaurant on the top of Fortress Hill. Maria's parents were trying to be good sports, though visibly disheartened that their only daughter would fade into matrimonial union with a divorcee and no traditional fanfare.

Despite the prosaic practicalities of living, a romantic air settled in as soon as they closed the door to his, now their room. Tibor's parents extended demands on his time as if he was more single than ever. As if he had married them. This crossed his mind, when almost breathless, grappling for words, he politely refused their request to drive them to Budapest.

"Mother," he threw his arms up. "I have no vacation left—"

She cut him with a reproach, "You promised to always keep a few days just in case—"

"That was before I got married," he sputtered. His arguments seemed to hit the wall bouncing back on him with a thud.

"That's no reason to throw us away. We took you back, ungrateful dog, remember?" She screwed up her eyes. "Besides, you should be happy to get away from the stench she makes in the kitchen—"

"Mother—"

"Soon I won't be able to use my own kitchen—"

"What got into you? Let's stop this. She'll be home soon." He glanced toward the door. It was time for Maria to stumble in exhausted. "Please, leave her out of this," he lowered his voice.

"You should tell her."

"Tell her what?"

"I don't want her in my kitchen."

"Is this about money? You don't think the rent covers what we use? No problem, just tell me. I'm doing my best to make our separate space. What else can I say?"

"I'll cook for you—"

"Look," this time his voice followed his mother's to the higher registers except his was thundering. "Don't make me choose. If you'd have any doubts, don't. I'll stick by my wife. I have no chance of getting an apartment. The waiting list to buy is just as long. We'll be out of your hair by the end of the summer. If you want to throw us in the street because Mari cooks differently, fine, we'll go—" Tibor couldn't finish his sentence.

Maria stepped in turning her back on the people in the kitchen as she closed her dripping umbrella. "What weather," she said.

Tibor sensed she was faking a cheerful tone. He took the umbrella. "Come to our room." He pulled the door. "Did you tell them?" he asked his wife.

"No."

"My mother flipped her lid—"

"I was outside. I couldn't come into the middle of all that. Tibi, let's move."

"Where?"

"Anywhere. A sublet."

"With the baby coming? I failed you Mari. I'm no good."

"We can move to Bistritza with my parents."

"From the fire into the frying pan? How about jobs?"

For weeks, Tibor had attempted to dig up Nora's last letter from the wreckage of their most recent move. Finally, when Maria unpacked a box, she found it. He read it again.

"Dear Tibor, I shall keep copies of my letters. This might sound strange. It seems that I lie and I forget what I lied about and to whom. True. You know why? Because life is so hard, it makes me hallucinate. Now here comes in Adel. I cannot tell her how hard it is for us. So, I lie to her. A dilemma is killing me. I don't know what is more difficult, working up to 100 hours/week or deciding whether I should convince Adel to come here.

You? I wish I could send you a rubber blow-up house equipped with everything you need. I understand your troubles, and I think it's good that you got away.

I am a wreck by the rare days when I have a day off. The children are going wild, it is not true what a friend once said, that kids grow up by themselves. They need more parenting than I can offer. Is there an easier way? I know none. I have to regain my right to practice medicine and this is the only way here. For a nice break, when they gave me my vacation, we went to Washington. It's a thrill for me to be able to get around without any particular difficulty. Sonya named the highway interchanges 'bowls of spaghetti.' You can't imagine how fitting this metaphor is in fact. She also said that the best things America had produced are the highways, the cartoons and the fast food restaurants. Just about sums up this country's essence. With all honesty I should add what they call here "country music," kind of ballads, we all are starting to like very much. Especially Daniel.

Best wishes to Maria with the pregnancy and hope to have the good news of a healthy baby and happy parents. With all the friendship, Nora"

Tibor was not inspired, but couldn't put it off any longer. He wrote a formal introduction that betrayed his discomfort. He politely acknowledged Nora's difficulties. It didn't come easy either in the view of his own problems. Then he plunged.

"In the few months since I wrote we went through hell. Maria almost miscarried. Now she's fine but confined to bed. A little more to go. Cervical incontinence, or something like that.

We moved in with my in-laws. It all came down to jobs. I wish everything could have been as good as my professional situation. But, for peace, I had to throw that away.

There is a fairly decent general hospital here. They hired me gladly. So much for my talents you discovered, my ambition that you fueled and my professional future that was but an illusion. A provincial masseur. I hate myself. I entertain some foreign ideas, if you know what I mean!

So, we're living with Mari's parents in a big house. Mari came by ambulance. Her parents seem nice, but old fashioned. Marika is well taken care off, but she's bitching all the time, she's picky, crabby and quarrels with her mother. With me too. She has changed a lot. But that's not the subject of this letter.

Maria usually knows when I write to you. I don't stick my letters under her nose, but I leave them around. Not this one.

This is hard. This is my last letter. I will live my life imagining what you're doing. Marika assured me she was never bothered by our tele-friendship, but sort of hinted that her parents have different views. Or maybe her feelings have changed and now is the moment to put an end to it. I cannot receive your letters here. I am sure you would agree that secrecy is not what you and I are about. I feel that I am losing you for the second time and it is my fault again. Your letters kept me going. Believe me, this is the truth. Hug the kids for me, Tibor"

"Tibi, do something about this," Maria complained about her own parents. "My father is chewing my ears off that we should name the child after my grandparents."

"Would it be so bad?" Tibor sat on her bed leaning with an arm on the other side of her protruding belly. He would rather have thrown cart wheels which he was never able to do, than act as the buffer between wife and parents once again. Tried once and failed. He felt like screaming, but instead smiled gently trying to untangle his wife's nerves.

"They pester me," she whimpered.

"What are those names again?"

"Arpad or Zsofia."

"I wouldn't mind either, sweetheart."

"You wouldn't?" She looked relieved.

Tibor felt warm around his heart. The prospect of this child banished all other concerns. Mostly the frustrations with his work. What they required of him was but a small part of what he was able to do. That was the lesser part of his problem. The provincial stick-in-the-mud hospital administration was refractory to anything not related to self-serving their paltry interests. He was barking up the wrong tree trying to introduce an innovative trend. Not enough patients, the administrator argued. True. He couldn't win and was totally discouraged. He had no shoulder to cry on. He couldn't bother Maria with his problems. "You shouldn't worry about me. A name is a name. The child will have to manage despite its name. On the other hand," he put on his joking grimace, "A little girl born as an old aunt? Zsofia?"

"See?" Maria snapped.

"I'm joking, silly. It's a lovely and serious name. But forget it. It's a boy. Isn't it?"

"Don't say that."

"You did a good hatching job," the obstetrician told Maria at her eighth month check up. "Now we have a good size fetus and I need you to make up for all the slacking," he said gently slapping the steep slope of her belly.

"I have not been idle," she protested in all seriousness.

I shouldn't joke, Tibor tensed up. One never knew when she would take offense. "She *did* a great job, Doc, didn't she," he interjected to divert any further joking.

"Well, of course," the doctor winked. "Now, I don't want you to start carrying stones or plowing the fields, but you can definitely start doing light housework, go up and down stairs." Maria nodded, looking occasionally at Tibor who also nodded in agreement. "We need your muscles active."

"I made sure that her muscles were as busy as if she was walking," Tibor said proudly.

"That's your luck, Mari," the doctor said, "To have a professional at your side. And isn't that great for you Tibor that you could contribute to the making of this baby more than just having a good time?" He cleared his throat. "But now we have some business to do."

Tibor took Maria's hand, he knew what was coming and was not sure whether it would hurt her.

"We'll remove the last ring from your cervix."

Maria took a deep whistling breath.

"Don't worry. This is nothing."

"Right now?" she asked.

"Sure," the doctor said while the nurse lifted her legs up into the slings.

The couple held hands. There was the subdued clink of touching instruments they were already used to. The metal ring dropped in the kidney basin sounding the signal of a beginning.

"That's a girl," the doctor said slapping Maria's thigh.

"You have golden hands," she said with a grateful expression adorning her face, now swollen and stained by motherhood.

"I hope not," he said."I couldn't move them."

"He's great. I really trust him," she said on the way home.

"That's good. You don't mind the hospital?" They had been considering delivering at the university hospital in Tîrgu Mures.

"What could be missing?"

"I hope you carry to term. If you deliver early the baby might need special care, you know that as well as I do."

"We'll be fine," she said with no hesitation. "It's better to be home."

By the time Maria tapped Tibor's back, her loud moans had awakened him. "It's time. My dear Virgin Mary, this hurts."

She rolled onto her side and sat up. "Wait." She was holding her underbelly. "Maybe it's a false alarm. I have two more weeks." He stood and watched. "No, it's not," she said in another five minutes.

A hushed breeze welcomed them out of doors. Maria waddled carefully to the car holding onto Tibor's arm. The late summer night was mild, though they had a few frosty ones the past week.

"I wish it was not the middle of the night," she said.

"You know what they say? Delivery starts when the baby was conceived. You don't like to screw in the morning, now you should be sorry."

"I got your point. Remind me in the future."

Tibor felt like a deserter pacing painlessly in the hallways; he cracked open the delivery room door but got the same response. "Don't worry, everything's going by schedule." The midwife gently pushed him back and closed the door in his nose.

He was unhappy and restless with that schedule stretching now in its tenth hour. But he was informed, he couldn't complain, the doctor told him when they reached the nine centimeter mark. That was a while back. The door opened wide and the midwife motioned him in with a funny wagging of her index finger. There was no doubt in his mind, it was a good sign. Maria needed him.

He stepped in to the most wonderful scene that had ever welcomed him in his life. A bundle of piled gauze sitting on his wife's chest, with tiny little hands and bent wrinkled fingers of the liveliest pink sticking out of it. Maria was holding her bundle, happy and relaxed as if pain had never touched her.

"You got a lovely and healthy little daughter," the midwife said. The doctor was sitting at the little metal table in the corner scribbling.

Tibor bent over Maria. "Thank you, darling. You are both beautiful, he said pulling the gauze away with a finger from Zsofia's face. Then he kissed the top of her greasy and wet head.

"We'll have you wait outside until we deliver the placenta," the doctor turned to him leaning his still gloved hands on his knees.

"Thank you Doc," Tibor said. "You better hurry, I won't let you kick me out too much longer."

"Give us half an hour," the midwife said.

Tibor was sitting in the dim hallway when the loud metallic clatter of a rushing pushcart startled him. He turned his head in that direction annoyed that anyone would be so rude as to disturb the maternity ward with such clamor. Tibor recognized both the man pushing the cart and the woman in a white coat running at his heels. They nearly broke through the delivery room door in their rush as Tibor felt a wave of nausea and dizziness consume him. His girls were the only ones in there. He walked with a shaky resolve to the door.

The midwife stuck her head out almost into Tibor's face. "We have an emergency. Maria is bleeding," she said.

"What's going on?"

"The placenta . . . the doctor thinks it's not normal . . "

They had to make room for another cart rushed from the other direction. It was the anesthesiologist whom Tibor knew.

"I have to—"

"I'm sorry Tibor. You'll have to wait outside—"

"Is she in trouble?"

"No. She's fine—"

"Why does she need the anesthesiologist?"

"The doctor has to extract the placenta manually—"

"Oh, my god . . " He pushed his way in.

The doctor was sitting between Maria's raised legs. The anesthesiologist was talking to her explaining the mask and asking her to count. He saw Tibor and motioned him to stay away. Maria was pale and listless; she gestured for help when she caught a glance of Tibor.

They nudged him through the door. He was shivering. Cold sweat dripped down his temples. His fingers hurt from cracking his knuckles. He glanced at his watch every few seconds. He had to sit down, his knees were ready to give way.

The door opened. The doctor, face flushed, gloved hands bloody, coat splashed with blood stepped out and motioned Tibor to approach.

"Listen carefully, there's no time to repeat. I couldn't remove the placenta. The bleeding is right now under control—" he stepped to the side as someone ran towards the door with another bottle of blood. "—with the infusion of stipticks." Tibor was not familiar with the term but understood that he could not interrupt. "We'll take Maria to the OR. I will attempt to remove the placenta and get a clean curette. We have to consider though the possibility that this won't be successful—"

Tibor opened his mouth soundlessly. They were too many questions that he realized made no difference. He was more helpless than ever. Finally his worst fear erupted. "Could we lose her?"

"No. But you have to know because she doesn't. We couldn't control the bleeding." He held down Tibor's hands which were flailing nervously. "Now we're fine. But we had to put her to sleep in a rush so I could attempt do the manual extraction of the placenta." He took a deep breath. "If the second attempt is unsuccessful, which I fear—"

"Doctor—"

"Please, Tibor. Let me give you the whole story. At the moment she is not bleeding with the Oxytocin infusion, but we have to taper that. I need the uterus relaxed for the procedure and that means she'll bleed again. If it gets out of hand—"

Tibor wiped his sweaty brow.

The doctor went on. "—not to the point of danger, but then it comes to emergency hysterectomy. That's what I want you to know."

They opened both wings of the double door and wheeled out the stretcher. Tibor only murmured, "I understand," to the doctor who was running in front of the group surrounding Maria who was hidden under the mask.

A nurse brought a glass of water and a pill for Tibor. He took the tranquilizer. The consolation of being thought of as someone who also needed attention came between Tibor and the last words he whispered to the doctor's back. Zsofika. An only child. They never talked about having more children, but in Tibor's imagination there were more than one. Not a row of kids like organ pipes. Neither he nor Maria had siblings. He felt it in his bones. He felt it in his flesh what was going on in the operating room. *That's not the issue,* he stopped his line of selfish thinking. *They can't lose her with the transfusion hooked up.*

An hour, an hour and a half passed, he was in a trance when the obstetrician emerged. "Sorry Tibor. It turned out that it was a very good reason why I couldn't extract that damn placenta. It couldn't be separated from the uterus."

"How's Maria?"

"She's fine. Five units of blood, she is stable. Still under. You'll see her in a while."

"So you did a hysterectomy?"

"Yes. I don't even need the pathology. This happens like one in six thousand pregnancies—"

"What?"

"That the placenta grows into the uterine muscle. If you want to know it's called *placenta accreta.*"

So, Tibor knew by the time they showed him the pathology report in the chart a few days later what that melodious lovely term meant: No more children.

Maria took a long time to understand. She required repeated explanations. She cried unable to get over her loss. Tibor was advised that his simple presence would be her best consolation.

Work, spending time with Maria and the baby in the afternoons, or at least the brief interval between coming from the hospital and going out to house calls knocked Tibor out comatose for the night. He could afford the luxury with a baby as considerate as Zsofi. She was happy with the little mother's milk they could get from a wet nurse. For a fortune. For the rest, she gladly took the diluted cow's milk. Baby formula had disappeared from the socialist market together with the rest of the food. Nothing spoiled her happily smiling lips curling over her dimpled chin.

"She's going to be a smart girl," Tibor said sounding mushy as he held the lacy bundle close to his face.

"How can you know that?"

"She doesn't take after me."

"Reproaching me that she's not a boy?" Maria was unable to respond to a joke, even when Tibor was earnestly self-deprecating. Maria's eyes followed the column of smoke rising to the ceiling. She had resumed smoking, stubbornly insisting that taking up her old habit would help her to recover. Another blow. Tibor gave up hope of saying anything right, or providing the means to help her mend.

It took almost more than he could muster. "Mari, you both are the most wonderful creatures I could wish for."

"A mother without milk and without a uterus. How wonderful is that?" She puffed again, this time right in Tibor's face.

3

The sweet fruit of maternity spread bitter seeds of over protectiveness around Maria. Tibor had long retired his own problems. Losing the handle on his recently gained sense of priorities made Tibor painfully disappointed at times. Maria projected her list of baby care rules from behind a wall of smoke. The size of the smoke puffs became the measure of her state of mind. Disdainful: small twisting puffs; angry: large puffs blown to the ceiling.

Four year old Zsofi, untamed and exhausting, deftly handed dishes one by one to her grandmother, and cheered at the suds rising like tiny soap bubbles from the overfilled sink. Zsofi was swift, her wispy hemp-like hair flew as she turned around quicker than the old woman could handle the plates. "Here I'm Granny. You make me wait."

"Where are you rushing?"

"I have to feed Baba." Baba was her doll patiently waiting in her little seat in the corner of the kitchen.

Tibor's adoring gaze lingered for a while on his graceful little daughter. Then he observed his wife pulling the washing machine from its niche and rolling it to the bathroom to connect it to the faucet. She was sniffling. He went to her and put his arm around her shoulder. "What's wrong, dear?" *Did I neglect my duty? I haven't thought about it lately. I've been so exhausted. Did she have a fight with her mother?*

"They called me to the principal's office," she said sobbing. The class of 30 pupils she had picked up two years earlier—when the whole family had been happy to see her back in the class—had dwindled down to 25. The real reasons for worry about the shrinking class had escaped them both until then. "Parents are upset about having a teacher with a Hungarian accent teach their children Romanian language."

"Wait a minute," Tibor snapped. "These allegedly complaining parents don't speak Romanian at all."

"Tibi. That's not the point," she said wiping her tears. "They have orders. It's the Transylvanian accent. The dialect. The Romanian I teach is perfectly correct. I'm bilingual. I told him as if he didn't know."

"Mari. You knocked me out. I didn't think it would happen to you too."

"What?"

"It's the same for both of us, can't you see?"

"Oh? What's happening with you?" She sat down wiping her wet hands.

"Not now. Remember how many times I tried for a job in Tîrgu Mureş?" He started to pace. Years back, he had gotten over the failure of his job hunting. But now it was an unwelcome revival. "Everybody there is Romanian. Brought from Cluj and Bucharest to fill top jobs. They don't speak with an 'accent,' they don't understand Hungarian, period. They can't communicate directly with more than half of the patients." Tibor was referring to the Hungarian minority population of Romania which in their region ranged from fifty to a hundred percent in different areas. He raised his gaze to the ceiling. "So, now we know which way the wind blows. It's the romanization we've disregarded. I don't want to be a victim of nationalism. Not even my own."

"I hate politics. They drive us to it."

"I hate this, damn it."

"What's for us to do?"

"Think about it. The least we can do is help ourselves."

The in-laws have contacted an old cousin in Budapest, whose former profession was passed under a ponderous silence.

Uncle Pista and aunt Boske, as Tibor was made to call the old couple, opened the door together as if the job was too difficult for either to handle. Tibor gave no second thought to sleeping on a cot in the small nook off the kitchen. His parents, who never missed a chance to pop over to Budapest, got the extra room, that had been sublet to a young woman. How lucky, little Vera, they said, had been recently married to an American, a little old for her, but never mind, he's lined with money.

To Tibor's surprise the furnishing was like out of the movies. The heavy, carved mahogany, brocade upholstery, though worn, had seen better days. So had the oriental rugs as far as he could tell. What had they been doing for a living? They must have done very well in their time. But, he had to move on, as intrigued as he was by these vestiges of wealth.

To the curious inquiry about leaving in a rush, Tibor replied, "Not wasting a minute dangling my legs, when I can wear thin the soles of my shoes on the pavement," he said with a tone that intimated this-subject-is-closed.

"Won't you come with us?" His parents had mentioned their need for a driver for the business. All his contribution, besides driving them there, was to buy up in Bistritza as much of the famous local plum brandy that he could round up. Not easy. It became a currency that bought favors. Of course the customs restrictions were for his mother a good joke one had to laugh at. She knew how to wrap the customs officers around her finger. On the way out she had filled the trunk with Romanian crystal, rubber sink stoppers, Carpati cigarettes—a few packs stuffed under the front seat ready to be administered as instant remedy to cure border guards suffering from exaggerated vigilance—Chinese lace fabric for curtains and terry cloth towels. On the way back, his car would be loaded with Vegeta, the famous food seasoning, salami and other smoked meat products, laundry detergent and whatever his mother could lay her hands on that had a chance to be sold in Romania for a profit.

He was not up to anything shameful. Having to watch his every word, every step, felt unfair. He was only about to make a fool of himself and not crazy about people consoling him for the expected failure. To his relief, no one remarked at his wearing a suit, neither his nor anyone else's common habit for sightseeing.

I should've stayed under the cars, I wouldn't have this miserable itch, Tibor thought as he stepped to the door of the administrative offices at the famous Gellert Hotel and introduced himself to the secretary.

"Have you an appointment?"

"My director, Doctor Kovács, had mentioned a while ago that I'd drop by." Tibor put on the most glamorous smile in his arsenal to leave no room for the woman's doubts. "No. Not for *today,*" he conceded with a guilty, but fetching smile. His best hope was to have one set up for the next day without having to prove in any way to this Kövi that he knew Kovacs.

"What is your visit about?"

He had to put his foot in the door. "I've been told that Mr. Kövi is looking for highly qualified . . " he threw around the director's name he had just learnt at the front desk, and swallowed hard because he hated to be called a ". . . masseur." *From abroad, to boot, but you needn't know that just now.*

"Take a seat, Mr. Rózsavölgyi," she said getting up and leaving the room through a heavy oak door. Within minutes Tibor was invited in.

The athletic figure of the Director of the Gellert Spa impressed Tibor more by his mild finely polished manners than by his size.

"I appreciate you seeing me so promptly."

"No problem. And how is our Doctor Kovács?" The man asked with a flourish.

Tibor was about to break out in a sweat. Would he ever find out whether these two men knew each other? "He's great and the best boss," Tibor said, prepared to make up a recent personal history for his director.

"Thank your luck, Mr. Rózsavölgyi. I'm going away for a three day conference to Karlsbad."

"Then you probably have no time to waste," Tibor said assuming his self-confident posture in the armchair and proceeding without delay, speaking without hesitation as if reading his bio.

Kövi nodded and said, "I guess I'm not wrong to assume that you intend to re-settle in Hungary."

"It's just a matter of time for the formalities in Romania and also here. I have made my decision. Yes," Tibor said and wished he could speak for his family.

"Naturally I'm familiar with the Hungarian minority's plight in Transylvania—"

"It's really getting out of hand," Tibor interrupted.

"You still have your jobs, don't you?"

"Finger right on the button," Tibor switched to a more informal style sensing he had audience. "*Still* is the key word."

"Well, I hope this will please you. I won't turn you away empty handed. Would you be available for a couple of days of work? Off the records, naturally. A test, if you wish."

"I'll take the opportunity. I'm at your disposal for as many of the following three days as you require."

Being passed from secretary to elevator operator to a young woman in a lab coat waiting for him at the concourse level, put Tibor in an especially reckless mood. The swing door opened to hallways filled with steam and resounding echoes. The mineral baths were close by. Someone held a lab coat for him, he slid his arms in. It was too tight and buttoned the wrong way. They walked along colonnaded passages that wound around pools, and through cavernous halls under arched ceilings. In unisex pools, people were bathing in suits; in the women's pool, most bathers were in the nude. He felt like an impostor. Embarrassed. He couldn't explain. Through the swing doors at the other side of the water maze, they walked along a corridor lined with doors. Some were open. Massage tables waited. One waited for him.

The variety of people he laid hands on totally astonished Tibor. While at home he typically attended to farmers with sciatica, and clerks with flabby atrophied muscles, here he worked on the lanky bodies of Italian movie actresses filming in Budapest and rich tourists staying at the hotel. Agnes, the supervisor, a corpulent matron, informed him why he was assigned to foreigners to prove his skills. "Our local permanents have their favorites. They wouldn't have you."

"That's a good idea." Tibor winked. "They might follow me home."

Strong hands slapped Tibor's shoulder vigorously. "You know what, Tibi?" Old Agnes said. "I saw what I needed to see and Kövi wants to know. I have a minister's wife here for her weekly appointment. I've been doing her for ten years. I'll tackle her. She's adventurous enough, plus she has problems. That's all I'll tell you. If she agrees, you'll tell me the rest. Do you mind?"

"Why should I? I'll take a challenge any time. Anything you say, Ágikám." The totally inappropriate term of endearment startled her for a fraction of a second only to make her burst into a belly-shaking laughter. "You're my kind of guy."

The client agreed. Even shook Tibor's hand, a gesture contrasting her thin tall aristocratic figure, turned up nose and tight lips that whispered 'Good luck' when she lay down on the table.

The crawly feeling in his fingers told Tibor that the hour could make or break his future. He didn't ask the woman what she liked or what her problem was, he didn't even ask whether she would like to chat or sleep. He had to find out everything as if it were a riddle.

He smoothed the white sheet fragrant with fine laundry detergent over the lady smelling less fragrant with the chlorine from the pool she had just soaked in. She was lying on her stomach curiously peeking at Tibor. Concentrating on capturing even a minimal reaction of her limbs and body, he moved his palms slowly, using his powerful, now relaxed, thumbs as sensors. His imperceptibly fluttering fingers, barely touching the sheet, were the transmitters of his will and capability to relax tension. From the sides of her neck down the sides of her chest, back on her spine, down to her hips. There it was. The slightest twitch, more a soundless moan, a tensing of her low back, as if she expected to be hurt by someone who did not know how to respect and deal with her ache. *Which side? It's usually only one, isn't it sweetheart? You'll let me know in a sec. I bet dear Agnes instructed you to guard your secret. If you can. Hah!*

Tibor let his hands slide down the back of her thighs and legs as if nothing happened, then ever so slightly he returned to her low back. He rested his hands for a fraction of a second. Then let his hands take the same road as before, but only on one side at a time. Nothing on the left. No reaction. Her right buttock, slightly more flacid, welcomed his hand with relief. A loss of muscle tension, a total surrender to a trusted healer who came to take the pain, and the sheet, away.

"You aren't sleeping yet, are you?" Tibor asked lowering his voice to a very calm register. He had to know.

"Oh, no. Not me."

"Do you mind if I ask you a question?"

"Go right ahead."

"I hope you'll agree to a special after the regular procedure."

"I won't even ask what it is."

"Thank you. In that case are you visiting the hair salon?"

"I didn't plan to. Do I need to?" she giggled coquettishly.

"That's not my place to say, but if you don't, I'll take a minute to wash the oil off my hands when I do your scalp. I think it's best left for the end, ears included," he cackled.

"I *must* have your special." The exclamation was Tibor's prize for going through this fuss he had just made up to impress her. Not his special, but rather calling it so. Pure cunning sleazy. He was role playing masseur to the influential. *I guess they fall for a little extra pampering no matter how ministerial they are.*

"So? What do you want me to tell you?" Tibor asked Agnes after the minister's wife left, slipping a big tip in his coat pocket. He aborted the reflex to push her hand away. *Why not?*

"Nothing," Agnes said with feigned offense. "She told me everything. You passed with brio. And she told me I can retire when they hire you."

"Don't upset me. Such a young lady to talk about retiring."

"You're a character that doesn't grow on every street corner," Agnes said. "Good luck. If it were up to me I'd hire you today."

"I wish you could. Thanks."

Carried by a surreal dream, along a straight line through a system that should have been complicated, straighter than the road he was driving on, Tibor refused to wake up.

"Should we keep your disappearing acts confidential?" His father's voice broke into his reverie.

Tibor felt like slamming on the brake as an answer. "What do you mean?"

"Well. Should it stay between you and us?

"You mean from Marika?"

"Yeah. That's exactly what he means," Tibor's mother said with disdain. "You behaved quite strangely, wouldn't you say?"

Criticized again, all his elation was smeared over with slime. He felt an urge to dump them right there on the roadside. He had to grind his teeth to remain civil. "What do you think I had a two day knockers escapade?" Then he tried to be objective. They could have thought that. "No. She'll be the first to know what I've been up to."

"Honestly, I don't understand your anger," Tibor's words fell short of helping, opposite Maria's rage. "I didn't tell you before I went, not to get you all worked up for nothing. I had no idea what the job market would be—"

"I can tell you a lot of things you have no idea about," she spewed. She had not heard the rest, he thought, and was wondering when to deliver the essential part she didn't care to hear. "You think you're on top of everything." She started to whimper. He wrapped an arm around her and lifted her chin.

"Isn't it better to tell you now when I'm sure of what we will do? Why do you think I took everything upon me? It would've been easier to share my worries. I wanted to spare you in case it turned out to be nothing."

She pulled away and lit a cigarette. He controlled his urge to grab it and throw it away.

"I have my job." Puff. "I'm happy here with my parents' help." Puff. "I know nothing about teaching in a different system. It's not like your job—"

"It's your mother's tongue, Mari. What's your problem? Teaching kids. How different could it be?"

"Maybe I would never be able to work."

"Maybe not from the first day."

"I'll give it a thought." She said softly.

"The formalities take a while." Tibor's mind took off to remote memories of the tribulations Nora went through with her emigration. Would it be the same? Just moving across one border? "We'll have time to think while we wait. Let's file."

He promised to let her get more comfortable with the idea. Life went on. Worms of restlessness started to gnaw at Tibor. Lead weights hung about him when awake, nightmares weaved into his sleep.

"I couldn't have imagined how perverse people are," Maria said one evening at dinner. She made an inventory of her family's puzzled looks, including the five year old always alert Zsofi.

"What's pe'ves?" Her question was expected.

"Nothing you can play with," her grandfather said.

"What's pe'ves, daddy?"

"Something bad people do."

"Breaking a window is pe'ves?"

"Yeah. Especially if it's the neighbors'"

Zsofi picked up her cup of milk. "Is milk pe'ves?"

"Not at all." He turned to Maria. "If you think it's not worse than breaking a window go on."

"It's worse. You know that in Hungary there is hatred against Hungarians like us?" She fixed Tibor with an inquisitive look. "Minority Hungarians from Transylvania."

"I've never heard anything as stupid as this. Why?"

"Because we're shits according to our brothers in the motherland. Because we never stood up for our rights. Because they have to raise a voice for us—"

"You certainly got into the politics you hate. Why don't we just look after ourselves, what everybody else should do and leave others alone."

"—because we are the reason Hungary lost Transylvania. I'm just telling you what to expect if we go there." Maria's tone dripped hostility.

"Look. Everyone I dealt with there was supportive. More than one could hope. Do we have to listen?"

"I don't know. It just sounds so hideous."

"All politics are hideous."

Tibor wished that his daily duties and troubles, pleasures and squabbles wouldn't leave him free time to torture him with the question of a last missing push. One day, it came from where he expected it the least. Until then, pressuring Maria had elicited only her venomous suggestion that he should emigrate by himself.

School vacation was nearing its end. Tibor could not fully enjoy his daughter's excitement about going to kindergarten, but he forced a delighted demeanor to make her happy despite his prevailing gloom. A day promising to be calm ended up in a storm like none before or after.

Maria called Tibor at work. "I have no class," she cried, then told him that the principal had called her into his office again. She was about to start the fourth grade with her group of pupils.

"What do you mean you have no class?"

She went on whimpering. "Remember Kati? The one who told us that she moved her daughter out of my class?"

"Sure." The realization of how gullible both of them were, punched Tibor in his stomach: they had disregarded a piece of information; they had paid no heed to the parent who had told them during the summer that she was transferring her daughter to the Romanian school. Fine, they had thought. The woman, however, seemed slightly upset that Hungarian language was not offered at the other school, so that the little girl's mother tongue was to become a spoken language to her; simply stated she would never read or write properly in Hungarian. She had argued, rightly, that she did not want to make her daughter's life more difficult. It was no secret that quotas became a reality one could not overlook. Certainly parents intending to send their children for higher education couldn't disregard the imposed quotas. Discrimination was all around. There was no doubt there was fire behind the smoke.

"These miserable bastards called parents to the city hall and talked them into moving their children to Romanian schools. The approved number of children per class is 18 to 30. They managed to send away enough kids to cancel three classes out of twelve only in our primary school this year."

"Did they offer another job?" Tibor hoped the answer was no.

"Now sit down," she said more collected. "Yes. In Moldova. Is that equal to being thrown out or what?"

"Moldova? What? A Romanian class?"

"Wrong. Hungarian. At the *Csángó*-s," she said.

Tibor knew little about the enclave of the stray Hungarian tribe native in the middle of remote Moldova, on the Eastern slopes of the Carpathians, about three hundred kilometers from their city. "Swell," he said.

"What do you mean, swell?"

"Well, isn't relocation your favorite subject," he said, not able to control his sarcastic gloating.

"You can't be serious."

"It's time that we think fast. By the way. did they offer you to teach at the Romanian school here? You *are* bilingual."

"I asked," she sighed. "I graduated from the Hungarian Teacher's Academy, so they say I can't."

Now Tibor sighed with relief. One obstacle down. He was grateful to the undeniable process of romanization for kicking Maria overboard into his waters.

It took a fast-rolling six months to have all the papers together, file and get the green light. The semaphore had to turn on the Hungarian side as well. Tibor was stunned to discover what the Hungarian government was the most concerned about, when taking in "repatriating" individuals: living space. Solid logic. If someone took you in, he wouldn't let you starve to death or evict you onto the street.

The only redeeming feature of their never ending moving—from a room in his parents' house, to one room in no particular sublet, to Maria's parents—was that they had not much to pack. The Rózsavölgyi family was not the first to emigrate to Hungary from the area of Romania where Romanian nationals were the minority, despite all government efforts to correct that quirk of history.

They were told at the post office where their belongings were inspected and registered, "You'll be notified in three to four weeks." Pleasant surprise.

The day came when the old Moskvitch that Tibor had been caring for like a family heirloom, was filled, overfilled, and top loaded to a testing capacity. On their way, the stop at Tibor's parents turned into a farewell party Tibor didn't expect. A pilgrimage. It was the nicest thing his folks had ever done for his family.

They traveled through known territory, the familiar road robbing Tibor of the thrill of the unique nature of the drive. In the setting sun, bursts of glare and darkness blinded him as the car rose and dipped following the ribbon of asphalt thrown over the hilly land. They left behind Huedin and Ciucea with their old mansions and legends sleeping in the golden dusk. He could drive now forever into the sleepy plain. But, arriving in Budapest in the middle of the night would make him feel as if they were sneaking in. Daylight served his ambitions better.

They pulled the car into the safe garage of the Dacia Hotel in Oradea, a mere half an hour from the border. Tibor shook his head as if waking himself from sleep when Maria mentioned that it was the place of their honeymoon. "It was nice," he said with a feeble hint of nostalgia. The imminent future claimed his undivided attention.

4

They left the brightness and clamor of the busy street, and stood in silence in the dim hallway at the threshold of their new home and new life. Tibor rang the door bell of the second floor apartment. The worst predictions couldn't have prepared him. But, he had no warning, only the memory of a visit as benign as a friendly greeting, and just as immaterial. Nothing to clear his name in front of his wife. What he had promised was not there. Maria's long resistance to the move seemed totally justified. He tried without success to avoid her panicky and chiding gaze that cried deceit, and sunk into a guilty shock.

An air thick with sickness filled and shrunk the dark rooms into bleak holes of decay. The furniture lost not only its luster, but its color as well, as if it were rotting under the layer of grime. Could the two years since he had stayed there do such damage? In people, in objects? The faded luxury, the vile proposition of scrubbing it all out of the crust of neglect was in unison with a sound from beyond the grave. A musty odor filled the bleak bedroom where an old man, Uncle Pista, sat on his bed wheezing. Gawking eyes reflecting a painful anxiety looked over the oxygen mask at the three newcomers standing in the doorway. A muffled grunt as he pulled away the mask from his face suggested words of welcome.

Holding sour smelling Aunt Boske in the entrance hall had squeezed out of the newcomers the last drop of zeal. They were empty of hugs by the time they set eyes on the old man.

They carried up their belongings from the car. They piled suitcases and boxes into the small bedroom. As Boske couldn't sleep with her grunting husband, the dining room was what she called her room now. Relegated to the little kitchen alcove, Zsofi's unhappiness soon became noisily evident.

Despite sullen Boske, Tibor moved the refrigerator out to the entrance hall. Blocking half of it was better than taking away half of the little nook Zsofi could claim as her own. She deserved a new start on a better footing.

❧

"How did she imagine having it both ways? Getting care, housekeeping, rent, *and* having us fade into the woodwork?" Furious, Maria complained bitterly right from the start.

"We'll have to get used to all this," Tibor said though the future escaped him.

"I don't know how long I can take this mean old bitch." Maria's foul language was a warning. Weeks into a new life, with Tibor at work most of the day, Maria was running around from store, to market, from taking Pista and his breathing machinery to the bathroom, to doing all the physical work. Boske more or less cooked for all, with Maria's expected help. Arthritic hands could not handle peeling and chopping vegetables, pouring oil and many other domestic operations. Maria did what Boske only pretended to do. A good word might have kept Maria going, but, "Is this the best you could do?" was Boske's kindest remark.

No circumstances could save the Rózsavölgyis from the emigration crisis all uprooted people have to suffer through. Grumpy Boske and the wheezing stinking Pista didn't help.

"Poor old man," Maria would say some other time. "He had it from her all his life. And no kids. That stinking Yid—"

"You speak in such anger." Tibor was taken aback.

"So?" She wiped her tears. "Sending money? Big deal. That will take care of them, right?"

"It's not our business. I don't want to defend a stranger, but when he left for Australia he gave the apartment as a gift to Pista and Boske. Well, if you ask me, he paid them fairly for hiding him in the tough times. What's wrong with sending money?"

"All we get paid is a stupid piece of paper."

Now the paper—without which they couldn't have immigrated—was stupid. It was obvious which way the wind was blowing. No doubt Maria regarded her burden an unfair share. It was not she who wanted to resettle. It was his idea. His need. And now she had to lift the old man's dead weight, wash him, feed the old wreck. Tibor was bracing himself against what he was sure would soon pour out of his wife's mouth. How would he pacify her? He was not about to contest that Maria was taking the brunt at home, including a growing youngster, who was becoming rebellious. Frighteningly so. Zsofia was coming of age prematurely, transplanted from the quaint countryside and grandmother's skirt, to the big city. The very bellybutton of a city torn between past glory, bloody history and present decline towards a worn-out victim of Socialism. Or was this Communism yet? Whatever it was, it was Hungarian style, with pretenses and snobbism that went far beyond what Tibor could ever have imagined. He would merely shrug lacking a more effective means to deal with his own culture shock. He was helpless on both fronts. *Pompous penury!* It became his favorite line, one he would dispense right and left as a comment on life's daily shortages.

Old Agnes was there for Tibor's debut at the famous Gellért Hotel and Spa's massage parlor. Her sturdy maternal presence and support gradually expanded the circle of his clients. The minister's wife had been a sample in advance, but how uniquely important she was in his life, Tibor couldn't possibly guess. Not even when she became his exclusive client.

Moonlighting came in handy; for Tibor, it was an easily defendable reason to stay away from home. The less he was around, the more he could avoid quarreling with his frazzled wife, but regrettably he missed the time with his daughter. The mother had the merciless duty of feeding the bad eater, shushing her for the sick old man's sake, and supervising her homework. She did not accomplish much; often the child would revolt and spoil her notebook in a rage. Aged eight, little Zsofi was blamed more often than not for anything that went wrong. She often welcomed her father by jumping from behind the door, and kept bouncing up and down like a boisterous puppy ready to be taken out. Tibor tried to make her understand that she should not blame herself for everything that went awry at home—as he was made to think in his formative years. How long it had taken to get his confidence back, and how great was the sacrifice?

Father and daughter left happily for Margaret Island across the river. Feeling energetic, they walked instead of riding the short distance. They crossed the bridge and took the leafy path along the road to the Palatinus open air mineral water pools. While waiting for Zsofia to come out of the locker room, Tibor bought two fresh pastries at the kiosk. Sitting on a bench they gobbled them up before jumping in the tepid water. Playful swimming belonged to the past. Tibor was more and more amazed at how Zsofia enjoyed the long laps that he would've expected to bore a child.

Spending Sunday at the closing day of the week-long Horse Days in the dusty plain at Hortobágy was a whole-family affair. The day was too short for everything Zsofia wanted to see. "Mom, I want another cotton candy," she screamed every minute for something else, stopping only when her mouth was full. She ran from the line of groomed pacers harnessed ready for the next race, to the stables where the foaming sweat of the previous race was being wiped from the trotters. In minutes, she was hanging from the fence along the racetrack, and to onlookers' astonishment, yelling and cheering for some horse she happened to recognize from the line-up. "Dad, I want to get in that buggy." A friendly jockey who had lost and was idle, kindly accommodated her.

As they strolled around the grounds, the scent of food attracted the crowds to the area where sets of three to four huge black caldrons hung on heavy chains from poles placed horizontally over tripods driven into the ground over log-fires. The procession of sides of beef and mutton to be carved, sacks of potatoes and carrots to be dumped in the caldrons was endless. Hefty cooks with small round black hats were already stirring the steaming broth, their long white sleeves rolled up their powerful arms.

By the end of the steeplechase, the goulash was ready for the hundreds of hungry folk drooling around the tracks. The air was redolent with the appetizing aroma rising from the bubbling stew.

Tibor and his family left the grounds after dark. Zsofia was sleeping on the back seat. Tibor felt chatty until he realized he was talking to himself although Maria wasn't asleep. "Wasn't this great fun?" he asked.

"Bearable." She said scarcely parting her lips.

With the conversation cut short, Tibor swallowed his next question. He clenched the steering wheel, then took a deep breath and willed his hands and shoulders into a more relaxed position.

He carried the sleeping Zsofia to the elevator. They found the lights on in the apartment. Boske sat stony faced at the kitchen table.

"They took Pista to the hospital."

Pneumonia wiped out his remaining functioning lung. He never recovered.

Boske moved back to the master bedroom. What seemed the most reasonable re-shuffling to Tibor, and what would have brought them closer to a vague ideal of home, was moving teenage Zsofia into the dining room which could have doubled for a few hours in the evenings as a massage room. In his eyes, this was the best of all possible worlds. He could start a decent practice, he would have no problem getting a license, and he could stop running around the city like a headless chicken. The balance of events, however, hinted to secret negotiations between the two women, that he was excluded from. Excited, Maria talked about something Tibor couldn't make sense of at first.

After an inspection, the National Tourist Board declared the dining room appropriate to rent as a guest room. Tourists would be sent from the central reservation bureau to their home which was changed overnight into a B&B.

Zsofia, a teenager coming of age, a flower with her petals scrunched, remained squeezed behind a folding screen, an unkind symbol of the forty square feet of her deceptive privacy.

A feverish planning and shopping spree lifted Maria's spirits out of depression, a reward that filled Tibor with hope.

He hadn't met the first guests. He sneaked through his own home with some irritation for having his movement curbed, but repressed his frustration when he saw Maria's elation the next day. "My love," she said. She was bouncy with joy. He welcomed this long forgotten term of endearment. "I can see this as a career," she said, then answered his questioning look. "Hosting, dummy."

"Ah."

"It's easy and pleasant. This couple from Prague? Really sweet, and quiet. I saw them looking around with respect—"

"What do you mean by looking around?"

"Like . . . like they're impressed. They love the room."

"How can you talk to them?"

"Easy. It's fun."

Her enthusiasm caught up with him. "You should spend the first money from the rental on yourself. You deserve it," he said.

"That's very sweet, but you helped a lot, painted the room, we both deserve it."

"Let's all take a weekend at the Balaton," he said.

"When I don't have guests."

"Of course. Zsofia's swimming is quite classy, she's—"

"With aunt Boske—"

"I was thinking more like family—"

"She's family, isn't she?"

He bit his tongue. He had no idea when things had changed and Maria's aunt was no longer the mean bitch. A weekend at the lake didn't look that attractive any more. Going out to the island, lying in the grass, swimming and mostly watching his daughter plunging and racing against herself would have been far better.

Tibor had to agree eventually that the investment had paid off. It paid for itself and became lucrative faster than Maria had expected. The irritation of having to tip-toe about in his own home was replaced by the comfort of coming home to a happier wife. Beyond that nothing was obvious to Tibor. Boske didn't mind the strangers. She mingled, especially with guests who spoke Hungarian. Some appeared to find the little old lady shuffling around and chirping like a carefree bird an icing on the cake. Romantic, as Maria started to call the whole affair. Both women were ebullient; they seemed to be recovering something previously missing in their lives.

The secret of success was not only the room, which was certainly more than welcoming. The real magnet was the location. It made guests feel special. An address as luxurious as the Hilton in Buda at half the price. Tourists everywhere pay gladly for the feel of elegance.

One Sunday morning, Zsofi scrambled to finish her homework for the promise of a circus show. Tibor sat across the kitchen table reading the paper and enjoying his daughter's intent face bent over her notebook.

Guests showed up to settle in for an entire week. Maria, dressed in flowery flowing silk, proudly showed the middle age couple to their room, pointing a long red fingernail to the bathroom in passing.

But Tibor? His chin fell. He couldn't recognize his own wife. An apparition from some movie screen? Embarrassed, he took his paper folded under his arm to the bedroom. It was not his show. Was this his place? His wife? Was Maria's elevated mood he welcomed in their intimate moments a mere trickling down from her exuberance she poured over the strangers?

It was not long before Maria ordered embroidered bed sheets from Vaci utca's most prestigious custom store. She redecorated their bathroom and by what magic, Tibor couldn't figure out, convinced Boske to let her, Tibor and the girl use hers when guests were present. That shot the price they could collect on the room way out of sight. Unshared bathroom, in St. Istvan Park, across Margit Sziget in the little paradise of the central city park!

Maria-the-hostess's new cool manner, left behind the lowly worries of

Zsofia's school, interest in her progress with swimming, or her husband's extra long hours. She reveled, inordinately so by Tibor's standards, in receiving *guests à la grande dame*—especially Westerners with advanced reservations. She would whirl around the house, fill the guest room with flowers, forget that anything else existed. She would often disappear soon after a phone call and throwing a short instruction list to the part-time help she had hired to take care of the almost crippled Boske. She would return late in the night with chocolates for "My poor dear Aunty," as she recently started to call the old woman.

Tibor was left to worry alone about an indistinct, but developing mystery, Zsofia. Not a little girl at all. At thirteen she banished her favorite ice cream to the past, instead filling a refrigerator shelf with cartons of yogurt. Even to the two sets of grandparents, who acknowledged her serene beauty with awe when they came a couple of times a year.

Annoyed, Tibor excused himself in the middle of a massage session as he pulled the sheet over the man's naked body. He went to take the call. "Love . . " he heard Maria's voice dripping with honey, ". . . could you have lunch with me today?"

He had but one choice. Be fittingly outrageous. "You break my heart, my darling," his sonorous voice resonated with sarcasm. "You make me feel so guilty—"

"That's all right," she interrupted curtly but sweetly.

Surprise left him speechless. He didn't think she was joking. He cleared his throat. "Think of me gobbling up my sandwich in the locker room in the half hour break."

"I certainly will, you poor slave." He couldn't dismiss the smiling tone in her voice.

Fighting through rush hour across Margit Bridge to Buda, driving from one house call to the next, Tibor concentrated all his attention and skill on his clients. Half paralyzed women. Few masseurs, even those who by the new fashion called themselves healers, could claim real experience in post-stroke care. His hospital training gave Tibor a confident bearing of competence that set him apart from his garden variety peers.

Late, he dragged himself upstairs, still looking for an explanation for his wife's morning call. The apartment was quiet and dark. He found a note on the kitchen table. "My angel." *My angel? My ass. What did she have for lunch? Maybe she's sorry for something.* Zsofia not at home either. Evening swim practice with a national swim coach, after recently having been selected to the team of hopeful youngsters. Nobody to ask, How was your day? He read on. "Warm up your dinner. I forgot to tell you about Charlotte's birthday party. Don't wait up. The guest room is occupied. Mari."

A husky snore filled the passageway. Boske. The guest room was dark. Perhaps they were sleeping, perhaps they were out. He tip-toed anyway, yielding to his exhaustion.

In the morning, Maria was sleeping sweetly next to him, sensuously perfumed. Was it a new fragrance? Contrary to his recent habits, he felt like enjoying an exceptional quicky. Lately his professional preoccupations invaded him as soon as he awoke, pushing intimacy out of the way. That morning, he felt his wife unusually exciting. Moreover, he was to realize, languorously but firmly refractory to his advances. *What the fuck's got into her?* Miffed, he flipped the blanket and got out of the bed as if thrown by a spring. He took a cool shower.

5

Spring with its cheery green fireworks emerging from the trees in the park could not disguise the worsening big picture. Tibor couldn't find the aura of glamour that had previously enchanted him when he visited the city where he now lived. Too much hassle. Never a really relaxing day. Pungent exhaust choked him as he crawled along with the slow traffic funneling towards the bridge. At times, Tibor longed to sidestep from the grinding routine. His job failed to supply the energized contentment he felt at the beginning. *Had I outgrown my own dreams that brought me here?*

Tibor felt heavy under the weight of his discontent as he stepped into the white Swedish clogs and pulled himself straight as he opened the door to the corridor. Cracking his knuckles, he rotated his head slightly before entering the treatment room. He started to work his way through a full schedule of flesh, old and young, lined up for him to pump up their vigor and lift their pain. His powerful arms grew numb by the end of the eight hours of kneading, rubbing, feeling, slapping, pulling. Not talking about how numb his mind was after all the entertaining talk expected of him. He usually had no problem faking interest in his clients' lamentations and sometimes he was genuinely interested. Lately, he found himself dodging their political views. Having hesitant opinions, or rather not being interested in any political platforms, he did sound a bit narrow-minded at such times.

Tibor was as restless as a dog during a solar eclipse. He would be hard-pressed to admit that six years into a new life he was bored to death while expecting to be jumping up and down with satisfaction. His days were robotic. Maria became a one-subject-wife: hosting business. At work, while everyone was sucked in by the large unfolding picture, he felt left out. Self-styled politician-citizens, even old Pali *bácsi,* the janitor, sounded like they were giving political lectures. Perhaps, motivated by loneliness, his resentment of politics started to decline into curiosity.

When he picked up the *Népszava,* the official party daily paper, and read that one or the other of his work mates had dropped in the locker room, he never got further than the headlines and sporting news.

A hot wind was blowing in Eastern Europe, coming of all places from Poland. The winter session of the Hungarian Parliament was brewing promises to bring in the year of 1989 with a bang. People were craving for a shake up. As the janitor said, "This is seriously explosive." But, they had spilled enough blood in 1956. No one wanted blood flowing again in the streets of Budapest.

Like a reactivated volcano bubbling in the depths under the heavy crust of official government politics, voices became louder and louder. The shouting on the floor of the parliament picked up the noise from the streets, and in turn, the crowds echoed and sustained the impetus coming from the Parliament. Tibor started to feel guilty watching from the sideline.

"Tibi, my friend, how are you going to let all this fly over your head?" Bodor, the supervisor, asked Tibor in January, when the bang hit the papers. The Parliament has just legalized independent parties and public demonstrations. "What a chance for you to make up for not being with us in '56."

"You'd have to teach me the first thing about politics—"

"I'd be happy as a lark to do just that. No effort is too much for me to have you join us," Bodor said with a glimmer in his eyes. That scared Tibor, for he intended his remark as an evasive one. He did not have one political bone in his body. He couldn't wriggle himself out of his skepticism, though he tried to build a feeling of political belonging and contribute to his new country's betterment.

Twelve year old Zsofia was wise enough to finish her homework as fast as she could. She was not crazy about school. She made no secret about being more enthusiastic about running to swim training than coming home, as she rarely avoided running right into her mother's palm that landed on her face. She no longer questioned her mother's arguments for the slaps. It was mostly about getting in late, though she always got home before her mandatory bed time.

Zsofia was one of the most vivacious youngsters amongst her peers. Not so at home. Tibor knew from what he saw around the pool that boys, less so girls, acted as strong magnets on his daughter's developing allegiances. She stood out with a physical maturity that opened doors to a slightly older company. This was not trivial, Tibor thought, observing that from under the baby skin, puberty brought forth attributes, equally enchanting and disquieting to a worrying parent.

Maria, in her ultimate inconsistency, was going full circle from slapping Zsofia—without an explanation, "The little twit must know by now what she's guilty of," to sharing some newly acquired Western cosmetics and making up her daughter's greenish almond eyes and high cheeks to look double her age.

"Dad, how do I look?" Zsofia asked, admiring herself in her mother's oval hand held mirror.

"If you ask me, terrible," he would say with a sorry grimace for having to deny her beauty. "Like any old lady hiding the signs of aging. What are *you* hiding? Your healthy color, your youth?" And his eyes would shift to his wife's face where make up seemed to serve that very purpose. What was she hiding? Perhaps, something other than her age, because her fullness upheld her features quite well.

"You're forgiven," Zsofia would giggle. "You're not modern."

On June 17, 1989, the warmth of a bright sun tried to lift the human spirit, beaten under the yoke of impending economic collapse. Tibor joined the million or so throbbing, tumultuous crowd that lined Budapest's streets leading to *Hösök Tere,* Heroes Square, where they would wait for the procession. The occasion, no matter how political, appealed to him. The process of Nagy Imre's rehabilitation and eventually the preparations that led to that day didn't leave any citizen of the country untouched.

Nagy Imre's appeal for Western help in 1956 during the October revolution was drowned by the rumbling of the Soviet tanks on the streets of Budapest and he ended up with a noose around his neck. He gave his life for the national freedom that was slow to come. Now, when that goal was close, his bones were judged by the Supreme Court as deserving the tribute that was denied his hunted and betrayed living body.

Since Tibor was a young boy in Romania, his vocabulary did not yet list the word politics in 1956. In retrospect, it seemed that he was not the only one who was ignorant then; at that time no one was let into the truth. Certainly not in a Romania—still unconditionally loyal to the Soviets—which as recent history has proved, was part of the traitorous ring extraditing the fleeing Nagy and returning him to his executioners.

Tibor's work pals, a talkative gang, not unlike everyone around, dwelled on the events that had led to Nagy's earthly remains being exhumed from the prison grave. The popular demand prevailed over the party hard-liners still in power who had no choice but to allow this national ceremony to take place.

"Only the blind can't see that nothing can stop the real liberation. The *Russkies* will have to go, my party will chase them out," Bodor, a member of the Hungarian Democratic Forum, the strength of the opposition, led the enthusiasts. The event kindled more than national feelings; it fueled the burner needed to flush the remaining Soviet troops out.

The very air throbbed with determination. If it depended on some more radical factions coming out overnight like mushrooms, blood could spill again, for they were not so patient as to wait for the wind of renewal to sweep through their country. Loud groups were reciting. *Talpra Magyar hí a haza!* Petofi Sandor's National Song, revolutionary verses fit for more than the National day for which it was originally written in 1848. Hungarians recite when in doubt, when full of verve, when in love with their country. It's in their blood, just like the penchant for vagueness and intricacy they seem to be born with.

There was promising news. People mentioned it overcome by emotion, like referring to the symptoms of a beloved recovering from a fatal illness. The barbed wire had been recently dismantled at the Austrian border by soldiers joined by an optimistic crowd. Tibor cheered especially at the piece of news that the Romanian government was engaged in driving concrete poles into the ground along the borders with Hungary and the Soviet Union to extend the barbed wire fences in the hope of stopping the tide of renewal. At least he was on the right side of that fence, a laughable line that history would cut away with its bloodied knife.

Shreds of conversation, amidst laughter, intimated that some raucous groups, going out on a limb, were removing red stars from the facades of official buildings. And no one was stopping them.

"When was it that Dubcêk was on our television?" Tibor remembered seeing the kindly looking old man, back in the limelight from the oblivion, not long before.

"About two months ago," a woman said. "April I think. See, we're ahead of the Czechs. He could speak *here.* Not there yet. I bet they'll have to give in too, those bastards."

"Why bastards? We killed our Messiah, they didn't. They're more civilized than we are," Bodor said, obviously not forgiving about his own history. "Dubcêk is alive and carrying the torch. After 20 some years. Do you know that after he spoke here they put him on the Soviet TV?"

"How can that be?" Tibor asked.

"How? Gorby is not the butcher Brezhnev," Bodor sounded proud and loving, using Michail Gorbachev's, the leader of the *Perestroika,* popular nickname. "They *did* reassess the *Prague Spring* just as here we won't let the Government off the hook until they rehabilitate completely our Nagy Imre."

"Isn't this absurd?" someone interjected. "Here we are, honoring these coffins and they're not rehabilitated yet."

The six coffins—Nagy's, four of his executed colleagues' and a symbolic one for the other hundreds killed between 1956 and 1961, when those trials finally ended—were being carried onto the monumental platform and placed amongst the tall torches.

"And our pigheaded leaders still hold the old position." Every decent citizen hoped that the review process under way could not stop before all were totally rehabilitated. After all, Walesa, Dubcêk, Havel, names held in high esteem in that crowd—just as the torches amongst the coffins—were alive and winning. Nagy's memory took the Hungarian people's initiative to a higher level at a more favorable time.

Bells from all over the city pealed above the speechless sea of people. The bold black and white drapes of mourning, hung over the columns of the facade of the National Museum, fluttered in the breeze like so many Phoenix birds, while the sound of broadcast eulogies filled the somber air.

By midsummer Tibor was convinced that Bodor, his supervisor, knew his politics. Tibor needed to pick his brain. He was wondering how common it was to have sports news other than big international wins on the front page. "What do you think, is there more politics in this than it looks?" It was the piece about the National Olympic Committee being restored, revived from its long forgotten ashes as the paper put it.

"Well," Bodor scratched his head. "It would be a long shot to call it political. It's more like getting back to reality. I would say it's more anti-political."

"Which in this case means what?"

"That sports will be free from politics. As it should be. That hopefully it will be managed by experts, not political commissars."

"It didn't seem to have suffered before. Wouldn't you say Hungarian athletes always did great?"

"There's always room for improvement. Besides, if you read between the lines, a subcommittee buried somewhere in the lower echelons of some ministry would never be able to attract financial sponsors. We're going free market economy big time—"

"I'm aware of that, and also of how badly it's going—" Tibor was interrupted.

"Nothing is for nothing." Then Bodor changed tone. "How come you notice such news? I wasn't aware of your interest in sports management."

"Nothing. The big headlines, I guess."

What was there besides the candid 'nothing' Tibor didn't know yet. As if his attention had a mind of its own, during the following weeks, his eyes slid over all news items seeking out anything even vaguely connected to the new Olympic Committee. The names of the newly elected—emphasis on elected, as opposed to nominated—president and secretary general meant nothing to Tibor. Shortly after the five sub-committees were announced, he couldn't explain his agitated state. Medical subcommittee. He couldn't ignore it.

As if his life depended on it, he strained to summon from his short list of acquaintances names he could elevate to the function of useful connection. The minister's wife? His first patient on Hungarian soil, the now not-so-young lady whose ancient mother at home in her wheelchair had also been his patient for quite a while, since her stroke.

He could barely contain his urge to talk to the minister's wife. He felt like a child craving a cookie and screaming if he didn't get it. *Should I call her? Too dangerous. Why? My ego, damn it. Not talking about secrecy. How'd I convey on the phone what I'm after? Too high a stake. Maybe she doesn't want to lose me as a masseur. I'll never find out whether she can't help or she doesn't want to. Give her the benefit of doubt. I should be fair. Why would I doubt her disinterest? Do I not trust anything or anybody? Why'd I be in such bad shape? Maybe I should ask for her opinion whether it's a good idea at all.*

She finally came for her massage. The three days marked on his calendar seemed to Tibor like a three years wait. *I have never been so impatient.*

Being on first name terms with Aranka, after so many years of such private nexus, helped. Tibor gave Aranka his prepared speech when she was lying on her back. He believed in the power of eye contact.

She acted surprised, even appalled at the idea that he was not happy at the spa. Aranka's wrinkle-wreathed kind eyes scrutinized Tibor's that were filled with noticeable sadness. He smiled at her as if in apology.

"I can't pull a name from the hat, Tibor. I'll talk to Árpád." She mentioned also that her husband was now retired, so he could count less on his connections. She patted Tibor's hands with encouragement. "And to answer your first question. I think you should go for it. There's more in it for you than here, for God's sake. We'll help you as much as we can."

Tibor had an inkling, or rather a sinking feeling in the pit of his stomach. He suspected that grapevines had side branches that transmitted information faster than the main trunk that failed to bring *him* any news. He was called to see Lakatos, the new director, who must have intercepted messages on one of the high speed branches that bypassed Tibor.

The man's courtesy extended just one step beyond gross directness. One sentence, then he plunged. "You know we have to cope with budget cuts," he was saying while Tibor counted in his mind his years of seniority. "It should make you feel good that you have saved someone else's job. It wouldn't have crossed my mind to lay you off. You're too valuable."

"May I ask why are you mentioning the layoff plans to me?" He was aware of the futility of his question. Ostrich policy.

"My budgetary obligations are pressing, Mr. Rózsavölgyi," Somogyi said. "You would agree I shouldn't fire someone who is not out looking for another job."

He knows, the miserable bastard. Who was the careless, crazy, stupid idiot to cut the branch from under my feet? Not only have I no other job. I practically haven't looked for one. I inquired, that's all. Not even an interview in sight. Maybe never. Is anyone out there who knows? Please, surprise me. The instant arithmetic of his moonlighting income yielded dismal results. Even together with Maria's B&B income, the number didn't add up to half of what his family needed for basic living. Tibor gasped for air, he was crushed. He desperately needed to spare his aplomb.

The official numbers that shocked the nation a few months earlier also flashed through his mind. The government admitted that 25 percent of the population was living in dire poverty. Just out of Communism and into poverty? No. Nothing had changed, save that they could publish the data, something that had never been done during the full blown Communist *well-being.* Soon they could add his family to the statistics.

What is he going to do about the reason that sprung him into action in the first place? He could hang himself. Tell this to the guy with his piercing gaze? Why would he care? "Don't mistake my words for complaints, but I want you to know that you're practically throwing me out in the street. And I'm not that young to—"

"You have no reason to worry." The stiff and cold figure of the director surprised Tibor with a suddenly softened voice.

Tibor imagined some talking going on behind his back. He hoped this sudden realization was the closest to the truth and said, "I hope you're right. I wish someone would tell me what's going on."

"I can't promise you, it's not up to me, but I advise that you be patient. I'll conditionally postpone your termination for two months."

Though Tibor could have thanked, he didn't. "I guess this is for now all the information you'll give me." He took his leave.

On the way home he decided to say nothing to Maria. Why should he? She had gotten into one of those *terrific* screaming fits when he had mentioned his intention to find out whether the Olympic team would be interested in hiring him. What now? Poor Zsofika with her dreams of making it to the top. Loving that swimming as she did. He would not be able to afford it.

He cracked his knuckles, tossed sleeplessly, lost his appetite, forgot an appointment. Never a chance to dazzle anyone on that grapevine with as little as an imploring look.

"A Doctor Dóczi wants you to call," Zsofia gave Tibor the message one evening. He looked at the scribble. Erzsébet. A woman. One of Aranka's contacts had mentioned that the doctor in the Olympic medical team, the next link down the grapevine, was a woman. Tibor started to ring his hands. No specified time.

"Is this a hospital? Are you all right, dad?" Zsofia asked.

He sat at the kitchen table. He wished Maria was there. Now he could talk about the noose he felt around his neck for the last four days. But she was out. At some tea party again.

"Zsofi, where's your mother?"

Zsofia stepped out from behind her screen. "I'm not my mother's keeper. Neither are you, I guess."

"Sweetheart, there is no reason to be so rude." He put on a mocking tone. "It's not good for your complexion," he smiled at his own joke and a young tall slender woman grinned back. She couldn't hide the glamorous smile that lit up her face. No make up. She had just come from swim practice.

"Did this doctor say what time should I call?"

"She said this is her home number."

He looked at his watch. Almost ten. He ran to the phone not to be out-of-bounds calling too late. Although not young, the kind voice sounded clear and beautiful. Of course, Tibor smirked. Anything she said was a poem. She wanted to meet him. After hours at the Central University Hospital. Tomorrow?

He couldn't sleep. He tossed, his bones ached. Maria slid into the bed around midnight. He wanted to talk. She wasn't interested though he said it was something especially important.

"I'm tired. I will be fresher tomorrow, then I won't miss a word," she responded condescendingly.

They settled back to back. He tried to harness his imagination confined by a wall of unknowns. *A life I can't imagine as a goal? What am I doing?* He was wondering whether he was in search of himself or an escape from himself.

His stride became springier, his expression rejuvenated as the down-sloping lines of anxiety mutated into lines of hope. When he knocked on Dr. Doczi's door he felt like a youth just out of school, full of motivation. *Of course, she'll quiz me. Didn't cross my mind. Do I remember any theory? I've no idea what this job involves. What job? I'll see, as the blind baron said.*

An hour later, he knew that Doczi was a consultant to the Olympic team, a leading orthopedic surgeon recently returned from the United States from a two-year fellowship. She had big plans to overhaul the system she was appointed to. Her enthusiasm carried Tibor to an ecstatic state of mind. She objected that the masseurs were not called physical therapists in sports circles. "Worse is *massers,*" she said, "but that's what most of them are, old timers and let me tell you, unmatched in their skills. But I would like a few people who would handle from the beginning, I mean my beginning with the team, the entire palette of modalities at our discretion," she added. In an unobtrusive way, she sounded Tibor's background and possible dislikes.

"Your training . . . I know about from those who spoke on your behalf . . . immediately piqued my interest. I don't need to see you at work, the references I got before you came speak for you. I'll report to the vice-president hiring new medical staff, but I see no problem. Naturally you will have to like what they offer you in terms of employment and I hope to see you around." She held out a strong hand for a hefty shake.

Back in the street he walked with his arms thrown high, his hands feeling for some hold in the air to stop him from flying over the buildings. He laughed out loud as he smiled back at people puzzled by his outlandish behavior. *Who cares who the careless inquirer was who could jeopardize my livelihood? They know what they're after. Do they? Or, would they hire anyone willing to join? Did Somogyi supply them with such irresistible references? Maybe he's a barking-dog-that-doesn't-bite type? If I'd like the offer? If I'd find it satisfactory, not because I've lost my top-notch job at the spa, not because I'd take anything, because . . . because, what? Why is this business filling me with such joy? It feels happy as a wedding, better, the birth of a child, not a job opportunity. No. They couldn't offend me with a poor offer. I could be offended at this point only with a pitchfork to my behind. His laugh rang out, then he sobered. They could still go cold on me. Maybe they can't hire right now. On the other hand, with two years to the next games, I bet they have to beef up all they can. Please, don't let me down, I won't let you down either. You, vice-president or whoever, you won't be sorry. Take me.*

6

Tibor squinted in the bright sunshine as he came up from the underground at the Octagon. He was not late. He hurried only to blow off steam. He aimed playful kicks at the dry leaves rolling along the sidewalk in the cool autumn breeze.

The new headquarters of the Hungarian Olympic Committee occupied a high floor of a baroque building. The facade, like many along the street lined with plane trees, boasted windows and doors framed in carved stone. He walked through an echoing lobby. A secretary asked him to wait in the corridor. He picked up a small brochure—*Facts at your fingertips*—from a table placed in the middle of a row of streamlined chairs. Dates and names traced Hungarian achievements in the modern Olympics. Names had been added since the recent advent of major reorganizing, the event that brought him here. Bombastic statements about rekindled hopes for more victories. Photos of venues Tibor never heard of. He had been narrow-minded, he realized. It seemed obvious now that the Balaton and Lake Tata were top choices for racers, as were tranquil country roads for cyclists. *What a snob I've become. Of course there's life outside this pretentious exhaust bin. What are these camps in Dunavarsány? Tata? They look like modern compounds. Training facilities? Living quarters? What purpose would that serve when one could commute to Budapest?* Just as well that the secretary led him into an office half furnished with brick-a-brack furniture. *The Vice didn't get his streamlined stuff yet,* Tibor mused. Piled in corners on the bare worn out parquet floor badly in need of polishing, boxes spilled papers that looked like records onto a coffee table. A man stood by the tall window reading a file. His file, as Tibor could see when the man stepped forward to shake hands.

"Mr. Rozsavölgyi, I'm pleased to meet you under promising circumstances," the man said.

"The pleasure is mine, Mr. Kiss," Tibor said then took the seat the man pointed to.

"We are full of hope . . . great things are coming . . . things to be done with the best of available knowledge. We are looking for devoted people."

It may be downhill from such lofty words, Tibor feared. He braced for an answer to match the vice president, who appeared to be waiting for some response. “In the short time outside I learned a lot,” Tibor said. “There is much more to know about our sports movement than an average fan can accumulate in a life time of rooting for a few favorite sports—”

“What sports would be your favorites Tibor? May I call you Tibor?”

The man could have been his father. Even their stature was similar. Both men were very tall, straight as pines; their square faces were open, honest; only Kiss’s hair was a sparkling white brush, while Tibor’s dark blond was short, but hugging his scalp. “Naturally,” Tibor smiled showing all his teeth. “As the illustration shows . . “ he pointed to his profile hardened by the jagged saddle of his nose, “. . . it used to be boxing. Nowadays, of course, it’s soccer, like everyone else, and also water sports. This is probably because my daughter shows promise in swimming—”

“That all sounds wonderful,” Kiss said picking up Tibor’s file again. “I understand from Doctor Doczi and your application that your qualification and skills meet our needs perfectly. Now the question is whether we can meet yours. I’ll be very realistic and straightforward about how I see your employment. Firstly, your job description. We’ll be very possessive of your time and energy.” He reacted immediately to Tibor’s eyebrows pulling up in bewilderment. “In other words, you will have to agree not to engage in any work outside your job. This decision is of course debatable, when actually people are trying to augment their incomes by moonlighting. We justify this request from our employees by some philosophical standards, which are beyond the scope of this meeting. We have already employed a few people who, of course agreed. Others who were not convinced they could kick the old habits we let go.” He put the papers on the desk again and clasped his fingers together. “At all times you would work with one or more coaches. Most of the time here in Budapest, most of the time according to a precise schedule of approximately eight hour work days. There is a twist here. While everyone’s private life is important and we respect it, there will be times when you might feel that . . . how should we put it? You will be a slave to a higher goal. This is a strong statement, so I hope it will look better in practice.”

Tibor nodded expressing his understanding. “The goal?” Tibor threaded his fingers leaning his fists with the thumbs extended against each other. “I guess, if one regards it as the *common* goal one won’t feel like a slave.”

"Tibor, that's great. One need not waste words with you. Briefly, before competitions, tournaments, the games, your services will be mostly needed at the training camp sites. Could be any, which are not that far from Budapest, but we'll adopt a policy of *quasi* sequestration. For weeks, at times." Now he raised his eyebrows as two hairy question marks. While waiting for Tibor's reaction to the prospect of such hardship, he added, "I can assure you that accommodation is civilized."

"So far, everything you said I kind of expected." He was so pleased with himself, undaunted by the prospect of a new lifestyle he hadn't even contemplated, that he was ready with some lofty statement himself: "Everyone involved should share in the pre-competition fever."

"Very good. However, there is another aspect I should mention. I'm afraid we treat this issue quite clumsily. You see, there is no experience that could help me out here, this is all very new." He rubbed his chin. "The National Olympic Committee intends to be a beacon, an example of apolitical organization. By remaining politically uninvolved we can secure our independence from any biased influence. In the past, we achieved this partially under the most unfavorable circumstances. We stayed above pressures to which sports leaders of other Communist countries caved in or made *a modus vivendi* out of—"

"I know exactly what you mean. I moved here from Romania. Sports organizations were extensions of the Communist regime—"

"Were you involved in sports there?"

"Only as an amateur, but the fact is of common knowledge."

"We cannot request individuals working for us to drop their political allegiances, but they would have to agree to keeping their beliefs and such activities totally outside and separate from their jobs. The same goes for our athletes."

Tibor jumped at what was the exact opposite of what Bodor was trying to con him into. He felt like crying out. *I'm your ideal chap, take me. I kept myself a virgin for you.* He said, "What appeared to have been a shortcoming of mine not ever being affiliated with any political party, sometimes, I can assure you, at the risk of my livelihood, comes in handy now. I have no objection to this requirement. I am apolitical by birth."

At this moment, Kiss smiled with obvious relief and came down to earth to discuss money matters and benefits. Tibor was pleased to hear the numbers, a decent compensation indeed for the lost opportunity to earn extra money. He accepted the package without holding his nose high.

"When would I start?"

"As soon as you are free."

The team was finally off to Barcelona in the summer of 1992, taking half of the dozen masseurs with them. That meant two weeks vacation for Tibor. Seniority was essential in determining who stayed and who went. Despite his key activity of introducing new methods of physical therapy, after only two years with the national team, he was still a novice. Besides, he hadn't really enjoyed going to preliminaries in Berlin, Moscow or even Torino. However modest his sightseeing dreams were, they always ended up the same. Collapse in some crummy dormitory after twelve hours of work. No breath left even for socializing.

Tibor came home at the end of an exhausting month being sequestered at Tata. The tension of the upcoming games had been one of the toughest times of his life. The athletes, with rare exception, were bunches of ruffled nerves. It was not the good adrenaline flowing in their blood. It was the kind that made them self-conscious, self-doubting anxious humans, no matter how hardened in discipline they were. Tibor worked up calluses on their *crunchies*. They were twice as sore and it took twice the time to relax their muscles.

Being left at home felt like releif. For that matter, not being in Barcelona was pure luck. He escaped the investigation that everyone there had to undergo after a manager absconded with the team's money.

On the other hand, his soul ached from guilt. Zsofi'a regional swim competition was her athletic crossroads. If she advanced (which she did) would she pursue a competitive career? He was not there for her. That it wasn't his fault made no difference. *Why can't sports organizations give priority to Olympic preparations?* On July the 18th the national team was at the height of feverish preparation and leaving in another few days for Barcelona for the July 25th opening ceremony. After all, the whole country scheduled their lives around the TV programs, which in turn revolved around the Olympic dates and events.

Maria wasn't there for Zsofi either. She was busy. No pleading could persuade her to skip her Saturday afternoon rummy game so their daughter would have someone to cheer her up if she lost, or share her victory if she won. He could see her willowy figure full of the sorrow of abandonment, her defiantly squinting, sulking gaze darkening her green eyes, denying to her pals that she was hurt by the absence of her family cheering squad.

Was his job worth the sacrifice? Zsofia was fourteen when he took it. They had made plans to travel together. She the champion, the flag bearer, he cheering from the sidelines as he did for all the strangers under his care. He'd failed her. He reshuffled old insecurities. Not knowing what to do as a father was worse.

More and more often treats appeared on the dinner table when he returned from Tata. Tired, but happy with work as it was, Tibor was enjoying an excited talkative moment. No doubt that his favorite mushroom soup with dumplings played a role. When the telephone rattled its rusty hoarse ring, he stopped talking. Zsofia jumped to answer it as if ejected by a spring. Maria and Tibor sat looking at each other, their spoons frozen in midair.

After stealing gazes towards the entry hall, and whispering behind a cupped hand, Zsofia returned to the table, slurped up the soup hastily, without answering either parent's questions. Then, she abruptly pirouetted out of her chair. Instead of an apology for leaving in the middle of the meal, she blew between lips tightened in spite, "Thanks for dinner."

"Where're you going again?" Maria asked.

"What difference does it make to you? It's vacation."

Tibor's spoon hit the soup with a splash. A sixteen year old with a bruise he thought he knew. He feared that noticing Zsofia's nasty remark would be a bad move. Instead, Tibor picked up on a previously unfinished subject in an appeasing tone, "Would you like a party to celebrate your success?"

"No way!" Maria snapped. The unfortunate interjection left Tibor's mouth agape with exasperation.

"See, what I mean," Zsofia raised her voice and pointed an accusing finger at her mother. "I can't bring anyone here because they leave marks on the parquet, not to mention the marks on my face after they leave." She waved in a gesture of helplessness and ran out slamming the door.

Tibor held his head, clawing his forehead with trembling fingers. "You can't keep slapping a sixteen year old," he said in a lamenting broken voice. A dream was foundering. A single absence wiped out all the times when he was there for his daughter. When he held her twiggy little kicking body learning how to swim. When he chaperoned her to practice for years. Oh, she was good. She had a future. All her coaches said so. And now she won't give him the time of day.

"She's the nastiest brat," Maria affirmed sounding conclusive.

"Perhaps she could use more support—"

"Sure. You're so smart from the distance. Who gives her a clean home? Cooks for her? I work my tail off so she can afford all the expenses to keep up with her hobby—"

"Wait a minute. Hobby? She has the fabric of a champion. Besides, you talk as if I don't exist. You want numbers? Hours worked? Money brought home? Why couldn't you go last week?"

"I have my miserable once-a-week game. You're having your fun around the clock. Don't you think I know why you switched to this job? I see through you. Kneading all those young bodies. I bet you get more hard-ons there than at home—"

"How can you be so vulgar? What is this stupid idea of yours all about? This is about how we are failing our only daughter and that's your excuse?"

"What's your excuse?"

"What excuse does work need? If you're asking for excuses why is it that Zsofi could come stay for two weekends with me at Tata and you didn't have time for that either? We had a good time on the lake, between work hours—"

"I don't swim."

"No, you don't. And don't visit either. I swear . . " he put his hand on his heart, "I would've never asked, though don't kid yourself, I *was* wondering why. Besides . . . I came home the other weekend, didn't I? And what did you do?"

"I did what I usually do on weekends."

Hungary was not immune to the deprivations and sacrifices of turning to a market economy, but in Romania people were taking the brunt of rising from the ashes of Communism. While before the revolution a kilo of nonexistent meat was cheap, now that it was available—not loaded in refrigerator trucks heading for Italy and Germany—not many could afford it. A week's salary for a salami? More than a month's rent? But that started to adjust too. Goodbye cheap housing. All prices were edging up to Western standards. Incomes were stuck in a past regime's unrealistic value scale, a discrepancy no one was prepared to understand.

Having spent eight years in a land where people were almost as unhappy with the new directions as in other former Eastern block countries, Tibor and Maria had the moral obligation to arrive with a loaded car. Because of the slightly better conditions in Hungary, their relatives in Romania regarded them as living in Canaan. They had to deal among other things with the sense of fairness. Maria's family was much more numerous, and not proportionally more modest. That infuriated Tibor and limited his generosity. He thought that was an objective assessment, and applied it also to his own cousins whom he barely knew. Why did he have to feel guilty about giving less to someone who was nothing to him when he was already stretching beyond his abilities? He started to hate the yearly visits. "What are we? The American Red Cross?" he mumbled while arranging the packages in the trunk like jigsaw puzzles.

The vacation meant a good chance for Tibor to redeem himself to his daughter. To his relief, the hostile mood at home faded to a forgotten nightmare when they put on their vacation hats. At Maria's family, they enjoyed a warm welcome. Some relatives thanked them for the salamis, cans of coffee, coolers full of fresh meat. Others took the gifts for granted. Tibor bit down hard, kept quiet, and put them on his black list.

The sight of the stores justified the sacrifice of spending a month's income on feeding hungry relatives in Romania. Though store windows were not empty any more, like they shamelessly were before the 1989 changes, they were a mere stage set for a drama performed in a language no locals spoke. In 1992, the language of numbers was understood only by foreigners. The numbers on people's payrolls did not translate to those of the merchandise in stores. Worse still was the discrepancy of the pensions frozen into pre-inflation numbers. Many people in their 50s had been conned into taking early retirement. Soon after, prices started to escalate rapidly. The same was happening in all former Communist countries, but in Romania the infrastructure had been pulverized in the phantasmagoric mill that the Ceausescus had been cranking for a long time. Their excuse? Paying off the national debt. There was simply nothing left to build on, only the warped stubbornness—called national pride—of refusing foreign capital to build up a healthy economy, the reluctance to yield to international experience and to prove themselves trustworthy of foreign investments.

This mentality was obvious from what simple citizens explained to people as ignorant in economics as Tibor was. Of course it all sounded more like whining, which was unfortunately justified.

Tibor and Zsofia set out on the trail behind the mountain chalet that was not there when he had camped with Nora and her kids. He couldn't resist going back after Maria had expressed her wish to spend time with old girlfriends. They were to spend the night at a shelter. They emerged in a small leveled clearing, a welcome break from the steep boulder-strewn trail. Tibor drew a deep breath.

"Dad. Do you know Ervin? Zsofia's detached question seemed inconsistent with the open vistas of the forested slopes rolling into the mist, or anything they talked about before.

"Ervin who?"

"The sailor. I met him at Tata when I visited you."

"Yes?"

"Do you know him?" Zsofia asked sheepishly.

"If I know him? I know every muscle in his body."

"Isn't he a nice boy?

"Barely a boy. He's almost through med school, twenty three I believe. Why?"

"I like him."

"As in?

"As in boyfriend."

"At sixteen? He doesn't make a good boyfriend. If it were up to him he would be every girl's boyfriend," he said. As if he were trying to register photos shuffled too fast to identify the exact scene or people they featured, he blinked. A loud group in front of the Olympic camp coffee shop. A couple holding each other walking at the lake front. A manager apprehending an athlete in his office he overheard in passing the open door. Same character everywhere: Ervin. The spirited, romantic, barely manageable, universally appealing Ervin. "You finish high school, then think of a boyfriend, all right, sweety?"

His inability to see his daughter as a young woman voided Tibor's need to further probe Zsofi's mind. She was just a child. A well developed, pretty, lively but serious and ambitious child. The time would come when no agony could free him from the remorse of his narrow mind. If there was salvation in the awareness of omission, if there were penitents embracing the relief of absolution, it was not to be Tibor.

Zsofi's high school diploma was lying on the table. The warm breeze blowing through the open kitchen window didn't touch the still life within. She had stormed out leaving behind a tremor of approaching disaster. Zsofi had politely excused herself from any celebration with family. Whatever party she was going to it was not her parents' business. It was not the prom that had already passed without getting Zsofi interested.

Tibor felt the bond with his daughter receding like a rainbow from the darkening sky of his hour of confusion. There was no way he could make sense of the apparent facts. Zsofi had had her room during her senior year, since Boske died. The apartment was now Maria's exclusive property, a fact Tibor didn't care to think about. He didn't really care. He cared about other things around him. He preferred to disregard what could have been too easy to grasp. Like Zsofi enjoying her space less and less, spending less time there than was available to her during the busy year. He stopped questioning her when her answers became elusive and redundant. She was studying with classmates elsewhere.

Tibor parked his car, pulled up the collar of his raincoat and hurried through the beating rain to the residential building at the Tata camp. He threw his duffel bag on the floor of his room and with it, he hoped, his less than comforting thoughts. He was back at Tata for the week and he was glad. The schedule was building up to the Atlanta games that lay two years ahead. He was ready to welcome with a gratifying serenity the restful order of the physical therapy room as he opened the door of the medical building.

Sitting on a treatment table, dangling his legs, was Ervin reading a journal. The thud Tibor felt in his chest seemed less out of context than the young man's presence.

"You can't possibly be here to practice in this godforsaken weather." Tibor tried to hit a light note. An empty echo bounced back an ominous invisible but hard wall.

Ervin stood now almost at attention in front of Tibor. Evidently uneasy. "I'm here on a mission. I hope that we'll be able to handle this . . . like between men . . "

Tibor had no intention of making it easier on the young man.

". . . We love each other—"

"For how long has it been going on?"

"More than a year," Ervin said averting Tibor's gaze as if holding his face for a slap which didn't come.

The lightening in Tibor's eyes echoed in the distant thundering. Someone came in. "Let's go to the office," Tibor told Ervin and led the way. "What's on your minds?" the father asked behind the closed door.

"Zsofi's moving in with me. She'd like your blessing." Ervin looked almost vulnerable. His candid look denied his reputation.

"I can't stop her, I guess." Tibor's voice broke. "Thank God this is not a marriage proposal that I could disapprove of only more. In time, you both will understand what you've missed out on and how much pain this causes me." He left the room to bury the ruin of himself in unconsoling solitude.

Part V

1

The sweltering air hung over the city like a musty, heavy dishrag. Whiling away the time in Maui suddenly seemed more appealing, though the day before, the idleness was burdensome, the shrieking parrots' wake-up call irritating, and she had been itchy to leave. Back in New York her new home seemed a superfluous luxury.

The ring of the phone was sheer relief. "The best of the two weeks was when they had no messages for me." Nora enthusiastically answered Sonya's quiz about the honeymoon.

"That doesn't say much about your vacation."

"Just kidding. Don't you know me?"

"Happy to say sometimes you surprise me." Nora found Sonya's words flattering. "Tell me about yourselves," Sonya added.

"We stayed at three different places during the ten days. Old world luxury at the Royal Hawaiian on Waikiki Beach, a pink marble charm. Rustic laid back beauty of a lanai in Kuaui, a green nest. The Hyatt Regency in Maui, a pretentious cliché. Let me think—

"All sound good to *me*—"

". . . my first choice is Honolulu . . . This sounds corny, but the feeling isn't at all. Touching history is rousing and humbling. Pearl Harbor, Diamond Head. It helped me become more American—"

"Nature and luxury wouldn't make for a fulfilling vacation, ha?"

"That's the idea. But, what's going on with you guys?"

"We shed a few tears in the airport . . ." Sonya said with a sweet undertone. Nora felt strings of kindred emotion vibrate along the fiberoptics that Sonya had chosen as her specialty. "My boss, George, was waiting for us—"

"A division supervisor from a company like GTU?"

"Why not? He promised when I interviewed."

"I'd talked to him on the phone, he sounded nice, but, how should I put it? I don't understand this friendliness—"

"Don't bother. People in California are a different breed. They do things you never heard of back East. He knew that I'm coming with my little brother, he made the choice of accommodation for me, and guess what? I accepted his suggestion. We're house sitting for someone away in Asia for the summer. You know what this means?"

"I'm afraid to guess."

"Why do you always doubt me?" Sonya snapped suddenly upset. Nora bit her tongue. Sonya went on. "We have it for free," she exclaimed with renewed exuberance. "They have us for free and everybody's happy. Therefore, your only expense is the car rental. Swell, ha?"

"You safe there, alone, two kids?"

"Mom, give us a break . . . get used to it. By the way, the owner didn't cancel the cleaning lady and the gardener."

"Great, but why do you object that your mother cares?"

"I don't know," Sonya sounded bored.

"How's your job?" Resilient, Nora switched subject.

"Exciting. I'm working on a fiber-optics project. Something I've never thought was possible. I can't imagine anything else I'd rather work on than communications. Mom, I feel as if California was invented for me. I was born to live here."

I hope she's not serious about moving out there. California was not Nora's idea of a safe place for her children. Didn't she run away from Israel, forbid them to go up in the tower of Pisa? Now she didn't want her children on the top of quivering land. "What's so attractive about a place where you can't trust the ground beneath your feet?" she asked.

"You never ever have to wear a winter coat or scrape the ice off your windshield."

"Is that a goal in life?"

"Twenty-three million people think so."

"I hope Dani doesn't." Nora spoke on impulse, as if averting a punch. Trying to save at least one from the siren song of California.

"He likes it, all right . . . only . . . he's too serious—"

"Wha'd'ya mean?"

"I've hoped he'd chase after skirts, true, that's difficult, girls don't wear skirts here," she giggled, "or mini-shorts—"

"What's he up to?"

"He met some other teenagers, with cars, they go to the city—"

"What city? How far are *you* from the city, your work?"

"We're in a canyon . . . around Santa Monica . . . my work's around the UCLA campus . . ." The pause sounded to Nora as if Sonya was looking for a subterfuge not to tell her. "Depends on the traffic," she said. "Twenty minutes give'n take."

Nora sighed. "On highways?"

"I'm not gonna get into this," responded Sonya dismissing the turn that the conversation took. "I'm having a great time, I made friends—"

"That's not California, sweetheart. You make friends in five minutes anywhere." Instead of being plain happy, Nora felt like a ridiculous and powerless Don Quixote, and just as angry. "I hope there's no one to keep you there," her mouth went ahead without the approval of her better senses, which were trained not to contradict Sonya too much. "Let me talk to Dani."

"He's out."

"Where?" Nora looked at her watch. Ten, meaning seven in Santa Monica.

"They went with the boys to Pasadena."

"Pasadena? What's there besides the Rose Parade?"

"Caltech."

"Sorry?"

"California Institute of Technology—"

"Now I know. What's he doing there?"

"Mom, Dani didn't tell you?" Nora could imagine Sonya's grimace of surprise. "He agreed to come out because it gave him a chance to check out the school."

In one sweep Nora felt like a negligible entity. Daniel, at sixteen, had his life, his secrets, to which she, the mother, was irrelevant, and possibly worse, deemed incapable of understanding. "No, sweetheart, but thank you for telling me," her voice faded. She couldn't let this happen. A few years back, overworked, exhausted, she felt like a dog kicked around, reacting to normal teenagers as if they were monsters. Nora was ridiculously aware it was never the children's fault. They were always just as great as now. It was always her over-wrought sensitivity. "I hope he won't like it there."

"Mom, why do you say that? It would be good for him and I hope you don't doubt that he would be good enough for them. He's brilliant and hardworking. What could be better? I don't get you. Just because it's far from *you?*"

Sonya's right. Dani's right. Everybody's right, but I. I'm a narrow-minded woman. But, what does she know about being a mother? "I guess," she said, unsettled between the remorse of not having stopped them from going to California in the first place and the ridicule she would have faced trying. She was desperately groping for comic relief.

Naturally, the more pressing the need the less chance of finding it. "When you have time, would you pity your Mama with a little more than just an address and telephone number scribbled on a picture postcard?"

Sonya laughed. "That's a photo of the house."

Nora reached for the pile of mail on the coffee table. "Where is this luxury villa again?"

"In a crack of the earth called Topanga Canyon."

"Well, enjoy. I'll spare you the mother-stuff this time. Tell your brother to call."

When he did, the conversation followed his agenda: divulge as little as possible, in the bounds of standard filial respect. The lack of information frustrated Nora, and threw her where she least liked to be: bugged down by repetitious, trivial questions. "You comfortable in that big house?"

"The bears are taking care of us."

"What bears?"

"You should have seen your future engineer daughter unpacking her knapsack. You know what came out of there?"

"Bears?" Nora asked and listened to the scuffle. "What's going on?"

"Mama," Sonya's voice choked by laughter came on. "Tell him to leave my bears alone. Dani, I'll kill you," she shrieked. Nora could imagine the scene. She smiled delightedly.

"All I did is check out their shiny little noses and—"

Another phone was picked up. "He would've pulled them off, I had to stop'im—" Daniel explained the rest. "Mama, she stopped me by sitting on the floor cross-legged, frantically hugging her bears. The worst? Neither of us could stop laughing until she had to go to work next morning. With the bears."

"I can *barely* talk," Nora said chuckling. "Dani, what did you unpack? I can't find your blanky. I wanted to wash it."

"See, that's why I had to take it. To avoid that sacrilege."

The summer was a balancing act between trying to unglue Daniel from the TV after his return from Los Angeles and Martin retiring to Tops in an attempt to appease his nerves before lashing out anyway at the rotten, lazy teenager.

Having just arrived home, listless, craving a short nap instead of putting dinner together—Nora couldn't foresee the approaching disaster.

"You can classify me with the dead birds," Daniel said after finishing his third helping of breaded veal cutlets, steak fries and creamed spinach.

"How's that?" Nora asked.

"I'm stuffed." He leaned back and kept slapping his bulging stomach. Nora received her son's uncouth display as a compliment to her cooking and she applauded both the appetite of the growing healthy boy and his humor.

"Perhaps it would be more civilized not to guzzle like a pig," Martin said with disdain while peeling an apple, going around it with the knife with elegant movements of his wrists.

Nora suddenly wished he would do something wrong. He never did. She was bursting with a desire to get back at her new husband. A tigress defending her cub. The air was woven with invisible chords they kept bumping into, all the more as they tried to avoid them. Was Daniel disrespectful and vulgar? If he was, certainly Martin's haughty remarks missed the target.

"Perhaps you should eat that apple unpeeled. It's good for your *guts.*" Daniel pushed back his chair noisily, also known as a no-no, and disappeared to Donjon despite it being his turn to wash the dishes. He would eventually, Nora had no doubts, but not before Nora and Martin had cleared out from the kitchen and too late to avoid at least a biting remark from Martin. She couldn't do the five minute job without hearing again about the need to curb Daniel's manners and attempts to dodge his duties.

"Dinner was delicious, love." Martin blotted his mouth with the napkin, pecked Nora's cheek and went to the living room.

"Marty," Nora approached him shortly, irate at herself for the trepidation filling and restricting her.

Martin was sitting in his Eames lounge chair, reading the New Yorker. Nora gestured, he made room for her on the ottoman, she sat down, put a hand on his crossed ankles. He reached over to the radio and turned the volume down.

How could she *make* a point *and* pacify? So much at stake. Was she wrong expecting this man, a boy too long ago, but a boy nevertheless, to understand the needs of one?

Martin broke the silence. "I could go easier on him. I try, then poof. As if I'm shot out from a canon."

I'm not alone in the ups and downs of the adjustment crisis. Obviously he's just as perplexed. "He's a good kid, a hard working achiever, responsible, honest, no vices. Nothing else's important. He has his personality, even if he didn't find it yet," she said. She was about to plead for Martin's understanding and patience, then she changed her mind. She shouldn't beg. That would humiliate them both. She had to trust that Martin would come around.

"I can't accept animosity. It renders me unfunctional. I'm not good at making up or stupid things like that—" Nora was interrupted.

"You're the greatest pacifist I've ever met."

She recalled hearing that before. When she got back with Tibor, he said something like that. She didn't welcome the memory. "But every time I have to make peace over some fight, it shortens my life. I over analyze—"

"There isn't much to analyze here," Martin said. The slight irritation in his voice startled Nora. She thought they were on the right track. He went on. "Dani is more disrespectful than the normal teenager, with a mother who deserves more respect than any parent."

"But, humiliating him won't help, Marty." She was intransigent with her husband on account of her child. With her head high, she decided her feelings were right. "Your opening helped. Thanks for telling me. I want everybody to be happy. We all need some help at some point. But, please don't misunderstand me. If it comes to making a choice for a more serious reason than a clash over table manners, I'd have no qualms standing by my son. We're a bunch of smart people behaving as stupidly as anyone whom we wouldn't hesitate to criticize."

"You certainly have your own personality." There was no provocation in his voice.

Nora felt the pressure bear down on her, shutting off her brain. "I must go sleep." She looked at Martin with a pouting sorry expression.

Martin was chatting with Valery, Nora's office mate, when she came in carrying a load of files, a textbook, her dictating machine and her now famous blue coffee mug with the inscription: "Please hassle me I thrive on stress" that many people took at face value. A rainbow of China markers stuck out of her breast pocket.

"What a surprise, love," Nora was genuinely amazed.

"It's your short day, isn't it?" He referred to the compensation for the prior long day.

"Do you feel like going to a museum?"

She shook her head as if to rearrange her thoughts. "Okay. I'll call Dani to tell him to eat some leftovers—"

"I took care of that, Nori."

She looked at Martin as if seeing him for the first time. "You did?"

"We took a walk to Zabar's and he picked out his dinner. We had a lovely time." Martin's face betrayed joyful countenance.

"That's fabulous. Thanks—"

"Don't mention it."

"Let's go see the Thyssen-Bornemisza collection."

"Surreal, all right," Nora had been going back and forth between the Magritte paintings. "He strikes me as more lifelike than conventional real life—"

"That's a strange way to look at it," Martin said tilting his head onto his shoulder, as if trying a different perspective.

"Really, or rather surreally," Nora said. They laughed. "Except my work which is organized and predictable, hopefully! What else is like that in my life? Any life. Isn't everything, not only memory, like this broken window pane holding snippets of a landscape we accept as reality?"

"I can identify with the idea . . ."

She stepped close to the wall to read the title. "I don't really care what the artist called it, and even less what this translation is . . . totally off the mark . . . *Free to roam.*"

"I bet what Magritte meant by *La clef des champs,* which would translate as *Key to the fields,* was the freedom to understand the nature of the double scene. Intact and broken," Martin said.

"I look at them as the two faces of anything. The real thing and its reproduction. On the canvas as in memory. Memory . . . always broken," Nora said dreamily." I saw this in 1969 in Lugano," she looked over to Martin. *Does he know what I mean?* "When we were touring Europe with Paul, you know." She nodded. "I carried tiny shards of memory, and a bigger one with that fantastic villa overlooking the lake, that housed the collection back then . . . I'd never imagined until then that a private collection could be that huge . . . well, I couldn't imagine a lot of things back then . . . All this time I was thinking of Magritte being my favorite painter . . . modern painter . . . now I know for sure."

"What are we going to do with Picasso?"

"You can keep him as your favorite," Nora said. They continued strolling from room to room at their own pace, occasionally locating each other to exchange impressions.

Next day Nora found Martin waiting in her office again. "What's this?" she asked him while unwrapping the roll on her desk.

"Open it," he sounded mysterious.

She carefully unrolled the Metropolitan Museum's poster of 20th Century Masters, the exhibit they had enjoyed so much. Nora registered the willingness of her mood both to soar at the slightest encouragement and to express her affection with ease. They kissed.

The table conversation amidst the animated crowd at the NoHo Star sparkled like a brightly colored stimulant drink poured from glass to glass. The Greens had recently returned from Scotland and were excitedly sharing their experience.

"What about the bug?"

"It's not *bug*. It's *bog*," Martin spelled it for her. "Can you hear the difference?"

"Sure," Nora said repeating with emphasis the vowel with wide-open lips. "So can I hear the difference between *bough*," she spelled, "*dough*," she spelled, "*bought*," she kept spelling, proud of herself.

"*Enough*," John shouted laughing. "*Although* we could go on'n on."

"Let us hear about the *louche* monster of *Lough*," Martin spelled, "or better known as Loch Ness."

"I got another one for you," Judy said. "The *goal* is not to get into *goal*."

"*Ouch!*" Joe said.

They hurried up Lafayette Street to the Public Theater. They took their membership very seriously and regarded with indulgence some flops for the benefit of Joe Papp's mostly great choices.

"Anyone heard about this dissident Czech playwright?" Judy asked."

"Václav Havel," Martin said. "Published only in the West, I believe. In'n out of prison for his ideas."

"Living in his country. I bet he'll make me feel like I was back *home*," Nora commented.

Audience, Private View and Protest, Havel's three one act plays stirred deep emotions. His subtle, but sharp irony sensitized the audience to the corrupt public life in his country, the dehumanizing surveillance of political prisoners, to fear as pathological obsession.

"Very human and so very poignant to the inherent responsibilities people tend to forget 30 years after the holocaust. Just remember Albert Camus! *The Plague*. The civilized world can't afford to disregard warnings," Martin declared.

With a surge of adolescent excitement, Nora turned around blocking Martin's way. They stood and kissed like a young couple on the banks of the Seine in Paris.

At home, there was a note under the hall phone. "Mama, I'm going with Elaine to a late movie." Nora had heard about Elaine, the chess player at school, as mentioned in one of Daniel's rare spells when words poured in a deluge of details. Now she welcomed the news of late night *whatever* instead of school chess club.

Alone with her husband of many moods, a perfect balancing force for her own extremes, Nora let her passions flare. Not a blind lust from the blue, not a revengeful urge like then, before the wedding, but just as urgent, made Nora lose patience over the little distance between the entrance hall and her bedroom. She found a resonating playmate. She had given up hope of having another chance in life to fall in love until she got really mad at Martin. Five months later, it was happening again.

"I'm trying to get tickets for Radu Lupu's recital," Nora told Daniel, while cleaning some string beans for dinner.

"Hah? Who's he? Or she?" Daniel left his mouth hanging open. He looked like disinterest incarnate.

"You don't remember that Radu is a Romanian male name?" He shrugged. "He's a famous pianist, classical music at Carnegie Hall—"

"So?"

"I'm politely offering to get you a ticket—"

"By the way, I'm going with my chums to the Madison Square Garden bash with Creem. You *must* know the rock group. Ar'ya interested? I'll get you a ticket," he gibed, then with his changing hoarse voice added. "And by the way, you're not being polite. You're trying to stuff classical music down my throat."

"Scuse me," she mocked in turn. "We have a gap here—"

"A canyon."

"Dani, can't we deal with our differences without hostility?"

"Wouldn't be half the fun."

"Okay, then let's patent a new term. Generation canyon."

Martin walked in innocent of the mood reigning in the kitchen.

"I need to dig . . ." Daniel said with total calm. ". . . how often's normal to have sex? Every other day, twice a week, once a month, every day?" He was intent as if drafting a comprehensive list.

"I'll pass," said Martin to Nora's dismay. The kid needed a male, not a mother, to deal with the subject. "It's individual," she said.

"That's a sensible answer," Daniel said simply, as if talking about putting on a raincoat. "I mean . . . at my age?"

"Twice an hour with whatever available," Martin said.

"Thanks for your blessing." Daniel left waving a victory sign.

"Did you have to encourage him?" Nora chided Martin.

"Makes no difference, Nori," he said, "Boys are boys. Until they learn to love someone else, they'll turn to themselves, whatever you tell them."

2

Nora had not given too much thought to the rapid turnover in the department. What the boss felt remained obscure. Most everyone had considered her intolerance with Andy's arrogant, but certainly not hostile attitude, a childish ego trip. Andy turned the situation to his favor and found a private practice in New Jersey that was easily more attractive than grumpy Helen. Two years after Andy left, Nora still missed the repartee of a peer with her brand of humor. Alan, a bright young man freshly out of a reputable fellowship in Chicago, took Andy's place. Happy to start in New York, he aimed to fulfill all expectations in an uptight, bow-tie way, as if joking would have come between him and his work. All one could elicit from him was a benevolent gaze that would've suited a grandfather.

After Jeff's farewell party (also leaving in favor of private practice), no one expected a simple replacement. Should Nora have been faithful to her philosophy, 'Too nice to be true,' she could have saved herself the forthcoming shock. The slate was clean for her advancement to head of division. Secretly she was hopeful.

Gossip was always her weak point. She would be the last to find out even the juiciest. Warren on the other hand, who had not one mean bone in his body, was blessed with big ears and a mouth to match. "You heard about Harriet I'm sure," he sounded Nora one morning.

"What about her?" Nora knew that said Harriet worked uptown as a cross-sectional radiologist. Her slowly delivered hedging opinions were an irritating corollary to an unobtrusive, reptilian personality. She slithered sideways as if she was hiding behind her own shadow. There were very few people Nora couldn't stand. She wouldn't admit it because she couldn't explain why, but she could never stomach Harriet.

"She'll grace our staff soon," Warren said.

"I see." Nora's voice faded. She had a sinking sensation as if she had missed her last train, out of breath after a hopeless sprint, as she looked at the back of the last car pulling out of the station.

The four years in the department flashed before her mind's eye. She was not sorry. Someone had to make things happen. If it wasn't her, someone else would have done the job. Ultimately, despite her defeat, she was modest and proud that it was *her* achievement.

When Nora had joined the staff of West End Memorial and its director, Helen Smythe, well deserving of her reputation for pioneering in the field of Nuclear Medicine, the division of cross sectional imaging was below recognized standards of practice. By contrast with the nuclear medicine division, the boss's darling, that *was* on the cutting edge, the CAT scan and Ultrasound divisions had obsolete equipment, much like orphans in rags. They were motherless too without chiefs of service to keep them running smoothly.

Nora had focused on the infrastructure as a prerequisite for improvement. She felt challenged and willing to invest her time in bringing about significant progress. Weeks after the idea had fully formed in her mind, she presented it to Helen.

"You'll have my support," she said wooden faced, her ascetic figure stiffly upright in the straight-back leather chair.

Nora felt uneasy. She held back the, "Wait, you're not doing me a favor," instead she asked, "Helen, what time frame do you predict for clearance after I have the data?"

"How long will it take *you* to come up with convincing data? You've preached to the converted so far." She fleshed one of her aborted, cool rudimentary smiles.

"For comparative data I need to go uptown." Nora meant Columbia-Presbyterian Hospital. "Even outside the system. Two or three days in each place."

"We can arrange that."

That sounded more promising. "I've never done anything like this. My expertise unfortunately doesn't match my willingness. Perhaps three months. The input of a bio-statistician would be useful."

"That's no problem." The chief lifted the receiver. "Zelda, please send in Kathy Wang," she told the secretary.

"The research statistician?" Nora asked. Helen nodded.

She had soon launched the campaign to demonstrate that the situation was untenable. Replacements would run in the millions. That was not her problem. Her goal was to make the administration realize that it was responsible for the division's current diagnostic inadequacy.

Some colleagues were unhappy about the extra work. Others, more appreciative, gladly lent a shoulder, not flinching at the questionnaires Nora had designed and that had to be filled on a daily basis. The technicians were an eager bunch, craving to put their paws on shiny new pieces of modern technology.

At home, when her fired-up elation over the slightest hope for good results did not elicit Martin's appropriately excited reaction, Nora reconsidered the validity of her enthusiasm. Martin was preoccupied, so Nora would stop, refocus, listen. He was at crossroads grappling with once-in-a-lifetime decisions. Nora's minor grievances against Daniel faded in the glowing halo of his Bronx High School of Science diploma. She would smile even in her sleep at the foolish fuss she had made over Daniel's disinterest in a science project. "Wouldn't it be great to get one of those famous Westinghouse prizes?" He had shrugged and took off for some harmonica gathering in the Village.

The project Nora had orchestrated finally produced a Certificate of Need, without which the bureaucratic tape could not start rolling towards the acquisition of the new equipment.

Then, the end of an age of peculiar innocence came to Nora as a slap in her face. Her struggles—especially the ones she experienced since her arrived in America—had inspired a realistic outlook that suited her personality. Of universal meritocracy she had never dreamed. But to have no credit whatsoever given to all she had done for the division was pure disillusionment, she couldn't deny no matter how she tried to avert the disgrace. What had befallen Nora was disgrace from an ingrate. An unknown side of Helen Smythe.

"It's probably my accent, don't you think so?" Nora asked Martin. When he denied the possibility, saying "Not in New York." That felt worse. "Then, it's my qualification."

She was not about to hang herself, but urges swept over her in waves. She craved to goof off like a teenager taking out her anger at an unsympathetic teacher. Or just get away, take off to the woods where beasts are beasts and you know what to expect of them. Instead, Nora set her face muscles in a new phony grin. "Happy to have you aboard, Harriet," she told the new Chief of Division while shaking hands. "What a relief not to have to run this damn division." *without a title.*

The more it became a pattern, the more Nora was angered by recurring remarks on some requisitions from the chronic care facility that sent films to be read at West End Memorial. She frowned at the scribbled comment: "*Uncooperative Russian patient.*"

Nora was not an immigrants' rights activist. Especially not if they were Russian. Her personal feud got in the way. She had suffered for not being one of them. Yet, she lost her cool. Signed: SS. How befitting. No doubt that an uncooperative patient could compromise the quality of an x-ray film. But somehow, the ethnicity of the patient should not be a factor. Same remark, same technician, same suboptimal films. Nora snatched the receiver. She identified herself. She was connected to Sally, AKA SS, and conveyed in concise terms her objections.

"They don't speak English."

"Sure! And you didn't bother calling a translator. Do you realize how hostile your attitude is?" Medical institutions are known to have a registry of employees speaking foreign languages.

"It's not my job to teach them," Sally snapped.

"Okay. Now listen close. I'm an immigrant myself. Are *you* an American Indian?"

"No." The woman seemed not to understand the relevance.

"Your ancestors came here not speaking English. Lucky you, to be born here. That doesn't make you better than the poor devils who come now."

"Look—"

Nora interrupted. "If you find me harsh or hostile, that's exactly my intention. You have absolutely no understanding or feelings and don't deserve any either. The fact that *all* your films, without exception, are crap, speaking no language any radiologist could understand, is the Russian's fault as well?"

"I don't have to listen—"

"No, you don't. And I don't have to read your crap. You better shape up, lady, or you'll have to deal with your administration which I assure you won't be any prettier."

Nora slammed down the receiver. Puffing, she threw her head back and blew off steam. Did she take out her own frustrations on just anyone? She was acutely sensitized to injustice. She returned the unread films with her own remark: 'Technically sub-optimal non-diagnostic study. Repeat.' She remembered the phrase she learnt early enough during her residency to save her a lot of trouble. 'A bad technician can make the best radiologist look stupid.'

She was feeling stupid, all right. Her blood was boiling. She left the reading room and the pitying gazes. She had overreacted, everyone around could hear, she had exploded—that it was for a reason didn't justify her loss of control—now she should cool it. Sure they could see through her, but surely not everyone would gloat. *My soreness is naked, damn it!* Did I *expect . . . Of course, I did. Otherwise why would it distress me so? I have to claim sour grapes.*

Martin's placid ways that enraged Nora at times, were not indifference after all. "A title doesn't make you," he said. Nevertheless, like a child who was looking for ways to hide her failing grades, she kept it from her children. *What a rotten role model I am.* Her disappointment could harness their impetus, she feared. On the other hand, keeping it secret was as if she took rain for a spit in her face. Run away like Jeff and Andy had? She had no talent for business and no matter what others said, private practice was in a limited way business and she was not about to get involved. To her mind, business and health care should not be mentioned together. What others did was not her problem and what all physicians would be forced to do in the not-so-remote future against their deepest ethical conviction was not yet evident.

"Only electro-shock could change me," she told Martin after a hard day at work. "Nothing could take away my credibility."

"This sounds more like you." He looked pleased.

"Remember that dilemma I had . . . the CAT scan Harriet had read and a gynecologist showed me the films and I happened to have a different opinion? And what she had to say when we went to corroborate with her? She said everyone is entitled to their opinion, true, but *Le tone fait la musique,* what a tone she used, she could drown in her own venom, and left us there looking at each other. He said something to the effect that the woman needs to be laid. I wondered whether he'll proceed based on my observation, which called for a totally different management? He did. Today he came to me right from the OR, in his scrubs, to thank me for my input. Anyway, not only is Harriet stubborn and superficial, but she has no manners and enrages most everyone."

"You're as good as they come. With all objectivity—"

"There's no such thing. The word objective is an artifice of the language. It has no counterpart in life," she said.

Nora's and Martin's new routine of talkative evenings was free of the problems she used to bring home, spiced with sheepish gloating over how spoiled Harriet's evenings must be.

Daniel, naturally high on the prospect of going to Caltech, the college of his choice, acted out the prototype of the carefree high school senior wasting time for a few more months.

Mellowed, Martin announced his decision. He was ready to resign from the editorial staff of the paper, leave behind his disagreements with the new management, and come out of a depressed state that had never been acknowledged, but hung in the air like a ghost.

Nora stepped out of the Jetway. Vexing thoughts were swiftly replaced by serenity, a sense of melting honey, as she hugged her two children.

Less than half an hour later Sonya turned from the palm lined boulevard into a narrow alley. Garbage cans stood sentinel between the rows of carports. Multicolor smears on the peeling paint of the dividers bore witness to close encounters of generations of cars with the confining pillars. They walked along the scarce planting under the catwalk to the unfinished rough concrete steps. The walls radiated the memory of the sun that had already set beyond the Pacific horizon.

Inside Sonya's apartment, a sea of folders, books, items of personal hygiene and clothing flowed into the living room. In one neat corner, a table was set for three. As soon as they entered, Sonya transferred a large fireproof dish with shrimp casserole from the refrigerator to the oven.

Nora hoped to meet her kids' significant-others. Sonya didn't tell her why, she had only warned her mother that her friend was not the intelligent and polished young man, the California blonde prototype, whom Nora had met on her first visit. She also knew that the next boyfriend, a riotously funny UCLA classmate had dropped out of class and her daughter's life after a few weeks of failing to bond with either. Sonya was a collector at heart. In childhood, it was the paper napkins, then came the honors in both the high school advanced placement classes and throughout the college years, and more recently the array of romantic involvements.

Daniel? All she knew was that there was a girl.

Next morning, Daniel opted out of a Newport Beach outing. "Count me out, I have an interview," he said.

"Interview?" Nora exclaimed. "It's vacation."

"Mama, people work here, they don't take vacations—"

"That's silly. I work and take vacations," Nora said.

"Because you're a slave." Daniel sounded serious. "These people don't feel like slaves, they don't need vacations—"

"Strange . . . What interview?" she conceded.

"I know already," Sonya yelled over the clattering of dishes. "Daniel Mann, the genius, tell your Mama what happened."

"Oh, gimme a break, you monkey." He stuck his tongue out at his sister while grabbing her ears in faked anger. She brandished a wooden spoon at his face.

"Why didn't you tell me on the phone?" Nora asked smiling at their friendly scuffle.

Daniel released Sonya. "So you don't have to look for another reason to criticize me." Nora shrunk at the rebuke as if scalded by the sudden change. "Greg, he's a grad student, my TA in Math . . . anyway, we were chatting in the food line in the cafeteria, you know, just the usual nerd stuff . . . so, this guy cuts in . . . rude, isn't it? He was eavesdropping on us, you see . . . and asked me how come he doesn't know me. How was I supposed to know whether that's good or bad, so I told him because I haven't been finger printed yet . . . he didn't punch me in my face, but he told me that he teaches all the juniors and seniors . . . devices . . ." Nora opened her mouth for a question, he waved her off, "No need to bother with that. So, I have an interview at his lab tomorrow."

"For the summer?"

"Mom, work is not seasonal here—"

"You forgot the fruit pickers—"

"All right. Other than that you work when you feel like, if that's around the clock, okay, if it's at three in the morning, or during the worst California mud slides . . . *capisci?*"

"So, you're not coming home?"

"Home?" He looked as if he was waiting for translation.

Dagger in her stomach. *What did I do wrong?* "Yes, home. Change of scenery. Goof off with old pals?"

"All right. If I get the job in that lab as an apprentice calculator, a shoe-shine, fruit picker, whatever, I could say that, *megfogtam az Istent a lábánál,* did I say that right?" he smiled at Nora to check on the Hungarian phrase, which asserted that grabbing God's foot was equivalent with great luck.

"Yes, sweetheart. Perfect," she laughed at his twisted pronunciation. "Is this whatever-his-name a big shot?"

"This guy, my guy, works in the shadow of Richard Feynman," he raised his eyebrows searching his mother's blank expression. "Let me put it this way. To be associated with Feynman's shadow is a million times better than working in the next guy's blinding light of wisdom."

"Your enthusiasm is proof enough—"

"Mom. Feynman is the greatest living mind and an inspiration to anyone breathing the same air with him," Daniel declared with a pathos quite uncharacteristic of him.

"Wow."

"Mama," Sonya interfered. "You realize what this means for Dani?"

"That congratulations are in order for being interviewed."

"Right. But I have to say this. I'm very proud of my little brother. He's being recruited for this group before anyone else could snatch him."

"Yeah," Dani said. "They have a whole nursery of minnows."

"How else would one grow into a big fish? A small fish becomes a big fish—"

"Dani boy is swimming in the right pond," Sonya concluded.

On the way from the parking lot to the restaurant, Sonya expounded confidentially to her mother: "He's a lawyer. The type I can see you getting ideas about. Don't get excited. His days with me are numbered. He's a selfish bastard . . . last time I slept over at his place, he ate my yogurt that I took with me for breakfast."

Daniel, unapologetic for failing to bring his girlfriend of a few months appeared to be seething all evening.

After dinner, they drove Daniel to Pasadena. The sidewalk cafes along Colorado Boulevard were still packed with a young boisterous crowd milling about under patches of light alternating with dark clumps of palm trees. They turned onto Orange Grove and soon Sonya was driving along the leafy Caltech campus in front of the arched Athenaeum. Preoccupied people hurried along the brick walkways snaking under the sprawling elm trees.

The three of them stood in the cone of the floodlight at the entrance to Daniel's dorm. Nora hugged his waist, looked up at his chin. A hint of stubs spoiled the baby skin. "When am I gonna see you again?" she asked with affection.

"Whenever. I'm sure we'll both enjoy it," Daniel said, pulled away, tapped his sister's head and turned into the shadow of the alley.

Daniel called a week later. "Remember the swimming in the right pond thing? Well, I'll be surfing this summer."

"It sounds very California." Nora was happy that he was up to something else than playing his harmonica like some romantic minstrel. She sometimes regretted ever buying the first one for him.

"Let me enlighten you," Daniel continued. "It's an acronym for Summer Undergrad Research Fellowship—"

"Oh?" She tried not to sound disappointed. "Despite that Caltech is not even at the beach?"

"Marginally funny," Daniel accompanied his words with a cackle. "I'll be starting in the applied physics lab as a research fellow—"

"Wait. Don't you need a degree for something like that?"

"Generally this is called a research assistant. Not here. You do what you can, you take courses that you can stomach, you kick around ideas with practically everyone willing to listen, you learn what you want, not necessarily by curriculum—"

"How about credits for a degree?"

"Yeah, of course, but everyone does more than just that. What it comes to is that I'll decide on my options, that's to say you'll hear by April what specialty I think I'll stick to."

"That kind of talk I understand."

"I'll be paid a stipend."

"Wow."

"I thought you'll like that."

"Don't you? That doesn't preclude your allowance, okay?"

"Thanks."

Martin's book was a success. His greatest surprise was, he confessed, that it generated more than the professionals' interest. "An unexpected bonus," he said. His subject—journalists' lives and work; what made or broke them—masterfully avoided a gossipy tone though a great part of the information could have been classified as such. Nora could tell, though she could have identified more easily with adversities encountered in raising vegetables on Mars, than with the cutthroat climate in the writing world. Indeed, she was appalled. "I never thought it can be as bad as medicine."

What transported Nora into an awestruck state while she held *The Dilemma Behind the News*, with its matte jacket suggesting light and shadow, was knowing the amount of research that had gone into the book. With its richly quoted writings and statements by the respective journalists about their own particular claim to fame, it was a well documented collection of biographical selections. Titled as a take off and homage to Martin's idol, George Seldes and his *The Truth Behind the News,* it was a declaration of allegiance. Nora couldn't agree more. It was Martin, with his quandaries, and all.

Nora was pleased to see in an elaborate but clear form many of the ideas previously discussed in her company. Yes, the thin line between public opinion and crowd hysteria, the overlapping zones between optimism, pessimism and cynicism and their frequent lack of impact or substance, a mental process that according to Martin was slowly being battered out of existence by the cyberspeed of daily life. That's why Seldes' name, a hero and victim of American journalism, Martin said, should be printed as a memento on the front pages of all major papers.

Nora deconstructed the damage of Martin's success in the company of friends. They found her exposé irresistibly hilarious. How the three years that went into the book, the know-how, the research expenses, yielded a paltry two dollars per hour wages. Naturally, counting the hours around the clock. Martin's mind had never been more than one degree off his book. Even in his sleep. "The satisfaction of a completed work can be doubled, and Nora deserves more than my grateful dedication," Martin had said. While he toasted her, she was glowing at the thought of having Martin back full time. Mind and body. She daydreamed of a Camelot reflecting in their nights and days of lightness. From the tiring seesaw of their moods she was happy to get on the phone and fill her social calendar.

Sonya received Nora and Martin in her arms, then showing off, she shook her mane of—this time—long frizzy hair.

"Is this my baby?" Nora spun around Sonya who had undergone a major makeover. Not that she needed one, but the new look was stunning. Nora could object to her high heels, but she knew better. "Where's your brother?"

"He's wrapping up some rush work. Sends his regards. You'll see him at the commencement ceremony."

The white structure of the Miramar Hotel was a few church-lined blocks away from Sonya's rental in Santa Monica. The window of their room looked over the lit Palisades to the darkness that would be replaced by the sparkling ocean in the morning.

"You're hired," Martin said. "I'll go anywhere you send me."

"Thanks. I might need a travel agent job—"

"That's the best you can do with your master's degree?"

"I can't keep my mouth shut . . . I wanted to tell you tomorrow. I *got* a new job."

"At GTU?

"In the overseas marketing division."

"That's impressive," Nora said.

"Congratulations and good luck," Martin said.

"Thanks. Right now, if you'll excuse me . . ." she pulled an envelope from her sloppy bag, ". . . your tickets for the ceremony. I'll pick you up at ten fifteen. Okay?"

Elaine, Daniel's high-school friend, not sweetheart—Nora had to avoid the term even in her thoughts, as Daniel put a ban on it and could be driven beyond the horizon at the sound of it—showed up, apparently with the intent of breaking the spell of Daniel's universal disinterest. Nora caught a glimpse of the buxom girl with her lopsided blond pile of curls, a narrow but shapely bust separated by a tiny waist from the oversized lower body stretching the seat of the tight jeans. Very feminine, very anti-fashion. Nora liked her. She would have liked anyone who could pull her Dani baby out of the dismal mood he brought with him that summer.

The music stopped in Daniel's room. Perhaps it was only turned down. With the air conditioner on, Nora felt excluded from the sonic world. Should she turn it off in favor of eavesdropping? Perhaps catch one of them going to the kitchen for a soda? Or offer them something? Would these grown up kids regard anything as meddling? Probably.

Animated voices seeped in disjointed shreds from behind the closed door of Donjon. Nora's subconscious agitation became manifest. Daniel poured his dejection into a reunion for which the girl must have been at least partially prepared, judging from his less than amicable tone on a previous phone conversation.

". . . a bitch . . . the nerve . . ." Elaine's high pitched voice carried disquieting snippets of conversation. ". . . put off . . . happily . . . what's to me . . . my room mate . . . your female dub . . . too seriously . . . —oly barrel . . . I don't . . ." Was she attempting to console? Put some amorous failure, consistent with Daniel's mood, in a more favorable light?

". . . no explanation . . . human would do . . . leave a heap . . . question for me . . . drawn in?—a cold shoulder. So I'd know what the hell's wrong with me." Daniel had opened the door and was talking with his hand on the door handle before he headed for the kitchen. "Nothing. Meaning that anything could be wrong with me."

Nora pricked up the ears of her soul. She discerned moans of growth pains. The question in her mind was not whether Daniel needed help, but whether he was getting it from that girl. She could trust no one to convey the right message. She was far from admitting that there was nothing she could do, or for that matter should do, as a mother.

Nora sat at the card table in the far corner of the living room looking through a stack of photos. Daniel crossed the hall carrying two glasses of soda. They looked at each other and exchanged no words. He pulled his door without closing it.

"As long as I unwillingly overheard your conversation, I can't disregard it . . . Are you willing to hear my opinion?" Nora said later.

"I can't use your opinion . . . you can't be objective," Daniel snapped at his mother.

"We can't and shouldn't avoid experience," she tried anyway in an appeasing tone. "Even if unpleasant, they serve a purpose."

"You might be right, but I have to figure out where my place is, whom I want to associate with . . . if at all . . . before I get wrong ideas, waste half of my life, then realize that I should have done anything but . . . Last year I would've told you I'm with the right person. I was clearly wrong. Who could tell whether I'm in the right place now. There's no more Feynman to tell me."

"Let's assume—" Nora dreaded the suspicion that Daniel never got over that girl. Is he going to have a fixation on Feynman's death too? How does his mind magnify these events, so minor to the onlooker? Why is he so prone to turn events to his disadvantage, to incorporate them into the mold of self-doubt he apparently has been developing?

"I can't afford the luxury—"

At 21, finishing junior year with brio, it was nothing less than painful to Nora to hear Daniel. "Do you not like the school?"

"Don't know. I can promise you one thing. I'll find out." He sounded ominous.

"What does Sonya think? I don't know whether she's bound by an oath or something, but she doesn't mention—"

"Good girl," he interrupted. "All right. She was a junior, I won't get into her academics, but take my word, she could use any help and I didn't mind . . . it's marginally irrelevant . . ."

It sounded to Nora that the girl used him, before whatever had happened. Probably she ran out on him. Was that enough to shake the foundation of Daniel's developing self-confidence into an unfamiliar, uncomfortable mold of erosive self-doubt? Nora wondered whether she knew and foolishly disregarded this side of Daniel.

Everything in the confines of the apartment felt contrived like a pantomime of unrelated characters dodging each other. Nora approached Martin. "Help me out here. I sense a lot of tension. Is there anything going on between you and Daniel that I'm not aware?" What started as pillow talk soon turned into another aborted sequence of the same pantomime she had tried to solve.

"Nothing. Let's go to sleep." He turned his back.

Nora got up. "Where're you going?" Martin asked her.

"I'm going herbal. Better than going ballistic, don't you think so?"

He questioned her with a silent gaze.

"Just making myself a Sleepytime tea," she said.

"How can I be sure that there's nothing I could do to help him?" She said returning. "He's laconic, so is Sonya when it comes to him. It has been a complete change for the past year."

"Your worrying won't help . . . *you* need help . . . I'm honestly annoyed and offended with your preoccupation with a grown up independent young man . . . you cannot control his life—"

"Control? That's what you think my problem is? I wouldn't fuss not hearing from him, only if I could be sure he's fine, happy, with whatever he's doing, with whoever he's doing it with."

She had never formulated it that way. With whoever? Is that his problem? Was that girl business a final mistake? Nora's brain was under assault.

"Sonya, this is a question behind your brother's back. What upset him so?"

"What did'e tell you?"

There was now a transcontinental pantomime creeping right at her through the receiver. Nora came to the realization that she had misjudged the scale. The extent of Daniel's problem was larger than she feared. "Look." She walked with the phone to the window, and looked over the Hudson as if she could get help from space. "I don't expect you to tell me what's confidential between the two of you. I'm happy that you're close. I won't be around for ever—"

"Let's change subject."

"Is he depressed because of the school?"

"He's not the depressed type. He's a thinker. Probably over-thinker. He'll be fine."

"He *will* be? So, now he isn't."

"Look, Mama. Don't get paranoid—"

"I'm not," Nora snapped.

"All you have to do is cross your fingers . . . and that only to keep yourself busy . . . He's been working too hard. Besides, Feynman's death got to him. He lost another male, or rather, father role model."

"We talked about that," Nora frowned recalling the phone conversation when Daniel sounded so distressed that she felt she should fly out to express her condolences in person.

3

The description in the guide books "Couldn't do justice to Budapest," as Martin said when they arrived on the top of Castle Hill in Buda. The Hilton Hotel, built on the ruins of a XIII century monastery, surpassed any imaginable architectural integration of modern slick glass with gothic buttresses and towers. They walked around the labyrinthine halls, up and down steps under medieval stone arches. Exposed ancient stones decorated the lounge where guests comfortably sunk in postmodern armchairs, absorbed local history as well as their drinks carried on silver trays by gloved waiters. Martin sipped his scotch talking to himself. "Perfect."

"I'm trying to get into your mood," Nora said, "It'd be easier without memory getting in the way. Not weak enough yet." She paused and squirmed, finding herself in a time warp of inner contradictions. She faced a tough dilemma of hate and love. "I like this city. Though I hate its past. I'm guilty of disloyalty. I wish I could enjoy and not analyze—"

"Good. Where do we start?"

"We'll hire a guide." Nora said.

"I have one."

"I take that as a compliment. I'll reserve the honor for later. We could use an erudite and amusing local."

The recommended guide, an old gentleman, tipped his fedora when kissing Nora's hand, then shook hands with Martin. "My name is Fazekas. Retired professor of contemporary history. Call me Pali *bácsi.*" Thus he set the mood. "I speak six languages including ancient Greek and Latin."

"No Russian, Pali *bácsi?*" Nora asked.

"We paid dearly enough for that. I don't have to speak it. I prefer more civilized, more natural languages."

"Not that I want to argue," Martin said, "but English is a made-up language you'd not call natural."

"Oh!" Fazekas exclaimed with a flurry. "That's different. It earned its place in Western civilization and more. Russian is a barbaric language."

"As in pagan? Like Stravinsky's Rites of Spring—"

"Well—" the professor tried to argue.

"It's a marvelous—" Martin stopped short when Nora pulled his sleeve. The old man was ultimately biased, she didn't blame him, but had no inclination to find out more. She intended to have fun, not political debates. To follow him up and down the cobblestones and catch all the information Professor Fazekas was pouring out in a continuous stream, without getting short of breath, was itself an intriguing challenge.

"These buildings," Fazekas pointed to the row of Renaissance façades facing St. Matthew's Cathedral that could be seen continuing into the streets radiating from the wide open square. "What do you think?"

"Well preserved?" Nora hesitated like a student caught unprepared. "I guess XVIIIth, perhaps XVIIth centuries."

"Ah, hah! You hit the nail on the head," the old man pointed a long crooked arthritic finger to a building with aluminum-framed windows. "Mostly. Not *that* one. Godless criminals. We don't have stone? Better leave the burned out building with the scars of war. Come, let me show you," he beckoned turning into Tárnok Utca. Amongst façades expertly restored, one building showed its mellowed stone face pockmarked by black bullet holes. A reminder of whatever one was able or willing to forget.

Nora squeezed Martin's hand. Don't scratch to find out what's under the luster of pride. They climbed the marble steps of the Royal Palace housing the National Gallery and the Budapest History Museum. Dominating the central hall, on the top of the stately central staircase, sat the Dozsa Gyorgy statue, a monumental metal structure that grabbed one with the pain of the burning flesh twisting into the scorched crowned skeleton, its contorted fingers clawing for freedom. A chimerical creation projecting the authenticity of human agony.

"History was not ready for him," Martin concluded after reading the plaque with the story of the XVIth century Transylvanian leader of the peasant uprising, caught and burned on a throne with a crown of thorns on his head. "Premature like any visionary. The lucky ones are those who the future would understand and approve."

Shaken, they walked out onto a grandiose terrace. Leaning on the stone balustrade, they took in the ribbon of the Danube, with bridges like gems strung along the most beautiful meandering section of Europe's greatest river.

"I'm hungry." Martin said. They ended up following Fazekas up the stoop at the Ruszwurm.

"Thank you Professor. This place escaped me for decades." Nora mumbled as she wiped from her lips the cream left by the best mocha-chocolate roll, then dipped her fork into Martin's towering fluffy Napoleon. The old man was quietly sipping his coffee over a crumbly Linzer. The sparkle in his eyes seemed to mock, as if saying, suit yourselves, if you like this better than history.

St. Matthew's Church, the pride of the city—one of its many—though undoubtedly an architectural beauty, seemed nothing else to the Ferbers than a nice piece of old stone. Nora and Martin agreed that it was a detail without which the city would be much the same, unlike Cologne which would be very different without its cathedral. Then, she realized she misjudged it. The church they were silently walking through had no doubt the power to transcend a visitor's spirit with awe for Hungary's most revered historic king, Matthias Corvinus.

"Remember Marty, you'll meet his excellence again in Cluj as the central equestrian figure, *quasi* the symbol of my city," Nora informed Martin. Despite her elation over the place, Nora turned down the offer to visit the church's famous treasury. "I'm not interested in seeing gold and gemstone chalices epitomizing how priesthood debauched on the world's best wines while preaching water," Nora pondered.

"Well said," Martin remarked.

The talkative, friendly taxi driver was polite enough to get permission to drive around some extra distance. Down Castle Hill, along and across the river, he listed the attractions—barely giving Nora a chance to translate for Martin—slowing down around the Parliament, turning swiftly left onto Margit Bridge, then right onto the island. "This used to be the most romantic spot on this entire round earth. Don't you believe it now. More than its share of mugging and drugs than Angyalföld," the district considered Budapest's most crime ridden, he explained.

They left the island with its spa hotels, summer theater, and outdoor pools surrounded by greenery. On the Pest side of the river the driver made another detour off a boulevard, namely the St. István *körút.* Another turn to the right brought them into what appeared to be a park made of squares of green separated by intersecting alleys. "Are we in Gramercy Park?" Martin exclaimed as the car quietly rolled around the square under the old elder trees allowing glimpses of slick Art Deco portals.

"This is so eery," Nora said, then noticing Martin's questioning look she added, "That we're here." Nora's pulse quickened. The memory of

Manci, her late mother-in-law who grew up right there, was out of proportion to her sudden state of agitation.

"Why?" Martin asked.

Nora told him. She asked the driver to stop. They were in no rush. She needed to get out. People hurried along, net bags with groceries or attaché cases in hand, dressed simply or in trendy clothes, old and young, sad and cheerful. Some returned Nora's stares. She looked at strangers intensely trying to pick out a familiar face from a crowd. Martin's remarks flew over her head; seconds later—or perhaps minutes?—she noticed his probing expression. Nora looked around before ducking to get in the car.

Half way down the side of the square, a man turned the corner from a side street. He passed a bulging briefcase from his left hand into his right, pushed the wing of his open trench coat back and reached into his left pants' pocket, continuing his impetuous walk. There was a jingling sound as he dropped his keys on the asphalt. The little incident seemed to startle him. He turned around to pick them up. The street light reflected on his glasses as he straightened. Shivers ran down Nora's spine. *Oh, my God. Not unless he's a Dorian Gray.* The man looked just like Tibor. A stabbing pain in her low back paralyzed her. A sign of ultimate tension. The man opened the gate of the next building and disappeared. It looked as if he lived there. Her shaking knees curbed her urge to run after the man.

"It's getting late." Martin called from the car.

"Nice, isn't it?" the driver asked.

"I guess so," Nora said as she slid onto the seat. Her heart was ready to jump out of her chest, she could hear her pulse pumping. She took a few deep breaths.

"Are you okay?" Martin asked.

"Why?"

"You act strange."

"I do?" She couldn't dismiss the shocking suspicion without at least acting bizarre.

"Nicer living one can find only in Buda. Up on Rózsa Domb," the driver said pointing across the river.

The Opera House on the imposing Andrássy út was an old building. They had read about recent restoration works, but what opened before their eyes in the foyer was beyond imagination: Proportionate beauty of colors and shapes, of bas-reliefs and columns, of marble floor and ornate doorways, caryatides and alcove muses, ceiling frescoes. "This is hard to top," Martin said awestruck. "Show me nothing else, I'll be happy."

"Wait with your praises until after the performance." Nora, calm once more, switched back into her tourist mode.

"You, pusillanimous creature," he mocked her.

"That means?"

"Timid, sort of cowardly—"

"I'm trying not to contaminate you with my excitement, that's all. Erkel's national opera in Budapest is a first for me too." But that was not the main issue on her mind. Not understanding words Martin used sometimes awoke in her an inferiority complex.

The curtain went up after the impetuous overture of *Hunyadi László.* A castle loomed on the dim stage, costumed figures moved around mysteriously, world class voices soared.

"This could be Verdi," Martin whispered.

"It was in the XIX century air," Nora said during the break. "Verdi and Erkel were exact contemporaries, if I'm not wrong."

"So humbling. There's so much here I never imagined, and you know it all," Martin mused after a perfect performance. Even if it were half the truth, Nora's gray matter said, it elicited pure gratitude in her heart, as Martin put her shaky ego to rest.

For years, Nora had not dreamt of Tibor. And certainly not of her father whom she knew only from old photographs. But in her dream, the image of a male character of non-descript features, with an expression the same time protective and violent, who held a house in his arms—her house she was sitting in—was a commingling of her father, Tibor and Martin. The dream would not leave her all day. She thought of her dream as a straightforward revelation of her life-long worries that she couldn't express better in a thousand words. It was like a whip urging Nora to return to St. István Park. There was no time.

The Great Synagogue in the narrow street, the dilapidated Dohány utca, gave Nora a pang. "Tight as a drum," Martin said rattling a locked door. The bell was followed by shuffling steps. A man as gray as his beard, and worn out as his clothes, opened it. Nora talked to him in Hungarian. He showed them around, then left them sitting in quiet consternation in the temple.

Nora closed her eyes and listened to her memories. There was music in the background and they were dancing. She could hear Paul's voice: "My mother convinced my father, a born Transylvanian, that we would be safer in Budapest. Her father was some director, not too rich but well enough to expect, in his thinking, special treatment. We got it . . . just as special as all the other Jews. Ghetto. Not my grandparents personally. They obtained an exemption, but nothing was done for the rest of the family. My mother's only sister, whom she adored, perished in Auschwitz. Dodging bullets and scouring for food, keeping my mother's wits together was what we did day after day . . . My father and I were trying to get to the building where we lived to get in before the curfew. We were running, We should've known better, Anyone running was suspicious, I was only thirteen, The Arrow Cross stopped us. My father had false identity papers just in case and I imagine he was so terrified and confused, he showed them. They made us drop our pants. After they saw what they wanted, they pushed us with their bayonets into a column going in the other direction. We jumped under a gateway and hid there all night. We were lucky. That column, we found out, was marched to the Danube and shot into the river. My father and I have lived through a miracle . . ."

Opening her eyes, Nora took Martin's hand. "Paul was in the ghetto around here someplace. I think it was Dob utca. It's near Klauzál tér, you know that infamous square shown in that movie with Jessica Lange—"

"You mean The Music Box?"

"That's it."

They walked out. A commemorative plaque in the small garden was unreadable under the overgrown weeds. Random carpenter's equipment blocked the museum entrance. "No fonds," the old man apologized. "We can barely feed the few hundred old Jewish destitutes who would die starving on their pensions. He took the money Nora meant as a donation. "We hope some day we'll restore the synagogue. Thank you." The sad queue in front of the canteen next door, a regular soup kitchen, was an eloquent illustration.

"Remember the Synagogue and the Jewish Museum in Prague?"

"The difference is shocking," Martin said. "I mean the attitude of two Communist countries toward their minority heritage . . . I guess for the Czechs culture comes before prejudice, if they have any. It's objectionable to classify people, but the evidence speaks. Remember that seven hundred year old wooden synagogue across the street from the museum?"

"And the old cemetery there? Here you have the pavement of Klauzal square for a cemetery," Nora said. Neither she nor anyone else could predict the future course of history, or rather market economy, that would put money above historical values even in Prague. A relique half a millennium old would be worth less than the land for urban real estate it occupies.

Approaching the Romanian border acid bubbled up into Nora's throat. She sort of expected this after the fish soup like liquid fire they had at the roadside restaurant on the banks of the Tisza. *Maybe it isn't the soup. I'm awfully nervous.* Martin drove through no-man's land. They contemplated the wide smooth plowed strip of earth accented every few hundred meters by a looming guard tower.

"You could see even a bird's footprint on this," Martin said.

"From closer you could see streaks of blood."

"Hmmm."

Nora rummaged in her medicine bag and popped two Maalox tablets in her mouth. She was still chewing when the border patrol at Bors, in his well fitting khaki uniform held out an arm across the road. Then he waved them towards the side under the corrugated metal awning. He stepped to the window. "*Bună ziua,*" he said. Nothing wrong with his official Good day, Nora thought, as Martin answered with a friendly "Hello" and she deliberated whether to respond in Romanian or not. Then she realized it was nothing short of stupid pretending she didn't speak the language with the place of birth clearly written in her passport. At the thought of her knee-jerk intent her heartburn rose right into her head as if propelled by an explosion.

"*Documentele, vă rog,*" the soldier asked for their passports.

Nora had no doubts they were well prepared. Visas in order. The trunk packed with extra-long Kent cigarettes, some handy in her purse to pacify unhappy officials. "Why 'Kent'?" she had asked friends who returned from Romania. "That's all they like. It's passed around like currency. They might not even smoke them. People knew cases when Pall Mall or Marlboro had been refused, or worse, trampled in spite," she was told. The soldier disappeared with the passports in the rundown one story building. Nora took a Tylenol. Martin got out of the car and started to pace. Another soldier gestured him back into the car.

In another lane cars slowly but steadily drove through after a brief stop for passport control and a more or less disinterested inspection of the trunks. They were from the Communist block countries, including Romanians returning home.

"I'm wondering what's going on," Martin asked after half an hour.

"If my aches and pains are any indication, we might be in trouble." She was serious.

"Are you blacklisted?"

"Isn't everybody?"

"Oh! I see. Show you, rotten imperialist traitor."

A guard passed the car. Nora got out. "What's happening with our passports?"

"Routine check," he answered without stopping.

"I'll start to fuss if nothing happens within the hour," Nora told Martin taking her place in the car.

Nothing happened except that their bladders filled up.

"Okay. Let's go." They got out, locked the car and headed to the building. At the entrance a soldier blocked their way. "We're going to the bathroom," Nora said in Romanian. The soldier grinned and told them to wait. They were stepping into the bare grimy vestibule. At a facing window with metal bars—*CASA*, for cashier—was a drab woman. On the left was a door with a sign *Vama-Grăniceri,* for customs-border. A half open door in the opposite right corner with its lock carved away, elicited Martin's more acute interest. "Is WC in Romanian what I think it is?"

"Yeah," Nora was leaning, one foot ahead, ready to dash.

"Only one of you at a time," the returning soldier told her. Inside she found two separate sections. Men and women. The stalls dripping with rust and mildew was the least blemish on the seatless toilets. No paper.

Martin went in. "Why one by one," Nora asked the guard.

"Orders from the major." His face was stony.

"Please come with me to our car," she told the machine gun carrying soldier. "I want you to look at something." She winked. He followed without a comment.

She opened the trunk. She knew where the half bottle of Duty free scotch was. She pulled it half way out of the bag. "Are you interested in this?"

He didn't bother pretending. "Yes."

"Well, enjoy and let us have those passports fast."

"I should've gone to the john sooner," Martin said when driving away.

"Sorry to disappoint you. That was not what inspired them. Don't look for the scotch."

"You gave it away? I should've passed it through me once. They wouldn't know," he said.

A display of Communist Party slogans dominated the roadside like rows of huge guillotines dripping bloody words of a nonexistent prosperity and empty promises of a bright future. Oxen with sadly hanging heads pulling carts, buses with drums of natural gas hoisted on their roofs, and occasional bicyclists was all the traffic of the dull present. The road was devoid of cars even in urban developments. At destination, trolley cars picked up crowds of gray individuals waiting in long lines.

Help was available at the most elegant hotel, the Belvedere, at the top of Fortress Hill, though not official valet type. "Remember the Return of the Pink Panther," Martin whispered when their luggage was whisked away. The venue was new, built since Nora had left. Two soldiers sat at a coffee table in the corner of the vast lobby, with their machine guns neatly placed across their knees. Next to them was a sparkling display case filled with the best Romanian crystal and folk art. A manager invited Nora with zealous gestures to his office behind the reception. He opened a folder containing Nora's American Express number adorning a tentative menu for the banquet.

"You actually have everything you need for this dinner?" Nora was candidly surprised. Cold appetizers, pork cutlets with braised cabbage and potato gratin, walnut cream torte and coffee were terms probably absent from the table, even erased from the vocabulary, of the population of Romania.

"Anything for a beloved visitor like you."

Or rather beloved dollars, you think I don't see through you. "Do you love me enough to prepare a *ciorbă de perişoare?* I'm dying for one with plenty of *leuştean.*" She craved the Romanian sour meatball soup seasoned with lovage.

Nora designed the banquet with eighteen of her best friends as a vehicle to reminisce in public. Westerners visiting citizens at their homes brought unnecessary risks. Nora didn't want to incite any trouble for her friends. Agreeing to a feast in an exposed place was harmless enough. At least they hoped so. The banquet was also Nora's chance to be generous without hurting anyone's feelings.

The elevator whisked them to a modern room on the fifth and highest floor, what Nora had requested. Her delight lasted until the first of the daily power cuts, when she had plenty of chance to demonstrate to Martin how Romanians did their daily exercise. Nora's customary bathroom check unveiled two skimpy-wispy towels and a tattered hemp cord hanging from the high reservoir over the toilet. The rest was of unremarkable basic comfort.

Standing by the window, the panorama of the city awakened Nora's nostalgia she suddenly needed to share with Martin. Their eyes followed a path drawn by her pointing finger. "See that blue building at the South-West edge of the city? That's the Triumf, the factory where Paul worked. There, beyond the river, see that park? Like a miniature central Park. But walking through it?" She sighed. "At the time when I was walking through it to and from school, it was safe. But then, maybe New York was safe too . . . and beyond . . . that cluster of buildings is my alma mater."

Soon Nora opened her notebook. How could she offend anyone with a call saying, I remember you, but you are not worth my time, so just hello, I have no time to meet you. One was Cornelia, the nurse. She could have asked about Tibor, maybe not in Martin's presence. Suddenly, she was sure she was not up to finding out. If she could keep away from such a powerful magnet, then her med school friends presented no temptation. She crossed out a few names and dialed the operator. She asked in fluent Romanian, "Would you please look up a number for me . . ." While she heard pages being turned the operator said musing, "You must have left the country long ago."

Nora's puzzlement seemed ridiculous. *They must know everything about their guests. Probably the room is bugged too.* "Why do you think that?" Nora asked. "You speak Romanian with a foreign accent." Funny, though a blow. And to the point. Displaced, hanging in limbo between languages and cultures. "You should hear my accent in English," she responded.

Martin looked up from Fodor's *Eastern Europe with* a bewildered pity on his face. Nora was blowing her nose and dabbing her eyes.

"We're going to meet . . ."

"Shouldn't you go by yourself?" He spoke with empathy.

"Didn't you want to see the mud huts?" She noticed his questioning eyes. "Silly." Nora's smile was knowing. Her husband's thoughts were uncovered. "The lunch invitation is in Gheorgheni, my old neighborhood."

His sigh betrayed a concern he had never mentioned. At that moment Nora knew it was the right decision not to look for Tibor.

"Now, we'll pick up Laci," she said already in the car.

"Who?"

""Laci, Hedi's husband, the man at the other end of the table from us last night. Great friends. Implying that sometimes they felt entitled, if not obliged, to bring to my attention my mistakes and lecture me on the right conduct. They—"

"—stuck their nose where it was not their business."

She nodded meaningfully. "Surely it was not their business and I hadn't asked to be lectured. Our friendship survived a considerable strain. He wants to come to the cemetery with us."

"I see."

She was not sure whether Martin did, but he certainly had the kindness to wait out the events and the subsequent impressions his wife's old friends would make on him.

She led the small procession from one lost family member's resting place to another. Paul's father died first, then Paul and Manci. Adel had died alone. Arthur's grave was a few plots away. Looking at the cement slabs, she waited for pain to stir, for tears to well up, but instead she felt comforted. Perhaps it was the well-kept condition of the sites. A deceitful proof of duties fulfilled.

They settled on the bench at the foot of Paul's grave. Then Nora gathered a few stones. She placed two at the base of each tombstone. The token changed the weight of remembrance to the lightness of relief.

Nora filled dutifully, as she had promised, the role of guide. "A little detour . . . this was my office . . ." She pointed to the trolley yard, a foreboding sight of a forest of ropes hanging like nooses from the forks atop the cars, looking abandoned behind a wire fence.

"Don't you want to go in?" Martin asked.

"No. I've decided against calling on anyone. I'm glad we won't stay longer. But we can stop wherever you want." They had already done so at the National Theater, and they walked across to the Greek Orthodox Cathedral. Both were closed. The square offered more. A view of the regional Communist Party headquarters located in a showy Art Deco building. It displayed its assets in patterns of fresh pastel colors. Further on, a few new buildings, also five stories high, emulated and complimented the clean architectural features in a post-modernist rendition.

"This is what our Budapest guide cried about," Martin observed. "How come in a small place like this they can achieve such remarkable unity of styles?"

She said with a droll expression, "We're having lunch at the home of the person who I think is responsible for this feat. We'll ask the host."

"How's that?"

"George is a genius and the chief architect of the region."

When George opened the door, it was much more of the genius than Nora knew. The years had piled around his body. His rotundity caused a surge of the adolescent affection they had shared in high school.

The lunch was made of ingredients from the overstuffed freezer—as Gytta, George's pretty and mock-aloof wife, easily the best cook around, put it, "I must buy up whatever's available, if we don't want to starve other times. True, sometimes we have to throw out spoiled stuff." The shelves in food stores at best loaded with cans of tomato sauce or canned fish, fully supported her rationale.

"Did you know that Tibor got married?" Gytta asked Nora in the kitchen.

"Yes," Nora answered in a neutral tone.

"And that he emigrated with his family to Hungary?" Gytta whispered.

Nora had the best intention of simply stating she didn't know. Instead she focused on keeping her knees from buckling under her. After she managed that, how successfully she was not sure, she broke out in an uncontrollable laughter and said, "I've seen him."

"How is he?"

"Or at least I think I did." Nora held her head in her hands and heard a jingle of the keys falling onto the sidewalk. *I should've checked the listing of the residents.* Then, at the risk of seeming ill-bred toward her puzzled hostess, she added with a wry smile, "Let's drop it."

As the Ferbers didn't miss any opportunity to "hop over to Europe," as Martin called their short trips, Nora had plenty of occasions to use her cherished American passport. Walking alongside Martin, bypassing the long lines waiting at the immigration booths, were always emotional moments for her.

Like everything else on the Mann's way to American citizenship, their dealings with the INS were not a delight. Neither on the phone, nor in writing, nor in person with officers after half days of waiting in crowded offices, nor the news, after five years of their arrival, that Nora was not eligible for the citizenship. Instead she was advised that her purification from her Communist past would be considered complete in another five years. Those were the five years of the stand-by joke, when Nora and Daniel, once in a blue moon, begged Sonya to adopt them. Sonya, eighteen, not being blemished, did not have to wait, and became a citizen before her mother and her brother.

Nonetheless, returning from Romania, getting off the plane on the soil of her new country, a feeling of belonging moved Nora to tears. However, the joy of feeling totally at home could not stop her recurring nightmares for months to come. She often woke exhausted after fighting beasts dressed in Romanian border guard uniforms that wouldn't let her work her way through thick fences of bloodied barbed wire.

4

Nora had always been lacking in understanding people who swore they wouldn't be alive without a shrink. "If your brain can't figure out the way around your problems, it won't be able to process what someone says who doesn't feel the stings of the bed of thorns you're lying on," she would argue.

She shrugged off again Martin's argument, "It would give you back your peace of mind—" The rest of his reasoning was closer to the target. "—based on experience and statistical likelihood offered by an expert. You don't make your own shoes, do you? You're not a cobbler. You don't try to fix your own mental health. You're no more of a psychiatrist than a cobbler."

How would statistics save her from being tormented over Daniel's choice of throwing everything away? Nora tried to put all the objectivity she could muster in accepting her son's decision. She failed miserably. It was not merely that she couldn't endorse Daniel's argument, but that she could not put it at the back of her mind for one minute. Not to mention the nightmares of the most awful catastrophes that could have occurred while she could not direct as much as a protective thought toward him. She did not know not where he was or what he was up to.

Nora pushed aside the dinner. "Admit it, my dear. You need help." Martin commented.

"*I* need help?" Nora's palms came down onto the kitchen table with a noisy slap. "I'd do anything to help Daniel. Jump in a well. Anything. But you tell me, how would that help *him* if *I* got help?"

"Has it occurred to you that you have to take care of yourself?"

"Nothing is wrong with me. I didn't run away from the world—"

"All right. You're fine. How about us?"

"I'm sorry. I didn't realize that I'm failing in my duties—"

"I must admit we've had better times."

Nora spent hours in an uncomfortable chair at the Barnes & Noble Bookstore on Broadway, picking up books one by one from the pile she had set on the floor. She had pulled an armful from the self-help shelves.

She studied the tables of contents, leafed through, turned them, looked at authors' credentials, turned them again. Then she dropped them on the other side of the chair in the reject pile.

"You know what I think?" she told Martin that evening after she had tried to switch off the worrying side of her brain and to be a more interested wife. "The titles of these self-therapy books are words picked from a hat. Take ten words, no more. Like: self-confidence, adult, want, failure, success, understanding, parents, peace, conflict, hope, and add a few prepositions and you got all the titles of these treatises, and probably the contents as well. So much hog wash—"

"I can see how they can turn you off," Martin said.

"Experienced psychiatrists, right? I went through three books on parents and children at war, or making peace with the situation that the former doesn't own the latter, etc, etc. I didn't find a measly ten percent that could apply to me. Anything, so I could say I didn't waste my time. Anything, to understand Daniel better—"

"If that's what you want."

"My point is that I didn't find anything in these books that I could use. Except that they talk down and irritate me. How would it help me to read a case report, about twenty pages long, about parents who couldn't get rid of their grown up parasitic children? Or parents who didn't want to hear about their grown up children because of their sexual orientation? Or people with different types or social incompatibilities."

"Don't read that. Read the ten percent that applies—"

"I didn't find it."

"So nothing came out of your book store research?"

"There was one book. How should I put it? I thought I'd like to open it once in a while and leaf through it. I bought it."

"Good. Can I see it?"

Nora got out of bed, walked to the entrance hall console where she had left her bag. She returned with a book. She handed it to Martin, who sitting on her bed, was dangling one bare leg from under the wrinkled sheet. He opened the covers, read the book jacket at the front and back. "All right?" he asked puzzled. "What makes this better?"

"It's the tone. It's not condescending. I think I could talk to this author. Of course, if she's still in Manhattan."

Nora rang the bell at the Madison Avenue address. She took the elevator without a call button sent for her from above. At the end of the long and obscure hallway on the third floor a maid in a pinafore opened the door. Nora followed her past the kitchen smelling of exotic spices, through a vast dining room leading to a sunken expansive living room area around a concert piano. They ended up at an elevated sitting area in a geometrically irregular end of the apartment. The maid motioned her toward a bench running against the wall and mumbled some words that might have been English disguised in a Spanish accent. Nora stepped up and sat at one end of the bench. The facing French window blocked by iron bars overlooked a narrow outdoor space.

Objects with a definite antique patina decorated the walls and lay on the irregular glass coffee table in no apparent order. Nora picked up a foot long scrimshaw. Amongst elaborate carved scenes, she noted the date of 1790. She lifted an appreciative brow and set the piece of ivory on the table. Next to the bench, on an ivory-inlaid Chinese side table, was a box of tissues, a writing pad and a sharpened pencil. Facing the elevated area, a modern leather office chair stood in bold contrast to the rest of the interior decoration.

At exactly six o'clock the Therapist walked in from the invisible section of the apartment. Dressed in a tailored lilac silk suit, she looked as if she had stepped off the pages of *Vogue* magazine, high heels, freshly coiffed short blonde locks and all. Her blue gaze poured warmth as the two women shook hands. "I am Ann," she said as she quickly sat on the office chair. In a posture of pure and trusting repose, she crossed her fleshy legs and placed her hands in her lap. No rings except a wedding band.

Nora wondered whether she felt uncomfortable because of the novelty of the situation. Was it the total lack of symmetry expressed in the surroundings? She couldn't decide whether it was a whim of taste or intentional and related to what she could expect. Was it perhaps Ann's classy appearance, in contrast with her own? She felt like Cinderella in her flat rubber soled shoes, sport suit and shirt blouse, less than fresh, after a day's work. Yet in the end, it was more Ann's poise than her high-fashion get-up. This woman exuded confidence. Was it the fact that in the position of a patient, she had to look down to the person she expected help from? Am I *placed higher to boost my confidence I lack?* Nora knew it was not the two hundred dollars for the introductory session. Her peace of mind had no dollar value at that point; her mind was open to any assistance, at any cost.

Soon, help took the form of well-paced questions. Nora didn't mind being led into a soliloquy on the reason for her seeking help, after she had explained in unequivocal terms that it was not her professional or conjugal situation that brought her there.

"I'm aware I should be a happy mother. For that matter I would be the worst ingrate to complain. What normal parents—I thought I'm one—aim for, is to raise independent children. I achieved that. I used to praise myself that I have an empty nest without the syndrome. But now I cannot make peace with what my children do. My daughter is successful, climbing the corporate ladder. I believe she's enjoying every minute of it. No family instincts. Perhaps it's too early. Individuals mature at their own rate. I'm not unhappy and certainly don't nag her. She's only twenty seven. It's my son, the twenty-two-year-old, who worries me to death. According to others who are able to be objective, and who have some background themselves that enables them to appreciate his abilities, he's simply brilliant. Do you think you want to see a picture, so you relate better to whom I'm talking about?" Nora realized how irrelevant a photo was.

"Certainly."

Nora took out a picture taken a year back in Los Angeles.

"Both are gorgeous." Ann scrutinized Nora. "It's mostly their eyes which strike me. They don't look like you."

"Their eyes take after the paternal grandmother."

Ann handed the picture back. Nora put it on her purse.

"Go ahead," Ann urged Nora.

Nora gave as objective an account of Daniel's three years at Caltech as she could. No adverbs, not even adjectives. "May 1988. That was last year. It seems ages ago. We were at a French restaurant in Santa Monica. It was Sonya's graduation, she chose the venue. One could have said everybody seemed happy, certainly us, the family." Nora paused. "In the spirit of the past year, since Dani appeared so changed, I paid more attention to his mood. He was sparkling. I was happy, if for nothing else, than for that alone."

"Did you make any remark to that effect?"

"I don't think so."

"Good."

"It was an emotionally animated party, we all toasted, I felt happier than I could ever have dreamed. Then I recall uneasiness setting in as Dani dwelled on his interpretation and meanings of commencement—how it refers to him who's not at the end or beginning of any definable period of his life. Honestly, even in retrospect I can't say I understood exactly how he put it, though now I know what he meant. He knew what he was talking about, I have no doubt, despite the fact that he was beating around the bush. Sonya avoided my eyes during Daniel's speech. I was definitely left out of their confidence. I have this belief that they never hide anything from me that's good for them—"

"May I correct you? What would meet your approval—"

"Perhaps. They either don't trust my judgment, or they're aware that something is not right in theirs. His, in this case. With Sonya's knowledge, blessing, approval, whatever. I felt an ominous tremor, and I was not even aware that the world was collapsing." Nora looked beyond Ann. Then she refocused to relate facts. "Daniel apparently had already quit his research position at the time of Sonya's graduation. They didn't tell me. Whether he had filed already for dropping out of school altogether is irrelevant. I didn't know when I left Los Angeles after the weekend that I'd be forbidden to see my son." Nora pulled a tissue from the box. She dabbed her eyes. She sniffled. She blew her nose. She smiled bitterly at the box of tissues, then at Ann. She had just fallen into the predictable pattern of the tear-dabbers taking turns on that bench. Ann remained silent and serious. "If it weren't for this . . . I'm selfish again, I guess, but how can I not feel guilty? Why do I have to be kept out of his life? What did I do wrong to cause him to isolate himself? To punish himself? Whatever he says—"

"What reasons did he give you?

"That he proved wrong all that time he thought he was right. Just because of one girl?" Nora waved off a question from Ann. "No. He didn't say that. But let me ask you. What else threw him off track? Why does he lump together his emotional insecurities with his professional status? He says he wants to avoid future mistakes, minimize failure. Again, there's no question that could elicit a straight answer."

"There are no straight answers."

"Well," Nora nodded in defeat. "He calls me once in a while. I have no number where I could call him. I assume Sonya has been forbidden to divulge the number where he can be reached." Nora sighed deeply. "Sometimes he sounds upbeat. Then I wonder whether he's covering a depression. Sometimes I don't have to wonder. He makes no secret that he's depressed. He took a summer job at a rafting center on the Arkansas River in Colorado. He's a hand. He doesn't have the qualification to be a guide. He lives in a barrack, a dorm with who knows what oddballs. Hopefully as harmless as himself." Nora's feeble attempt for comic relief didn't work. Both women were too deep in their thoughts. "At Labor Day, rafting stops. Then, Daniel apparently just crossed the state line into Arizona." Nora paused. "How would you like your borderline genius son to be promoted to stable hand at a dude ranch? Please, don't think for a minute that I'd like him back on the track he's born for just so that I could be pleased. No one could convince me that this life could make him happy."

"Are you afraid that he would embrace this kind of life instead of an intellectual life?"

"Well? His class mates are seniors now. And what is he doing? Cooking up future plans knee deep in manure? Ann. Tell me anything I can believe."

"Is he still at the ranch?"

"No. I guess he was over-qualified. He had elevated himself to the title of *body valet.* I don't know what exactly you call the handsome young men who go around the pool area of a luxury hotel to cool the sunning ladies spraying them with water from bottles." Nora tried not to be appalled by Ann's smile. She looked like she would like to be one of those ladies. "He's at the Marriott in Desert Hot Springs outside of Palm Springs. He's back almost full circle. At least geographically speaking. I hope it's the magnetism of the school." Now Nora smiled sheepishly.

"Do you suspect he wanted to be close to Sonya? Did they stay close? Their rapport?"

When Nora told Ann, "Yes and no," she had no idea how accurate her contradictory assessment was. "I hope that the two of them are close. More meaningful than to be close to an old mother, though that's like a lifeline to me." Nora was working the ball of tissue between nervous fingers.

By the end of the session, Nora knew she had to let Ann's words permeate her tortured and stubborn brain, if she wanted to gain anything. First tenet: She was not supposed to worry about her son. That would be the safest way not to *show* worry. *That's a good one,* she mocked Ann wordlessly. It was all right to tell him—*Easier said than done!*—that she's saddened by his problems causing the setback. Her chance to influence her son passed.

"You have to build a rapport—" Ann said.

"I thought we had one."

"That takes a vigorous approach, but with utmost caution not to cause him to further withdraw—"

"Further than disappearing without a forwarding address?" Nora became feisty in trying to assimilate the absurd notion of being vigorously cautious. Especially after she sensed that her attitude of resistance didn't touch Ann. Nora started to respond with sharpness, antagonizing Ann without preambles of politeness.

"He's not seeing the facts through a conventional prism," Ann went on fixing Nora with an insistent gaze. "He measures events against a standard of his own which eludes him right now. Whether his current view is temporary, or the beginning of a new life concept, is very difficult to say. In this state the last thing he needs is help from *Mother.* Part of his problem is being too close to you and starting to despise his feelings as a handicap—"

"Isn't that a little strong?" With difficulty Nora kept her growing frustration under control through Ann's lecture. *She's telling me that all I was afraid of is real, that Daniel might decide to trample on his own life, disregard his potential and future, throw away knowledge, turn into a bum.* How could Daniel's wasting his most beautiful years leave her cold? That with his intelligence he could turn his disappointment with a girl into repulsion toward his mother?

Nora considered making this the last session with Ann. Should she say so? Wouldn't it be more honest?

She heard Ann's words shattering her thoughts. "Not strong enough to express what you both go through. He will be able to re-connect with his own feelings, to adopt a new direction only if he's not interfered with. Certainly not by unsolicited people." She looked at the clock, a superb contraption of enamel and bronze sitting on the mantelpiece. Probably Meissen, Nora thought. "Time is up," Ann said. "I have a favor to ask you. Would it be acceptable for you to schedule the next session in two weeks? It might get hectic here with some house guests."

"Ann," Nora wanted to thank her for her help so far, but Ann's last words still vibrated in the air. "You gave me so many new ideas today. I need time to work them out anyway. Let's skip a few weeks."

"Very well. I only want you to know that whatever you decide, I'm here. And something else. Keep in mind that parents don't own their children."

"Show your support, I'm told. What course should my support take?" Nora sounded desperate and clueless, as she indeed was, when she returned to Ann in a few weeks.

"Assurance that you're there if needed. Simple as that. I'm here if you need me. Don't express fear. Fear means lack of trust in his judgment. Lack of trust undermines his self-confidence which right now is under siege. You can express sadness that he's not feeling more confident about himself. You cannot tell him you desire that he should feel better. That's taken as criticism. He doesn't need to hear that he's not doing well enough. Saying that he's not good enough, is naturally out of the question. Besides, it's not the case."

Later, Ann engaged herself more. "It's unethical to interpret and diagnose a person whose symptoms I have no direct knowledge of. I can go as far as advising you in order to help you through a difficult period. This naturally implies some consideration of his status. The way I see it, this should help you. Daniel would fit the criteria of an adjustment disorder. It is probably a thin line between a transient Adjustment Disorder, and a full-blown Anxiety Disorder. The separation in Daniel's case is not quite clear to me, because I'm getting the information secondhand. The difference would reside not only in the intensity of the symptoms, but mainly in the onset and the expected duration. I need to emphasize that I'm getting close to the core of his problem only to alleviate your anxiety. You, for that matter, share a diagnosis with your son. He might have displayed signs in his teen years of some behavioral predisposition for anxiety. Or phobia, if you wish. Here we're getting into guidelines, or rather, requirement restrictions. An Adjustment Disorder would have to be limited to six months. If we put the onset of Daniel's symptoms at the time of dropping out of school, *not before,* he should be approaching resolution. He might have passed that turning point. He might have made peace with the past stressor, he might have found the solution for his fears in a radical change in lifestyle that would avoid any future insult of the same nature, he might be happy and doesn't want to hear any criticism. Especially not from you. Also, he might be agonizing, feeling handicapped, frightened by a life that he thinks he's destined for, so to speak, the only one for the long run. Or, as most likely is the case, he's taking his time to conclude an episode of Adjustment Disorder and return to his previous normal life."

"Hi, Mom." Sonya was not supposed to be back from Greece.

"Where are you calling from?"

"I came back yesterday." No specifics given. "I wanna fill you in with the big picture and the current events—"

"Are you getting married?"

"Mama, please, this is serious." Now she paused as if she expected to be interrupted again.

"I'm trying to be silly because it's the only way to keep me from screaming from the end of my rope," Nora said.

"Please, listen. Things are not as bad as they seem."

"I was talking about my worries with Daniel."

"Well, that figures. We're on the same wavelength . . ." Sonya paused, as if to underscore her own words. "Before I left, I spent a long weekend with Dani. I was exhausted anyhow after finishing a large project, so I thought I deserved a rest in Desert Springs. Dani had already decided to leave. He says he saved enough money to be off anyone's payroll for a bit."

"What's wrong in letting me finance his education?"

"I think it would be a setback."

"Tell me honestly. Do you understand and support his ideas?"

"It's not an idea. It has been his problem, you realize—"

"So I'm told. But—" Nora's worst premonition flared up.

"Daniel wants you to know—"

Did he delete my phone number from his memory? I'd fly—literally—to be at his side if he wants to talk to me. I'd welcome anything that would make him happy. Why does he need a mediator?

"We're in Seattle. He's fine. He had an accident."

Nora took in a wheezing breath, covered her gaping mouth with a hand and squeezed her jaw. "What happened?"

"They were hiking on Mount Rainier. There was an avalanche. The rescuers were very good—"

"What's his condition?"

"He's in no danger. He has some fractures, nothing critical . . . Exposure too . . . I can't give you medical details—"

"Do you have—"

"Have paper'n pen?"

"You don't need to know everything," Daniel declared when Nora called back.

She held the receiver in her gently cupped hands as if supporting her son's broken arm, happy just to hear his voice.

"Tell me what you want me to know."

"You'll be glad to hear this," he chuckled. "This experience cured me from going for the Everest."

"That's a pity. Your doctor said that you're fully baptized now for such an expedition," Nora said with relief that finally a moment came, even if at great cost, that they could joke.

"So, you talked to the doctor. I must admit, you're fast."

"There's really no danger of nerve damage. That's something that one automatically fears when hearing of an injury to the spine. It was pure luck that the rock hit you where the spine is the strongest."

"I know."

"Then you know that you don't need to be immobilized, for your back, I mean. The two broken spinous processes as they call the posterior projections of your vertebrae will heal by themselves. Possibly you'll have some pain. The forearm is just a matter of patience . . . I trust them, though I'd feel better seeing the x-rays for myself—" she paused exercising self-control.

"There are two ways . . ." he spoke slowly, weighing every word.

Nora held her breath. She couldn't get on a plane and visit him without his consent. Nothing had changed and she knew it. Once she had mentioned, "I wouldn't abuse your confidence," to which he had answered, "That's the best thing we have." Now, if he didn't say it, she couldn't go.

There was some fidgeting, Nora heard some crackles coming through the line. She kept quiet. "Sorry, I had to scratch my nose. I tried with the receiver. Highly unsatisfactory." Daniel cleared his voice. "One way is to have them send you my x-rays—"

"Copies, you mean," she said. Her heart raced as she realized he would finally say what she wanted to hear. What else could've been the other alternative?

"Yeah, yeah," his interjection scared Nora for an instant. "The other is that you look at the originals here."

"I'll be there tomorrow even if I have to flap my arms for three thousand miles."

The day was exceptionally clear. The plane flew past floating clouds, like superfluous ornaments around the immensity of the snow cap covering the rounded top of Mount Rainier. Nora's eyes were not tuned to the picturesque; they were searching for a point lost in infinity, where the forbidding mountain had turned against her son.

Time melted in the rush of the taxi and her own thoughts. She looked up at the facade of the Harborview Hospital on Capitol Hill. Soon she stepped through a door. The room was filled with Daniel's expectant gaze; it seemed as though he had done nothing for the last 24 hours than wait for that moment.

Nora bent over him, put her arms around his shoulders, kissed his forehead, wanted to lift him and cradle him in her arms. "Hi, baby," was all she could say between tears.

"Thank you for flapping your arms, Mom," he said with an attempt at joking. The clearing of his throat was more telling than the disclosure of his budding plans later.

That's how Sonya found them. Mother and daughter embraced. A long and tight embrace. "Thank you for everything. You're a marvelous sister and daughter. Are *you* all right here?" Nora whispered.

Later, watching over a sleeping Daniel, they stood at the window overlooking the grand panorama of downtown, the bay beyond, and made plans. Nora was not interested in sightseeing, she felt no calling other than be with Daniel and to get some sleep in the modest B&B room located at walking distance from the hospital. Sonya had to return the same day to Los Angeles.

5

With time on their hands Nora and Martin wandered aimlessly, dragging their carry-ons around in the San Juan airport. The glassed corridors offered a view of planes with bellies open, luggage trains circling underneath, food service trucks waiting. A soundless canvas of oil-stained tarmac.

"I'd rather fly for six hours straight," Nora's remark bored.

"Have you digested the plastic breakfast yet?" Martin asked.

"We could wash it down," Nora said looking toward the elevated platform of a snack bar.

They sat down at the tiny table behind the chrome railing. The soft calypso caressed her eardrums and her brain beyond. Picking a nacho from the bowl, she dipped it in the dish of salsa, and enjoyed it as her mood swung towards sheer euphoria even before Martin offered the slice of orange and the little paper umbrella from his glass of mai tai. She held his wrist and pulled the fruit off the tooth pick with her lips.

"To fun!" He lifted his glass and winked.

"To a perfect vacation." She sipped her mineral water and leaned back. "So, prime me," she said. He had never taken charge of arranging what they called a mindless vacation, claiming he lacked experience. He preferred to organize their many European trips, the cultural ones. Like the one when he got fired up by the opening of the Opera Bastille in Paris. She got her choice of hotel on *Ile St. Louis,* he got to choose the performances. Since Nora had been on the treadmill for the past few months, she couldn't possibly carve out enough time to organize this vacation she craved.

"Well, for starters, on approach, we'll get a glimpse of the geography," he smiled at her enigmatically, for she hadn't had the time to even read the description of the place they were going to. "Surprise me," she had said when he tried to show her.

His attitude was stimulating, his smile open. He visibly tried to get Nora into a vacation mood and to coax her to begin unwinding after all she had gone through with her work, with Daniel. She had kept the stabs of anxiety to herself. That Daniel rejected the family, unwilling to share the joy of his graduation, took on an ominous meaning for Nora. She knew that the Seattle reunion a year earlier was no opening, but a mere crossroad. She couldn't accept that he simply didn't care for formalities. She had been grateful to Martin for his cool head then, and now she looked at him as if she was seeing him after a long absence. Tenderly. She couldn't take her eyes off his face. She held out a hand, and he lightly hooked his fingers over hers. She gave him one of her all teeth and eyelashes, tenderly loving smiles.

From the bluish mist reflecting the turquoise waters below a vague mirage unfolded into a strip of land. In minutes, the straight gray line grew undulating outlines, bays and coves trimmed with white caps along the shore, green mountain peaks holding the blue skies. Two foreshortened green sugar loafs stood on the shore.

"What a pity we're not staying here." She felt sorry to leave that land behind as the plane passed the island's South tip. She took his hand, a gesture she usually did on landing. "I've never seen such mountains in the Caribbean." Then she realized that the hand-holding must have been reflex, as if triggered by the loss in altitude. They were in a sharply curved landing pattern as the aircraft turned. Only the screeching of the landing gear was missing, but shortly it came on. "Marty?" She looked at him with mock reproach.

"Yes, dear." His calm voice could not hide his thrill of master-minding a real surprise.

"You rascal. This *is* St. Lucia then."

"I hope I chose well. The best of all possible worlds." She knew he meant their different passions. His fondness for snorkeling made up for his dislike of sunning. Nora took more slowly to snorkeling, with only her natural curiosity making the sport interesting through the new world it opened; in her soul, she always craved the mountains.

An expansive landing strip lay under the shimmering noon heat. "Wow, some oversized airport." Nora exclaimed.

"US military air base."

"Active?" She was ready to learn.

"Not really," he said leaning over her to have a better look at the tarmac. "On the other hand, wouldn't you say it's awfully well maintained for a little island nation that doesn't have resources?"

"I see. And we never needed it for Cuba, did we?"

"Here we go." The plane touched down bumping along the cement slabs with grass growing in between.

Hurled around in a van that might never have had suspension, along a road difficult to discern from the string of pot holes, they were looking at the mud splashing at every bounce. The overflowing bougainvillea, lush banana groves surrounding modest, but clean, rural dwellings, sporadic passing islanders were mere images skipping in and out the window like a broken strip of film.

"Rehearsal for *Purgatorio*," Martin spit the words fast. They didn't talk for fear of biting their tongues.

The little parking lot not far beyond the *Anse Chastenet* sign, and the set of tight serpentines, looked over a lower shaded terrace partly concealed in cascades of greenery. Above and below the small low-walled platform of the registration office the steep slope of the mountainside was hung with buildings showing between the foliage. Young women dressed in island attire, colorful scarves twisted in the shape of little birds on top of their heads, were replenishing baskets with fruit and pitchers with juice.

"We must be in *Paradiso*," Nora said, following an employee up the climbing stone alley bordered with exotic flowers.

"You said you don't mind the steps."

"Uhum," Nora took a deep breath and looked up. Villas revealed themselves behind dense clumps of trees. "I'm glad I tried to keep in shape," she puffed, then realized that her words sounded like a complaint, so she added, "Marty, this is 'A' plus so far."

The employee turned onto a narrow path that led to an unlocked wooden door. "The key is inside, you can lock if you wish."

A knobby old tree with lacy leaves grew from within the corner of a high fence. Inside the villa, was a large tiled bathroom with a shower under the open sky under that tree. The sprawling, also tiled, bedroom couldn't get its deserved praising, for the man immediately led them out to the large terrace lavishly furnished and surrounded by hanging citronella candles. "You have a full view of the *Pitons*, as you requested." He pointed to the twin green sugar loaf peaks they had spotted from the air.

"Is everything here made with my wish in mind?" Nora asked elated. They reached the tracery of the brick banister. She sighed trying to breathe in the panorama, then hung her arms around Martin's neck.

"Thank you, love." They kissed. The staff retired discreetly. They stood there, gazing at the twin peaks jutting high over the forest canopy. The bird song suddenly stopped. A soft steaming rain started to pour, dance and polish the leaves. They stood mesmerized. After a few minutes of soaking downpour, the sun chased away the fleeting clouds.

"It's the price to pay for the luxury of such vegetation. It rains ten times a day," Martin said apologetically.

"I won't ask for a refund." Nora wanted to fly like the birds in the dripping foliage.

Faithful to custom, they hurried for an inaugural dip. As if the tartars were after them, they ran down the stairs carved in the mountainside. A tiny flowerbed marked each turn. They stepped on the warm sand. Nora took a deep theatrical breath. The sun peeked under the beach-grape bushes from a lavender-blue cloudless horizon. The glossy rock behind the dark, matte sand was painted with the long silhouettes of the palms. When he was working out the details Martin had asked her, "Would you mind volcanic sand?" She kicked it up now, it felt just as silky as any other. She had encountered sands in all shades from the bleached white of Mamaia on the Black Sea and the Hamptons on Long Island to the pink of Hawaii; another dark volcanic beach in Maui provided a perfect background for the infinite colors of the fish swimming around her feet in the crystalline water. No, she didn't mind the earthy brown sand. Perhaps, in contrast, she appeared whiter than an unripe cheese, but she planned to change that during the week to follow.

"Marty," Nora called out, her hands pressed against her chest. "Marty." He stirred. "Sorry to wake you." She was covered in sweat, breathing with some difficulty and taking her pulse. "I didn't intend to . . . I had such a strange dream . . . I must have woken afraid . . . I couldn't stand being alone."

"What can I do?"

"Just be . . . It must be the sun exposure . . . I was being like pasted to a rock . . . like the back of the beach here . . . a hot rock, I couldn't move . . . I was like glued . . . From the dark a light headed towards me, twisting, getting closer and bigger than the sun itself . . . it was dropping out of the sky, drilling its way towards me through a thick air, like oil . . . when it hit me in my chest the entire heat was concentrated on one point. . . ." She pressed with the fingers of both hands the middle of her sternum. "I don't have chest pain, don't worry," she told Martin who got up, walked around the bed and sat next to her rubbing her back.

"First thing tomorrow morning, I'll rent a car to take us around to the beach," he held Nora's protesting hand, "shush . . . I think the steps are too much for you. You're tired—"

"Why on earth would I be tired? An hour of snorkeling, half an hour of splashing around . . . I'm perfectly fine . . . I'll stay out of the sun tomorrow."

Every day they swam further away following the rainbow path of the forests of beckoning fan coral, banks of bonitas, myriads of parrot and angelfish no color chart could do justice to, squadrons of reef squid peering at them as if frozen, swinging sea horses, threatening sea urchins. Martin was a good swimmer, despite his age; it was the male, Nora decided, that had the better resistance. She kept quiet about getting slightly out of breath, but suggested they return to the beach.

A man darker than the darkest of his mates, with a bigger smile than Nora herself could produce, sauntered along the beach, with his sunglasses pushed midway down his nose. He was simply irresistible with his bare hairless chest and narrow waist, and a cap as big as a caldron covering his Rastafarian hair. He introduced himself uninvited, "I'm Francis." How he used his persuading power remained his secret, for next morning Nora and Martin were sitting in the prow of Francis's outboard plying in a straight line across the bay to promised mysterious sights. With cotton hats pulled down to their ears, Nora and Martin returned Francis's broad smiles.

They landed on a gravel beach littered with soda cans and candy wrappers marking the natural gem into a tourist spot. Francis exchanged cordial slaps on the shoulders with a chum waiting on the beach. "What's this?" Martin asked. "Don't worry, man, all included, Savion will take you to the water fall," Francis *reassured* them. They followed their new guide up the mountain path in the dense tropical rain forest. The young man picked up a fallen coconut and turned to Nora. She almost ducked startled. "You like this?" Savion asked. Nora nodded breathlessly. He split the fruit with a strike of a big rough stone, and drank the milky water, then scooped out strips of tender white pulp with a switch-blade. Nora and Martin exchanged meaningful glances. They sat for a while munching.

"Not long," Savion promised, climbing in front of them, just before they could hear the thundering waterfall. A group complete with children, was frolicking under the warm spray. Nora and Martin joined in feeling like kids again themselves, giggling, jumping around and sitting in the warm pool, until Savion ordered, "Enough now."

Francis, who was waiting at the beach, suggested a detour to Soufrière. The fishing village embraced a tiny bay, and was embraced in turn by the green mountain. The market was in full swing. Boisterous haggling, running dogs and no toilet in sight for the weary and bursting. There was no other choice than the police station; at first Martin doubted that Nora would actually ask to be admitted.

"How long should I wait for you?" he said in jest as Nora disappeared behind the metal-grid door.

"Are you released now?" he welcomed her as she re-emerged.

The steady loud motor propelled the boat over the ripples with speedy jumps and splashes. A knock made Nora grab the rim to avoid falling. Her anxious look found Martin calm, his face welcoming the breeze, eyes closed. "What was this Marty? Did the motor stall?"

"What motor? What stall?" He answered with some puzzlement.

"It almost knocked me over." She had made a connection with her strange dream the night before when he denied any malfunction.

She turned her left palm up. It appeared smooth in the bright sun. No deep long lifeline. What a pity. She knew no more than that her lifeline was short and she was destined to get married young and have two children. How did that gypsy figure out, after the war, that the little skinny girl standing in front of her was to get married young? Right on the button. Shrewd old woman. The statistics were of course with her. She was much too young at twenty two. Two children. Bingo. Isn't that the average? Nora had not lived in permanent terror, she didn't even think too often about the gypsy's prediction. Yet she was known to joke about it now and then. She would rarely contemplate her palm and that only when some symptom of vanishing wellness would call for an explanation. Like that instant in the racing boat. No matter how strongly she felt against superstition, she could not discard the childhood memory of the palm-reading gypsy.

Is it now? It's not a sun stroke, that's for sure. I can't catch an irregular pulse. Maybe I'm having a Transient Ischemic Attack? She pictured areas of her brain transiently under the duress of impaired blood flow. *Neah! Hopefully it is something like my numerous cancers or exotic infections that cure themselves after they're done torturing my mind. We're going home tomorrow. I'll go from there. I'll take it easy, which of course could worry Marty all the same.* She disengaged herself from probing the configuration of her palm and she found no difficulty admiring the vertical panorama of the mountainside exhibiting the entire resort hung between the turquoise sea and the white-splattered blue sky.

Between the pressure of the approaching spring demanding her attention on the rooftop garden, and her work with all its ramifications, Nora wished she could trim her schedule like her hedges on the terrace.

In that mood, she called her internist from her office. "Hi, gorgeous," Nora told the receptionist. "Make it an emergency? No. Gary would be after me. Perhaps urgent . . . Uh? . . . Put down rule out TIA. Of course I'm too young for that, thank you . . . of course that sounds like an emergency, but you see, I must work today, and tomorrow, and after. So, let's do it tomorrow."

Work felt much better the next morning. Everything was under control and rolling smoothly; the resident was ready with pre-reading a whole stack of scans, so there was not much need for jumping up and running to the scanner. Nora settled in her chair in front of the multi-viewer. Abi, a senior resident came over later. She was preparing rounds and Nora being her discussant, had to review the material. "How is today after work? Oh, wait." Nora slapped her forehead. "Okay. We'll look at your slides briefly, so you can work on them tonight. I've an appointment. Why don't we come in early tomorrow morning, okay? I'll have a busy day. Three biopsies, unless they hit me with some extras."

"What happened to you, Doc?" Stan, the forward CT tech asked looking over his lowered half-glasses at Nora, who was wearing the Holter monitor under her lab coat. "You're getting fat on one side."

"You better watch what you're saying. I'm wired." She didn't joke the day before when Gary outfitted her, she didn't claim the monitor was overkill, she was pleased to get the whole annoying business of her spells over with.

The resident on the CT rotation, David, signed the informed consent of the first scheduled patient. The elderly man listened as Nora reassured him against complications. "The biopsy itself is done with such a thin needle that even if it touched a vital structure it could not cause any damage. I'm confident that we won't have any difficulty. One or maximum two sticks. The worst is the little numbing injection. Just think you're in Alaska and one of their mosquitoes bit you. A little burning, that's all," she said, patting the smiling patient's hand.

After a quick set of scans and marking the point of entry according to the grid, Nora put on the mask, sterile gown and gloves, and nodded to David to do the same. Nora explained every step so the patient would be aware of what was going on, at the same time teaching the resident. They prepared the sterile field, draped the patient, and went back to the control room to review the localizing scans on the monitor. "Perfect. Let's go."

The procedure progressed like clockwork. Nora inserted the needle for the first pass. They scanned for position. She stabilized the syringe, explaining to David in a low voice the reason for the position of each of her fingers. "Mister Davis," she said loudly. "Take in a deep breath, hold it." She nodded her head slowly five times. "Now breathe out. This was a rehearsal. Now we'll do the real thing. Take in a deep breath . . ."

She acted quickly, then withdrew the needle and scrutinized the syringe. The aspiration yielded no blood, no visible material. "Perfect," Nora said again. "How do you feel Mister Davis?"

"You've done it already?"

"For now, yes. Please relax." The nurse reached under the drape, folded it up and took the patient's blood pressure.

Nora walked into the control room holding the syringe high and addressed the pathologist who wheeled in her cart as if on cue. With an engaging smile, she took over the syringe. Nora leaned against the wall and looked relaxed. Finding the cells was now up to the experienced cytopathologist preparing her slides.

Nora motioned to David. "We might be told that there isn't enough cellular material and have to go back for another sample, but we might not, if Pat got the answer. Are you ready to perform the second pass?" she asked him.

David nodded and a grin of expectation lit his face.

"Good," Nora said.

"Just go over your aspiration technique which seems so effective," David requested of Nora.

No problem . . . no problem . . . then why am I getting dizzy? . . . scared to death . . . is it a crime to let a second year resident . . . That's how we all learn . . . Why is the ceiling light in my eyes . . . falling on my face . . . on my chest . . . heavy . . . sliding down on my sides like rivers of hot mercury in the grooves of my ribs? . . .

At that point her mind went blank.

Nora's gloved hand brushed the CT console, the Holter monitor caught on the edge slowing her fall as Stan pushed his chair back with a kick, grabbed Nora's torso and eased her onto the floor. Pat looked up, grabbed her cart and pushed it into the hallway. Other people squeezed to the wall in the tight space.

In the hubbub that instantly erupted, it took seconds for those present to make a connection between Nora's joking about being wired, the heavy box harnessed to her and a severe cardiac event. The nurse unfastened the blood pressure cuff from the patient's arm hastily reassuring him that she'd be back. David tried to identify a carotid pulse with not much success, and yelled, "Code! Call a code!" while jumping up to unhook the Ambu bag from the wall. Stan and David were kneeling on the floor giving CPR as smoothly as they could manage. The nurse ran down the hall yelling to a passing clerk, "Code! Send the recovery room nurse quick!" She wheeled the crash cart to the door, and unlocked the padlock. Just a little over three minutes after the call, the code team pushed into the room ordering everyone out.

Scissors were the first life-saving instruments in use. Coat sleeves, dress, bras were quickly cut away. In the absence of a palpable pulse the paddles were applied to Nora's chest. The team leader projected a commanding voice. "She's in Vee fib. Defibrillator ready?" He waited for the confirming nod of the senior medical resident in charge. "Everybody clear? Clear everyone," the resident ordered. Nora's body contracted like a rag doll thrown in the air. An instant of tense silence. Everyone with a favorable angle had one eye fixed on the small monitor of the defibrillator. Nora coughed and grabbed for the face mask. "Sinus rhythm," the monitoring resident announced.

"Stan," Pat called. "Do what you have to do with the patient. He's done. Nora did a good job, as usual," she said, looking into the control room teary eyed, then pushed her cart to the elevator.

I am being dangled by the arm from an immense red zeppelin dripping blood. From a deep black trap in the belly of the balloon heavy white boulders spill but don't crush me, instead they levitate in the abyss around me. I have to find a hold, I am weightless . . . Nora grabbed at her face mask. Her eyelids fluttered, her eyeballs took slow turns, until she realized, not more than two minutes later (as she would be told) that it must have been the burning in her arm where they had inserted the intravenous line, the emergency physician's pointed red turban blown up to the size of a dirigible, him talking and showing his pearly teeth, that triggered the dream in her waking brain. "I'm Doctor Mohan. Doctor Mann, can you hear me?" He was gently slapping her face. "Doctor Mann? You're all right now."

"Uhum . . . hah? . . . uhum . . ." She was flying again, over a warm sea where corals grew out of the water and held her on a comfortable bed, her aching arm splashed by the cool waves. "Where . . . I . . . am?"

"You're all right now," Mohan repeated still alert to the monitor. The nurse reported a normalizing blood pressure. "You'll have to be admitted—"

"What happened?" Her eyes were fully open. She lifted her head.

"We found you in ventricular fibrillation, doctor," he said and waited for her to process the information.

"Do you know more?"

"No. But in your case it won't be a problem to find out. Who gave you the Holter?"

"Yeah, yeah. Garry . . . Garry Herman."

"We'll notify him right away. Paula," he called to the recording nurse, "Page Doctor Herman, would you?"

Nora closed her eyes, but the tracing on the monitor did not cause any more commotion.

In the twilight of fading alertness rolling on the quiet rubber wheels of the stretcher toward the telemetry floor, Nora felt relieved. Delegating her worries to her colleagues was as soothing as suckling mother's milk. She stopped fighting.

Sonya and Daniel flew in from Los Angeles. Martin picked them up in Newark and drove them directly to the hospital. The white-haired, young-faced reputable Chief of the Arrhythmia Service at the West End Memorial's Cardiac Department was more than amicable explaining to the family.

"Nora is Nora." He stood at the end of her bed with folded arms. "It happens once in a million that we get such help from a patient. So thorough, wouldn't you say? Is she always so well organized?" You bet, everyone's vehement nods said. "Making sure she gets the possibly fatal heart block in the hospital, on a Holter monitor—"

"That's our luck," Daniel, until then very quiet, interrupted. Nora looked at him with adoring eyes.

"Thanks Dani. It was worth dying a little just to hear this. I love you too." As Daniel was not near her—he was leaning on the window sill, standing behind Doctor Frish—Nora took teary-eyed Sonya's hand instead. She gestured a little droll peck to Martin standing at the foot of the bed, so he wouldn't feel left out. He wiggled his fingers raised to his shoulder.

"I hope everything is clear now. I'd like to take advantage of serious and involved witnesses, Nora. You cannot ignore your high cholesterol any longer. It's never too late. Especially that your coronaries have been standing the assault pretty damn well. So, with your documented arrhythmia, probably multiple and worsening episodes, out of the way, you should do your best to maintain your coronaries."

"I'll be a good girl." Nora raised a hand in oath.

"That's a girl. And go ahead with your life as if nothing happened. I don't expect the pacemaker to cause any problems."

"We're very grateful for the way you took care of Mom, doctor Frish." Sonya stood up. "Please explain to a simple minded engineer what caused the problem if her coronaries are fine." She stepped by her brother's side.

"It's wear and tear. With bad luck little defects in the heart's conduction system interfere with the transmission of the impulse from the atrium to the ventricle, if you know what I mean." Sonya nodded. "The ventricles don't have their own reliable autonomous centers to keep them going. In essence, that's what happened, heart block. The ventricles stopped, then went into fibrillation, which is basically irregular worthless contractions that lead to death if they are not reversed to normal or at least some kind of efficient rhythm."

"Thank you, now I understand," Sonya said.

Frish smiled at everyone around, shook hands with Martin, then left.

After an undue taste of purgatory, Nora was back in paradise. She visited her children who went normally about their business, at least according to conventional concepts. Hers, as it were.

To Nora's satisfaction, Sonya was enjoying a break from too much traveling, that she had become tired of. Though her comments continued to fall on deaf ears, Nora kept bringing up the subject of her friends enjoying their grandchildren.

Daniel, with an address, a phone number, and a lifestyle that didn't defy all known definitions, stayed on at Caltech.

"The rotations you wanted?" Nora asked him on the way to Sonya's apartment. "Did they work out?"

"Sure. The people at the Palomar Mountain Observatory got bored and were more than happy to have a harmonica player cheer up their long and silent nightly vigils." He laughed throwing his head back.

"In fact, they also needed a poet in residence, so in me they got a two for one deal—"

"May I show Mama your verse?" Sonya exclaimed excitedly.

"As if you didn't so far—"

"That's offensive. Did I ever break a promise?"

"All right, point taken." Daniel sat down in a mauve leather armchair. From the lacquered coffee table, he picked up an album of Japanese prints that lay next to a bonsai tree, while Sonya returned from her study with a piece of paper.

"It's not finished," Daniel mumbled loud enough for Nora to hear. She read.

IN NEED OF A BIG BANG

(Or some other eyeopener, like a telescope)

From the mountain top man's seeing arm
stretches and fails to grab a star.
Will never reach, will never touch,
Lofty puzzling affair.

Like a cyclops the earth gazes at the stars
Through one huge glary eye.
Stars that haven't come'th to me
Elusive sparkles of a squandered big bang.

Snow flakes of lighted fleeting matter,
How do they withstand the gaping black holes
That could attract, hold back or swallow.
What? My antics, or the whole Astrophysics?

My feet are scrawny roots the earth feeds,
My head's worth less than a charmed quark
Locked in a bottle I can't uncork.
Is anything wrong with dreams?

"Don't!" Daniel raised a protective arm, elbow pointing to the ceiling, as Nora assumed the threatening posture of kissing him. Instead, she punched a firm muscular shoulder.

"You wanna hear about the observatory?" Daniel asked as if nothing had happened. "It was an old dream of mine and they obliged. I set up my curriculum. They're accommodating when it comes to my problems about decision making." He waved off Nora who opened her mouth intending to reassure him. "Nothing I can, or for that matter, I want to fight," he added with some irritation. "Going from observing through a telescope to projecting with a rocket—"

"How's that?"

"A few weeks at the JPL—"

"Meaning?"

"Jet Propulsion Laboratory. The NASA affair next door. Of these two power house applications . . ." he nodded as if to his own thoughts, ". . . I'll probably stick to theoretical Physics."

"And stay in academics?"

"That's too far down the road. I'll tell you around graduation next spring whether I feel like going for a PhD. That's the only way to stay in academics."

"I'm going to risk a prediction here." Sonya looked up. She was setting the table in the dining alcove of the elongated living room of her new, small but luxurious, apartment on Linda Flora in Bel Air. She liked to toss around the address as a subtle underscoring of her success. The reflected light of the Pacific waves filtered through the tenth floor picture window suffusing the room with lightness. A bunch of slick silverware in her left hand, Sonya stood tall, slim and shapely, dressed in a wispy long dark green lounge dress, with her hair gathered in a pony tail. "A PhD is definitely in the cards," she declared, and gestured Daniel to silence. "You won't even have to make a decision. The stream will carry you."

"I expect your stream will wash ashore a thesis too."

"Wouldn't that be nice." She clowned an adoring smile. Daniel returned a super-sweet sarcastic grimace of affection.

Nora basked in her children's rapport. She was not aware of how Sonya had contributed to Daniel conquering his insecurities. She was happy observing the bond first hand. Her own rapport with her two children, though undoubtedly present, was different. It was packaged in a breakable wrapping that threatened to disintegrate at the touch of a word and spill the precious contents. An innocent word perhaps, at the wrong time that touched the wrong button.

While he was in Desert Hot Springs, Daniel had started to commute on his days off to a therapist in Los Angeles. He would get a ride, or rent a car, or once (at least from what Nora knew from Sonya) he flew from Palm Springs for an appointment. Undoubtedly, it had been Sonya's influence, though never a verbatim statement from either of them. Did he just follow advice, or did his sister effectively find him a shrink? As long as it worked, Nora had come to understand, she should stay out. Long live Ann! She had been praying that whoever took Daniel's temporarily disturbed mental health in hand should know what was right for him. Wasn't that part of her own problem in seeking help? The lack of trust, the misleading, even injurious advice wafting around psychiatrists' and psychologists' offices, like a miasma infiltrating and corrupting vulnerable brains?

What had been labeled an Adjustment Disorder occurring on the sensitive background of a slightly artistic personality now looked like a re-adjustment. As long as the Los Angeles therapist didn't mention depression, Nora would be the last to use the word. Some fragility of Daniel's state of mind still persisted. Was it a phase towards full recovery? The outcome was unpredictable.

"It's bad enough to have to do things, why would one have to also make decisions?" Daniel said. It was not his cynical self. His tone was tainted by his residual tendency to see potentially hurtful factors through a magnifying glass.

Did he emerge with a weakened self-confidence? If it was so, would his trouble have surfaced sooner or later as a response to some stressor other than that no-name female disappearing on him? What was eventually the most helpful? His high intelligence and willpower, his sister's support, her own enlightenment through therapy not to nag Daniel, therapy itself, or time? Nora was wondering, but was also aware of how unlikely and irrelevant it was that she would have her questions answered. She was hopeful—and cautiously happy—that he was back on track.

6

The bustle of two hundred people—stripping their wrinkled warm ups after 11 hours of flight, and changing into freshly unfolded beige two piece suits—abated in the flurry of zippers pulled, buckles fastened and the hushed jitters of arrival. The non-stop Delta flight from Budapest landed at Hartsfield Atlanta International Airport.

The large Hungarian delegation pulling Jurassic size, worm-like duffel bags on rollers reassembled at the carrousels. The immigration and customs check was surprisingly swift and efficient. A caravan of *seven* buses dressed in diaphanous garbs of their sponsors was waiting. Tibor got into a huge Coca-Cola bottle.

Curiosity wiped out the distance along featureless highways and streets. With roads and city flagged to the teeth, it was difficult to tell what was Olympic venue and what was not. The opening of the doors was more an indication that they had arrived at the Olympic Village. Led by officials, the delegation headed to a multi-story, brick building; their home for the following two weeks.

Tibor and his fellow masseur, Joska, stacked their luggage which tested the limit of the aisle between the two beds in the small bedroom. The small living room furnished with pieces of furniture in primary colors, and the tiny bathroom were to be shared with two other guys in the second bedroom. In the kitchen, all four men raised their eyebrows at the sight of the sign, "Enjoy, Coca Cola" hanging on a magnet on the refrigerator that seemed huge by their standard. They each grabbed a soda and were on their way.

The instant tour dazzled with the ordinary and the extraordinary. Not used to, or prepared for what to expect, Tibor was speechless. Music spilled onto the street from the Coffee house. The translator was rattling on about pleasures awaiting them in their free time. Given any. Complimentary goodies like coffee, tea, soft drinks, day time performances—perhaps that's what they were hearing; dancing in the evenings; theater. The Dance Club, they were told, was already promising to be the most frequented place in the village.

"Vertical practice for a horizontal performance," Joska whispered to Tibor who frowned saying, "Yeah, fast."

The dining area in an astronomic size tent, Post Office, policlinic and pharmacy buildings, Day Spa and Health Club, Video and Recording Center, the recreational pool, were only pointed to from the distance. They were late and running.

They filed into an amphitheater covered in flags. Reporters flashing their cameras as the delegation filled the circular standing room lined the rear platform. TV screens displayed text in French, Spanish, German and Arabic. Tibor couldn't identify the languages.

Three elegant men stepped up to the podium. A blessedly short speech in English welcomed them. The translator hummed in the background. The Hungarian national anthem followed by the raising of the flag put Tibor (and apparently most everyone else) in a festive mood, even before the Village mayor presented the Chief of the delegation with a colorful traditional American southern quilt. This was a gift of the Atlanta Committee for the Olympic Games. *Lots of things to learn.*

They were escorted in groups of ten to the security station where essentials like picture taking, hand geometry recording and credential presentation were completed. They were informed about how the Security ID badge was part of the high-tech security blanket virtually invisible to the casual observer. While most of the information was over Tibor's head, he felt assured by the attention to detail. Accreditation badge with radio frequency identification chips embedded, bar code storing all personal data including a compressed digital template of the users hands sounded awesome and unique, never experienced anywhere else.

Tibor had a similar feeling as in flying. There was no control over one's fate, one could only pray that the people running the show knew what they were doing.

In practice, what promised to be an annoying procedure every time he would pass a security gate—though not an unreasonable price to pay for safety and a good night sleep—turned out to be a barely noticeable slow down. The machine unobtrusively read the data stored in the slightly cumbersome, but smart ID badges, the light flashed when they placed their hands on the little window at the entrance to the Village.

On the fifth day into the games, Tibor left behind the Aquatic Center with its solar energy heated pools, swimmers with nerves choppier than the wakes they left in the water, the village with its bustle, and for a moment, he hoped, his worries as well. Feeling carefree, he jumped off the bus at the giant glittering Georgia World Congress Center. The mirrored side of the building stretched into the distance and receded into the alien horizon of the hazy Atlanta skyline. The landscape dwarfed people to sci-fi proportions.

He reached the entrance reserved for the Olympic Family. The opening door blew frozen breaths onto the melting sidewalk, stirring the vibrating heat. The steaming Atlanta caldron—Tibor was happy not to spend much time in it—suggested something out of a nightmarish vision of hell. Thanks to the modern and, as he imagined, expensive technology of mass producing artificial cool dry air, the whole setting evoked the extreme beating of a powerful Swedish massage. Hot and cold, hotter and colder, aimed right into the lungs.

It was the same dealing with people. Hot and cold. Like the most obliging volunteers milling all over ready to help, who shriveled in confusion as soon as they tried to figure out a question he had so carefully uttered. By the book. It happened several times during the first days along the sky high lobby of the WCC, where banners hung like rain clouds, polished marble floors reflected the silenced footsteps, guides sat in their highchairs shouting down directions in a shower of words Tibor could not understand. Was that English he had learned at home? *But, hey. I'm not complaining as long as the gap is mutual.*

A bored second-tier security guard leaning against the door of the reserved lounge summarily looked and nodded at Tibor's badge. Tibor walked in looking forward to a respite of half an hour. Climbing greenery draped a stone column behind a corner coffee table. The caramel color arm chairs melted into the light cocoa of the carpeting in an appealing blend. In one corner, a group of Germans were using the Info'96 computer terminal. Between two miniature palm trees, an archway led into an alcove with the omnipresent refrigerator showing its colorful display of a variety of cold drinks that far surpassed any picky person's needs. Suddenly thirsty, Tibor stepped behind the figure of a woman in a wispy cream dress. She picked a Diet Coke. He swiftly stepped back as she turned with the freedom of movement of a person knowing herself alone in a space. He saw her cream-colored straw hat and recognized the outfit of a medal bearer volunteer, the lovely young ladies who carried the tokens of victory on flower-laden trays to the stands of happy victors.

"*Ezer bocsánat,*" Tibor excused himself in Hungarian, then realizing the slip he said, "Excuse me."

The girl tilted her pretty face to look at Tibor from under the wide brim. "*Én értem,*" she acknowledged, in Hungarian with an American accent as far as he could tell.

"One can't be careful enough around here," he joked and a long lost carefree expression took over every inch of his tired face at the sight of the girl's beauty.

She returned a delighted smile, then focused on his badge. "Tibor Ro . . . o . . . . Ooof! Too long name. I'm Shirley. Hungarian name Tibor?"

"Not really," he had no intention of explaining the origin of his name in the Latin Tiberius, a piece of information that he himself was not aware of half of his life. "But *I* am. How about you?"

"My father from Hungary. And Granny. 1956 exodus, you know."

"Smart people," he said while they settled in the chairs. "You think?"

She can't be that unaware, he thought. "Some kids of your generation are trying to make up for their parents," he said and realized he was not free of the heavy burden of his thoughts and the dilemma of his immediate post-Olympic future. The lightness he felt minutes earlier proved but a mirage.

"Ah," she was visibly at loss.

He added. "I meant my daughter. She lives in Canada."

"Smart girl." Now she nodded. "What you do with team?"

"I'm a masseur."

"Interesting. I study *physical therapy.*" She named the occupation in English. He looked at her tiny hands and wondered.

"Quite interesting indeed, because I'm a PT myself, but with the team I got used to being called just a masseur."

Tibor kept crossing and uncrossing his legs expressing his amazement over the unlikely conversation better than any words could. He talked about the exhaustion of long work days, sometimes twelve hours long. More than during pre-Games times. Shirley spoke about being home from school and giving up a trip to Russia with her parents in favor of volunteering for the Games. He talked about how spoiled he felt by the table of plenty, as he called the cafeteria in the village; by the magic carpet, the buses running door to door, even though some drivers had no idea where they were taking their load of hurried Olympians, giving them apparently un-scheduled spins, which was no big deal, as the one he was on one morning still made it to the event on time.

Shirley wanted to know more. She had no access to the village. How was security? Did Tibor feel threatened? He didn't and said so. For that matter he just realized how reassuring the presence of the military patrol was, positioned unobtrusively along the double perimeter fencing behind the campus, the invisible system that was not supposed to omit anything or leave anything to chance. No human error at entry points. High tech match, perfect match or you were stopped. Flashing lights whether one belonged or not to a particular venue at a particular time.

He talked about his small, spartan room. "I'm not complaining. At the beginning, years ago, when I started to travel with athletes I was enraged that my age didn't get any respect—"

"Age? What age? You're maybe 40?" she made an inquisitive pouting circle of her lips.

"I wish."

"I'm twenty two—" she said.

"Looking 18." He knew it was the minimum age as a medal bearer.

"I heard this before." She looked proud and didn't giggle. An 18 year old would've giggled, Tibor thought. "*What* wrong with your room?" she seemed highly interested.

"My friend's snoring." They laughed and drank their sodas. He looked at his watch. "I can't believe it. Sorry, I have to run. Nice talking to you. Attila must be ready for me."

Shirley popped up, obviously not interested in who Attila was, her ample light skirt flew and revealed shapely ankles and calves. She picked up a napkin from the bar counter. "Do you have a pen?" she asked Tibor.

"Am I glad someone is using it?" Tibor mumbled to himself as he rummaged through the side pocket full of the bunch of unwritten postcards.

"Here's my phone number. I show you around when you have time." She kept a coquettish eye on him while she reached for the soda can on the table.

"Thank you," he said. "It's very nice of you, but I could never be sure how my one day off a week will work out and maybe you won't be free."

"Yes, I will. I make sure." She got up on her toes. "Now you can give me a kiss," she said. Intending to kiss her on her cheek, his lips were intercepted by her eager mouth.

A day that was fine so far, did not look that way any longer when Tibor, tipsy from Shirley's flirting, stepped into the back room of Hall E.

Attila, the promise in his weight lifting category, was sitting on the bench, hunched over in pain, squeezing his right thigh with both hands. "Tibikém, help me," he almost cried.

It meant real trouble to be addressed with so many words, even a suffix of endearment, by the word-bound young man. "What's with you now?" Tibor asked. It wouldn't have been the first time that Ati pulled some muscle an hour before a competition during an overly-eager warm up. That's why he asked for Tibor, that's why Tibor was pulled from the busy aquatic events. Attila had a chance at medaling. Tibor was the one who had worked his muscles back into place before.

"It's my quad."

"Let me see." Tibor knelt and slowly and gently felt around Ati's thigh. "What do you think?" He asked the coach.

"His foot slipped, the bar touched. It might be a contusion."

"I felt the pain during the slippage, before the bar could've come down on it," Attila said.

Tibor hoped for a bad spasm, not a tear. He saw no depression. "It's just a cramp," he said, but let me see your whole leg. "Yeah. Worry not until you see me," his joking tone was supposed to put Attila's mind at peace. "You'll be fine in an hour. Slip off your warm-ups, Ati," he said. Turning from hip to hip with Tibor's help, he did. The usual fifteen-minute through-the-clothes pre-performance massage didn't seem enough to solve the current problem.

Tibor popped an instant ice pack and placed it over the sore quadriceps muscle. Then, hurriedly, in the corner, he changed his team uniform with his work clothes. There was not one minute to be wasted. *The case might be worse.* Certainly much worse than he could let Ati or even the coach know. He had to take all the tension upon himself, he had to make Attila's pain go away. Tibor started to work the muscular back, then proceeded to the front of the powerful torso and the upper extremities. They were fine. His pectorals and deltoids were smooth and relaxed, ready for the supreme effort no other man on this earth of Ati's medium weight category could perform. Hopefully. His previous successes at shouldering raised expectations and made the athlete nervous. If only he could improve his wrenching, he had lamented the past few days.

"You concentrate, my friend," the white haired coach urged Ati, gently rubbing his forehead. "Close your eyes. Don't worry about your body."

"But the prediction. Did I not—"

The coach didn't let him finish. "Prediction is the worst sport an Olympian could ever go for. It spoils your youthful complexion." He smiled looking over Ati's handsome frowning face and throwing a silent questioning wink at Tibor, whose nod was non-committal.

By the time Tibor lifted the ice pack and placed it under the painful limb, he could work on an almost anesthetized thigh. He sprinkled talcum powder. Very carefully, keeping his hands flat, moving them softly, pressing down in feeling waves, he started to roll the firm muscle. Employing utmost caution he moved to deeper tissues expecting reaction to pain at any careless pressure. Avoiding pain completely would be the triumph, both physical and psychological; that is what Tibor aimed for. It would reassure Ati that there was nothing to fear back on the platform. He was lying still, eyelids slightly fluttering, taking deep breaths, doing his focusing drills, no doubt, just as Tibor concentrated his skills in supporting him in his goal.

Attila had to go. The vicarious stress Tibor took upon himself wore him out. He walked into the busy foyer. He would check out the wrestlers in Hall G. He suddenly realized that Ati might need him and promptly ran back. Breathless silence alternated with the weight lifters' groans followed by the thuds of the weights falling on the mattress and the roars from the audience. Tibor listened to the loudspeaker cutting in. He peered at the glistening backs of the competitors. Everything blended into a loud image. One muscle—Ati's right quadriceps—was flashing in his mind like an alarm signal. He crossed his fingers, then uncrossed them and cracked his knuckles. His temple poured sweat as if he was the one lifting six times his own body weight.

By late afternoon, Attila stood on the podium with a childish happy smile on his face and a bronze medal on his chest, looking over at the two Asian athletes at his left.

With his job done, Tibor was just as pleased, modest and proud of his achievement behind the sets. He was free till next morning when he would resume his long hours with the rows of hopefuls filling benches in the warm-up rooms at the Aquatic Center. Swimmers, jumpers, polo players would wait for masseurs to relax their muscles and lay their nerves in perfect readiness for the ultimate race.

Until the evening libation, solely in Attila's honor, Tibor excused himself and was out of the WCC first. He needed critical information before he would call Zsofia. A day pass for her was in his pocket. It had not been easy to squeeze it out from their manager; the team's allocation was a meager eight passes a day for the entire delegation.

In the Village, Tibor walked in the long shadows streaking the moisture-soaked dusk. Immersed in his own world, he stepped into the travel agency. With less difficulty than he expected, he made himself understood. The price of the ticket was out of sight, but it was worth every penny of his savings. Only if she'd agree to fly down to Atlanta. Two days before, when he tried first, she didn't. He left the office with a printout of possible round trip flights.

The failing of his memory, when he tried to bring alive Zsofi's rosy features of a carefree girl, terrified Tibor. He could only see her dispirited face when she'd moved back home the year before. Maria had acted so disoriented, so shaken, that she even canceled her contract with the National Tourist Bureau for the guest room. Maria and Tibor moving back together from the two separate bedrooms was no longer an option. Zsofi had assumed for weeks a hermit existence. Trying to cheer her up seemed hopeless. Dejected, cheated, disillusioned, she sat, sunk into the meaning of those new words she had learned the hard way. She hardly talked, but when she did it was only about her misery. Being in love and loving, having a devoting Zsofia there had subdued Ervin to the extent that a fresh innocent love could harness an unbroken mustang born to roam.

While the affair lasted, Zsofi was so full of her soon-to-be-physician boyfriend that dates fell out of her calendar. She had missed college registration. Her ambition ebbed, her muscles slackened, as Tibor imagined, because she abandoned swimming altogether. She had disguised all of that in a happy-go-lucky tender smile when visiting her father in Tata. As it turned out, she had never been happy with Ervin. When she was barely recovering from the abortion Ervin had no qualms arranging for, she discovered that he was no longer interested in her. Zsofia's love turned into the mature pain that was too much for her tender age. Daddy felt like a wounded animal when his prophecy came true. Of course, statistical probability was behind him, though it was not arid statistics that dictated his warning, but a pained father's useless plea.

Then Zsofia's soul was an open wound crying out for a solution. She found it herself. It was ultimately Maria who made it possible. Though, at the time she was devoted to help her daughter achieve a goal, Tibor couldn't help suspecting his wife of doing it just because it suited her to know her daughter was far away. Maria found remote cousins who lived in Toronto. They remembered Maria and were willing to put her daughter up. Temporarily. This was a year ago.

Tibor hoped she was happy now in Toronto, though he couldn't imagine how. Though Tibor never saw the couple who were now his daughter's surrogate parents—truthfully landlords—he liked to think that it was reassuring to hear them say how seriously Zsofia was taking her waitressing job in their downtown Hungarian restaurant, how amazing her progress was in the English class at the community center, how sorry they were that she resisted going out with other youths, how she kept practically to herself. *Sure. She burned her lips with hot soup, now she blows on yogurt,* Tibor had thought.

Next door at the Village Post Office, despite his trepidation, Tibor stepped to the phone. The Smart Card did the trick. It paid for the call as for everything else.

"Dad, I have an idea." His daughter talked as if they had parted yesterday.

"Zsofi—"

"Dad, please call me Sophie. Is that a deal?"

"Of course." He would have agreed to whatever she wanted. He didn't know her any more. She proved creative and Tibor wanted to prove to himself that he was ready for anything just to see her.

"I haven't had a chance to visit New York," she said. "Let's meet there."

"What an idea," he said and was afraid that hesitation tainted his enthusiasm as he was trying to figure out the cost.

"Don't worry about getting me there. I can manage. I earn as much here as . . . well . . . about ten times as much as I could at home."

Tibor felt switched on, as if his motor barely idling under a layer of dust and rust has been cleaned, oiled and tuned. So fine was the tuning, that under the penalty of a heart attack, he couldn't stop dancing through the evening of celebration. This was a new, funny and agile Tibor, bursting with happiness to everyone's unmistakable delight.

7

"Pride in a superior and moral health care system is not justified any more," claimed a physician whom Nora met at the same friends' BBQ a year before and who had retired since. "The compromise with mercantilism borders on amorality. I'm perfectly happy not being part of it any longer." The group around the grill under the maple trees behind the old country cottage, was keeping the hosts company while enjoying the aroma of the rosemary and sizzling leg of lamb.

"What triggered this setback?" another guest asked. He looked familiar too, but Nora had no idea who he was. Judging by his long wispy hair he might have been the painter she had heard about.

"The general tendency of our society is to give everything a dollar value. Only that which can be expressed in dollar numbers is appreciated, everything else has no value," the doctor said.

"And doctors know it only too well raising their fees all the time. Doesn't *that* tendency need to be curbed?"

"This is the biggest misconception," Nora said. "Let's take a TV set. It's around $400. If it becomes a monitor attached to an Ultrasound machine with an additional safety gadget valued at $15 it will cost $3,000. Because the manufacturer knows that the doctors will make a lot of money with it. Right? So the doctor will have to charge a lot of money for the test run on the overpriced equipment, not talking about the astronomical malpractice premiums, which is another calamity plaguing the health care cost. And what costs the most in a hospital run by bureaucrats? *They* charge in the ball park of $1,000 for a bed per day."

People's approving nods gave her impetus. "Another thing. Tell me another profession that requires years of training after school, weeks of up to 100 hours of work, held to a double standard all their lives? Just being a reliable slave around the clock won't be enough soon. Administrators, profiteering parasites, will dictate to physicians how to do their job."

"Only in managed care," someone said.

"That's not the point. Not only because managed care is on the rise, but because it's a powerful lobby. The point is that health care should not be a profit-making industry for string pulling, leg dangling, lobbying CEOs putting millions in their private pockets, while you say that the doctors make too much money working their tails off. Parasites make millions on sick people's skin. Whoever participates in this system, to whatever degree, is an accomplice. This renders the whole nation immoral, or at least amoral, for allowing it to happen. It's not the only example that people in general are losing their sense of priorities," the retiree said.

"What's your solution?" the painter asked.

"It's obvious. Single-payer insurance system."

"Is there any one that works?"

"There are several that are far from perfect. We should be able to put together enough know-how to analyze the systems of different developed countries, learn from their experience and come up with one that could work for us."

"Wasn't that tried?"

"Oh, yes. You refer to Hillary's famous task force? She squandered a historical momentum three years ago. It was not even an honest try. The issue shouldn't have been to make it a playground to prove the first lady worthy of public service. For free. Remember what Bill said during the campaign, that the nation will get two for the price of one. That's for you to learn a lesson. Nothing is for free. Whatever is free isn't worth more. She certainly proved that point."

"She bullied the task force around," Nora said.

"How do you know?" Someone asked.

"Some pundit comes from Washington to conferences and updates the audience on the health care politics of the day. Apparently, the experts who were supposed to contribute their know-how to the task force were not even allowed to take the material out from the premises of the meetings. They were expected to give an opinion on thousands of pages they could *only* look at there. What was she afraid of? That someone would appropriate her ideas? It's a pity. I put too much hope in her. She let me down, she'll have to go a long way to redeem herself in my eyes" Nora said. "The process of working out a health care system should've been conducted for as long as it takes. Years if needed. Knowledgeable people presiding. Not necessarily C. Everett Koop, but someone like him comes to mind. Someone with principles and vision. Every voice that raised issues not on her agenda was silenced by the bossy matron. Her ears bent to the whispers of insurance moguls sitting by her side. Wasn't that a message for everyone but the blind and demented? When the Aetna president sat by her in the house, when Bill was praising her abilities?"

No topic was significant enough to suppress the rising aromas and appetizing sight of a row of bowls filled with salads, baskets of country breads, platters of sliced roast, amid the clinking of drinks. Health care was sacrificed on the altar of universal salivation.

It was the first time the two women set eyes on each other. Martin and Tom were lifelong friends since they shared a room at Princeton. Enough grounds to bring about this vacation. Nora, and Julia, Tom's pleasantly plump and joyful wife, had had no disagreements on the phone line between New York and Montreal discussing their plans.

In the Calgary airport, Martin flipped a coin twice for the first driver. Which couple, which spouse. Then, they would all take turns in alphabetical order. The spouse of the driver would navigate. Nothing more fair. Personal indisposition subject to collective approval.

"Sorry, I forgot my driving glasses," Nora said with a straight face to underline the good start.

"If our intelligence is correct you can drive blindfolded," Tom responded to Nora challenging the rules.

The scenic drive was the right start. The pine forested slopes, gurgling brooks and photogenic caribou grazing on the roadside and posing for a group of tourists were almost wasted on the four busy occupants of the rented Ford Taurus. The August day was a scorcher, alleviated somewhat by the crisp dryness of the air, becoming purer and purer as they gained elevation. Nora unbuttoned her striped polo shirt, pulled up the legs of her light denim pants. She got hot as they circled the second time and again they ended up in a grassy dead end instead of the Post Hotel they were looking for.

"It's not my driving—"

"I'm not used to a metropolis like Lake Louise," Martin argued. "The directions they sent us stink."

"I'll take the rail tracks, they should lead somewhere at least."

"The hotel isn't supposed to be near the tracks. The choochoo whistle is not included in the rate," Julia said. It was she who made that reservation.

They finally turned into the parking lot hanging high above the railroad. Nora checked out the electric outlets at the parking spots. She had never been so far North where the car engines had to be kept warm overnight. The half-timbered gabled facade of the building with a rough stone base and balconies trimmed with red geraniums fitted right into the narrow rocky valley.

They were offered a tour of the public areas before going to their apartment. The cozy sunken bar with soft music wafting in the dimness, the sunlit airy dining room overlooking the babbling stream, the thick rust red carpeting on the hallway earned nodding approvals. A bellhop took their luggage to their two bedroom housekeeping unit. The pine furnishing, the brand new utilities in the thoughtfully equipped kitchenette seemed too nice to be true for a rental. "Great choice Julia," Nora said. "I hope my choice in Jasper will be half as good."

Rain or shine, nothing could stop them from sampling all the blessings nature and humanity had to offer. Seeing the famous lake had to be postponed for dusk had set in the valley accompanied by the sound of growling stomachs.

"It's touching," Nora said watching the evening news.

"Even if the flame is merely a wick?" Tom commented picking another fistful of peanuts from a wooden dish.

"Tell me, why do they call Mohammed Ali the greatest athlete of the century?" Nora asked without irony.

"His achievements, usually a corollary of raw physical force and similar personality, in Ali's case are associated with high intellect, impeccable character and a rare sensitivity," Martin said.

"Has nothing to do with his medical martyrdom?"

"Absolutely not. He was always a man of courage, took risks no one else did, he justified his decisions better than people in charge could."

They looked in silence at the parade of colors, muscles, youth and smiles, as national teams made the tour of honor in the Olympic stadium in Atlanta, before filling the stands.

Later, they crossed swords over the bridge table in front of the fireplace. Tom dealt the first hand.

The vacation was shrinking much too fast. A day trip and a romantic dinner, followed by a little hike the next day and a picnic on an alpine meadow. The restful evening and update of the Olympic events. A visit to Banff and shopping along Main Street.

A rustic two bedroom cottage at the edge of wilderness on the shores of Jasper Lake invited a more rugged kind of activity of Nora's design. Horseback riding along the continental divide, despite Julia's desperate protest against climbing on top of the towering animal. She got into a wet suit and clambered into the raft bumping around on the rushing icy waters of the Atabasca River with more feeble protest. She ended up asking for more, and more she got, like fishing for whitefish on Lake Minnewanka. What a dinner the big one that Nora caught would have made if only they had had a net to cajole it from the hook into the boat, before it got away. Well. Instead they rushed to save their hides from the sudden downpour, just before returning the rental boat at dusk. Barbecued ribs at a roadside diner was a pretty hearty consolation.

When they sprawled in their two separate spacious and elegant rooms at the Wedgewood in downtown Vancouver, the credits went to Julia again. Martin remarked, "You have a definite knack for luxury, Julia."

"My Inuit grandmother grew up hating her parental igloo. I got it from her." She laughed copiously at any joke, including her own.

The shock wave reached them on July the 27th when the news of the Centennial Park bombing in Atlanta claimed all front pages and news hours.

"This is the silliest thing you'll hear from me, I promise," Nora told the company in the middle of the apprehensive mood. "I had a dream last night."

"You had too much salmon and Gewurtztraminer last night," Martin said.

"I didn't eat that much. And drank even less. Really. I was trying to swim through drifts of snow—"

"Surely the rafting in glacier water—" Martin interpreted.

"Wait till you hear the whole story," Nora shushed him. "Not going anywhere, of course, though I knew I have to get beyond a huge fire to this man—"

"You don't have to fight your way through snow and fire. Here I am." Martin spread his arms wide.

"I love you too, but . . ." Nora put her palm tightly over Martin's mouth and went on. "A man with no face who was my father whom I barely knew, a lover from a lifetime ago and my husband—who was definitely not Martin, who says—you're all my witness—that he loves me. I had no feelings other than the need to get there and I couldn't. Now I have the strange feeling . . . I'm awake," she pinched herself, ". . . that there was the bombing last night. Now you can talk."

"Firstly it is incest, which would be highly uncharacteristic of you . . . Secondly, a husband *is* a lover. With your forgetting this, I have a problem—"

8

Two days before the closing ceremony, the only remaining activities for the Hungarian team were field finals at the Olympic Stadium and races on Lake Lanier. Athletes and supporting staff who were finished with their programs were generously offered the choice to stay and cheer for their compatriots or have a chance to look around. They were not promptly shipped home as they had been previously to save cost. Tibor opted to leave.

He would give Shirley a courtesy call from the airport. He had nothing to say. He was finished with Atlanta. Zsofia didn't come to enjoy Krisztina's victories; the star of Hungarian swim team was a great role model to the junior team that Zsofi had abandoned. Whatever he was thinking, Zsofia was in the foreground.

Mental images galore paraded just like the cityscape left behind the airport bus. His mind drifted back to his only day off. Afternoon of July 26. Shirley waiting for him at the Olympic spray fountain in the International Zone. Legs bare, tight mini-shorts hugging her tanned thighs, a lacy tank top—more revealing than concealing, sensible sneakers for the planned tour.

How would Zsofia like the cheap circus-like hullabaloo of the entire show bursting in a million colors and sounds, the nomadic look of tents flowing from one into the other around Centennial Park, the changing face of the huge Swatch clock covering a whole building? Would she go on a ride, or play with the computers in the AT&T pavilion? He found these more confusing than pleasing no matter how he tried to look at it. Would Zsofi enjoy the foods he was sampling? Cooked bananas they called plantains, spicy sausages Southern style? Funnel-cakes he so much loved in his childhood! Would she have asked for some souvenir pins laid out on sheets along the sidewalks, like the hundreds of people hovering over them completely absorbed in trading. Like children.

The afternoon dimmed into evening. Tibor let the festive mood carry him; yet every now and then, guilt disrupted his new selfish emotions. Snippets of the conversation with Shirley, an irrelevant foreplay squeezed him into the mold typical for the time and place. Shirley asked for his impressions of the opening ceremony to make conversation.

"I didn't get the roar at first," Tibor said. "Busy with the gift kits we found on our seats in the stadium, you know. A gift for every participant. Memorabilia, you know. Quite touching little souvenirs. The rest too long. So many people—"

"Bigger show than ever, right?" she sounded proud.

"Then we understood what caused the noise. Mohammed Ali took the torch from what's her name?"

"Janet Evans."

"That's right. Then I cheered too. You know, I never grew impartial to boxing, you can tell why." In his typical way he pointed to his crooked nose.

"I like your nose," she replied and looked up endearingly.

"You know," Tibor said, "we can be friendly, but I'm not sure I want you to like my nose." He laughed at her mildly shocked silly expression. "I had a wonderful day and I thank you for that."

"You know what Tibor?" She held her arm out in a forbidding gesture. "*Nem vagyok én gyerek,*" I'm not a child. I know what I like and what I want. I don't like just anyone and you shouldn't be so uptight. Let's go to my place and have dinner."

"Can you call a taxi there?

"I don't see why not, but the buses start running very early in the morning," she mixed English with pidgin but improving Hungarian.

In the morning? After years of hearing only complaints from Maria, and lately sporadic one night stands, perhaps he had lost his touch and the ability to last till the morning bus? he mused. The lust that the twenty-something year old had whipped up successfully, made him nervous. As pretty as she was, and as much as she clung to his arm all day long, he pretended to regard Shirley as a friendly local guide. He did his best to keep it as far from erotic as he could. After she had spelled out her plan, it would have been more difficult to get out than to go along.

So be it, he had thought, when with the pretext of a heartburn—well justified by all the samplings of cajun spices he was not accustomed to—he ran into a pharmacy. He was one of many. His teammates were right after all about the Games' powerful aphrodisiac effect.

Dinner at Shirley was sandwich style. With a mature approach Tibor curbed Shirley's youthful rush. In turn, she surprised Tibor with choices that left the overnight stay his only choice. With undeniable pride, he checked his watch around midnight. And not without being thankful for Shirley's insistence to sleep over. Then he fell asleep.

The radio was on filling the room with sentimental music. He had been shaken awake. Shirley sounded alarmed. Did her parents show up unexpectedly? No. An emergency broadcast. A bombing in Centennial Olympic Park, the place they had left only a few hours before. It felt as if the shock waves shook the room. It was not even two in the morning.

Tibor called his manager. He was ordered to return to the village. Getting a taxi proved to be a trying experience.

The bedlam he found when he stepped out of the car resembled an ant colony freshly poked open, with people pouring out of the lit dorm buildings. Coaches and managers were hurrying around yelling, people in night attire were running from floor to floor, from building to building in an attempt to round up missing mates who might have hit the sack somewhere else than their rooms in the international sex showdown. ID cards dangled over bare chests or loose and wrinkled T-shirts.

Tibor went to bed with vague remorse over leaving Shirley with inelegant haste. There was also a tinge of greed for having missed waking up with her. He stirred and stretched before the memory of pleasure lulled him to sleep.

He almost slept through the seven o'clock alarm next morning. Gossips reigned the streets like an unstoppable wind. The juiciest were the ones about the Americans who were in the worst shape at the post-bombing head count. Impossible to locate by the hundreds. Beepers out of order, discharged, turned off. "AWOLs", Tibor heard, and someone had to explain the term to him. Many (totally oblivious of the explosion) were brought back in the morning by reveling buddies.

At the Delta terminal in New York's La Guardia airport, Tibor yanked his extra-long duffle off the baggage conveyor. Self-conscious because of its size, he carefully maneuvered it so as not to run over anyone's toes at a careless turn.

He was still awaiting the glamour of the city to hit him when he got off the Carrey Transportation bus at Grand Central Station in Manhattan. No skyscrapers were visible in the dark alley. Only a smell of musty rancid oil from some cheap restaurant that turned his stomach. The saving grace went to the precise directions he was given and he could follow. To his surprise, finding the number 6 train uptown was as easy as child's play. He got off at the 77th Street station.

The people renting a room in the high rise building on East 75th Street, a busy few blocks from the subway station, came well recommended by Zsofia's landlord. The doorman made a call, then pointed to the elevator. He spoke a different English than people down South. What a language bending in everyone's mouth like rubber they try to push out with the tip of their tongues.

Sophie came out a door at the end of the carpeted hallway, her light green sundress with cherry blossoms shone like a sunny spring day. Tibor abandoned his duffel at the elevator. They took off running, arms outstretched. He picked her up by the waist and spun the tall young lady around as if she were a little girl. He felt strong and happy. She hung onto his neck even after he put her down.

"My sweet little girl," he kept her at arm's length marveling. Tears rolled down their faces. Sophie's high cheeks glowed with the radiance of smooth china. The shiny cascade of shoulder length dark blond locks framed her face, her eyes seemed more slanted than he remembered. "I hope you're as well as you look," he said.

"Looking good yourself, Dad." She walked around her father to get a better look at him.

"Is this my Daddy?"

"Your old geezer."

They both pulled the duffel into the apartment. Sophie gave her father the grand tour in less than two minutes.

When Tibor realized that New York was not just a bigger-phone-book-city than Budapest, but five bigger ones, and these yawned at him without giving up Nora's name, he felt cheated.

"I'm trying to find an old friend," he told Sophie on one of their walks.

"Here?"

"I checked an old New Jersey address."

"What's he doing?"

"She's a doctor from Romania."

"You worked together?"

"So to speak."

"I have an idea. Talk to a physician who might know of her."

"Where do you get such ideas from?

"See? That's our problem. Mother and you too. You don't think I can have my own ideas. From where?" She jokingly faked anger. "My head. You want to understand me. I don't understand you often and that's fine. We are different—"

"You'll be surprised to hear how glad I am."

They sat with their snacks under the shady tents around the round, marble-ringed fountain of Lincoln Center. Tibor's mouth was agape with awe at Sophie's knowledge. She was explaining the Chagall paintings on the Metropolitan Opera facade. Then, she pulled a Manhattan Transit brochure from her knapsack and folded it backwards to expose the bus map. With her finger on the page she looked up. "We'll go that way." She pointed uptown.

"I can't believe you haven't been here before."

"No, but all I did for two days before you came is study the city so I can impress you."

"I'm impressed." Her pregnancy came to his mind, when he was not impressed. His heart wept. Where was she heading?

"We'll go to a hospital library to find your friend," she said as if answering in jest his unspoken question.

Hand in hand, they waited to cross Broadway to catch the crosstown bus. They talked. Sophie noted the WALK sign and shook Tibor's hand. "Let's go, Dad." She stepped off the sidewalk.

His leg muscles, positioned for a similar step, suddenly contracted. He buckled from the waist, his left hand yanked by Sophie's right. Her hand flew in front of his face following her body. It flew in an arc and hit the pavement. Her head smashed into the curb where the pavement and the Belgian blocks form an angle. She lay on her face motionless. Her beautiful wavy hair spread out in the gutter.

A pizza box and a bare-chested youngster flew off a bicycle at the same time. The boy bounced back on his feet at once, as if catapulted, grabbed the horns of his fallen bicycle, yanked it upright, appeared to briefly measure up the inert girl and pedaled away at an astonishing speed before anyone could regain their breath.

Tibor recovered his balance. Two women with arms reaching out leaned over Sophie. Tibor jumped by her side and kneeled on the ground pushing them away. He put his hand on her back, he was sure she was breathing. In vain he called out to her. He was almost lying next to her. A trickle of blood smudged a lock of hair on her temple. He wished the blood he saw was his own. Terror crushed his head in a vise. He looked up from the circle of sandals and sneakers to the wreath of faces around a patch of whitish sky. A man talking loudly into his cellular phone made an irritated gesture and frowned with attention. The traffic whooshed by. The cars in the right lane slowed down and squeezed to the left. The man on the phone yelled out and made a nervous gesture to Tibor.

"They say she shouldn't be moved."

"I know," Tibor mumbled.

"The ambulance is on the way," the man on the phone added. The circle opened and closed as he stepped back hurriedly.

Tibor sat on his heels, stooped, head hanging limp, hands cupped over Sophie's head.

A police car pulled to the curb followed by an ambulance.

9

“Unpronounceable diphthongs. Must be Polish,” Nora heard Warren commenting as she passed his viewer. He was looking at a CAT scan of a head with a large intra-cranial blood collection shining like a floodlight in the night.

“Welcome back, Nora,” she mumbled to herself.

“Let’s consult our Eastern European expert,” Warren went on.

“Hello to you too,” Nora was annoyed. Readjusting from vacation to work was bad enough. Being pigeonholed didn’t help.

“Too short for Polish?” He poked the film with a China marker. “Only eleven letters. What do you think?”

Nora turned her eyes to the ceiling in defeat and stepped next to Warren. To get back at him, her tongue ahead of her mind, she said, “Right again. It’s not Polish.” By the time she said, “It’s Hungarian,” a sudden stabbing pain in her low back sapped all the strength from her legs. She had to sit down before her knees buckled. “Oh my god. Rózsavölgyi,” she cried out.

“How did you say that?” Warren continued jesting.

Occasions flashed before Nora when she had been on a wild goose chase at the sight of a name that had personal meaning. Like her own. Or when she had a patient with Martin’s ancestors’ name, Farbermann, and she found common roots going back to the same sub-Carpathian village, once part of the Austrian empire, currently in Russia. Looking for connections across continents and generations felt like finding lost life. She sat with her hands in her lap. Zsofia Rózsavölgyi. Nineteen. No name had ever elicited such emotion. She covered her face with her hands. She had not been haunted for years until that past week. What was happening?

“Are you all right?” Warren sounded worried.

“Yes, thank you.” The anxiety of her own reaction grabbed her. “May I see the requisition?” With a trembling hand she took the slip of paper Warren pulled from the pile.

The requisition from the Emergency Room was dated Saturday,

August 3; stamped in the Radiology department at 5PM; scan initiated at 5:40. *Pedestrian hit by bicyclist. Rule out intracranial hemorrhage,* she read. The resident's reading was correct: Right temporal *epidural* bleed; underlying brain edema; midline shift, non-depressed right temporal scull fracture.

Nora returned the slip with a whispered "Thanks." She stepped to the phone. The patient Rozavolghi, a clerk tried to pronounce, had been taken to the OR the same night. "The patient Rosa-something has been transferred to ICU," the recovery room clerk informed Nora.

Except for a slow recovery from the general anesthesia, Zsofia's brain appeared to escape general edema and she was recovering consciousness, slowly. They had taken her off the critical list. Nora processed the information with a cool professional mind. The private side of her brain took over as soon as she hung up. Jitters sent her right away to the ICU.

The young lady in Bed 10—head bandaged, nose and forehead discolored and swollen, IV running—was asleep. Nora stood by the bedside, her hands clutching the rail, her eyes on the long eyelashes turned up over high cheekbones of a distant lineage. Probably blonde, Nora thought, looking at Sophie's peachy complexion. Her lips were parted, shiny with the ointment applied to heal the trauma of the endotracheal tube. Nora's eyes traveled down her body. Her arms rested on top of the cotton blanket. Slender. The sizable feet in the beige anti-slip terry cloth socks belonging to a tall person showed from under the blanket. *How would she look if she was mine?*

Nora couldn't find the chart on the rack. She inquired.

"Doctor Smith must be writing the transfer note in the conference room," the nurse said.

Smith stopped scrawling and gave Nora the surgical details.

"The collection had been drained. No underlying brain contusion. The edema? Under control, responding well to decompression and medication. Stable all around."

Nora sat at the other end of the long conference table with the chart. The paramedics' note described a 'Canadian tourist hit by a bicyclist on Broadway. According to the eyewitness, her father, she had lost consciousness at the moment of injury and had not regained it since. Time lapse: approximately 30 minutes.'

Nora's pulse quickened and throbbed in her neck almost choking her. Eyewitness father? Her eyesight blurred. *They live next door? Never a sign!*

She turned page after page through color-coded sections. A white plastic tab indicated the ER records. *Next of kin, should be here.* Father: Rózsavölgyi, Tibor. Phone number. 212 area code.

It can't be. My dream in the Canadian Rockies. Was it some obscure magnetism? What do they call it? Paranormal activity? ESP? Nora looked at Smith. "Have you met this patient's father?" Nora asked him from across the table.

"He left the unit just now. Some kind of therapist. Was inquiring about some physician. I couldn't understand him quite well. Mann, I believe."

Nora's first reaction was to point at her badge. Or better, jump up and smother the young neurosurgeon in a grateful hug. She looked down at her badge. It was turned picture and name in.

"He'd asked about the medical library," she was told at the front desk.

Nora ran up four floors. She stepped out of the staircase slightly out of breath and stood in the shaft of light falling on the floor from the narrow window. The top floor, the fourteenth, housed only the library and the medical board room encircled by vast terraces. This under-utilized space worth millions was a fact that never failed to intrigue Nora. Not now.

Posters and brochures covered the glass panels of the library door. Nora opened it with caution, as if expecting a blazing fire. The shades were up, diffuse bright morning light flooded the room from the panoramic westerly windows. Two men, middle age, probably attendings, were reading papers at the round table behind the equally round librarian.

"Hi, Elaine." Nora scanned the room with a hesitant gaze.

"Long time no see." The lively librarian's high pitched voice and inability to whisper should have disqualified her for the job, Nora thought for the millionth time.

"I've been away. I'm looking for a man about my age who—"

"Ah! That handsome foreigner over there whom I helped with the Directory of Medical Specialties?" She pointed a finger towards the remote corner of the room and the back of the man facing the window.

"Bingo." Her lightness a facade, Nora's smile ran from ear to ear. A scenario flashed through her mind as she tiptoed amongst the hutched tables. They could've passed each other in the street, not knowing of each other's presence. The broad shoulders and longish hair tied at the neck in a ridiculous little tail—still dark blonde or was it gray?—didn't give him away. Blue jeans and sneakers. An outfit she'd never associate with Tibor. His face was lowered in his palms.

Should I tap his shoulder? Maybe he's not Tibor. For sure he's not tuned to play games. His daughter just escaped death. I'll whisper his name. Thrill replaced anxiety with the tingle of surprise while the memory of her body and past frame of mind overwhelmed her.

"*Uram, nem beszél véletlenül magyarul?*" She whispered in Hungarian, Sir, do you by any chance speak Hungarian? Standing behind the still figure, her heart was pounding.

Tibor lifted his head. His hands stopped in midair at shoulder level, as he turned. The hesitant and low female voice reached him through a dense fog. His wordless, unshaven face and his posture were those of a statue of stupefaction at a seance of spiritism faced with the ghost he never believed in. A life size ghost talking Hungarian, stood in front of him. The ghost of his life. His pupils widened visibly.

"This can't be true." His hands slowly came down and froze at some distance from Nora. Afraid to break the magic he didn't dare say her name.

She placed her hands in his and looked mesmerized at an almost unchanged Tibor. More rugged despite the glasses, more handsome and somehow taller and thinner than she recalled. *Glasses?* The glitter in the dimness of the Budapest evening appeared to her.

"Nora, am I hallucinating?"

"You're not, Tibi. I work here. I just missed you in the *ICU*—"

"Nori, I just found you in the book—" He was still in shock at the realization that they were in the same building.

"You *were* looking for me?" She sighed with relief. It didn't depend on the chance of her seeing Sophie's CAT scan. Her fingers tightened around his. He pulled her close. They hugged softly. "Can you believe now that I'm real?" For a fraction of a second, she surrendered to the feeling. Nothing changed since twenty-thousand-years-ago when she'd picked up Tibor in the street on her thirty sixth birthday. Shivers ran down her back as Tibor put his arms around her.

They stepped on a land mine buried deep in the dust of the past. It exploded with instant chemistry.

Never in his life had Tibor felt desire to be such an ordeal.

She desperately struggled to change her bearing. Assume the angle of an outsider. "I ran to the unit as soon as I saw your daughter's x-ray."

"You? Her x-ray?" He could barely believe it. He bit his lip appalled by guilt for feeling anything else than fatherly anguish even for a moment. "They told me she has a good chance for complete recovery."

"She'll be all right. And she's beautiful—" His stare that seemed to say, "She should be yours," stopped Nora in mid-sentence.

Nora stepped into the quiet apartment. Martin was absorbed in his work at his desk. She couldn't be happier. "Hi, love," she was content that he barely acknowledged her. For her own inner peace she added while heading to her room, "I'll talk to you later."

The computer seemed slower than ever to boot up. Finally, she could double click on the *Compuserve* icon, then the address book. She typed: Dani, are you there? She sent the message.

Yes, she read the reply in an hour when she checked the mail the umpteenth time.

Nora rang her hands over the keyboard, then wrote and sent the following message: Dani, this is very serious and urgent. I need to talk to you. In person.

It wouldn't have been a breech of her promise not to call him at work, barring a real emergency. She could've screamed: *Help. I'm losing it.* Daniel might not have agreed that that was an emergency.

While waiting for Daniel's reply, Nora emptied the medicine cabinet in her bathroom and started to wash the glass shelves. It was the only way of getting an inner turmoil under control. Or trying to. Doing a mindless and if possible a totally unnecessary job. She was not ready to put dinner together or to talk to Martin. What could she say to sound reasonable?

When the phone rang, Nora lost one slipper in her rush and tripped.

"Impossible," Daniel said. "I'm busy and we have important project meetings the next two days. What's the problem?"

"Do you remember Tibor?"

"Vaguely. Romania?"

"Yes. He's here. With his daughter. She had a bad accident. She's at my hospital."

"You got her in there?"

"No, but that's irrelevant—"

"I can't do anything for them," he said curtly. Then, as if his mind changed, he asked. "How bad is the girl? Any danger?"

"No," Nora drew the word out into a sigh. "Not any longer. *I* am in danger. Get it?"

"Not really."

"This is not for the phone. Take my word for it."

"Can't Sonya help you?"

"She's in Thailand, remember?"

"Oh, yeah?" There was a pause. "I'll tell you tomorrow after the meeting."

Autumn had not yet cooled the mornings. Nora walked to the hospital. Soon after sitting down in the reading room and trying to concentrate, she was paged.

"Is there more to your call than needing my advice?" Daniel asked with gravity.

Nora was awestruck by Daniel intuiting her inner commotion—more in her soul than mind—that she herself would not dare acknowledge. The Canadian dream. She needed an unbiased observer. The outsider she couldn't be. Foreign to the ghosts of her feelings. Someone able—and willing—to reevaluate a person she couldn't measure with lucidity untainted by past passion. It felt as vital as Sophie's recovery. She said, "No hidden intentions, if that's what you're insinuating." *Did I blow my cover?* She relaxed only when she heard Daniel say, "I don't know why I'm doing this. Better have a good reason." His words, though agreeable, sounded like a warning.

"That's subjective and open to one's angle," Nora said self-protectively.

"To a certain degree," he admitted.

"When can I expect you?"

"I'll get started around eight."

"Take our space in the garage."

Nora had no intention of keeping anything from Martin, nor did she think it would be mature and dignified. Facing him at the kitchen table over dinner, serving him her trademark cold cherry soup, she told him, "Dani took a few days off. I asked him to come home," she almost blushed, happy to have passed the difficulty of an opening. She felt so much more at ease that she immediately added, "This way he can meet with my ex. You have no choice," she managed to lighten up.

"Are you telling me that—?" His intended remark was enough incentive.

She talked, effusively dramatizing Sophie's misfortune. Then she grimaced. "Martin, I find this difficult to word. It borders on the occult. All I can tell you is that I have this premonition."

"I'm not sure I understand."

"Trust me on this," she said. And hold me tight, she thought, but she said nothing to that effect while hugging Martin.

"Did you have anything for dinner?" Nora asked Daniel when he got in after midnight.

"A coffee New Jersey Turnpike style so bad I don't want to remember what it came with," Daniel said searching the refrigerator with hungry eyes while Nora set a steaming plate of leftover cod Florentine on the kitchen table.

She rested adoring eyes on her famished son. The flickering columns of light of the Fort Lee apartment buildings filled the window behind him. "How is your project going?" she asked.

"Okay," he said with a full mouth. "That's irrelevant now. Tell me, what's this about?"

After the shock of seeing Tibor, Nora had found herself transposed in a disquieting virtual reality. Relived past sensations surrounded and invaded her. She felt vulnerable although during their conversation and serene after-dinner moments, Martin was the one to offer shelter from and give reason to her confused and stormy world.

"Can you be more specific?" Daniel asked after a swig of Bud Light.

"I always wanted to talk to you more about things past. We rarely found the right mood or time."

"Is it different now?"

"Well," she nodded. "Yes. I'm selfish now. I need a buffer."

"You mean punch bag?"

"No. Silly. Tibor's sudden appearing threw me off balance—"

"Which way?"

"I don't know. He makes me restless—"

Daniel raised his eyebrows. "What do you want me to do?"

"Prevent me from losing it."

"He'll disappear as soon as his daughter, what's her name, is out of the hospital—"

"Sophie. Her name is Sophie," she hurriedly said, then changed the subject. "You know everything consequential about my life. I'd be the ultimate ingrate to complain how my life, my own in a narrow way, turned out. I couldn't hope for better. And now I'm eaten by unreasonable doubts."

"Well—"

"Well, what?

"Well. Doubt is what keeps *me* going."

"May I correct you? It's reason what you call doubt. You're the strongest member of this family—"

"How did you figure this?"

"Because after what you went through in your formative years, then submitted yourself to a year long test, probably—"

"Assuming again? You know nothing about me."

"I'm always ready to listen."

"Not now. Now it's about you. What does Sonya have to say?"

"Remember? She's away."

"I forgot again." He slapped his forehead then said with irony. "Who can keep track of her?"

"She would be too far and too busy anyhow."

"So, you want me to keep Tibor busy?"

"Yes. Take him around. Talk sports."

"Why sports?"

"He is here as support staff with the Hungarian Olympic team."

"They came with their own cars?"

"You keep saying you don't remember anything. It's funny you remember this."

"That's right. It *is* strange. Wait! You meant Romanian team?"

"No. They emigrated to Hungary."

"He must have gotten the emigration itch from you."

"I hope he's better off there. Pleased with what he does, I understand."

"He must be good at it—"

"He has hands of gold—"

"Let's not get into that."

"You, bozo. Nothing like that. He used to massage my back."

"Just what I said."

"Yes, but that's not what you meant."

"All right. Go ahead."

"I was madly in love with him. That I never knew much about him made no difference. I'd never pull anyone's tongue—"

"But you try, even if not always successfully." Daniel used his mischievous winning smile.

"I can't possibly know what's going on with him."

"Do you need to?"

"That's what I need you for. To ask the right questions for me.

Apparently he's separated, apparently Sophie has some feud of her own with her mother. I don't know what he has become."

"Again. Do you need to?"

"It's the only way I can make peace with myself."

"Because of a coincidence? You wouldn't remember his name if he didn't happen to cross your path. Just forget it."

"I envy you if you could."

"You'd be better off. Things like this couldn't happen to me. I've built up an immunity as you put it."

Nora felt a stab in her heart. Immunity. To life? To repressed emotions, crippled urges?

"Would you spend a day with Tibor, please? In the name of all the baby-sitting he put in with you guys?"

"I'm no tour guide."

"Gimme a break. Go places you'd like to see yourself."

"You know how much I like Manhattan. Besides, he's probably a seasoned traveler. With a national team. Boy!"

"Not according to him."

10

After Nora had properly translated everything for him at the hospital, the doctor's words didn't sound like the doomsday bell to Tibor. He was looking at Sophie. Her eyes opened and closed lethargically, her mind appeared to navigate with difficulty the dark waters of retrograde amnesia that separated the sunnier islands of clear moments. She had difficulty remembering that they were in New York, and she missed her Budapest swim pals.

He found Nora's office. Waiting there for Daniel, he tried to find some short sentences to say to the young man. Though Nora showed him a photo, he still saw both him and his sister as skinny little kids. He feared his English wouldn't be good enough to express his urgent need for a friendly tie.

Daniel appeared in the doorway. Tibor stood up standing a tad taller. They shook hands.

"Hello Tibor," Daniel's baritone resonated in the small room.

"Hello Daniel," Tibor's tenor answered, then he asked. "*Emlékszel rám?*" Do you remember me?

"Honestly? No." He hooked his thumbs in his pants pockets. "How is your daughter today?"

"*Jobban van, köszönöm.* Have you no problems with Hungarian? Nora told." Tibor wanted to make sure Daniel understood that Sophie was better. "My English no good. *Nem tudom mit csináltunk volna Nora nélkül.*" He praised Nora for her help.

"We'll manage. *Jó lesz.*" Daniel tried to hide his impatience.

"You like we stop in Sophie's room *elöször?*" In the corridor Tibor said, "Nora not changed." As he got no answer, he looked at Daniel and saw a stern expression. The subject of the past was obviously taboo.

"I've never been to a patients' floor," Daniel looked around with interest, turning his head after nurses, exchanging a friendly greeting with a particularly pretty one who forgot her eyes just one second too long on him.

"I not that lucky," Tibor said.

They both stood in the doorway. An old woman clad in a hospital gown sat in an armchair and looked out the window. Like a child, Sophie was sleeping on her back with her head turned on the pillow all the way to the left. The shaven side of her head and the row of staples were in full view. The remaining long hair tied with a piece of gauze lay on the pillow.

Daniel became aware of the twinge of pity in the pit of his stomach when the concerned father's insistent gaze made it clear that he had been looking at the sleeping girl for a long time.

"We can't bother her now," Daniel said and turned around.

Facing the bustle in the street, Daniel asked, "Would you like to go to a museum?"

Both men carried the conversation mixing the languages, Tibor more Hungarian, Daniel more English. "I'm afraid it would be wasted on me. *Pláne most.*" Tibor knew he couldn't pay attention now, on the other hand, he welcomed Daniel's suggestion to take a bus uptown and work their way back along the Hudson River. He always needed to walk and never had enough time.

They crossed the busy two way traffic of West End Avenue. The sight of the landscaped slope of the riverbank was not what Tibor expected. "Beautiful trees here, Second Avenue all cement, lots garbage bags. This is pretty mixed old and not old."

"They're better examples of mixture of old and new, I'll show you later. Let's walk first."

In need of a subject for conversation and remembering Nora's advice, Daniel thought of how the Olympics had passed him. He wouldn't invest time in the biased trickles of commercial television. He never read the sports section of the *Washington Post* either. It struck him as of marginal interest to find out about the big sporting event from an insider. Tibor obliged, as much as he knew from the narrow view of a laborer stuck with his nose in his work, as he put it.

"This is where Mom lives," Daniel pointed to the wrought iron glass-backed entrance door. "Pretty spiffy if you ask me."

Tibor stopped and looked up at the turn of the century facade. It was like standing on Andrássi Ut in Pest. He felt like a stray dog kicked in its side.

"No point in going upstairs now," Daniel said. "Marty, Mom's husband, might be working. Believe me, we don't want to disturb him. I learnt my lesson when I lived with them," explained Daniel lips arched down.

"What does he do?"

"He's a writer, but mostly he's just a super smart guy."

"Oh! Then you two get along."

"What did Mom tell you?"

Tibor realized that's how he remembered Daniel. But that was the past and it was taboo. "What do *you* work?"

"Nothing I could show. I don't make things. I show people who're smart enough to listen a better way to do their work."

"Then, you are smarter than the smart people—"

"Not really, but such people were my teachers. Here we are," Daniel said, urging Tibor along to catch the Northbound 5 bus pulling into the station.

They got off at 122nd Street. Daniel led the way to General Grant's Tomb and engaged in giving Tibor an idea of the American Civil War with his personal touch. "This monumental *thing* here is for a figure I can't respect much, and I'm not alone. A bad general for whom lives were just numbers, a drunkard for president, in something like this," Daniel's sweeping arms meant to exaggerate reality, and carry his own verve, "overlooking such grand scenery. But, one of the truly great men, if not the single greatest man in the history of mankind . . . right . . . not only American history, rests under a modest tree, away from show." Daniel face was radiant. "The Potomac," Daniel didn't notice Tibor's totally baffled look and went on, "is also majestic at the bend where George Washington is buried at Mount Vernon." Daniel registered Tibor's nod. "That's the place where he lived until his death. It's not far from Washington, you know. I have been working around there lately." Daniel laughed realizing he must come down from his clouds. "Did Mom tell you anything about me?"

"That you're a doctor of some sort, not *orvos.*"

Daniel looked at Tibor with a suspicion meant for his mother. "Very well. It's called *PhD* here. Since I got my degree I've been working, amongst other places, around the capital—"

"Good job?"

"For me it is. I dread to be tied down by anything or anybody, you see?" The two strolling men exchanged understanding glances. "I do a job, I take my attaché case and move on. I don't leave anything behind. All I have I carry in me. No one has a right to . . ." he realized that he was confessing to a total stranger. If anything was more foreign to him, it was confiding in anyone, except his sister. *Where are you funny face?* "Anyway, what I wanted to tell you about Washington's tomb is that it should be visited by everyone in moments of doubt. Instead of going to a . . . how do you say *psychiatrist?*"

"I don't understand the word."

"A doctor who treats mental disorders."

"Aha. *Elmegyógyász?*"

"It must be it. We call it a *shrink.* One should rather go there, go through the modest house, walk down the hillside to the shade of the trees, and sit in the grass, and think of everything one does wrong, of all the self-serving, narrow-minded, terrible things that could be avoided by mere modesty. And vision. I did this more than once. I take my harmonica. Nobody minds. As they walk by, some people's looks soften from indifference to understanding the place they're walking through." Finally Daniel understood that he was barking up the wrong tree. He didn't see that change in Tibor's look. Perhaps he should take Tibor to Mount Vernon, his favorite place on earth. But why?

They arrived at Riverside Church. The cool, crepuscular interior hung over the flickering candles. The air resounded with the sounds of the carillon. Grand accords took off, then died out absorbed by the cold stone.

Tibor nodded apologetically, stepped ahead and sat on a bench. He crossed himself, his head reverently bowed. Daniel raised his brows, stayed back and paced. Shortly, Tibor came towards Daniel who couldn't miss the serenity in his eyes. Daniel felt almost envious. They resumed walking South on Riverside Drive.

Tibor began to talk. "My daughter said, *leckéztetett,* had been lecturing me, that I don't need to understand her . . . that *I* should *benojjön a fejemlágya,* like grow up—"

"It's called generation gap," Daniel grimaced in an effort to explain in his pidgin Anglo-Hungarian. "The differences in tastes, choices, I don't know how to say *concepts,* between parents and children."

"*Mentalitás?*" Tibor asked basking in the warmth of a kinship that defied the partial language barrier.

Daniel hasn't expected much from the man. He was ready to write off the whole day as an act of good will. Slightly abashed for his condescending thoughts, he found himself suddenly interested in Tibor. Also, he was amused that one word from him could cause such a dramatic shift in his own attitude.

From the shelter of his life—sanitized from all possibly troubling emotional contamination—Daniel summoned his dormant perceptions. With another surprise bordering on shock, he welcomed feelings that came to the surface with the ease of a ping-pong ball released from a tight fist under water. "Good word . . . mentality . . . it puts the issue in a pacifist light. Both sides achieve a non-confrontational legitimacy," Daniel mumbled to himself.

At 72nd Street, Daniel asked, "Am I wrong thinking you don't want to go near Lincoln Center?"

"No. You're right," Tibor said and gave Daniel a grateful look.

"Then we'll take the bus to Fifth Avenue. The bellybutton of the world. If you want guidance with stores, you'll have to stop someone in the street. I don't know much about the glitz other than that every tourist has to see it. Well, Rockefeller Center is not bad, or Saint Patrick's. There is old and new for you there." Daniel dropped two tokens for the fare.

Tibor lost his eyes on the crowd filing in and out of Trump Tower. "Would you like to sit down for a coffee?" Daniel asked.

"That's always a good idea," Tibor underscored his answer patting his lips.

In the hushed torrent of the waterfall towering atop the indoor scenery, stirring his coffee, Tibor talked first. "I have to tell you how much I appreciate Nora's and your support. The guilt is still killing me for dragging Sophie here."

Words, empty words, words conjured from a vocabulary of fiction, clichés without consoling power, didn't fit Daniel's no non-sense style. What was he to say? He kept quiet. Let Tibor find his outlet talking about his daughter to a good listener. For more than half an hour Daniel did just that. Clearly interested.

"Tibor is your second ex-boyfriend I have the honor to set eyes on," Martin said, hugging Nora from behind as she was busy putting dinner together.

"But who is counting?" There was no hint of hostility.

"What are you making?

"Mère-Nora's famous omelets and a chicken *Dijonnaise.*" She lifted a lid, sniffed in the rising aroma and stirred. "Don't tell anyone that the sauce is courtesy of Knorr." The idea of the tiny omelettes that Nora had been making for company came *from Mère Poulard* at *Mont Saint Michel.* The original, also served as an appetizer at the famous restaurant at the bottom of the well-known French cloister-mountain had the quality—at no extra cost—of weighing Nora down with a rock in her stomach for the entire night, when they had sampled it a few years earlier. Nora improved it by reducing the size of the omelette by a factor of ten. Naturally she had neither French maidens handy to beat and toss the eggs in copper skillets with a meter long handle, nor was her fireplace suited for frying. So, she cooked the mixture of eggs, mushrooms and spices in the cups of the egg poacher.

"No dessert?

"I ordered a *kuglóf* from André's in Queens."

"You'll make him feel too much at home."

"Whom? Daniel?"

"You know who I mean, silly."

"Are you jealous?

"Should I be?

"Not more than I should—"

"I doubt he's my type," Martin said.

She hugged him and smeared her wet hands on his face.

"I hate that." He rubbed his face in disgust.

"It's supposed to be sexy."

"I'm serious. It's cause for divorce."

"You file." She said with a clownish smile.

"Tibor is clueless and worried," Daniel told Nora and Martin when he returned from sightseeing.

"Sophie will be fine and he knows it," Nora said matter-of-factly.

"But he has to go home. His job. He can't take Sophie for three reasons. One, she can't travel yet, two, she's not in any condition to decide, three, if she would be he's sure she wouldn't want to go home. If I understand correctly, the precedent was that she had stopped talking with her parents after such an irresistible offer. He called his wife in Budapest and she couldn't be located. What I understood is that she's a hopeless loser. So, he can't count on her to come and take care of Sophie during her recovery," Daniel reported.

"What is the girl doing in Toronto, Daniel?" Martin asked with unmistaken concern.

"Tibor is crying that he's practically in the dark." Daniel quick glance at Nora said more than a thousand words. Mother and son had no misunderstanding there. They both knew she was just another parent in the dark. "Tibor knows from the people Sophie is staying with, that she goes to school, works as a waitress, jogs and listens to music on her walkie-talkie. No friends. That's her life. Probably a thousand percent better than at sweet home—"

"Plans?" Nora asked.

"Hers?" Daniel pursed his lips. "Your guess is as good as mine. Or the father's. Someone has to talk to her. Would you do it?"

"I'm a parent," Nora answered. "She'll identify me with him. Or worse. With her mother. What good would that do?"

"You got a point."

"You try. She won't bite." They exchanged ambiguous smiles.

"Wait here for her concussion to clear? No thanks. I have to go back to work tomorrow."

The evening on the terrace was hot and muggy despite the breeze. Nora set the table for four in the dining room. She was moving about like a robot. Her mind was on fire and her eyes tried to capture any minuscule sign. Especially from Martin. Nothing. His eyes were not wandering like hers. He had surprised Nora during the last couple of days with evermore generous suggestions. She didn't lack generosity herself, but her position called for a more careful handling of the situation. Everything he had said recently, seemed to her a triumph of her own transported will.

Daniel retired to his mother's bedroom to work on something he had brought with him. He appeared more serene than ever, his brow unclouded. *Perhaps pleased with the day's activity,* Nora hoped. *No cynical comments that would have suggested otherwise.*

She has been meeting Tibor exclusively in the hospital setting. Now an old friend was coming for dinner.

The door bell rang. A sudden animation jarred Nora's thoughts. Her stomach fluttered. Martin opened the door. It was two minutes after seven o'clock. Nora heard the exchange of names in the entry hall as the two men introduced themselves. Nora controlled a surge of hyperventilation that was supposed to repress momentary tears of weakness. She faced the three men in the hallway lit by the slanted golden rays of sun setting across the river, looking composed to any, but the most probing eye. And those were occupied. Tibor's eyes roved around Nora's American home. Then, he looked at her with those probing eyes she had altogether forgotten and handed over the long slim cellophane cone with three yellow roses.

11

Daniel parked his car under a dogwood tree. Two a.m. flashed on the dashboard. The dead end street in Bethesda's residential area, where he had been renting a tiny one bedroom at the top of a family home, was deserted. The brick walk to the back of the house along trimmed boxwood bushes was poorly lit. After a few months of living there he was still not familiar with the trickeries of the old lock. He fumbled with his keys, his soft bag thrown over his shoulder.

Upstairs, on the coffee table, a pile of CDs, some Aaron Copland scores he had been practicing lately, and his harmonica looked foreign. At twenty-nine, well appreciated at companies whose problems became his mind's playing field, he was still toying with his harmonica. He would pick it up and play it, alone in this, or another, furnished apartment, in cities across the country, wherever he would take a job. He wouldn't play in company any more. Not since the Palomar days. After years he couldn't get over the pang of weakness. He couldn't believe they wouldn't pity him for his amateurish skill. He liked to follow Rampal's flute, or Winston Marsalis's trumpet, in a round of baroque tunes. It served his mental health. Now, looking at those objects waiting for him in disarray he knew he had grown out of the pretense of it all. The occasional people who gained temporary access to his fortified world formed a tight circle threatening his self-sufficiency. Women who wheedled their way in retired after the message hit their lascivious brains that they didn't belong there for more that the night that had already passed. Now, his harmonica, the old trustworthy friend, was following those people. It became a brick in the crumbling walls of self-defense. The realization was liberating.

Tibor slept in New York in the small room which Sophie had used for fewer days than planned. On a bed of thorns. Friday morning, getting up early was a relief, taking the crowded 79 cross-town bus a diversion.

He found his daughter perkier than the evening before when they had walked along the hospital hallway and talked about her being discharged the next day. Her helpless, sorrowful smile had filled Tibor with pain. Not seeing clearly added to his predicament. Did he accept too easily the generous offer? Did he grab a favor he would never be able to return? Nora was stepping into the shoes of his daughter's mother. He ground his teeth. Thinking of how he felt in the beginning about Nora's husband, Tibor felt guilty. Martin was more amicable than he, the old boyfriend, could've expected in his wildest dreams. Martin with his serious attitude had made him humble and steered him free of the initial overwhelming emotion that, if it were up to him would've . . . no, he couldn't afford even to think. He had to protect what little was left of his self-esteem.

"The doctor said I will be able to travel soon after the check up," Sophie said. Tibor nodded. *Soon? A month away. Travel? Where?* He said nothing. There was not much to say. Not much he could say to convince her of something he couldn't hope would serve anyone.

"Nora is so nice," she went on. "Sorry to say, but none of your friends at home come up to her pinky."

"Of course not. Her whole family . . ." a squeezing feeling in his stomach made him pause, ". . . is nice. Though her husband is the only one here."

"Tell me again about her children." She sat on the edge of her bed, head cocked, long hair combed over the top of her head to cover the bald spot and the scar.

"There's Daniel whom you met. I wouldn't have recognized him. He's some important scientist—"

"How old is he?"

"I think," he paused, "twenty-nine or thirty—"

"How important can one be at such an age?"

"We're not going to argue," he laughed, but not sincerely. "Then there's a daughter, Sonya, who is not married either and she's away a lot of the time."

"How old is she?"

"Thirty-four I guess. A successful engineer." His eyes searched Sophie's. He saw only a childish curiosity. "Nora's husband is funny." He cut short his smile that felt too sweet, too false. "He said you're doing him a favor staying with them. Nora would give him a break and use her mothering instincts on you."

"I'm not a good subject," she said bitterly. "Not used to it."

Tibor seemed to shrink looking at his hands lying idle in his lap. He knew no words he could say to this child whose parents had failed her.

The four of them sat and moved around the apartment like pieces of a puzzle pushed around with their proper places yet to be found.

"It's a pleasant evening," Nora said to break the silence. "Wouldn't you like to take a walk with Sophie, Tibi?" Noticing his bewildered look, she added. "Oh, just to the park. You're ready to walk, aren't you," she smiled at Sophie.

"I'm ready to jog," she giggled.

While they were out of the apartment she asked Martin. "What do you think?"

"I think we did the right thing. She's a lovely person. She even has a sense of humor which was not in the bargain."

"And we'll put up with the father?"

"For twenty-four hours I can put up with anybody," Martin said.

In Martin's bathroom, Tibor moved around as if afraid to break something. The most breakable seemed his spirit. His ineptitude took unsuspected proportions. He could not speak or hear what was important. Nora. A powerful magnet through the meter thick wall of his self-control. Martin was solid, didn't threaten to collapse, unlike his own imploding confidence. When he left, Daniel took away the kinship that seemed to sprout and nurture. Strange enough, for he knew very well that the pivot was Nora. A pillar of strength and comfort, as Daniel had put it. While he craved to hold out his hands as a feathered cradle to Sophie, his failure made him feel like a useless stranger.

He tiptoed to the couch in the living room, stripped his T-shirt and jeans and laid them on the armchair on top of his gaping carry-on. He slipped into the cool sheets that burned his skin. Nora had made his bed. Not a wrinkle.

With the restless night and the flight next day ahead, the image of Nora breathing under the same roof, but so far away, separation again from his daughter . . . all he could do was to invoke composure.

Nora stood in her bathroom and saw in the mirror not her own face, but life-long unanswered questions that flickered like elusive August stars. She pressed a washcloth over her quivering lips trying to cover her anguish for her children's future, for they filled her with trepidation;

trying to erase her pride for Tibor's present, for it was too remote; trying to disregard her past desire, for the fluid heat was too intense to bear. The only remedy was to invoke composure.

She emerged cool and settled. She walked into the bedroom. The man that her flesh trembled for was not the one in her bed. The man in her bed who took her hand with one free hand—the other clutched a book—was the man with whom she had started to make a lighthearted inventory of their changing age. A man with whom she found it easy to look at those sometimes disturbing changes with dignity and good spirit that subdued the burning desire of the flesh.

Like a hiker on the top of a mountain collecting her reward, she took in a panorama gilded by the setting sun. She wanted to stay where she was. As the sun was setting. It was all there, the manifold love and balance, in the squeeze she gave Martin's hand and the smile that passed unnoticed.

The crimson mums in the large wooden planters were in full bloom. Nora checked the outdoor temperature. Perfect for a leisurely breakfast on the terrace. She found Sophie setting the kitchen table. Wrong plates, wrong place. The girl was not lost in her new environment, a fact that denoted an observant mind and a willingness that didn't escape Nora. She wouldn't undo what Sophie had initiated. "Good morning, Sophie." She touched the girl's back lightly.

"Good morning, Nora."

"You had a good rest?"

"Thank you. I slept much better here. You mind if I help with breakfast?" she said with a modest smile, and smoothed down her loose blue T-shirt covering almost completely the white denim shorts as if she wanted to appear as neat as possible. Her English was surprisingly good, her accent light, a comment one could barely avoid when listening to a Hungarian.

"Not at all. I appreciate any help," Nora said without mincing her words. She was not talking down to a child. She couldn't. Sophie was much taller. Athletic too, in her shapely slimness. "We'd like you to feel at home, you know."

"Thank you. I'm sorry that my father has to leave so soon. It's been so long . . . I wanted him to come to Toronto with me." She said in one breath, thoughts obviously from the top of a long list of her worries.

"I promised your father I'd wake him at nine. He might not have had the most restful sleep on the sofa."

"You want me to go wake him, eh?" Sophie was already walking to the closed door of the living room before Nora could answer.

Like a busy-bee out of control, Nora opened and closed the refrigerator, pantry and cabinets; she took a skillet, beat some eggs with milk for French toast in a glass bowl, efficiently cut with the kitchen scissors the *unwrapable* wrap of a pack of bacon. While sizzling sounds filled the air, she twisted off the crown of a ripe pineapple, quartered it and cut it out of the rind with a curved paring knife. She handled the dishes as if they would break at the slightest touch, making the least noise possible. The men were not to be disturbed that quaint Saturday morning, when the heartbeats were not to be measured, and lying eyes had to be prepared to meet unknowing ones.

"I don't want to be trouble in case I get tired or something," Sophie said.

In jest Martin placed a white plastic bowl on his head in lieu of a nurse's cap, as Sophie's nurse.

Tibor held back his tears with difficulty as Sophie kept him in a long hug in front of the elevator.

Then, the two of them, Nora and Tibor, were alone. And speechless. Nora took the GW Bridge. Neither could avoid thinking of a conspiracy. And neither felt at ease with the two loaded hours until check-in. Too short a time, and just as long. The car rolled soundlessly. Tibor's comments on the car were meaningless. Nora searched for words of meaning that would not stir any waves. By the time she had crossed the upper roadway and pointed out to Tibor the Manhattan skyline, they were both burning on the pyre of their repressed emotions.

They stopped in the passageway leading to the metal detector. Tibor pulled off the rubber band holding his hair and started to smooth out the length to redo his ponytail. Nora reached for his wrists and pulled them towards her. "Leave it," she said. She put her hands around his determined face. "Don't worry. We'll be fine here. You take care of yourself."

"Thank you for everything," his voice dampened as he embraced her.

She stayed and said, "We'll call you often." Her fingers combed through his hair, as soft as ever, her arms ended up wrapped around his neck. Their eyes locked, forgetting the worries and scruples for a long minute, transported to their past selves that didn't exist any more.

"What have you missed?" Daniel returned his sister's question. "Why do you think you've missed anything?"

"Because Mom's account of the events was remarkably journalistic."

Sonya's matter of fact interpretation brought a sarcastic scowl to Daniel's face, which until then was quite pensive. Let her keep guessing, he thought. "Let me hear what you know," he said.

"Oh?" Her voice conveyed suspicion. "An unhappy father, who mind you, once stood on a high pedestal of the ultimate lover, a fact I can appreciate, it's not something easy to come by—"

"Could you stick to facts?"

"Excuse me," she smirked. "And an unhappy runaway daughter reunited with the aforementioned unhappy father who met her fate at the hand of a careless bicyclist. Or should I say feet? Taken away from her ambitious design of making it in the New World all by herself—"

"OK. Let's drop it then," he cut her short with undisguised irritation. "Tell me about your trip which was one of the worst timed, if I may say so. It took me two days to—"

"Since when are you in such a rush?"

"Since now, if you must ask."

"Should I hang up?"

"That's not what I meant—"

"Fine. The father is, so to speak, successful, and between you and me, from what I can recall, that's to Mom's credit—"

"How so?" Daniel faked ignorance, as he had to hear a second side of the story even if indirectly.

"Mom met him in his loser period and gave him the idea and the push, I think."

"But she didn't do his homework I imagine."

"I'll give him that. He probably worked hard. Okay. The girl. She lives as a boarder with the restaurant's owner where she works when she doesn't go to school, or jogs, or listens to music. I can't help not making deductions that she apparently, one, has more than cabbage juice sloshing in her head, and two, she treads the right waters in Toronto, where opportunities for a hard working girl abound in a supportive Hungarian community—"

"Yes, it—"

"Don't interrupt. She wants to go to school. To study Physical Therapy.

Be an Athlete's Trainer in professional terminology, I believe. Following in daddy's footsteps, mind you . . ."

That was a new piece of information. He rubbed his chin and listened more carefully to what else Sonya might have to say.

Daniel wrapped up the project to the company president's undisguised satisfaction more than a week before the anticipated deadline. Now they could go ahead and present the contract proposal to the Energy Secretary's commission on their Delta 45 Solar Energy System, a key component of the Millennium Solar Energy Project.

"It's almost embarrassing," the president said. "The glitch, or I should say glitches," he chuckled, "are so obvious and simple now after you've pointed them out. I should be grateful to Mr. Jarvis for making the connection with you."

"Same here," Daniel said sitting calmly and comfortably on the leather couch facing the stout man sitting on the edge of an armchair. "I had a great six months here working for you."

"Dr. Mann," the president probed now deeply into Daniel's eyes. "I am not aware what your plans are after the expiration of our contract—" he gestured to Daniel that he was not expecting an explanation. "The hearing is set for September 25 to 28 with an option of extension for another couple of days if needed. You've made everything clear for us. Your work is done. However, it would give us more confidence having you on the team, just in case. I ask you to consider staying with us for the duration of the hearing at a daily compensation of three thousand dollars."

Daniel didn't even blink. He considered thanking him for the offer, then changed his mind. "Mr. Burrow, it's impossible for me to answer your offer just now. I'm starting on an open ended project with built in potential ramifications." Daniel turned his palms up and tilted his head in resignation. His face radiated an expression of proud equanimity he knew very well was not stemming from the professional aplomb that the president surely attributed it to. He was only happy not to have another job lined up at the moment.

"Mom," Daniel's voice was hesitant, weighing down the receiver in Nora's hand. "How's Sophie?"

That was like a punch. Nora pressed a hand on her chest hopeful that her pacemaker wouldn't fail her. "She's amazing. The check-up went fine. She's fully recovered."

"Is she able, or rather, is it safe for her to travel?"

There was a stampede in Nora's mind, snippets of information running over her racing thoughts, secondhand fragments of the few phone conversations that Daniel and Sophie had had over the past month. "She's ready to go back to Toronto, though advised to stay out of work for another couple of weeks. To tell you the truth? We're going to miss her around here," she said.

"Look. I definitely want to meet her . . . when she's herself, you see . . . you've said she's fine—"

"Oh, yes," Nora said and could barely hold back, but the training of years helped, she was an expert in holding back, she wouldn't say that Sophie was more that fine. She was very special. How gracefully she moved around, demure but self-confident, but not taking herself too seriously. Nora would cloak her admiring gazes and wonder over Sophie's unfailing common sense and tact.

After more hedging from Daniel and more holding back of the need to scream for joy, Nora knew for sure that she will soon be a happy mother enjoying the rare company of both her children.

After the phone conversation, contentment enclosed Nora in a halo as she walked around; astonished to feel the floor under her feet, when she thought she was weightless and flying. As if all her life had been but a rehearsal, and the tension of a difficult premier was finally over. She could measure the reward for all the pain of holding back. She had made neither a suggestion, nor one single invitation, although she had been feeling like an erupting volcano. She knew better.

"Sophie dear," Nora said as they walked along the leafy sidewalk, enjoying their usual evening stroll. "I can't tell you how happy I am that Sonya and Daniel have a chance to visit. They're coming in two days."

"I'm happy too," she said shaking her hair and assuming a proud poise. "Do they come often?"

"Oh, not really." *Perhaps you shouldn't know that it is a very rare occasion indeed.* "It just happened that Daniel finished a project and Sonya was dispatched to New York on business."

"If you need Martin's room, I should—"

"Don't be silly. Just think of the old saying that good people manage in a small place," Nora laughed as Sophie swayed her lopsided mane.

Daniel loved to play the game of synchronization and mostly hated to wait. He didn't mind that much if others waited for him. Not too much anyway. Never abusively. That afternoon he was only too eager to pick up his sister at Newark Airport and get the road to New York behind.

Sophie's features unfolded from his surmised haste . . . a face complete with the blemish of black and blue (the only face he knew) waiting for him, and only him . . . opening the door of his mother's apartment . . . and welcoming him with a twinkle in her eye . . . and her warm voice . . . that smiling face, as he saw her weeks ago before his return to Washington, when he went back to the hospital room with Nora and Tibor. There were not many words he had said then, other than that it was not his first visit . . . that the first time he found her sleeping. How she had said that she was very glad not to be asleep again. It was a bonding smile . . . and words of courtesy that Daniel couldn't remember, as he didn't recall any of the many phone conversations they had since. No words could have any particular bearing on his present state. He knew no words to express what he was feeling.

THE END

Acknowledgments

I am deeply grateful to my husband, George Gabor, whose support and insightful opinions helped me focus, and get through this project while keeping my sanity. I hope not at the expense of his own.

My heartfelt thanks go to George and Martha Gotthard for their friendship steeled by inclement times, their unfailing support, and also their invaluable clear-sighted critique of this book.

To my editor, René Breier, I can only say: I am indebted to you, Mother of All Editors.

I want to express my gratitude to George and Agota Adler, also Judy Balas who offered their time to read my manuscript, and their encouragement. They should know that my request to clobber my blabber was genuine. The shortcomings they pointed out in my writing woke me from mindless wandering and strengthened my determination to cut out the nonsense.

I take this opportunity to thank my cousin, Bernard Breier, for his feedback during the years of my meddling with writing.

I owe special thanks to my daughter, Emily Gabor, for her gracious help.

Composition: Agnew's, Inc., Grand Rapids, MI
Typeface: New Caledonia
System: QuarkXPress 4.04

8 ~ 6/10/03